The Five-Year Plan

CARLA BURGESS

ONE PLACE. MANY STORIES

HQ
An imprint of HarperCollins*Publishers* Ltd
1 London Bridge Street
London SE1 9GF

This edition 2020

First published in Great Britain by
HQ, an imprint of HarperCollins*Publishers* Ltd 2020

Copyright © Carla Burgess 2020

Carla Burgess asserts the moral right to be
identified as the author of this work.
A catalogue record for this book is
available from the British Library.

ISBN: 978-0-00-837879-0

MIX
Paper from
responsible sources
FSC® C007454

This book is produced from independently certified FSC™ paper
to ensure responsible forest management.

For more information visit: www.harpercollins.co.uk/green

Printed and bound in Great Britain by
CPI Group (UK) Ltd, Melksham, SN12 6TR

For Mum, thank you for everything x

Chapter 1

Present day – London, UK

'How did you get invited to this exhibition, Orla?' Emma turns to look at me, her loose black hair streaking back from her face as the wind howls down the street towards us. It's a horrible night, and I feel bad for inviting her out in such awful weather, but she seemed eager enough when I told her about it this afternoon. 'I can't believe you've got an opening night invitation to Aiden Byrne's exhibition. *The* Aiden Byrne! Do you know him or something?'

'Yes, kind of. Well, used to, anyway,' I say, side-stepping a sodden newspaper that takes sudden flight and tries to wrap itself around my legs. That'd be all I need, to see Aiden again with wet paper stuck to my tights! It's bad enough my hair feels like it's coming loose from the glamorous up-do I had done this afternoon. I'd intended to arrive looking chic and sophisticated, but at this rate I'm going to look like I've come on a motorbike. 'Why? Have you heard of him?'

'Of course I've heard of him!' Emma says. 'I wouldn't have agreed to come out in this storm if I hadn't!'

'Really? How?'

Aiden's not that famous, surely? Okay, he's getting bigger,

otherwise he wouldn't be having an exhibition at the Hayward Gallery, but still, I'm surprised Emma knows who he is.

'Are you joking?' Emma throws me an incredulous look. 'He's done all those wildlife documentaries! Everyone knows who he is now. Besides, I have lots of friends who are environmental activists, and they think he's really cool.'

I absorb this information with some amazement, though I shouldn't really be surprised. Aiden had a bit of a cult following even when I knew him five years ago, so it stands to reason that will have grown, especially with the documentaries being televised. Of course, I knew about them, and though I've not watched any myself, I'm aware they've been well received.

'You can't know him very well then!' Emma says, crossly. 'I thought you were going to introduce me to him. I wanted a selfie! I told all my friends and everything!'

I can't help laughing. Emma's our new trainee reporter, and even though she's impressed me with her sparky enthusiasm and intelligence, on occasions she'll revert into stroppy teenager mode. I like her though. Her cheekiness reminds me of my younger sister, and I've kind of taken her under my wing since she started working on the paper. Hence the invite to tonight's exhibition. She can do a write-up for the *What's On* section, and I get a wingman that will make this feel like a work assignment instead of a social event.

And I badly need this to feel like a work assignment.

No one was more surprised than I was when the invitation arrived in the post five weeks ago. As soon as I saw it, I decided not to go, intending to write a polite note wishing him luck. But the note never got written, and somewhere along the line I realised I couldn't not go to such a major exhibition when I'm a newspaper reporter with an entertainment section to fill. So instead I confirmed my attendance with a plus one, thinking I'd ask my boyfriend James. But that didn't seem right either. After all, I'd hate to meet Aiden's girlfriend.

2

Oh no, what if Aiden has a girlfriend? Or a wife!

'We don't have to go, you know.' I stop walking abruptly. 'We can just go home, pretend it wasn't on. I doubt we'll actually speak to him.'

'Oh no!' Emma sounds contrite, thinking her stroppiness has caused my sudden change of heart. 'I didn't mean it. It'll just be good to be in the same room as him, really. I don't care about talking to him, or the selfie! Ignore me, you know what I'm like.' She carries on walking, and I feel duty-bound to follow, all the while thinking of excuses why Emma should go in on her own. But before I know it, we're at the gallery doors and my pulse is going haywire in panic.

I can't see Aiden again, I can't see Aiden again, I can't see Aiden again.

'You must know him a little bit though,' Emma's saying as she pulls open the door and steps inside. 'I saw the invite on your desk and it was addressed to you personally. It wasn't just for random newspaper staff or the entertainment editor, it was directly to you. In gold embossed lettering.'

'Well, I knew him a long time ago, but he probably invited lots of people that work in the media. He must want the publicity.'

The nerves I've been battling all day threaten to overwhelm me as we go inside and join the queue for the cloakroom. I didn't sleep last night, and I haven't been able to eat since breakfast. Now I feel hollow and light-headed, my hands shaking from the day's excess caffeine consumption. At least that's the reason I tell myself they're shaking.

'Did you guys fall out or something?' Emma asks, curiously.

'No, no. Nothing like that,' I say, my eyes darting all over the place. To my relief, the gallery is full of people and the air is buzzing with laughter and conversation. Of course, Aiden has a huge number of friends. As a wildlife photographer and conservationist, he travels all over the world and his kindness and friendly nature naturally draw people to him. There are bound

3

to be all sorts of people from all sorts of places here. He's going to be so busy catching up with other friends that I'm sure I'll be able to avoid him all night. I square my shoulders, feeling slightly calmer than before. Maybe I could manage a friendly wave from a distance, just to say I've shown my face. My stomach dips as the thought of any contact, however small, sends my heart racing.

Just knowing he's here in London frays my nerves. All week I've been thinking that I've seen him out of the corner of my eye, standing at bus stops or walking down the street, but it's never him when I've turned to look.

I hate the hope. I hate the disappointment. I hate that I still feel like this after all this time.

When Aiden and I said goodbye five years ago, I vowed never to see him again. We hadn't fallen out or anything. Far from it, in fact. We parted amicably, lovingly, but we'd run our course. Aiden had an assignment in India, and I was just starting out as a newspaper reporter. Our lives were going in different directions and we always knew our relationship was temporary. We needed a clean break. Emailing him every week and seeing him whenever he came back to the UK wasn't ever going to help me move on.

Not that I've done a great job of moving on anyway. Still, there was no need for him to know that. Aiden's a free spirit. One of life's wanderers. There's no question in my mind that he'll have moved on by now.

He probably barely remembers me.

'Wow! Nice dress!' Emma says as I peel off my coat and pass it to the girl behind the desk.

'Thank you.' I glance down at it, pleased she thinks so. It's knee-length and black with sparkly silver embroidery. It cost a small fortune but I wanted to look good tonight, for my own self-esteem more than anything else. I chose a dress that made me look sophisticated and successful, as different from the girl he used to know as possible. I pat my hair self-consciously. 'Is my hair alright? It hasn't come down, has it?'

4

'No, it's fine.' Emma checks round the back. 'Just a bit wispy at the front, but nothing bad. Just sexy. Can we find the toilets? I need to brush mine through.'

'Yes.' I feel like hugging her, I'm so relieved that I get a few minutes' grace before entering the exhibition. We find the toilets and I reapply my lipstick as Emma brushes her hair.

'I'm nervous,' she whispers. 'I've never been to one of these before. You won't leave me, will you?'

'Of course not.' I smile at her, making an effort to pull myself together. Emma's young, and she's bound to find this all a little overwhelming. 'It will be fine. There'll be champagne and nibbles and we'll look at his amazing photographs. And if we get a chance to speak to Aiden, we'll ask him some questions and get that selfie, and if not, no big deal.'

Please don't let us get a chance to speak to him. Please let him be too busy.

I take a deep breath in. 'Right, let's go.'

She beams at me and I smile bravely back as I pull open the door and step into the gallery. The hum of conversation is much louder here, accompanied by the clink of glasses and tinkling piano music. Aiden's photographs are displayed on huge canvasses on the white walls – the first is a huge owl with enormous amber eyes, its feathers so textured and lifelike that I feel I could stroke it.

'Wow!' I hear Emma say from behind. 'These are amazing.'

A waitress passes me a glass of champagne and I accept it gratefully, downing it in one long gulp as Emma sips hers slowly, looking around with her huge dark eyes. My glass is instantly refilled by another waiter and I try to take more measured sips, aware that getting plastered would not be wise.

Aiden's photographs are captivating. Emma and I move from image to image, discussing them as we go. They're linked to the devastating effects of climate change, and between the beautiful striking images of animals, there are photographs of wildfires, deforestation, flooded villages, dried-up river beds, and emaciated wolves and polar bears.

'These images are so powerful,' Emma says, her eyes full of tears. 'I can't bear it.' She's looking at a photograph of a dead rhino, its horn removed by a poacher, while I'm still staring at the forest fire with fear stirring my gut. All I can think is how close was he to that fire? Did he put himself in danger for these images? Exactly how far will he go to get the perfect shot?

It's hard to believe that Aiden has been to these far-flung places and seen all these amazing things. He's lived a whole other life since I saw him last. It doesn't seem possible the small part I played in his past could mean anything to him now. If ever I needed confirmation that Aiden and I are completely incompatible, this is it. Tears burn behind my eyes and I struggle to keep my chin from wobbling. I should never have come here. I want to go home.

But Emma is talking animatedly to me about the photographs, drawing me on to the next one and the next one. I'm glad she's with me, with her bright, bubbly personality distracting me from my thoughts. We turn a corner and find a wall covered in a montage of images of plastic-covered beaches, and plastic floating in the ocean. There are terrible photographs of animals trapped in plastic and plastic trapped in animals. It's horrifying and we stare and stare.

'I'm definitely going to reduce my plastic usage,' Emma says. 'It's so difficult though. Everything is covered in the stuff these days. Have you seen those eco bricks?'

'Where you fill a plastic bottle with unrecyclable plastic and they get used for building things?'

'Yeah. I'm so going to do one of those.'

'Orla?'

I freeze. Aiden's deep Irish voice makes every hair on my body stand up and I turn slowly, my heart lodged somewhere near my throat. I've prepared my face into a smile, but I can't help the shock that registers when I actually see him. His beard and his long dark curly hair are gone, and instead he's clean-shaven with short back and sides. Even stranger than that, he's wearing a black suit and tie. I can't believe my eyes.

'Bloody hell!' I laugh in disbelief as pure joy courses through my veins at the sight of him. All thoughts of being friendly but distant are instantly forgotten. 'What's happened to you? Where's the hair? Where are the clothes? What have you done with the real Aiden?'

He laughs and scratches the back of his neck, looking embarrassed. 'I thought I'd better smarten myself up. How are you? You look beautiful.' Stepping forward, he kisses me on both cheeks, a light hand on my arm. My heart kicks in my chest and I feel hot. So hot.

'I'm well, thank you. This is … all of it … is just amazing.' I indicate the photos on the walls with a swirl of my arm. 'Congratulations, Aiden. I'm so prou … pleased for you.' My throat constricts with emotion and I swallow hard as I turn to Emma. 'This is Emma,' I say, my voice wobbling slightly. 'She works on the newspaper with me. Emma, this is Aiden.'

'Hello, Emma.' Aiden smiles and shakes her hand. 'Thank you for coming tonight.'

'Oh, it's my pleasure!' Emma looks like she's going to explode with excitement. 'I couldn't believe it when Orla asked me to come with her tonight. I was so excited and your work is just amazing. Your photographs are just like *wow*! I'm going to be writing a review of your exhibition in our *What's On* guide, if that's alright with you?'

'Sure. That'd be wonderful. Thank you so much.' His eyes return to mine and my stomach fills with butterflies. 'You achieved your five-year plan, I see. You're living in London and working on one of the big newspapers?'

'I am!' I say, proudly.

He opens his mouth to say something but Emma speaks first, diverting his attention back to her.

'Can I ask you a few questions? They won't take long. I know you must be very busy tonight, with lots of people wanting to speak to you.'

He gives her a lopsided smile and shrugs. 'Of course. I'd be happy to answer your questions.'

I stand to one side as Emma takes her phone from her bag, checking it's alright to record him. He agrees and she begins the interview. I can't stop staring at him. He's looks so *together*. Like someone who actually lives indoors and knows what day of the week it is. It's hard to believe this is the same scruffy, shaggy man I fell in love with all those years ago. But his eyes, as green as a forest pool and ringed with thick black lashes, are the same ones I gazed into when we made love, and he still carries the same gentle air of deep calm he always did.

He turns his head and catches me staring, and my stomach turns over as I drop my gaze.

It was a mistake to come here and see him again. It does no good to stir up all these feelings. Aiden belongs in the past. A beautiful memory. Hazy summer days spent lying in his arms in shady green woodland, the sound of birdsong and the river running next to us filling our ears. Butterfly kisses on my neck, and a feeling of such utter love that I could have died then and there and been happy. My Aiden. I loved him so much. Will seeing him tonight affect my memory of that perfect time? I'm disturbed by how different he looks. Disturbed by how much I'm still drawn to him. But I know there's no going back. Not now, not ever. Our lives are too different.

Tears threaten once more and I turn away to look at the photographs on my left. Emma's only got four questions about the inspiration behind the subject matter and how long it took to compile the material for the exhibition, and as she finishes, I hear her ask him for a selfie. I cringe a little, but he just laughs and agrees.

'Are we having one with Orla too?' he asks, and before I can protest he takes my arm, drawing me closer, and suddenly I'm pressed against his side with his arm around my shoulder.

It's so strange to be this close to him again. Even after five years apart, he feels familiar. The scent of his cologne makes my head spin, which is strange considering he never wore it back then. He smells completely different in fact, but there's something underneath the spicy aromatic scent of his fancy cologne that my senses seem to recognise. Some pheromone, perhaps, or something else uniquely Aiden that gives me a pang, deep down inside.

'Aw, that's a lovely one!' Emma says, peering closely at her phone. 'Thank you so much, Mr Byrne.'

'Call me Aiden, please,' he says pleasantly.

He's still got his hand on my shoulder, and I wish he'd let me go because I don't want him to know how much I'm shaking. From the corner of my eye, I spot a man hovering, obviously waiting to speak to Aiden. As soon as he sees Emma put her phone back in her bag, he darts forward and draws Aiden away from us.

'I'll come and speak to you later, Orla,' he calls, before crossing the room to join another group of people.

'He's lovely!' Emma says. 'I've forwarded you the recording of the interview, by the way. And the selfies.'

'Why?' I pull a face. The last thing I need is to torture myself by listening to his voice. I didn't watch his documentaries because I knew it would awaken the painful longing I've tried to repress all these years. Just like seeing him here tonight is doing now.

'Because of your face. And the fact you've barely taken your eyes off him since he went to stand with those other people.'

'I have not! And what's wrong with my face?'

'Nothing,' she says innocently, ducking her head. 'Anyway, I've just had a text from my boyfriend asking me to meet him for a drink, so I might go soon if it's okay with you?'

'Oh!' I'm dismayed she's leaving so early, but maybe it's for the best. It's the perfect excuse for me to slip away too. 'Okay. That's fine.'

'Thank you so much for asking me tonight. My friends are going to be so impressed. Especially with the selfie!'

I laugh, still incredulous that Aiden's become something of a celebrity. He's probably completely unaware.

'I'll look around the rest of the exhibition then I'll get going,' she says, checking her chunky silver watch. 'You're going to stay, aren't you?'

'No, I don't think so.'

'Are you sure? He keeps looking over at you, you know. And he said he'd come and speak to you again.'

'He doesn't keep …' I look over at Aiden just as he looks up at me. Our eyes lock for a fraction of a second before I look quickly away.

'See, I told you. He definitely wants to speak to you. How friendly were you guys, anyway? Was there a bit of romance?'

'Maybe.' I feel myself flush slightly and turn away to hide my embarrassment.

'Really? Wow, wait until I tell my friends. Do you think you'd get back together?'

'No!'

'Why not?' Emma jiggles my arm excitedly. 'Look at the way he's looking at you. He's surrounded by people, but it's like you're the only person he sees.'

'Stop it!' I turn my back on Aiden, determined not to look. 'Come on, let's look at the rest of the exhibition.' We move on to the next section of photographs. 'I suppose you're one of those romantic girly girls, who believes in true love that lasts forever and ever?'

'Of course I am. Why, aren't you?' She cocks her head, incredulous that I might not be.

'No,' I say, equally incredulous that she'd think that I would be.

10

'That's so depressing! Why not?'

I hesitate. That's a good question. Especially considering my relationship with Aiden. 'It's not that I don't believe in love, I just don't believe it can last forever.'

'But that's so sad. My grandparents have been married forever and they still hold hands. My mum and dad are still happy too. The old couple who lived next door to us when I was growing up died within a week of each other because they couldn't live without each other.'

'I doubt it was like that really. They must have both been ill. Did they check the carbon monoxide levels in their house?'

'Don't be mean. She died from cancer and he had a heart attack a week later because he couldn't cope with the grief.'

'Oh.' I wince. 'I feel bad now. That's really sad.'

'Exactly. There are examples of everlasting true love everywhere you look. You just have to work at it. My mum says that's what people these days don't understand. They expect everything to be perfect all the time, and at the first sign of trouble people bow out. But life's just a lot of ups and downs, and you get through it together.'

'Well, I'm sure she's right,' I say, 'but finding someone you want to spend your life with is a challenge in the first place. I've certainly had no luck so far.'

'What about Aiden? What was wrong with him?'

Unable to stop myself, I look back over my shoulder to where Aiden's laughing with someone. I can hear the rich, warm tones of his laughter from here. 'Nothing was *wrong* with Aiden. He was pretty perfect really. But we only had a short time together. Just one summer, when I was about your age, and neither of us was ready for a relationship. Our lives aren't compatible.'

Emma pulls a sad face. 'That's a shame. Maybe you should start over again. See where it goes now you're both older and wiser.'

'I have a boyfriend, remember. Besides, Aiden travels the world

11

pretty much constantly. You know he lives in a tent, right? No thank you. There's no going back now. Besides, Aiden might have a girlfriend now. He could be married for all I know.'

'If he is, he shouldn't be looking at you like that.'

'Like what?' Glancing back at Aiden, I find him looking at me again. Our eyes meet and he doesn't look away, nor smile, and neither do I. Instead, we just stare at each other and even though there are people all around us, it's like we're the only two people in the room. I'm rooted to the spot, my blood fizzing in my veins, heart thudding so hard I can feel it in my scalp, my fingers, my toes.

'Ha! Told you.' Emma laughs and nudges me with her shoulder so that I break our gaze and look at her, blinking like I'm just waking up from some kind of hypnosis. 'And you're looking at him in exactly the same way he's looking at you. Right, I'd better go or else I'll be late for the love of *my* life.'

'Wait, I'll come with you.' I look around for somewhere to leave my empty champagne flute.

'Don't you dare!' She touches my arm. 'Aiden invited you. He obviously wants you here. He'll be offended if you leave so early. Besides, think how much money you spent on that dress and having your hair done. You can't waste that.' She winks, seeming suddenly older than her twenty-two years. And my twenty-seven, come to think of it. 'I'll see you in the morning.'

'Well, be careful in this storm!' I call after her. She raises her hand and then she's gone, weaving her way through the crowded room and out through the door.

I feel lost without her. Standing on my own in a room full of strangers isn't my idea of fun. But she's right, it would seem rude if I left early. Aiden might belong in the past, but he's an important part of that past, and I owe it to him to be here, cheering him on and supporting him on his big night. It doesn't matter that being in the same room with him feels dangerous. I'm a grown woman. I'm strong enough to cope.

Glancing up, I find his eyes on me again. Christ, why does he have to keep looking at me like that? Feeling flustered, I move away towards the far corner of the room. It hurts me to do so, but I don't need his lingering looks making me believe the impossible is possible. We can't go back; we can only go forward.

'Hello, Orla.' A woman with long dark hair taps me on the shoulder. 'Do you remember us? Mia and Keaton?' She indicates a tall guy behind her, his long dreadlocks tied up in a ponytail.

'Of course I remember you!' I say, recognising them at once. I'm happy to see them again. I only met them once five years ago when I was with Aiden, but they were absolutely lovely. 'It's so lovely to see you. How are you both?'

'We're great, thanks! We've got a little boy now, and another one on the way.' Mia smooths her hands over her bump proudly.

'Congratulations! When are you due?'

Mia and I chat about babies while Keaton fiddles with his tie, looking like he wants to rip it off along with the suit he's obviously been forced to wear.

'Have you managed to speak to Aiden yet?'

'Just a few words.'

'He'll be so pleased you came. He was hoping you would. He's never got over you, you know.'

'Mia!' Keaton hisses.

My stomach gives a painful tug and I feel the gallery slant, slightly. 'I'm sure he has,' I say, forcing a laugh.

'No, he hasn't.'

I smile tightly, not wanting to hear this. It's too painful and it doesn't change anything. Aiden and I can't work.

Luckily, Aiden chooses that moment to make a speech so I don't have to answer. Someone brings out a microphone and Aiden thanks everyone for coming. He's adorably humble and sweet, and I'm sure everyone in the room is in love with him, not just me. As soon as he finishes, people flock towards him,

13

eager to congratulate him and say goodbye before making their way home.

Oh no, I don't think I can say goodbye to him. Just the thought of speaking to him again sends my pulse spiralling upwards.

'I'm going to have to go,' I say, checking my watch. 'Can you tell Aiden goodbye from me? I'm sorry. He's so busy and I'll miss my tube if I don't go now and I have to be up early in the morning.'

'You can't leave yet!' Mia gasps. 'You need to talk to Aiden.'

'He's busy,' I say, already drawing away from her. 'I don't want to interrupt.'

'Give me your number, then,' Mia pleads. 'I'll get him to call you. He's staying in London for at least another week.'

I hesitate. 'I'm sorry but I don't think that's a good idea. Good luck with the baby!'

I feel bad as I rush away, but not bad enough to stay. Collecting my coat, I hurry from the building into the storm outside. It's raining now, and the bitter wind feels like it's trying to drive me back inside the gallery, but I put my head down and push on, determined to get to the tube station in time for the next train.

I'm glad of the rain because it hides my tears when I start to cry. I knew I shouldn't have come tonight. To see Aiden again after all this time, to have him so tantalisingly close, to share lingering looks and then have to leave, is pure agony. A small voice at the back of my mind tells me I needn't have left. Tells me it was cowardly to leave. But what was the alternative? To stay and risk crying in front of him? No thanks. I'd like my dignity to remain intact.

I reach the entrance to the tube station and run down the steps to my platform. The train's already there, its electric doors wide open, welcoming me into its brightly lit interior. I hesitate, knowing that the moment this train leaves, there's no going back. I'll have left Aiden behind forever.

There's no going back anyway, I remind myself, only forward.

I step onto the train with seconds to spare before the doors close. Someone else is cutting it fine, too. I hear a shout and running footsteps, and they make it onto the train just as the doors slide shut behind them. I turn to say something about them almost getting chopped in half, but my words die on my tongue when I see who it is.

'*Aiden!*'

His eyes fix on mine and all the hairs on the back of my neck lift as he steps towards me. He can't be here. He's supposed be back in the gallery, at his own exhibition. He'll have to get off. He'll have to go back.

But even as I'm opening my mouth to speak, the train starts forward, rumbling onwards into the tunnel, and it's just me and him staring at each other across the carriage.

Five years earlier

Chapter 2

Five years earlier – Hawksley Village, UK

'Orla! Orla, where are you?' Phil bawls across the office, making several heads turn and me jump and spill the coffee I'm carrying back to his desk.

'I'm here, I'm here,' I say, hurrying forward as coffee dribbles down the side of his mug, burning my fingers. I hold it away from me so as not to stain my white jeans before placing it gingerly on his ring-marked desk. 'What's the matter?'

'Oh, there you are. I just wondered where you'd got to, that's all.' Leaning forward, he peers at his computer screen, stabbing the delete key several times with a short, chunky finger.

'I was just making you another coffee. You asked me to, remember?' I'm slightly concerned that he's drinking too much coffee. I've made him about seven already today and it's only 2 p.m. All that caffeine can't be good for his blood pressure. He's already a funny purple colour and I don't want to be the cause of his death.

'Oh yes, sorry, I just got a bit excited for a moment. There's a fire at the recycling centre. The whole lot's gone up in flames. We need to get down there and see what's going on. Come on,

16

grab your stuff.' He's already on his feet, pulling on his jacket as he downs the coffee I placed in front of him.

'But we're supposed to be interviewing that wildlife guy at three, aren't we? Have we got time to do both?'

'Oh shit, yeah, I forgot about him.' Phil swigs down the last of his coffee and sets the mug down on the desk. 'Can you ring him and postpone? Or do you want to go on your own?'

I hesitate. 'I can go on my own, it's not a problem.'

'Sure? Do you know what you're going to ask him?'

'I've got a list of questions ready. We talked about it last week, didn't we?'

'Of course, we did. That's great. Good girl.' He fusses about him, pulling his bag from beneath his desk and checking he's got his notebook and pen. 'He sounded like a decent guy when I spoke to him on the phone. Irish fella.'

'Oh good, I'm sure I'll be fine. Don't forget your keys,' I say, scooping them up from where they're nestled behind his keyboard. 'Have you got your phone?'

'Yep.' He pats the pocket on his shirt and smiles at me before turning to leave. 'See you later then, hon. Good luck.'

'Thanks. You too.'

I feel excited as I go back to my desk. In fact, I want to jump up and down and squeal. This will be my first solo interview for the *Hawksley Gazette*. I started working here six months ago, and every other time I've been shadowing Phil or one of the other reporters. But I feel like I'm ready and I'm pretty sure it won't be taxing. It's just a short interview with a guy who's photographing otters down by the river. My biggest concern is not being able to find the farm where we're supposed to meet. How unprofessional would it be if I turn up late to my first proper assignment? Or miss the appointment altogether? My stomach tightens with nerves as it gets closer to the time to leave, and I go to the toilet to check my appearance and reapply my lipstick.

I know I look younger than my twenty-two years. When I got

the job, I had my long blonde curly hair cut so I'd look more professional, but the short bob has made me look like a school-girl. I don't want this photographer to think I'm on a work placement or something. Having the job title of trainee reporter is bad enough. Not that I don't love the job or anything. I do. I really do. Every morning when I walk through the big glass doors into the building, I feel so happy I could do a twirl like Maria Von Trapp on a mountain. I suspect it might not go down too well with our ferocious receptionist though, so I never do. But it's my first job after graduating, and I feel so lucky to be working here. It may only be the local paper, serving Hawksley, a small rural town in central England that no one's heard of, but I know it's great experience.

After applying another coat of mascara and some blusher, I give my stupidly short hair one final rake through with my fingers. It's no good, I still look about 16. And it's not just the hair; my freckles don't do me any favours either. Nor my big, wide-set eyes. Mum says they make me look like a doll, which is hardly the image I want to project in my job. I fish out my black-rimmed glasses and put them on. I feel foolish wearing them when I have 20:20 vision (they're just clear glass lenses), but I think they make me look more intelligent. I slip them on and look at myself, before pushing them up to my forehead. On or off? I spend another couple of minutes pushing them up and down, trying to decide, then I pout a little and frown to see if that helps make me look less innocent. I'm just baring my teeth in a fierce snarl when the door opens and Chrissie from accounts comes in.

She stops and looks at me in surprise. 'You okay, love? What's up?'

'Nothing! I'm fine. Just off to interview a photographer,' I say, slightly hysterically.

'Oh, great.' Her face clears. 'Good luck!'

'Thanks.'

She goes into a cubicle and I roll my eyes at myself in the

mirror. It's time to go. I shove the glasses back in my bag, decision made. I'm not wearing them. I don't want to have to worry about them on top of my first solo assignment.

Hawksley is quite a new town, made up mostly of redbrick buildings and a pedestrianised town square with a good quota of high-street shops. There's still the odd original black-and-white timber building nestled in with the new, but mostly this town now belongs to the young couples and new families that are moving here in droves. The residents in the surrounding villages are furious about how Hawksley has grown in recent years, eating into the surrounding countryside as developers build new housing estates and schools to meet demand. I feel slightly bewildered by it myself; having lived here practically all my life, I can't wait to get out of the place. To see all these people moving in is weird. But then looking at it through their eyes I can see the attraction. House prices are lower than the nearby cities, and the town has a semi-rural but touristy feel about it, mostly due to the river that winds round the outskirts of the town centre.

The village where the photographer is staying is only a twenty-minute drive away, but I leave early to give myself plenty of time to find Lark Rise Farm where he said to meet. I've programmed my sat nav, but from past experience, I'm not overly confident it will find a farm. As luck would have it, once I'm through the village, Lark Rise Farm is the first place I see, and indicating right, I pull into the driveway and park in a neat stone courtyard next to an old red pick-up truck. Several chickens are pecking around near the house, and even though I'm ten minutes early, I climb out and head up to the front door, ready to interview Aiden Byrne.

A plump, smiling lady of about 50 answers, and I'm surprised by how well she fits the stereotypical image of a farmer's wife. Her dark hair is drawn back into a bun and she's wearing an apron with her sleeves rolled up, and flour all the way up to her elbows.

'Hi,' I say brightly. 'I'm here to see Aiden Byrne. He should be expecting me.'

'Oh, he's not here, my love. He's down by the river.' She raises a floured hand and points to a gate at the corner of the courtyard. 'If you go through there and down the hill, you'll find him.'

'Oh, great. Thank you.'

'You're welcome, my love. And you can tell him I'm making scones if he wants one later. They're his favourite.'

'Okay. Will do.' I grin as I leave her standing in the doorway, and head down towards the gate. I'm slightly alarmed by the steepness of the path down to the river, not to mention the muddiness, and looking down at my heeled patent leather Chelsea boots, suspect that I may not have chosen the most sensible footwear for interviewing a wildlife photographer.

Still, at least they're boots and not stiletto heels. Bravely, I make my way down the path, which is lined with purple foxgloves and tall, overgrown shrubbery with spindly foliage that snags on my clothes and catches my hair. A sheep baas suddenly from the field on the other side of the bushes, making my heart leap in fear. Clutching my chest, I laugh breathlessly and carry on down, holding on to branches as I go so as not to slip on the slimy earth. I'm relieved when I reach the bottom and find the ground flat and dry beneath my feet, sheltered by the trees that tower above me. I see the river glinting ahead, but no sign of Aiden Byrne. For some reason, I'd expected him to be waiting for me at the bottom, ready and waiting for his interview. I look around before spotting a khaki-coloured bell tent nestled between the trees.

'Hello?' I call, my voice sounding too loud in the quiet forest. A crow caws above me before taking flight, causing bits of greenery to fall from the tree.

I wait for an answer but there is nothing but birdsong and the rush of the river. Confused, I take another look around me before walking over to the tent.

'Hello? Mr Byrne?'

The tent flap is open and I can't help but see what's inside. There's a camp bed with a sleeping bag and two canvas storage cupboards; one with clothes spilling from its shelves, the other neatly stacked with pots and pans and tins of soup. A basket of vegetables sits on the floor and a folded-up camp chair lies on its side. Surely he doesn't live here? I stare for a moment, shocked that anyone can live so sparsely. I don't mind camping, but I like to have a few home comforts. There's not even a tent carpet on the floor, just a plastic groundsheet. I wince and back away, realising I'm intruding on his personal space.

There's still no sign of him, so I walk down to the river and watch the water rush around the rocks and boulders on its way downstream. It's much shallower here than in town, and the water is so clear you can see the flat brown pebbles lying on the bottom. In town, it's brown and so deep that all manner of dubious items lurk in its depths. You wouldn't want to swim in it, let alone drink it, but here the water looks so fresh and clean that I'm tempted to scoop some up and taste it.

The opposite bank of the river looks much wilder than this side, a dark tangled place where ash and sycamore trees compete for space, their roots poking through the river bank where the water has eroded the soil. A few trees have become so unsteady they grow outwards, their boughs and sometimes even their trunks leaning out low across the water. On this side of the river, the trees are more spaced out and uniform, growing upright, tall and proud. It's a very pretty spot. Peaceful. I spy a small waterfall a little way upstream and decide to get nearer to take a photograph.

Unfortunately, further on, the trees that I thought so nicely spaced and uniform grow as wild as the ones on the opposite bank. Leaves brush my face and brambles snag on my trousers, winding around my legs as though they're alive. As I push one away, another one takes its place. It feels like the vegetation is

21

out to claim me for its own and I'm already regretting my decision. My heels sink into the soft earth and catch on the gnarly roots, making me stumble as I struggle with the brambles. Deciding the waterfall isn't worth it, I turn to go back the way I came and put out a hand to steady myself on a nearby tree trunk. I expect to encounter rough bark, but instead feel soft material and the unmistakable warmth of a human arm.

There's a man standing against the tree in full camouflage, wearing a balaclava.

My scream rips through the air and everything is a blur of leaves and sky and ground as I try to run. There is no calm appraisal. No logic. It's fight or flight, and I choose flight.

I only get a few metres before I step in a rabbit hole. A blinding flash of pain and a crunch, and the ground comes up to meet me, knocking the air from my lungs.

'Owwwww! Ow, ow, owwwwww!' I clutch my lower leg. The pain from my ankle is unbearable.

'Hey, hey, hey!' The camouflage man approaches slowly, palms outstretched to show he's no threat. 'Shhh now. Calm down. I'm not going to hurt you.'

He speaks softly with an Irish accent, and dimly, through the panic and pain, it dawns on me that this is bloody Aiden Byrne. Oh Christ, why did I have to get the weirdo to interview on my first solo assignment? I think of all the normal people in normal places I've interviewed when shadowing Phil and think how unfair it is that I get the guy that plays hide-and-seek in the woods.

Aiden squats a few feet away from me and removes the camo-print balaclava. He doesn't look so scary without it. He's in dire need of a shave and his dark hair is crazy long and wild, sticking out in all directions, but his green eyes are kind and creased with concern.

'I'm so sorry,' he says. 'I was asleep, else I would have let you know I was there.'

'You were asleep?' I prop myself up on my elbow and peer at

him, still panting with pain and shock. 'But you were standing up!'

'Makes no difference to me.' He shrugs. 'I can sleep anywhere. I was waiting to photograph the owl that lives in that tree. It'll occasionally come out in the afternoon and sit on a branch but I'd been waiting for ages and must have drifted off. Are you hurt?'

'Yes, *obviously*! My ankle …' I try to move it, but pain slices through me making me close my eyes and gasp.

'Oh shit. You don't think it's broken, do you?'

'I don't know.' I feel like crying, but I can't, not here, now, in front of the man I've come to interview. It's hardly professional behaviour.

'What are you doing down here, anyway?' he asks. 'Are you lost?'

What? For crying out loud!

'No, I'm Orla Kennedy, from the *Hawksley Gazette*. You're Aiden Byrne, right? You agreed to an interview?'

'Oh! Friday at three?'

'That's right.'

'But today's … Wednesday?' He looks questioning, like he knows that's probably not right but he doesn't have a clue what day it is.

'No, today's Friday.'

'Really? Christ, I'm so sorry!' He pushes back his hair from his face. 'I completely lost track of what day it is. Here, let me help you up.'

'Oh no, I don't think I can.' I shrink away from him, not wanting to move or be touched or anything. I feel sick and dizzy and just want to sit here for a minute and compose myself.

'Well, you can't stay sitting down there like that. We'll have to do something.'

'Yes, I know, but just give me a minute. Maybe it will pass.'

He raises an eyebrow and stands up. He's very tall, at least six foot. For the first time, I notice the camera that hangs on a cord

23

around his neck. He's younger than I expected. For some reason, I thought he'd be about 40 or so, but he looks to be in his late twenties. Maybe I should have researched him more thoroughly before coming out here.

'I was expecting a man, actually,' he says. 'I spoke to someone called Phil on the phone.'

'Yes, he had another appointment so you've got me instead.' I shuffle backwards slightly and bend my good leg ready to support my weight. 'Okay, I think I'm ready to try and stand. Can you help me up?'

'Of course.' He reaches down and pulls me upwards so I'm standing on my good foot. As a rule, I don't like getting too close to people I don't know well. I like my personal space. But I feel so light-headed and unsteady that I need to lean against him to steady myself. Gingerly, I try to put my left foot down but can't put any weight on it at all.

'Oh, sweet Jesus! You can't walk, can you!'

I shake my head, teeth gritted with the pain.

'Here, I'll help you. Come on.' Hitching my arm over his shoulder, he wraps his arm around my waist, supporting my weight as we hobble forward. I don't know how I'm going to get back to his tent let alone my car. We shuffle a few more paces but the pain is too much and I have to stop. 'Alright, okay,' he says, and then scoops me up into his arms. With a yelp of surprise, I wrap my arms around his neck in case he drops me, but he's surprisingly strong and carries me easily through the trees, stepping over the foliage that caused me such difficulties a few moments ago.

It's a strange sensation being carried by a total stranger, and if it wasn't for the pain, I'd be screaming for him to put me down. I can hear him breathing and feel his heart beating through his shirt. It's much too intimate for my liking and I hold my breath in case he smells bad. He looks a bit grubby and his hair might be unwashed. But when I eventually have to breathe, he doesn't smell unpleasant at all. He just smells like the forest: of wood and leaves and fresh air.

We arrive back at his tent and he stands there, just holding me, deliberating what to do with me now we've arrived. 'Thank you,' I say stiffly, hoping he'll put me down.

'What for? Scaring you to death?'

'Not leaving me lying on the floor, waiting to be eaten.'

'Ah, I never thought of that. That could have been an idea.'

'What, eating me?'

'Not me.' He chuckles and sets me down in front of his tent. I stand on one leg, clinging on to his lean, sinewy frame as he reaches inside and brings out a dark green camping chair. 'Here, sit on that. No, I was thinking more of the animals I could film eating you. Foxes and badgers and stoats and—'

'Charming! Thanks very much,' I say, sinking down into the chair. 'Badgers are herbivores, aren't they?'

'No, omnivores.' He fetches a small folding stool and gently lifts my bad leg to rest on it. 'Can you take your boot off?'

'Yes.' Leaning forward, I unzip my boot and ease it off. It hurts like hell and as I slip my sock off, I see it's already starting to swell. A purple and yellow bruise is spreading across my foot.

'Can you wiggle your toes?' He squats and peers closely at my foot and ankle. I try and though it hurts a lot there is some movement. 'Ah good. I doubt you've broken it then, but you'll have to get it checked at the hospital.'

'I don't want to go to hospital! Besides, how would I get there?'

'Same way you'll get home, I expect. I'll take you. The main problem is getting you up the hill to my truck. You saw how steep it is when you came down so I don't know if I'll be able to carry you all the way up.' He places a hand gently on my knee as he peers again at my ankle, then removes it quickly as though realising what he's doing. I'm not offended by his touch though. It doesn't feel inappropriate, especially since he's just carried me

25

bodily through the trees. 'Really you should ice it. I'll run up to the farm and see if Ivy's got anything we can use, but in the meantime I'll wet a towel in the river. The water's pretty cold and it might help with the swelling.'

'Okay. Thank you.'

He roots in the cupboard in his tent and pulls out a blue towel before going down to the river. I watch him through the trees, squatting on his haunches as he submerges the towel, long hair falling around his shoulders. He looks like how I imagined Jesus when I was a child. I'm hoping he can perform a miracle and make my ankle better so I can drive home. I really don't want to go to the hospital.

The wet towel is freezing cold and I flinch and squeal when he lays it over my ankle. He cringes and squats next to me. 'I'm sorry. I'll get the ice.'

'No, leave it. This will do.' I pant a little as I get used to the sensation of coldness and he reaches for my hand and squeezes it. Strangely, it seems to help and we sit for a few moments in silence, just holding hands. 'We may as well do the interview now,' I say when it starts to feel weird. 'Who knows, I might feel better by the time we're done.'

'Christ, how long's the interview? Two or three weeks? Have you seen the size of your ankle? That's definitely a hospital job.'

I scowl. 'No, it's probably just a sprain. I'll be alright. Actually, I've got some paracetamol in my bag. That will help.'

Aiden laughs. 'Ah, optimism. I like it.'

Ignoring him, I find my tablets and pull my notepad from my bag. 'Okay, are you ready?'

'No.'

'But I need to do this interview.' There's a note of pleading in my voice that I don't like, and I cough to try and cover it up.

'I think you should just rest.'

'I think I should work. It will take my mind off the pain. Besides, this is my first solo interview. I need to complete it.'

26

Aiden's eyebrows shoot up. 'This is your …? Oh my God! That makes this so much worse.'

'Yes, I know. Thank you for pointing that out.' I flip open my notebook. 'Anyway, it's really important that I get this interview otherwise I'll look like a complete failure.'

'No one can blame you if you're hurt.'

'I'm pretty sure they can. So if you wouldn't mind, I've only got a few questions and they're not especially taxing.'

'Okay, go ahead.'

'So, your name is Aiden Byrne and you're a wildlife photographer, is that correct?'

'Yep.'

'Can you tell me a bit about what you're doing here?'

'I've been commissioned to film and photograph otters, so I made some enquiries and found that this was an ideal spot. Ivy and Bill up at the farm have been great letting me stay down here.'

'I didn't even know there were otters around here.'

'Yeah, they've made a big comeback in recent years, and now can be found all over the country. But they're very secretive animals, coming out mainly at night to hunt and play. It's not so much that they're nocturnal, they're just shy of humans. Around here is great because it's part of the farm so there are no dog walkers or kids playing or anything else that might disturb them. It's very quiet so I have more chance of seeing them in the daytime.'

'Have you seen them?'

He hesitates and scratches his beard. 'Yes, but not for a while. When I first got here a couple of months ago, I got some great shots of a male and female mating. It's a miracle really. The timing was perfect. I mean, I was tipped off by the local otter watch. They have people monitoring otter activity along the river and they'd seen the pair together. Not right here' – he waves his hand at his little stretch of river – 'but a bit further upstream. So, they phoned me and I got here just at the right time.'

'How long do they mate for?' It's not on my list of questions, but I find myself fascinated by what he's got to say.

'A couple of days or so. It's quite brutal, really. Not the nicest courtship in the world. I was really lucky to capture some of it on camera. The male moved on straight after, so he's gone now and I doubt I'll be seeing him again, but I got some good footage of the female on her own afterwards. Some great underwater shots of her hunting for fish too. But then she disappeared, presumably to have her pups, so …'

'How did you get the underwater shots?'

He turns and looks towards the river. 'I've got underwater trail cams set up in the river.'

'Oh wow.'

'Yeah, they stream to my laptop so I can see what's going on down there. I've got hours of footage that I'm still going through. But like I was saying, she disappeared so I assumed she went into her holt to give birth. The problem is, they stay in the holt until the pups are three months old, so basically all sightings of the female have dried up.'

'Why three months?'

'Their coats have to be fully waterproof before they can swim, so then the mother brings them out and teaches them how to swim and survive in the wild. That's the moment I'm waiting for. I'm desperate to get that on camera. I went away for a while, assuming she was giving birth and therefore I had about two months before she reappeared, but I came back early just in case I've got the timings wrong or she reappears. So now it's just a waiting game. Anyway, sorry I'm going on and on. I'm sure you don't need to know all this for your article, and I told that Phil on the phone that I really don't want people knowing exactly where I am. I can't afford to have day-trippers coming down to see what I'm doing or trying to catch a glimpse of the otters. It's blissfully quiet here at the moment and when I first saw the otters they seemed really relaxed, even coming out in the day. I don't want that to change, especially if there are pups about.'

'Okay, that's not a problem. But I can mention they're present in Hawksley River?'

'Yes, of course. Use it as a way to educate people. If they have dogs, let them know they need to keep them on a lead if they're near a stretch of river where otters are known to be. There are lots of signs people can look out for that tell them if otters are present. Five-toed footprints on muddy river banks, flattened, smooth patches of grass or soil going into the river where the otters have slid in, dead fish and fish scales left at the side of the water, and spraint.'

'Spraint?'

'Poo. They mark their territories using spraint, and well-used areas usually get a good coating. There's a rock along the river I can show you – another day, obviously,' he says, nodding at my ankle, 'where the spraint has built up from continued use. Otters are solitary animals, so they don't share their territories with other otters.'

'Really? I always imagine them living in big groups, holding hands in the water and looking cute.'

'That's sea otters. These are Eurasian river otters. A male otter will have a territory of about eleven miles, and there will be females living within that, but no other males.'

'Oh, I see. So, who's commissioned you to take this footage?'

'A wildlife magazine, and the BBC are interested in any film footage I might get for a wildlife documentary.'

'Wow, that's impressive.'

He shrugs and then frowns at me. 'Are you alright? You've gone a funny colour?'

'I feel a bit sick, but I'll be alright.' I shift on the chair and suck in a breath as pain shoots up my leg. 'Have you contributed footage to any documentaries before?'

'Yes, several in fact. I've filmed bats for a kid's nature

29

programme, contributed to *Springwatch* and *Autumnwatch*, lots of things. I'm never short of work.'

'Great. What did you do when you left here for a while? Did you take a holiday or do more work?'

'I just went home to see my family. Usually I'm halfway around the world so it's great being closer to home and feeling like I can pop back whenever I need to.'

'Where is home? Dublin?'

'Close. I'm a country boy. Wicklow. Can I make you some tea or get you something to drink?'

'No, thank you. Oh, I meant to tell you that the lady up at the house said she's making scones if you want some later.'

Aiden laughs. 'Aw she's good to me. Her cooking's amazing. I love her scones.'

'Do you eat all your meals up there?'

'Not all, but she invites me up for Sunday lunch and the odd meal in the week. I think she thinks I'm mad for living down here on my own. She thinks I'm going to starve to death or something. I tell her I'm used to living like this. This is my life.'

I glance back at the tent with a raised eyebrow. 'You live like this constantly?'

He nods. 'I'm always working.'

'Can't you stay in hotels?'

'Where's the fun in that?' He laughs. 'You can't beat sleeping under canvas.'

'You can. I'm sorry, but sleeping on a camp bed? That's no fun, surely?'

He laughs again. 'Like I said before, I can sleep pretty much anywhere.'

My eyes get very big as I try to absorb this information. 'But what about in the winter?'

'I just use a thicker sleeping bag. Although to be honest I usually work it so I go somewhere warmer. If the weather gets really bad and I don't need to be out filming, I do stay in hotels.

Ivy and Bill have let me stay in their spare room a couple of times when it's been stormy. It's nice to sleep in a proper bed once in a while. And I shower up there so it's great to be able to wash.'

I shake my head slowly. 'I just don't get it. Why would you want to live like this?'

'I love it. I love my job. I don't have to camp, but I feel more connected to nature when I do and that helps me in my work.'

'Oh.' I tip my head on one side, considering. 'That's kind of beautiful.'

He smiles and lifts the towel to look at my ankle. I flinch slightly and put my hand out to stop him, but he's careful not to touch my foot. 'I've got to tell you, that's not looking good. It's more swollen than before. I really think we should get you to hospital.'

'But ...'

'No buts. I insist. I can't be responsible for you hurting yourself and then not take you to hospital. I won't have it.' He stands up and starts to remove his camouflage jacket and trousers. I watch, slightly alarmed that he's stripping off in front of me, but luckily he's wearing jeans and a blue T-shirt underneath. Somehow, they make him look a lot more normal. He ducks into his tent and grabs a hooded sweatshirt. 'Are you cold? Do you want to wear this?'

'No, I'm okay,' I say, though I do feel a little chilly.

'You've got goose bumps on your arms. Here, put it on.' He holds it out for me to slip my arms inside and once it's on, I feel glad of the soft material. 'Right, let's do this,' he says, lifting the towel from my leg and then my leg gently off the folding stool. I hold my breath, not wanting to move at all, but Aiden is all business as he ties up his hair and then turns and bends down, one knee on the floor. 'I'll have to give you a piggyback.'

'Are you sure?' I say, with some uncertainty. 'I don't want to hurt you.'

31

'Don't worry about me. I'll stop if I can't manage it and you'll have to stay in my tent until you're better.' He laughs wickedly.

'Don't say that!' I have a very real fear that it actually will come to that. I can't believe this tall spindly man will be able to carry me up that hill.

'Don't worry, I won't make you sleep on the floor. You can have my camp bed and I'll sleep up at the farm.'

'Wonderful.'

He smiles. 'Come on, climb aboard.'

Heaving myself out of the chair, I stand on my good leg and wrap my arms around his neck. Aiden hooks his arms around the back of my legs and stands up. Pain shoots through my ankle as it brushes his side and I shout out and bury my face in his neck.

'Sorry,' he says, standing very still. 'Shall I put you down?'

I shake my head against him. 'No, go on.'

He starts to walk and I keep my eyes closed, teeth gritted as my ankle dangles and bobs with each swaying step. It's agony, but there's no way I'm staying in his tent tonight. I start to feel nauseous from the pain and I keep my mouth tight shut, imagining the horror of vomiting down this man's collar.

'I hope I don't smell,' he's saying. 'I did have a shower this morning so I should be alright, but I don't tend to wear loads of deodorant because I don't want the animals to scent me.'

'Do you want to go and put some on?' I mutter, my stomach turning over queasily. 'You might get a bit sweaty walking up this hill.'

'Nah, it's okay. It's up at the farm.'

'Great.'

He laughs cheerfully as we start to ascend the hill. He's got long legs and thick-soled walking boots, so he's able to cover the muddy ground quickly. His breathing becomes noisier and more laboured the closer we get to the top and I feel bad that I'm putting him through this. The swaying motion of his walk isn't doing anything to settle my stomach either, and I have to swallow several times as my mouth starts to water ominously.

'Right, we're here,' he says, letting me slither gently to the ground. As soon as I'm standing on my good foot, I turn and vomit into the dirt.

'I smell that bad, huh?'

I'm a mortified, trembling mess. My good leg wobbles and Aiden holds me firmly upright while I fumble in my pockets for a tissue. 'No,' I say, eventually. 'It's the pain.'

There are black spots at the corners of my vision, and I feel weak and light-headed. I'm only dimly aware of our surroundings – the square courtyard, the large, white farmhouse, the blue sky overhead, the red pick-up truck – but they're all spinning. Aiden swears softly as he struggles to hold me up while opening his truck door, then he lifts me up and onto the cracked black leather seat inside. The door slams, then he's sitting beside me and the truck's rumbling out of the yard.

'I'm sorry,' I keep repeating, my eyes tight shut.

'Don't be sorry. Tell me if you need to be sick again and I'll pull over.' He changes gear and the truck shudders. 'Sorry about the truck. It belongs to the farmer, Bill. He lets me borrow it whenever I need to. I don't really like driving her because she's such an old wreck and I can just imagine the amount of pollutants coming out of her exhaust.'

I can't answer him. My mouth is clamped shut and all I can do is murmur slightly. Every bump the truck encounters judders through me. Aiden keeps talking, and even though I don't listen to the words he says, his deep, soft lilting voice is soothing. After what seems like hours but is probably only minutes, we reach the hospital and Aiden parks the truck. I start to tell him that I don't want to be here, I want to go home, but he doesn't listen and instead gets out and opens my door. 'Come on,' he says, scooping me into his arms. 'Let's get you sorted.' He shuts the door with his shoulder and then he's striding across the car park to the accident and emergency department.

Some kind of miracle has occurred and the waiting room is almost empty. There's only me and a boy of about 12 holding a compress to his swollen eye. I give the receptionist my details and Aiden and I sit together in the waiting room. We've been sitting there for at least five minutes before I realise I'm holding his hand. I stare down at our entwined fingers, wondering how and when it happened. His thumb moves steadily back and forth against the back of my hand and I'm amazed by how comforting this contact is. It makes me realise how important another person's touch can be, even when they're essentially a stranger.

'Would you like some water?' Aiden asks quietly.

I nod and he gets up and goes across to the water dispenser in the corner of the room. He comes back moments later with a small plastic cup and I take it gratefully. The cool liquid washes the sour taste from my mouth and I lean against him, feeling weak. He takes my hand again and resumes the gentle massage with his thumb.

The doctor examines my ankle and then sends me for an X-ray. He says he thinks it's probably just a sprain, but he can't be sure.

'Do you want me to phone someone for you?' Aiden asks as we wait in the X-ray department. I'm in a wheelchair and I'm sure he's glad he doesn't have to carry me everywhere anymore.

'No. It's a Friday night, everyone will be going out and my mum has to take my sister to her drama club.' I look at him, realising perhaps for the first time that he might not want to be stuck here in the hospital, waiting around with me. He has owls and otters and badgers to photograph, after all. 'Don't feel you have to stay with me, though. You should go,' I add.

'No, no, that's not what I meant at all.' He looks earnest as he takes my hand again. 'I want to stay, I just thought you might prefer someone else other than me to be here.'

It's weird, but at that moment I can't think of anyone better than him. My mum would fuss, my dad would just be useless and my best friend wouldn't stop talking. Aiden's quiet, calm demeanour and gentle manner are just what I need right now. I smile and shake my head just as the door to the X-ray room opens and they call me in. Aiden pushes me to the door in the wheelchair but stays outside while they X-ray my ankle.

To my relief, my ankle is just badly sprained and not broken, though I'm amazed that something that's not a break could hurt so much. They bandage it up and give me advice about keeping it iced, elevated and rested before letting me go. Aiden wheels me to his truck and then returns the wheelchair to the hospital before driving me back to my flat.

I live on the ground floor of a new-build apartment block. It's just one bedroom, a bathroom and an open-plan kitchen and dining room, but it's home. I see Aiden sag with relief when he realises he doesn't have to carry me up another flight of stairs.

'Are you sure you don't want me to call someone for you?' Aiden asks as we enter my flat and he deposits me onto the sofa. I shift sideways so I can keep my leg propped up. 'I really don't like thinking about you on your own like this. How are you going to get to the toilet? What will you do if you need something to drink?'

'It's fine, I'll text my friend Katie. She only lives upstairs.'

'What if she's out? Do you want me to stay? I'm happy to stay with you overnight.'

'No, you've done enough.' I smile up at him, touched by his kindness. 'Thank you so much, and I'm sorry for causing you so much hassle.'

'Can I do anything before I go?'

'I tell you what, you can help me into the bedroom, actually. I'm really tired so I'll just go straight to sleep. And the toilet is within hopping distance so I'll be okay.'

He helps me up and supports me across the room and into

my bedroom. I love my bed. It's all white: white frame, white duvet, white fairy lights entwined around the headboard, but it's never looked more welcoming and comfortable than it does now. I can't wait to get into it. Aiden sits me down then goes back to the kitchen to get a jug of iced water and a cup of tea to keep me going.

'Anything else?' he asks, hovering in the doorway.

'You couldn't get my pyjamas out, could you?' I point to the chest of drawers across the room. 'Second drawer down.'

He goes willingly, looking huge and masculine in my very feminine bedroom. 'These ones?' he asks, holding up a pair of candy-stripe pyjamas.

'Yes, perfect.'

'Do you want me to help you into them?'

'No!' I give him a look and he grins as he backs away, hands held up in surrender. 'I'll be going then. Nice to meet you, Orla.'

'Nice to meet you too, Aiden. And thank you for looking after me.'

'My pleasure.' He smiles, hovering in the doorway like he doesn't know whether to stay or go. 'Well, have a nice life.'

'You too.'

The front door closes with a final click.

Chapter 3

My mum's appalled when I phone to tell her what's happened.

'You were stranded in a forest with a man you'd never met before?' she says. 'Anything could have happened to you! What's your boss playing at, sending you into dangerous situations like that on your own?'

'It wasn't a dangerous situation, Mum. I just went to interview someone for the paper. Phil had to be somewhere else so I volunteered. It wasn't his fault. Besides, I was glad to do it. It was my first solo assignment so I was really excited.'

'Your first solo assignment? And you didn't even get the interview?' Her voice switches from concern to disappointment. I assume she's disappointed on my behalf rather than disappointed in me.

'Oh, I got the interview. I just got a sprained ankle as well. It'll be okay soon though.' I look down at my bandaged foot, hoping that it really will be soon. I'm still in my pyjamas and have no intention of struggling into any sort of real clothes today.

'You're lucky the man was kind. What if he'd been a rapist or a murderer? You shouldn't be meeting strange men alone in the woods. Even without you falling and hurting your ankle, that was a dodgy situation to be in.'

I suppose I hadn't really thought about it like that, I just thought it was the job.

'Lots of journalists die, you know,' Mum goes on. 'Didn't you hear about that woman who went to interview some inventor and never came home?'

'Yes, Mum, but it wasn't a dodgy situation really. I think I was supposed to meet him at the farm, but he'd forgotten all about it and when I spoke to the farmer's wife, she sent me down to where he's camping by the river.'

'Well, it all sounds most peculiar to me. Why is he camping?'

'I told you, he's trying to photograph the otters down there. He lives out in the woods so he doesn't miss anything. He's a really interesting guy, although I don't know how he lives like he does. I couldn't do it.'

'Sounds like a bit of a weirdo to me.'

'Mum! He took care of me. He took me to hospital and stayed with me and then brought me home. He was lovely.'

'Was he handsome?'

I roll my eyes. There it was, the question she always asks any time I mention a man. She's desperate for me to get a boyfriend, though I've already told her I don't have time for a relationship right now. 'Well he wasn't ugly, but he wasn't my type.'

'Why? What was he like?'

'Tall, scruffy, long hair, beard.' I feel a sense of shame for selling Aiden so short when he'd been so lovely, but when it came to my mother, it was best to nip these things in the bud.

'Oh dear, well perhaps you could smarten him up a bit. Unless he was old? Was he old?'

'No, late twenties, I think. But look, I doubt I'll even see him again. We did the interview already and it's only a short piece, really to inform people that there are otters in the river. It's not a massive deal, although he's working for the BBC so perhaps our local otters will end up on TV.'

38

'Oooh!' Mum says, as though impressed we have potential celebrity wildlife. 'That will be exciting.'

'Yes, Mum.' My ankle is starting to hurt again and I reach for the painkillers from my bedside table. 'So, I know this is a bit cheeky, but I was wondering if you could pick up my car for me? I've left it parked at the Lark Rise Farm, just past Innswood village.'

'Oh, yes, I can do that for you, love. It'll have to be later on this afternoon though, because Ray's out. I'll call in for the key on the way past and you can give me the directions then.'

Ringing off, I slide across the bed to go and make myself a cup of tea. It's slow progress but I manage to get to the kitchen by hopping to the doorway, clinging to the frame, then hopping the rest of the way to the worktop. I'm quietly celebrating my achievement when the doorbell chimes.

'Hold on,' I call, stealing myself to get to the door.

'Take your time,' a male Irish voice calls back.

Aiden. What the hell is he doing here? It takes a minute or so to cross the short distance from the sofa to the door, but I can't help the smile that spreads across my face as I open it and see Aiden standing there. He's leaning against the side of the door-frame, holding up the boot I left behind yesterday.

'I was going to make a comment about Cinderella, but I'm guessing this isn't going to fit you right now.' His eyes twinkle from between thick black lashes as he smiles down at me.

'No, I don't think it will.' I look down at my fat foot and laugh. 'Thank you for bringing it back. That's really kind of you.'

He shrugs. 'You're welcome. I wanted to see how you're doing, anyway. Are you managing okay?'

'Yes, not too bad.' I hold the door open wider. 'I was just about to make a cup of tea if you'd like one?'

He raises his eyebrows and smiles. 'How about I make the tea and you sit down and rest.'

'That sounds like a good plan. Thank you.'

39

Shutting the door behind him, he takes my arm to support me as I start to hop to the sofa. Now the shock has worn off and the painkillers are working, I feel more self-conscious about him touching me, but as soon as I'm on the sofa he lets go and his matter-of-fact attitude makes me relax. He moves around my tiny kitchen, setting down mugs and opening doors and drawers in search of tea bags and teaspoons. I watch him curiously. His hair looks less wild today, as though he's brushed it recently so instead of wild spindly curls, it falls in soft thick waves around his face.

'I thought you might have someone with you today,' he says. 'Did you call anyone?'

'I phoned my mum before. She's going to collect my car for me.'

'And what about helping you around your flat?' He leans on the kitchen counter and looks at me, drumming his fingers as though he already knows the answer and disapproves.

I shrug. 'I'll manage.'

'You know you need to rest so that you heal quicker. You heard what the doctor said at the hospital.'

'I know. I'm not about to go for a jog!'

He rolls his eyes. 'That's not what I meant but glad to hear it.' The kettle boils and he pours the water into two mugs. 'Have you eaten breakfast?'

'Not yet.'

'What do you want? Toast? I've got to tell you, it's about all I can make.'

'Just a bowl of cereal will be fine.'

'I'll make you toast and cereal. How does that sound?' He brings the mug of tea over and pulls the coffee table closer to the sofa so I can reach it easily.

'You're very thoughtful,' I say, touched by his kindness. 'You really don't need to go to all this trouble, you know. I caused you enough yesterday.'

40

'It's no trouble,' he says, returning to the kitchen and putting bread into the toaster. 'Really, I have purely selfish reasons for doing all this.'

'Which are?'

'To alleviate my guilt for scaring you half to death. Honestly, I feel awful.'

'It's okay. You didn't mean to. You were there just waiting for your owl.' I lift my tea to my lips and blow on it before taking a sip. 'Although you were in full camouflage which is rather scary. Do you always dress like that?'

'To photograph animals, I do. It helps me blend in with the surroundings, which is kind of the point of camouflage.'

'Well, it works.' I laugh. 'I was just telling my mum about you actually, she said I shouldn't be meeting strange men in forests when I'm on my own.'

'That's probably good advice. Your mum's a wise woman.'

'I told her how good you were though, and she's very grateful.'

'Anyone would have done the same.'

'No, really, you went above and beyond. You didn't have to stay with me in the hospital, nor bring me home.'

'Of course I did.'

'And you definitely didn't need to go out of your way to bring my boot back and make my breakfast,' I say, accepting a plate of toast from him. He goes back to the kitchen and pours the muesli into a bowl with some milk. 'Feel free to help yourself to anything you fancy.'

'I've already eaten, thank you.'

'I feel like a pig eating all this in front of you.'

'Don't be daft. Eat up or I'll be offended.' He smiles as he sits in the armchair opposite. The sun coming through the window shines on his hair, making the soft frizzy bits glow like a halo around his head. 'Did you sleep okay or did the pain keep you awake?'

'I managed a bit of sleep, but I woke up a few times.'

41

'I felt bad about leaving you here alone last night. I kept imagining you stranded in your bed. I gave you loads of liquids then offered you no assistance in getting to the loo.'

'If it's any consolation,' I say, crunching through my toast, 'I wouldn't have let you take me to the loo.'

He laughs. 'You know what I mean. I was just concerned about you. And I was hoping you'd have someone with you today.'

'My mum's coming later.'

'I thought she was getting your car.'

'She is, but she's calling in first to see me.'

'Well, make sure she knows you need help. You shouldn't struggle on your own when I'm sure you have people around you that want to help.'

'How do you know that people want to help?' I wipe toast crumbs from my mouth with my pyjama sleeve before reaching for my mug of tea.

'Why wouldn't they?'

I shrug. 'People have their own lives. You're very kind, but I'm fine, really.'

'Sure you are. Is that why you look so pale and tired?'

'Cheers!'

'Well, you do. You've got dark circles under your eyes.'

'It's probably yesterday's mascara. I didn't remove my make-up last night.'

He shakes his head and picks up a newspaper. 'You look knackered.'

I laugh. 'Any more compliments?'

'Nice pyjamas?'

'Thanks.' I pick up my bowl of muesli and start spooning it into my mouth. I hadn't realised how hungry I am until I started to eat. Milk dribbles down my chin and onto my pyjama top and I'm relieved that Aiden is reading the paper and not watching me. 'Can you put the TV on?' I ask, after a while of sitting in silence. Not that it's uncomfortable, I just want to watch the news.

'Of course.'

As he gets up, the doorbell rings. 'Ah, would this be your mother, do you think?'

'It's a bit early. She said she wouldn't be able to come until later.' I sit up and try to peer through the window to see if there's a car parked outside, but I can't see one. 'I bet it's my friend Katie. Can you get it for me?'

Obediently, he goes and answers the door. Sure enough, it's Katie. From my position on the sofa, I see her jaw drop as she stares up at Aiden in amazement.

'Hi,' he says easily. 'If it's Orla you're wanting, she's laid up on the couch with a badly sprained ankle.'

'Oh no! Really?' She peers around the door into the room and looks at me with big round eyes. 'What happened?'

'Some eejit jumped out and scared her half to death,' Aiden says, making me laugh. Katie glances up at him, and I can see she's wondering who he is.

'I got my foot stuck in a rabbit hole,' I tell her. 'Come in, Katie. This is Aiden. He helped me when I fell and took me to the hospital.'

'Oh good. At least you had someone with you!' She comes into the room and sits in the chair that Aiden's just vacated before leaning forward and peering at my bandaged ankle. 'Look how big it is! Is that just loads and loads of bandage or is it really that huge?'

'Bit of both, I expect.' I spoon up another mouthful of muesli. 'Katie lives upstairs, Aiden,' I tell him, covering my mouth so he can't see the food inside. 'See, I'm not totally friendless.'

'Glad to hear it,' Aiden says, turning to Katie. 'She needs help, though she won't admit it or ask for it.'

'No, she never does,' Katie says.

'Ah, a common theme then?'

'Definitely.'

'Hey!' I say, annoyed they're talking about me like I'm not in the room. 'I'm okay. I can hop, it's fine.'

'I'd like to see you hop holding a cup of tea or a bowl of cereal,' Aiden says.

'Shut up and sit back down,' I tell him. 'You're making the place look untidy.'

'Ah no, you've got a friend to help now,' he says. 'And I've got some things to get from town so I better go. Here, I'll leave you my number.' He stoops to scribble his name on my notepad on the table. 'Call me if you need anything.' He smiles at me as he straightens up then turns to Katie. 'Nice to meet you, Katie. Bye now.'

'Oh my God, who was he?!' Katie says once he's gone. She goes to the window to watch him striding down the path towards his truck. 'He was like … oh my God!'

'Like what?' I say, bristling defensively in case she says something negative about him.

'Totally sexy.'

'Really?' Well, that was unexpected! I didn't think she'd think that at all.

'Hell yeah! Why? Don't you think so?' She turns and looks at me in surprise.

I shrug. 'I haven't really thought about him like that. He's the guy who got me to hospital, watched me vomit, and now has seen me looking like death in my pyjamas.'

'You don't look like death! You look sexy and rumpled.' Sitting back down in the armchair, she tucks her legs beneath her.

'Well, he told me I did.'

'I bet he didn't. What did he say?'

'He said I looked knackered.'

'Knackered isn't like death, Orla. Knackered is sexy and rumpled.'

'It is not!' I laugh in disbelief. Katie's positivity and optimism never fail to amaze me. 'So, tell me, how did your date go last night? Any good?'

'Well, let's put it this way' – she smiles mischievously – 'he's only just gone home.'

'That good, eh?'

'Oh, Orla he was just perfect!' she says dreamily. 'We got on so well and he paid for my meal and everything. He's going to call me tonight and hopefully we'll go out again.'

Suppressing the urge to roll my eyes, I smile and nod encouragingly. This is not an unusual occurrence. Katie goes on lots of dates with men she meets on dating websites, and they are almost always 'perfect', until they stop being perfect a few days or weeks down the line. To her credit, she doesn't spend much time moping about them, she just moves on to the next. Personally, I couldn't be bothered with the hassle. I don't even know why she wants a boyfriend so badly. Boyfriends just complicate things. I like being single and not having to share my lovely white bed with some stinky man. If I don't feel like shaving my legs, then I don't shave my legs. I can do whatever I like when I like without having to consider anyone else's feelings. Besides, I'm just too busy for a boyfriend. I often work late in the office, and even go in on the weekend if needed.

Katie's still talking about last night's date and I'm happy to listen while I finish my breakfast. She makes more tea and helps me to the toilet, then we watch TV until my mum calls around to collect my car keys.

Katie opens the door and Mum looks horrified when she sees the huge bandage over my swollen foot. 'You didn't tell me it was this bad!' she says, running her hand through her curly blonde hair. That's where I get mine from – and the wide-set blue eyes. Everyone says we look exactly alike.

'Well, I did tell you I'd been carried into the hospital by a stranger, so that should tell you a little bit of how bad it is.'

'But you said it wasn't broken. I thought you were just being a drama queen.'

'According to the nurse at the hospital, a sprain can be just as painful as a break,' I say indignantly. I'm annoyed about the drama queen comment. When have I ever been a drama queen? Well, maybe when I was a teenager, but certainly not recently. 'It should heal quicker, though,' I add when I see the worried look cross her face.

'Do you want me to stay with you? I can take time off work and look after you.'

'No, you don't have to do that! You've got Ray and Keeley to think about.' Keeley's only 10. She's my half-sister, and I know Mum needs to be at home for her. My stepdad Ray works long hours so it wouldn't be fair to commandeer her time like that. 'Besides, I've got Katie upstairs if I need help.'

Katie beams and nods. Mum watches me worriedly. 'Well, I really feel like you should have someone with you. Why don't you stay with us for a while?'

'You haven't got room for me, Mum. Your spare room is full of junk.'

'We can clear it.'

I laugh, thinking of the car parts that Ray stores in there, and the general junk they've accrued over the years. It stopped being my bedroom as soon as I left to go to university at 18. 'No, you don't have to go to all that trouble just for me. I'll be alright.'

Mum gives me a worried look. 'Well, I can come and sit with you tonight. I'll get us a Chinese takeaway.'

I perk up at this. 'That sounds good. Are you sure?'

'Of course I am. Right, Ray's waiting outside so I'll go and get this car of yours. Have you got the address?'

'Yep.' I've jotted it down on the pad Aiden used to write his number, and I glance at his ungainly scrawl before flipping to the page with the address and ripping it out. 'Thanks, Mum.'

'No problem, see you in a bit.'

Katie leaves soon after, and I grab my phone and add Aiden's number to my contacts. For some reason, having his number gives me a warm feeling inside, and I stare at it for a moment before sending him a text message:

46

Thanks for everything. Thought you'd like to know that my mum is staying tonight. Orla x

The instant the message goes, I regret the kiss. I want to snatch it back, but it's already gone, zinging through the ether to his phone. I console myself by thinking he probably won't receive it anyway; being out in the woods like that, I doubt the phone signal is any good. But within seconds my phone pings with a message:

Good x

Chapter 4

'So, you're not coming in today then, Orla?' Phil says when I phone him on Monday morning and tell him about my ankle.

'No, I'm sorry but I've really hurt my ankle and I won't be able to make it into the office. I can work from home though.'

'Is it broken?'

'No, just badly sprained, but I can't walk on it yet. It should be better in the next couple of days though.'

'How did you do it? Out dancing?'

'No, I did it when I went to interview Aiden on Friday. He'd forgotten we were coming so I went to look for him in the woods and stepped in a rabbit hole. He was really lovely though. Took me to hospital and everything.'

'Oh my God! Orla! That's terrible. I'm so sorry.'

'It's alright. Just one of those things. I got the interview anyway. Just about to email you the article now.'

'Oh! Well done!'

'How was the fire?'

'Good. The whole place burned to the ground. I got some great photos.'

I laugh. 'Do you know how morbid that sounds?'

'Of course, but it'll make a good story. Besides, no one died so I'm golden. So you're not planning on suing this guy then?'

'Why would I sue him? He carried me up a hill to his truck, drove me to hospital, carried me into the hospital, then drove me home afterwards. He couldn't have done more for me than that.'

'He could have been up at the farm like he said he would be. Honestly, Orla, if a situation like that ever arises again, don't go alone. Never put yourself in danger.'

'I thought that was what being a reporter was all about? Pushing yourself to the limits to get the story.'

'Maybe when you're a war correspondent, but not when you're a trainee reporter for the local rag. Think what would have happened if he was a rapist or a murderer!'

'Yes, thanks, Phil. I've already had this lecture from my mum.'

'Yeah, well, she's right. And I feel bad too. I should have cancelled it and we could have gone together another time.'

'Oh no!' I say, panicking that he'd think I wasn't good enough to go off on my own and do solo interviews. 'It all worked out fine. He was great.'

'Apart from you injuring yourself.'

'Yes, but I didn't break it. I'll soon be back to normal, I just can't get into the office today. Is there anything I can do from home?'

'I'm sure I can find you something, although you can't make me cups of coffee from home, can you?' he says gloomily.

'I'll make you extra when I come back, how's that?'

'I'll hold you to that. There's some stuff on the website you can do. We're supposed to be starting an eco-blog and there're some old articles on the main website that you can link to it. I'll email over the details.'

'Okay, great.'

The web stuff keeps me occupied for the rest of the day. I like doing the web stuff. Phil hates it, but I love the immediacy of it all and the design side is fun. I don't realise how late it's got when there's a knock at the door and Katie lets herself in with the key I've given her. She's just back from work and still dressed in her dental nurse uniform.

'Hiya!' she says cheerfully, throwing herself down on the chair opposite. 'You'll never guess who I saw walking through town today!'

'Who?'

'Your sexy coffee guy from Frothy Coffee.'

'Ooh did you?' I perk up. Sexy Coffee Guy is the new barista in the café I call into on the way to work. He's the most handsome man I've ever laid eyes on and always gets my day off to a great start. I don't know his name and I'm not interested in knowing his name either. I just like to look at him. He's kind of Italian-looking. Dark hair, dark eyes, smooth dark skin and whiter-than-white teeth that seem to glint when he smiles. He has a lovely smile. Not to mention impressive biceps and pecs that are clearly visible through the tight black T-shirts he always seems to wear. 'Whereabouts was he?'

'Just walking past the chemist. I think he'd just finished his shift or something. Here, look, I took a photo on my phone to cheer you up.'

'You did? Aw that's so sweet. Not to mention slightly stalkerish. How did you get away with that? Did nobody notice?'

'Nah, I just pretended to take a selfie. Look, here you go.' She passes her phone across the table so I can see the slightly blurry shot of Sexy Coffee Man walking down the street.

'Ooh!' I peer at the photo, feeling slightly disappointed. It definitely doesn't have the same effect as seeing him in real life. 'Is he wearing leather trousers?'

'Yeah. Rock 'n' roll, huh! He has a seriously nice butt.'

'Maybe he rides a motorbike or something?' I say, doubtfully.

I'm not sure I like the whole leather trousers vibe. I don't normally see the bottom half of him because he's always behind a counter.

'Maybe.' Katie takes back her phone as a message pings in. She spends a couple of seconds reading it before firing off a text and turning her attention back to me. 'How are you feeling today anyway?'

'Not so bad. I've been working from home.'

'That's no good! What's the point in injuring yourself if you can't take time off work!'

'It's too busy for me to take time off. Besides, I feel fine, I just can't walk, so there's no reason why I can't work.'

'Hmm, at least you get to stay in your pyjamas all day. Have you even brushed your hair today?' Katie wrinkles her nose at me. Her own super-straight brown hair hangs glossy and thick to her shoulders.

'No.'

'It's looking a bit greasy. Do you want me to shower you?'

'No!' I'm horrified by the thought of her in the shower with me. 'I'll shower myself when I'm ready.'

'Are you sure? There's no need to be embarrassed, you know. We're friends, and I used to work in a care home so I'm used to naked bodies.'

I shake my head. 'Are you trying to say I have the body of a pensioner? No, I'll manage by myself, thanks.'

'What if I run you a bath?'

I pull a face. 'I really can't be bothered.'

'Orla! What if that sexy Aiden calls round again? You can't let him see you like this!'

I frown, feeling offended. It's her that thinks he's sexy, not me, and besides his hair wasn't looking too great the first time I saw him.

'Besides,' she goes on, 'it'll do you good. You'll feel better after you wash.'

51

'It sounds like far too much effort,' I groan. 'Even making something to eat and drink is too much effort.'

'Well, I can sort that out.' Katie gets up and goes into the kitchen. 'What do you want? Coffee?'

'I'd love a tea, please. And biscuits. Bring me biscuits.'

My phone rings and seeing it's my mum, I snatch it up and greet her cheerfully. 'Hi, Mum,'

'Hello, Orla. Just calling to find out how you are today.'

'I'm okay, thanks. I worked from home.'

'Ah that's good. Better than having to struggle in. Have you managed to have a wash yet?'

I pull a face. What is this? Some kind of conspiracy? 'Not yet.'

'Because you were looking a bit grotty when I popped in yesterday.'

'Are you in cahoots with Katie, or something?' I say, annoyed that she phoned me especially to tell me to wash.

'No! I just think you need to keep on top of your hygiene. I've been telling Keeley this too. She never wants to go in the shower, but she's 10 now and really should get into the habit of washing regularly, otherwise she'll be an adult and still not be washing.'

'Mum! I do wash usually!' I say, annoyed to be compared to my pre-pubescent sister. 'I'm going to have a bath now, as it happens. Katie's going to run me one.'

Katie beams across the room at me and gives me a thumbs-up.

'Well, that's good to hear. Have you heard from your father?'

'No. Why?'

'No reason, I just wondered if he'd been in touch recently, that's all.'

Mum and Dad divorced when I was 14. Mum started seeing Ray soon after and then Keeley was born. Dad moved away and works as a long-distance lorry driver, so I don't see him often. We talk on the phone occasionally, and he always seems to be in some kind of crisis, lurching from one difficulty to the next. Last time we spoke was about a month ago. He'd just broken up with his girlfriend and was looking for a new place to live. My heart jerks with guilt as I realise I haven't checked to see if he found anywhere.

'Have you heard something?' I say, anxiously. 'Has something happened?'

'No, no! I just wondered if you'd told him about your ankle, that's all.'

'No. He won't want to hear about that. He's got enough on his plate. I'll phone him though and check he's okay.'

Mum makes a vague noise of agreement. 'Right, I'd better go. Enjoy your bath.'

'Thanks, Mum. Bye.'

Katie goes through to the bathroom and I hear water gushing. I'm annoyed at how everyone's interfering. Surely, I should be allowed to stew in my own sweat for a few days while my ankle heals. That's one of the best things about living alone: there's no one to judge. Unless, of course, you have an interfering friend who lives upstairs.

'Do you want me to put bath oil in?' she calls.

'No thanks, I need to wash my hair.'

'Whoops, too late.'

I roll my eyes. Why ask if she's going to do it anyway? 'Never mind. I'll use the shower hose.'

'I can wash your hair for you.'

'There's no way you're washing my hair for me, Katie. I'll manage.'

'I told you, I don't mind nakedness.' I think of the endless stream of men she has in her flat and think that sounds about right. 'The human form is a beautiful thing.' She reappears in the doorway, holding a towel.

'That's lovely, Katie. But I can manage, thank you.'

'Well, if you're sure.' She shrugs and then bends her knees to peer through my window. Outside, a red Vauxhall is pulling up in the car park. 'Oh my God, that's Danny. He's early! Why is he

53

so early? Sorry, Orla. I'm going to have to go and change before he sees me in my uniform. Give me a call if you need anything.' She runs out in a blind panic.

The lad in the car seems to be combing his dark hair in his rear-view mirror, so I think she has time to change. Struggling to my feet, I hobble and hop to my now steamy bathroom and am almost in tears by the time I get there. According to the Internet, I should be trying to use my foot more now, but it's so painful I can't face it. I think about giving the bath a miss, but then catch sight of my grotty hair in the mirror and realise I've got baked beans down my pyjamas. I am pretty gross.

Getting into the bath is awkward, but I manage. I prop my bad ankle on the side so the bandage doesn't get wet and set to soaping the rest of my body. I even manage to reach the shower head and wash my hair. I'm feeling pretty good about myself when I realise that actually getting out of the bath is not going to be easy. The bottom and the sides are slippery with bath oil, and I can't get enough grip with my good leg to push myself up. My first attempt ends up with me slipping back down and jolting my bad ankle, and I howl in pain. I'm going to have to call Katie to get me out. The indignity of it makes me cry and I spend a couple of minutes feeling sorry for myself before realising I can't actually call Katie because my phone is out of reach on the closed lid of the toilet. I get angry then, cursing my mother and Katie because this is surely all their fault for making me wash in the first place. And why did Katie put bloody bath oil in? How stupid can you get!

My anger gradually subsides and I realise I'm being ungrateful and need to think logically if I'm going to get myself out of this predicament. Perhaps if I empty the bath of water, it might be easier. But then, if it isn't, I don't want to sit here cold and wet. I could always refill it, but I know my hot tap comes out at a temperature close to boiling, so that runs the risk of scalding.

It's better than sitting here in rapidly cooling water though.

I'm floundering around, trying to pull out the plug when the doorbell goes. I freeze, wondering who it is. Katie has a key, so it can't be her.

Maybe it's Mum? 'Mum?' I shout, and then realise I sound like a child and stop immediately. Whoever is out there won't be able to hear me from the bathroom anyway.

The doorbell chimes again. I try and fail to get out of the bath one more time. Water splashes over the sides and I whack my elbow and swear at the pain. My phone vibrates violently from the toilet, its face lighting up with Aiden's name.

What does he want now? The man's a nuisance!

There's a long loofah on the side, and it occurs to me that I might be able to use it to draw my phone close enough to reach. I edge it closer, my tongue between my teeth, and just as it gets to the point where it's about to drop from the seat onto the floor, I manage to reach it with my fingertips.

Aha! The phone is mine!

I'm not sure Aiden's the best person to speak to in my current situation, but I answer it anyway.

'Hello?'

'Hi, where are you?' Aiden sounds put out, which annoys me because what right does he have to expect me to be in when he didn't even tell me he was stopping by? He doesn't even know me! And what's he doing here anyway? Is he some kind of creepy stalker?

'Why do you want to know?' I snap.

'Because I'm ringing your doorbell and there's no answer. I've brought you something.'

'What have you brought me?' I'm no less suspicious and I know I sound it but can't help myself.

'It's a surprise,' he says, and I'm surprised by how cheerful he sounds when I sound so crabby.

I rack my brain for what he might have brought for me. I hope it's not flowers or anything cringey like that. I detest being given sentimental gifts and hate opening presents in front of anyone. Even my mother. I know I'm weird, but I can't help it.

'So, are you at home or are you out?'

'I'm at home, but I can't come to the door right now.'

'Why? Are you okay?'

I pause. Should I tell him or not? I don't want him to think I'm incapable of looking after myself, but then I do need help, and maybe he can get Katie to come and help me out.

'Yes. Well, I'm kind of stuck in the bath.'

'You're stuck in the bath?' He sounds alarmed. 'What are you doing having a bath? Can I help?'

'You could go and get Katie from upstairs.'

'I've just seen Katie. She's just gone off in some guy's car.'

'Nooooo she hasn't!' I groan and put my head in my hands. 'I tell you what, can you put a note through her door telling her to come and get me when she gets in from wherever she's been?'

'Orla, you can't stay in the bath until she comes home! You could fall asleep and drown.'

'I won't fall asleep. I don't feel sleepy in the slightest.'

'Don't be stupid. Have you a spare key hidden anywhere?'

'No! I don't want you to come in, anyway!'

'Well, it's either going to be me or the fire brigade. Which would you prefer? One guy who has already had you vomit over his boots, or three or four burly firemen?'

'Now that you say that, that's the stuff of fantasies. I choose the firemen.'

'Orla, be serious. I can help you.'

I scowl at the wall for a moment. 'Did I really vomit on your boots?'

'Just a bit of a splatter. Nothing much.'

'Still gross.'

'Yeah, so I've already seen you acting like the exorcist and have no interest in your body other than getting it out of that bathtub.'

'Well, you still can't get in. Katie's got my spare key.'

There's a noise like the rattle of the door handle. 'Yeah I can. The door's open.'

'What?!'

'Yeah, you really should watch your security. Anyone could walk in while you're naked in the bath.'

'Don't just walk in,' I shout in a panic.

'I can't leave you stuck in the bath, Orla! Is there a towel to hand or anything else you can use to cover yourself up?'

'Erm, yes.' I grab the bathmat from the floor and submerge it in the water, covering up the front of my body. It's a pretty obvious solution really, and my panic subsides. I can hear him outside the door. 'Okay, you can come in now,' I say.

The door swings open and Aiden fills the doorway. I glance up to see he's wearing a faded blue denim shirt and black jeans and then look back down at the bathmat that's covering me. I feel so vulnerable and humiliated right now, I can't even look at him.

'Hi,' he says, as if he sees me sitting in a bath every day. 'How do you want to do this? Do you want me to pull you up from under your arms or lift you bodily out?'

'Under the arms is fine,' I mutter.

'Okay then.' He takes the bath towel from the radiator and tucks it under his left arm before bending to help me out. I feel his hands under my armpits before he lifts me up so I'm sitting inelegantly on the side of the bath. My backside squelches on the wet plastic and Aiden giggles.

'Child,' I say darkly.

'Sorry.' He straightens his face and wraps the towel around me so I can drop the sodden bathmat back into the bath, and then he supports me so I can swing my good leg over the side and stand up.

'Thanks,' I say stiffly. I know I should sound more grateful, but I feel so embarrassed and ashamed I can't even look at him.

'No problem. Do you want your robe?'

'Yes, please.' I've never been so glad to put an item of clothing on in my life. Annoyingly, I need his help for that too, and he holds it out to me so I can put my hand into the sleeve while I use the sink for support.

'Your present's outside,' he says, smiling at me in the reflection of the mirror.

'I don't want a present,' I say ungraciously. 'I hate presents.'

He looks at me for a moment as though I'm from a different planet. 'You'll like this one,' he assures me. 'I promise you.'

I growl at him. I don't even mean to, it just happens. Luckily, he doesn't seem offended and helps me out of the bathroom and into my bedroom. There, leaning against the end of my bed, is a crutch. It is the most beautiful thing I've ever seen.

'Ta-daa!' he says. 'I found it in Ivy's garage. She had no idea she had it, but said she'd broken her foot back in the Nineties so it must be from then. Anyway, I thought you might be able to use it, unless you've got one already? They should have given you one at the hospital, really, but I think they thought we lived together so you'd have help anyway. Maybe we should have been clearer that you lived alone and were a stubborn idiot who refuses help of any kind. Anyway, shall I put the kettle on while you get changed?' He waits for me to answer but I can't actually speak at that moment. I feel as overwhelmed as I would be if I'd just been given the keys to a new car. 'I'll take that as a yes,' he says, and disappears into the kitchen.

The crutch is clearly old and a bit battered, but I don't care. I stroke its length lovingly and then pick it up and try it out. It takes a bit of practice but I'm able to move around my bedroom and then make my way to the kitchen. Aiden is unloading the dishwasher. I watch him in amazement for a moment before hobbling over and wrapping my arm around his waist with my face pressed into his back in an awkward hug.

'Thank you,' I croak.

'It's no bother at all,' he says pleasantly.

58

'And you don't have to unload my dishwasher,' I tell him.

'I know I don't, but I want to.' He smiles down at me then moves over to the kettle as it starts to boil. 'You should let people help when they want to help, Orla. It makes them feel good about themselves. So you see, you're actually helping me by letting me help you, because it makes me feel good about myself.'

'Oh, okay then. In that case, you can make me some soup too.'

'Soup? Is that all you're having for tea?'

'I don't want toast, and you told me the other day that was all you can make. I figure opening a tin of soup might not be too difficult.'

'Come on, Orla. You can't live on soup.'

'I like soup.'

'What else do you have?' He opens a cupboard door and peers up at the empty shelves.

'Nothing. I haven't been shopping, have I!'

Shutting the cupboard door, he turns to look at me. 'I'll go shopping for you then.'

'You can't go shopping for me!' I laugh incredulously. 'Why would you go shopping for me?'

'Because you need to eat, Orla. And besides, what did I say before? You're making me feel good by letting me help, remember.'

'Yeah, but this is your time. I'm sure you've got better things to do than go shopping for me.'

'Orla, make a list and shut up.'

My stomach growls loudly and he raises an eyebrow. 'I tell you what,' I say. 'I'll do an Internet shop and get it delivered tomorrow, but right now, you can go to the chippy and get us both some chips.'

He thinks for a moment. 'How are you going to unload your shopping tomorrow?'

'I have a crutch now. I'll be okay.'

'I tell you what, I'll go and get you some chips, and while I'm out, I'll get you bread and milk and some bits and bobs from the corner shop.'

'You don't have to do that.'

'I know I don't, but I want to.' He picks up his keys from the side.

'Are you going to eat with me?'

His eyes dart to the side as though he's trying to decide what the correct response would be. 'Yes?' he ventures.

'Good.' I smile and hand him a twenty-pound note from my purse. 'Get whatever you want. My treat. As a thank-you for rescuing me from the bath.'

He looks at the twenty-pound note for a second, and I see him weighing up whether he should take it or not before he plucks it from my fingers and folds it into the back pocket of his jeans. 'Okay, I'll be back shortly.' He takes my cup of tea to the coffee table, then points at the sofa. 'Sit down and put your ankle up.'

Chapter 5

I watch him go out to the pick-up truck and drive off before using the crutch to get to my bedroom and change into my pyjamas. I'm astounded by his kindness. I don't think I've met anyone like him before. Especially as he's a near stranger.

Aiden returns about half an hour later, with a shopping bag full of supplies and chips for us both. I watch from the sofa as he gets plates down from the cupboard and opens drawers looking for cutlery. 'What have you been doing today?' he asks as he carries the plates over and sets them down on the coffee table.

'I worked from home. What have you been doing?'

'Just going through trail cam footage and looking for signs that the otters are out.'

'And are they?'

'Nope.'

'So it's just a waiting game?'

'Yep.'

'Sounds like it can get pretty boring.'

'It can do, but it's also wonderful when you do get some footage so it's well worth the wait. I've got a friend who's setting up a sensory forest for children with special needs and he wants me to help, so I might go and help him for a couple of days. It's only local. You might be interested in that for your paper, actually.'

'Oh yes, that sounds good.'

'I'll let you know when I'm going. You can come along.' He bends to eat the chip on the end of his fork. 'How did your boss react when you told him what happened to your ankle?'

I sigh, still worried that Phil's not going to let me do any more solo interviews. 'He said I shouldn't have gone down to meet you on my own. Like you were the big bad wolf or something.'

'Well, just about everyone you know has told you the same thing now, so ... you know.' He shrugs. 'At least you know not to do that in future.'

'Hmm, yeah, well I'm worried he's going to insist I accompany him everywhere for another six months now. This was my chance to show him I could manage on my own, and I blew it.'

'Oh no, don't say that.'

'It's true though, I have,' I say gloomily. 'I wish I hadn't told him what really happened and just made something up instead.'

'It's always best to be truthful. I can phone him and tell him you did a fine job of interviewing me, if you want?'

I laugh. 'No, it's alright. I sent him the article and he was happy with it. He's just worried about my safety now.'

Aiden smiles. 'Do you like working on the newspaper?'

'Yes, I love it. It's what I've always wanted to do. Well, not work on the *Hawksley Gazette*, specifically. The aim is to get one of the bigger, national papers one day, but this is a great start.'

'So, you're how old?'

'Twenty-two. This is my first job after graduating. I did a journalism course and then got taken on by the *Gazette*.'

'Do you not find all the crime and stuff depressing?'

'What do you mean?'

'I flicked through Ivy's paper the other day and it was full of bad stuff happening, people getting arrested for drug dealing and robberies. There was a story about a road closure because of a fatal car crash and then a stabbing and a factory closure. Even the lighter stories were about the hospital parking prices going up and a beloved oak tree being cut down in the park.'

'Oh, I forgot about the tree in the park.' I scribble a note on the pad. 'I need to link that to our eco-blog section of the website.'

Aiden shrugs. 'It's only a small town. How can there be so much bad shit happening in such a small town? I don't get it.'

'There's always bad shit happening. Where there's people, there's shit. I know what you mean though. I spent last Monday compiling a list of local people who'd been convicted in court recently. I'm sure there are more good news stories out there, it's just that readers seem to want to read the bad stuff.'

'Really? Now that's depressing. See you covered the tree being chopped down, but not the story about the three thousand trees that are being planted on the old landfill site two miles away. All the bad stories fuel people's paranoia and make them want to isolate themselves.'

'Yeah, maybe you're right.' I sigh, feeling a bit despondent. 'But it's important that people know what's going on on their doorstep. So what about you, then. Did you always want to be a nature photographer? How did you get into it?'

He shrugs and chews on another chip. 'Where I grew up in County Wicklow, it was very green and rural. I used to spend hours bird-watching with my father, out and about among the mountains so it grew from that, really. I suppose I never set out to be a photographer, it was just a natural progression. I studied ecology and conservation at university and my student job was in a wildlife park. Just in the gift shop – nothing to do with the animals, really, but I started going out and photographing them during my breaks and it grew from there. I entered some competitions, sent my photos off to magazines, made myself a website, Instagram and Facebook page, and went travelling with my camera.'

'Where did you go first?'

'I travelled around Europe at first. I had no money so I got jobs in bars and restaurants to pay my way. Stayed in the cheapest accommodation possible and just took photos of the local wildlife when I could. I started in France then worked my way down to Spain. Nothing happened for a while and my parents weren't happy. Then I found a colony of wolves and started photographing them and that was when I started to make a bit of money and make a name for myself. Since then, I've been all over the world. There are still places I want to see, and things I want to photograph, so it's not like I'm saying I've done it all already. But I've been to some amazing places and seen some wonderful things and I'm still as excited about it as the first time I picked up a camera.'

'Wow, that's amazing. What's been the highlight of your career so far?'

'Finding the wolf colony, because it was a complete accident. I was out walking, photographing the landscape, and suddenly there was just this wolf. Luck was on my side and I was positioned just right so she couldn't see or smell me. Here, give me your laptop and I'll show you. I am so in love with wolves it's unreal. Honestly, they are the most captivating animal. Just the expression in their eyes and the way they interact with each other. I could have lived there, watching them, forever.'

Pushing the plate aside, he takes my laptop and brings up the web browser. He types in his web address and brings up a gallery of breathtaking photographs. 'Here,' he says, turning the screen to face me. There is a photo of a wolf with bright yellow eyes against a backdrop of a sapphire sky. 'This is the alpha male of the pack. I called him Hercules. And this one here,' he says, scrolling through and bringing up a photograph of a wolf cub licking its mother's chin, 'is the image I was nominated for an award for. But I didn't win, so it's bollocks. And here ...' He gets up and moves around to sit on the floor in front of me. 'Here is the pack on the move, down the mountain.'

He takes me through the rest of his photographs. There are stunning shots of birds, lynx, bears, beavers and deer. There are landscape shots too, and photos of him on location, sitting outside his tent on a snowy mountainside, wrapped up against the cold, and another of him next to a river, tinged green by the forest canopy above his head. I'm fascinated and enthralled. He talks at length about all the different places he's stayed and the animals he's seen. The friends he's made along the way. I don't have to prompt him to tell me anything.

'It's so wonderful to see your passion for nature,' I say, when he comes to the end of the photographs on his website. 'It's clear that that's what drives you to do this work.'

'Of course, and I want to inspire that passion in other people too. More than that, I want to inspire compassion for these animals and the planet itself. I want to show people how magnif-icent it is and educate them on why it deserves our protection.' He flicks through more of the photographs. 'It's so amazing. I want to take everyone on a journey, educating them on what's out there. People are so wrapped up in their own lives, their own worlds. So many people living in cities. I could never live in say, London, for instance. I don't know how people can breathe.'

'I want to live in London,' I say. 'One day, anyway.'

'You do? Why?'

'It's such a wonderful place. So vibrant and exciting. Plus, that's where I'd need to be to get a job on one of the big nationals.'

'More doom and gloom?'

'Probably,' I admit. 'But on a bigger scale. I don't want to be stuck here in Hawksley for the rest of my life.'

'You don't have to be stuck anywhere, Orla. The world is your oyster, as they say.'

'Yes, if you're prepared to live in a tent! Honestly, I don't know how you do it.'

Aiden sighs and clicks off his website. 'Yeah, it's not for everyone.'

'Have you ever had your own flat or house or anything?'

'No.'

'Do you think you ever will?'

He's silent for a moment. 'I don't know. Maybe. I suppose there may come a time when I can't or don't want to live like this anymore, but for now I like it.'

'Where do you store all your equipment though? Surely you must have hundreds of pounds worth of photography equipment. Who's going to insure you if you keep it in a tent? And what about the camping equipment for different climates. You had at least four different tents in those photographs. Do you just throw them away?'

'Sometimes, if they get damaged in storms or what have you. Otherwise, I store them at my parents' house.'

'Your poor parents.'

'Yeah, I leave a lot of my stuff with them, to be honest. But they're very good about it.'

'Do you go and see them a lot?'

'Not a lot, I suppose, but when I can. At least three or four times a year, and I go home for Christmas.' He looks towards the window, and I sense he's about to leave. It's gone nine o'clock and the daylight is leaching from the sky. 'I suppose I'd better go,' he says. 'It'll be too dark to find my tent if I leave it too late. Besides, you need to rest.'

'Okay.' I feel disappointed. I could carry on listening to Aiden all night. 'Thanks for showing me your website and telling me about yourself. It's been fascinating.'

He laughs. 'I hope I haven't bored you.'

'Of course, you haven't. And thank you for all your help tonight, and for the crutch. It's officially the best present I've ever had.'

'Steady on now.' He laughs and gets to his feet. 'Well, I'll be seeing you, Orla. Take care of yourself.'

'You too. Good luck finding your way back to your tent.'

Chapter 6

The crutch changes everything. It restores my independence and I feel like I can move again, however clumsily. My ankle is still swollen and painful, but I no longer feel like I'm stranded on the sofa or my bed. I place strategic chairs in the kitchen and bathroom so I don't have to stand while making drinks or brushing my teeth, and I even manage to hobble down to the corner shop where I replenish my stocks of milk and bread. I work at home for another day and then return to working in the office, more because I'm still trying to prove I'm good enough for the job, rather than feeling fully fit.

'Alright, hon,' Phil says as I move slowly past him towards my desk. 'Good to have you back.'

'Hi, Phil.' I smile at him. 'Thank you.'

He holds out his mug. 'Milk and two sugars, please.'

'At least let me get my coat off!' I say, feeling dismayed.

'Ha, I'm only joking! In your own time, doll. No hurry. How did you get here, anyway?'

'Taxi.' I struggle to get my coat off and hang it over the back of my chair, then sit down to turn on my computer. I'm knackered already and I haven't even done any work yet.

'You're still struggling with that ankle, then?' He peers at my bandaged ankle with a frown. I can't get my shoe on over the bandage, so I've covered it with a big fluffy sock. Unfortunately, the only fluffy socks I own are covered in pandas, so I'm not looking particularly professional today.

'Yes, it's really sore.'

'Give it a few more days and I'm sure you'll be back to normal. Here, I'll make you a cup of tea this time, to say welcome back.'

'Oh, I'd love one. Thanks, Phil.' I pick up my unicorn mug and hold it out to him.

'No problem, hon.' He winks as he ambles away in the direction of the office kitchen.

My computer tells me the system is updating, so I sit and wait while the fan makes alarmingly loud whirring and grinding noises. I water the spider plant that sits on my desk and rearrange my sticky notes around my monitor. The office is open-plan and I hear snatches of people's phone conversations and the tippy-tap of fingers on keyboards.

'So tell me about this Aiden fella then,' Phil says, arriving back at my desk and placing my mug of tea down next to me. 'You said he was good to you?'

'Yeah, he was brilliant. He brought this crutch round and everything.'

'Oh, so you're still in touch with him, are you?'

'Yes. I haven't seen him for a couple of days though.' For some reason I can't quite fathom, I feel disappointed about this fact. 'He said his friend is setting up a sensory forest near here, actually, and wondered if we'd be interested in covering it in the paper. I thought it might be of interest?'

'Sounds alright to me. When?'

'I don't know yet. I'll find out.'

'Good stuff. I was going to send you out on a story today, but I don't think you're up to it, are you?'

I start to insist that I am, but Phil holds his hand up to stop me. 'No, you're really not, and there's enough work to be getting on with in the office anyway. Someone else can go. It's nothing big so don't worry. It's just a broken window in a coffee shop. Your otter story was good, by the way. Well done.'

'Thank you!' I beam before realising what he said about the coffee shop. 'Wait, which coffee shop?'

'The one with the stupid name. Frothy Coffee or something crap.'

'Oh God, that's my favourite one! How bad's the damage?'

'Dunno. Just broken glass, I think. Nothing much.'

'Why would they target that place?' I ask, feeling stricken. What I want to say is, 'There's a really handsome man that works behind the counter in the mornings and I really wouldn't mind going to interview him for the paper.' Stupid ankle!

Phil chuckles. 'Who knows why these thugs do the things they do. It's usually just mindless vandalism. They probably didn't even think about what they were doing.' He looks at me and frowns. 'Hold on! Is that where your sexy coffee man works? Ha ha! What a shame you can't interview him because of your ankle.'

'It's only down the high street. I'm sure I can make it on my crutch. I'm getting good now. Please, Phil. Pleeeease!'

Phil frowns down at my fat fluffy foot. 'You sure you want to see him wearing penguin socks?'

'They're pandas. And why not?' I stick my leg out and smile, careful not to bang it on anything.

'I really don't think you should. In fact, what am I saying? Definitely not! No, Orla. No.'

'Oh! But …'

'No!' Phil's already walking away, back to his desk. 'I'm doing you a favour, anyway. You're not looking your best, hon. I've got to be honest.'

'Hey! What do you mean?'

'I'm not loving those trousers, doll,' he laughs, deep and rumbling. 'I need my sunglasses to look at you.'

70

'Thanks!' Cheeky sod. These palazzo pants were the only ones I could get over my ankle without causing me pain. So what if they're bright pink and flowery? They're summery and felt appropriate when I saw the blue sky this morning. The fact that that blue sky is now rapidly filling with grey cloud is beside the point. I want to say something about his stripy shirt but can't think of anything mean enough. Or anything that won't get me sacked, anyway. Defeated, I slump in my seat. Today is officially the worst day ever, and it's not even nine o'clock in the morning yet.

But wait, I didn't really want to interview Sexy Coffee Guy anyway. I'd much rather keep him a mystery stranger who's just pretty to look at. It's not like I'm looking for a date with him. My stomach turns over at the thought. Oh no, no, no. I'm far too busy for such nonsense. Feeling better, I sip my tea and get on with my work.

'Bit of a change of plan, Orla,' Phil says, arriving back at my desk ten minutes later. He's red in the face and out of breath from walking across the office.

'What's that?' I look up with some concern. Phil is terribly overweight and unfit, and I briefly consider talking to him about seeing a doctor. He shouldn't be that red in the face. Maybe he should have his blood pressure checked.

'No one's free to go to the café, so why don't you give them a call and I'll send Martin the photographer down to take a few shots of the window. He's moaning, saying he needs to be somewhere else, but it will only take him a couple of minutes. It's only down the bloody road after all.' Phil rolls his eyes. He's not a fan of Martin, but neither am I for that matter. He has an air of being too handsome and important to work on the *Hawksley Gazette*, and spends most of his time with the sports editor talking about football.

'Okay, do we have a contact name?'

'Hold on, I'll just get it.' He goes back to his desk and retrieves a sticky note from his monitor. 'Frankie de Campo. He's the manager. I said I'd try to send someone but I didn't promise, so you can just smooth that over by telling him about your ankle. Get the number from their website.'

'Okay.' I pick up my phone to make the call, pleased that I get to do the interview after all. The phone's answered on the second ring by a male voice.

'Yeah?'

I'm so surprised by the abruptness of the tone that I think I must have rung the wrong number. 'Hello, is that Frothy Coffee Café?'

'Yep.'

'Hi, this is Orla Kennedy from the *Hawksley Gazette*. Can I speak to Frankie de Campo please?'

'Yeah, hold on, I'll just get him.'

I cringe slightly. That's no way to answer a business telephone. Luckily, the actual manager has a much better telephone manner and I'm able to ask him a few questions about the broken window. I hesitate, wondering if I should tell him that whoever answered the phone in the first instance should never be allowed to answer the phone again. I can't believe it would be my sexy coffee guy. He's always so polite when he serves me in the morning.

'Can I just ask who answered the phone to me?' I say as we're wrapping up the interview.

'Oh yes, sorry about him. That's my son, Fabio. He's useless on the phone but easy on the eye so I keep him on anyway.' Franko laughs heartily. 'Well, thank you for your time, Miss Kennedy.'

'And for yours, Mr de Campo. Bye now.'

I ring off and read over my notes. The window was broken at three o'clock this morning, and the whole family was woken by the security alarm going off. It's not the most exciting story in the world, but it's the latest in a spate of windows being broken

72

in the past few months. It's probably just local yobbos, coming back from the pub and looking for a bit of fun. Annoying for the business owners though.

'How was the café story?'

'Oh alright. He was nice and didn't mind me not being there in person. He said the window guy's there already so I don't know how good Martin's photograph will be.'

'I'm just going to make the lazy git go anyway,' Phil mutters darkly.

I laugh and turn back to the computer. 'How long do you want this then? A quarter? Or less?'

'Write a quarter, but be mindful it will probably get cut to just a few lines.'

'Okey-dokey. There have been a few shop windows broken recently though. If we get any more, we could print a map showing when and where they're being broken. See if there's a pattern.'

Phil gives me a look. 'Calm down, Sherlock. Let's not get ahead of ourselves. We know it's mindless vandalism, nothing more.'

'Oh. Well I just thought we could spice things up a bit.'

'Keep your spice to yourself, girl.' Phil laughs and mutters something about phantom window breakers to himself, then laughs some more.

'You may laugh,' I say, wryly, 'but there could be more to this than meets the eye.'

'Oh yeah! Right!' Phil jeers. 'Like what? A protection racket?'

'Oooh yeah!' I say, my eyes getting big with excitement. 'Maybe the de Campos are actually mafia, and they've done their window as a cover-up to convince the other shop owners that they need protecting.'

'What kind of protection racket advertises themselves as protectors by getting their own window smashed in?'

'They haven't got it up and running yet, obviously. They'll do more shops one by one and when the shop owners are scared and cowering, that's when they'll move in.'

Phil stares at me, deadpan, until I stop talking. 'Finished now? I'm fairly sure that accusing the de Campos of being mafia just because they have an Italian name is racist. And also, why wouldn't the shop owners just get metal shutters to protect their windows, instead of paying into a racket?'

'Ooooh! Maybe it's the shutter company—'

'Stop with the conspiracy theories, Orla. There's no way of making this story more interesting, so don't bother. Just give it a couple of inches and move on with your day.'

'Huh, okay, boss.' Laughing, I turn back to my computer. 'You know, the person who answered the phone was quite abrupt. When I asked who it was, Frankie said it was his son, Fabio. I think that might be my sexy coffee guy!'

Phil laughs. 'Fabio? Great name for an Italian Stallion. Why are you looking so disapproving?'

'He was so crap on the phone! I was going to say whoever it was should be sacked on the spot, but I couldn't really when it was his son.'

'Is Sexy Coffee Guy Italian?'

'Yeah.'

'Ah well, there you go then. You've yielded a name. Congratulations! Fabio the Sexy Coffee Guy.'

'Woohoo!' I say in a flat voice. 'Fabio the Ignoramus. Fabio the Rude.'

Phil splutters into his coffee cup. 'My, my, what exacting standards you have, Miss Kennedy. Is that one of your stipulations in a man? Must have good sense of humour and great telephone manner.'

I giggle. 'Well, a girl has to have standards.'

Phil laughs again and slurps some more coffee. 'Just get writing.'

It's frustrating being stuck in the office all day. Usually I get to go out somewhere, even if it's just to the sandwich shop for lunch, but today I brought my own sandwiches so I sit at my desk, watching the clouds roll across the sky. It looks blustery and fresh out, and seeing the people walking up and down the high street with their shopping bags makes me long to feel the wind on my face. I've been stuck inside too long. So when it's time to go home, instead of phoning a taxi straight away, I limp into the town centre instead. It's probably not a great place to get a taxi seeing as it's pedestrianised, but I want to see some life other than that inside my flat or the office. It's not hugely busy, but there are enough people about to give it a buzz.

And then I see him: Fabio, the handsome coffee man, riding past on a bicycle. It's such a surprise that I stop and stare, his crappy telephone manner forgotten. He rides slowly, weaving in and out of the groups of people walking by, occasionally ringing his bell to warn them he's coming. He looks so happy and smiley, that I think it must have been someone else on the phone before. A man calls out to him and he waves, then stops his bike so he can talk to him. Realising I'm gawping at him in a slightly disturbing way, I pretend to rummage in my bag and then peer at him surreptitiously from the corner of my eye. I don't usually get to see his bottom half, hidden as it usually is behind the café counter, but he's wearing tight black jeans that make his backside look …

'Hi, Orla!'

I jump so much that I almost drop my crutch. Luckily, Aiden catches it before it falls to the pavement. He grins down at me and I can't help but smile back. The wind is blowing his long curly hair around his head like some kind of crazy windmill.

'Hi! What are you doing here?' The jolt of pleasure I get at seeing Aiden takes me by surprise, and I feel my cheeks heat.

'I've just been into the camera shop.' He inclines his head towards the shop I'm standing directly outside of. Its window display is filled with all kinds of photography equipment I'd never even noticed before. Aiden explains he's looking for a specific

75

kind of lens for his camera but they haven't got one in, despite saying they had when he'd phoned earlier.

'Can you order it?'

'I have done, but they can't get it until Friday. It's so annoying. Are you in a hurry to get somewhere or do you have time for a coffee?'

'Yes, if you like.'

'Great! Here, give me your bag.' He takes my bag from my shoulder and walks next to me up the street, chatting about a fox that appeared last night and walked right up to his camera. 'Shall we go in here?' he says, as we reach Frothy Coffee. The window is now fixed and there is no sign of the earlier damage. I tell Aiden about it as we go inside and find a table.

'I come in here all the time,' I say when Aiden comes back to the table with the coffee, 'but I don't think I've ever sat at a table. I just get a takeaway coffee on my way to work.'

'Reusable coffee cup, I hope?'

'Of course.'

'Good!' He grins. 'I come in here occasionally when I'm in town. They make good coffee.'

'Yes,' I agree, leaning forwards and lowering my voice conspiratorially. 'And there's a very handsome man that usually works in here. He perks me up no end in the morning.'

'Is that so?' He rests his chin on his hand and looks at me, a spark of amusement in his eye. 'Ah, you see, I've not noticed a handsome man, but there is sometimes a very pretty girl that serves me at lunchtime.'

'Really?' Maintaining eye contact, I lift an eyebrow and smile at him. 'Maybe my handsome coffee man goes on his break when you're in.'

'Maybe so. Or maybe I just don't notice him because he's not my type.' He laughs lightly as he pours milk into his coffee, stirring it round with a teaspoon. 'Perhaps we should meet one lunchtime and check them out together.'

'I like your thinking.' I smile at him before taking a sip from my coffee. 'Ooh, I've missed this,' I say, closing my eyes to savour the taste. 'The instant stuff at work is no comparison.'

'Was today your first day back in the office?'

'Yes, and it was okay. I'm fed up of being stuck inside though. I could have come here to conduct the interview this morning but had to do it on the telephone instead.' I glance round to see if Mr de Campo is in evidence anywhere, but there's only a couple of girls serving today. 'I feel a bit bad now I'm actually here. Maybe I could have made it earlier after all.'

Aiden shakes his head. 'I doubt you should be here now, to be honest. You need to rest it as much as possible. Give it a few more days and I'm sure it will improve.'

I smile at him. 'Have the otters appeared?'

'Not that I know of,' he says, looking disappointed. 'I was talking to a girl from the otter watch this morning and she thinks it's still early so I've rung my friend that I told you about. You know, the one with the sensory forest?'

'Oh yeah, I told Phil about that. He said we'd be interested in covering it.'

'Yeah? Great. I'm going down tomorrow to see how he's getting on so I'll let you know more after that.'

We chat for a while longer and then he offers me a lift home.

'You're such a gentleman,' I say, as he takes my bag and then holds the door open for me to walk through. 'Thank you so much.'

He looks slightly confused, like he doesn't know what I'm talking about. 'No bother. I'm parked in the library car park.'

Outside, the blustery wind has ushered in grey clouds that spit great dollops of rain at us. They're so large and the wind is so fierce that they sting my face. Aiden turns the collar up on his jacket and I feel bad that he has to walk slowly because of me. He shows no sign of minding though, and chats amiably as we make our slow way up the high street and through the alleyway that leads to the library. Aiden unlocks the passenger door and opens it for me before lifting me inside. I want to protest that I don't need lifting in and out, but I know that I do. The truck is too high for me with my damaged ankle.

'I'm glad I'm not you tonight,' I say, as Aiden climbs into the driver's seat. In the time it's taken for Aiden to walk round the truck to the driver's side, the rain has intensified so much that it hammers violently on the truck roof and I have to shout over its machine-gun roar. Aiden leans forward and peers up through the windscreen.

'Ah, it will pass, most likely,' he says, switching on the engine. The truck judders into life and the windscreen wipers slap backwards and forwards as Aiden drives out of the car park. The sky has got so dark, he has to switch on the head lights.

'Thanks for the lift,' I say. 'I'm glad I didn't have to wait for a taxi in this.'

He shrugs. 'Just call me if you ever need a lift.'

'You could be working.'

'I spend hours and hours waiting for something to happen. If I nip out for half an hour, what's the difference?'

'But that might be the very moment that something happens.'

'So what? I'll never know about it, will I? I can't think like that or I'd never do anything. Besides, I have camera traps set about the place anyway, so I've pretty much covered all the bases.'

The rain eases slightly as he turns into my street and pulls up in the car park outside my flat. My window looks dark and miserable, but there's a light on in Katie's on the floor above. Somehow it makes the dark façade of the 1960s building look a little less stark and unwelcoming.

'Do you want to come in?' I ask as Aiden comes round to lift me down from his truck. My heart quickens slightly as his arms go around me and I laugh self-consciously.

'No, I'd best be getting back.' He smiles as he sets me down on the floor. 'But I can meet you for lunch on Friday, if you like? I've got to come into town to collect my lens.'

'Okay. One o'clock?'

'That'll be great. I'll wait outside your office for you.'

'You know where it is?' I ask doubtfully.

'Sure, I do.' He retrieves my crutch from the back seat and hands it to me. 'See you Friday.'

Chapter 7

It's Friday lunchtime, and Aiden is waiting for me outside work as promised. He's wearing a grey hooded sweatshirt over a white T-shirt and blue jeans. I've been looking forward to seeing him again all morning. I'm surprised by how quickly I've come to regard him as a friend during the last week. It's exciting to have a new friend.

It's another drizzly day and his curly hair is huge and fuzzy with the extra moisture. I can't laugh at him though, because I know my hair would be exactly the same without all the product I've slathered on top of it. I'm wearing a bright yellow raincoat and his face lights when he sees me as though the sight of me has cheered him up.

'Nice coat!' he says.

'Thanks. It'd be no good for watching wildlife though, would it?'

'Probably not. It matches your personality though. Sunny and bright.'

I laugh. 'Really? Is that how you see me?'

'Of course. You're a very happy person.'

'And you can tell that how, exactly? I'm always moaning about my ankle when I see you.'

He laughs. 'Ah, no you're fine. I can just tell that you have a naturally sunny disposition. It's a mystery to me why you want to be a newspaper reporter, dealing with doom and gloom all the time. I'm a bit worried it will wear you down and make you cynical. How have you been anyway? You seem to be moving a little easier.'

'Yes, it feels like it's getting better. I can actually put some weight on it now. I'm still using the crutch though, just in case I overdo it.'

'Good idea. So, are you ready to see your handsome coffee man?' He quirks an eyebrow as he shoots me a searching look.

'I am.'

'Do you think he'll be there?'

'I don't know. I've never been in at lunchtime. Do you think *she'll* be there?'

'I think so. She usually is.' He holds the door open for me and we join the queue for the counter. Aiden lets me go first and sure enough, behind the counter, stands Fabio. Sexy Coffee Guy. He's looking hotter than ever and I feel my face start to flush, mostly, I'm sure, because Aiden is with me and knows I fancy him.

'Is that him?' I hear Aiden's low voice in my ear.

'Yep.'

'Humph.'

'Humph? What's humph meant to mean?'

'Nothing. Nothing at all.' He straightens up, arranging his face into a more innocent expression.

'Tell me!' I hiss, poking him in the side.

'Hey! No, it's just that he's a little dark and brooding for you.'

'Maybe it's the dark broodiness that I like.'

'Yeah but you're like … and then he's like …'

'What? I'm like what?' I stare at him, offended.

'Sunny and happy and bright. If you were one of the Mr Men, you'd be Mr Happy. Or Little Miss Sunshine, rather. But him? No. He'd be Mr Mean and Moody. Mr Miserable. Mr Nasty.'

'Any more names you'd like to give him?' I give him a look and turn my back on him.

'Mr Stabby,' he says into my ear.

'No.'

'Mr Drug Dealer.'

'He doesn't look like a drug dealer. Anyway, what does a drug dealer look like?' I hiss.

'Like him. He's my drug dealer.'

'Aiden!' I start to laugh. 'You don't have a drug dealer. Do you?' I glance back at him, suddenly unsure.

'No, I'm joking, but look at him.'

'Oh, I am.'

'Has he smiled once in all the time he's been serving?'

'He usually smiles at me.'

'Tenner says he won't today. Look how surly he is. He hates his job, and he hates all the customers, and that includes you, Little Miss Happy. He hates you and that yellow raincoat. He wants the world to be black. As black as his soul.'

'Will you stop? Geez.'

Aiden chuckles in my ear.

I pout a little and raise an eyebrow at him. 'Where's your girl then?'

'Operating the coffee machine along the back wall.'

I stretch a little to see her. 'Don't look!' Aiden hisses, making me giggle. The girl is oblivious to everything other than her coffee machine. She's small and blonde with a cute snub nose. 'Hmm!' I say, tilting my head to one side.

'Hmm? What's that mean?'

'Nothing. She's cute.'

'Yeah, see.' He nudges me gently in the back so I move forward slightly. 'Nicer than Mr Gloomy behind the till.'

'At least I'm big enough to admit she's pretty,' I say. 'You can't admit that about mine.'

'Well, I guess he's just not my type. Oh, here you go, you're on.' He makes low cheering noises, like my very own personal cheerleader – 'Go Orla, go Orla' – and of course I'm giggling and pink in the face by the time I get up to the counter.

'Hello, what can I get for you?' my luscious, delicious coffee man asks me in a bored voice, not even looking up from the till.

'I'll have an americano and this,' I say, placing the salad baguette I'm holding onto the counter and getting my card ready to pay. It's then that he glances up and smiles.

'Oh hi, you usually come in in the mornings, don't you? Tall skinny latte?'

'That's right.' I beam happily. 'I haven't been in recently because I've hurt my ankle.'

'Oh no.' Leaning forward, he peers over the counter at my foot, and I'm pleased that I've managed to find a plain black fluffy sock instead of the panda ones. 'What have you done?'

'Just a sprain. It'll be back to normal soon.'

'Good stuff. It'll be good to see you every morning again.'

'Ha ha! Yes, the sooner the better.'

I pay for my meal before moving to the other end of the counter to wait for my coffee, all the while grinning like a lunatic.

'See, he smiled at me,' I mutter, as soon as Aiden comes to stand next to me.

'Christ! I feel soiled after watching that exchange.' Aiden lowers his head so he can speak directly into my ear. '*It'll be good to see you every morning,*' he mimics. 'If that's not an invitation to spend the night with him, I don't know what is.'

'Oh shut up!' I scoff. 'He was just being friendly! It just happens to be that I usually see him in the morning. But he smiled. Didn't I tell you he smiled at me? He doesn't look so dark and dangerous when he smiles.'

Aiden snorts, eyes dancing with laughter. 'You keep telling yourself that, honey.' Moving towards the counter, he leans over it so he can make eye contact with the girl who's making the coffee. 'Hey, how's it going?' he calls, to attract her attention.

'Oh, hiya!' she replies cheerfully. 'How are you?'

'Good, thank you!' He glances back over his shoulder at me and nudges my cup of coffee towards me before turning back to the girl. I see from her name badge that she's called Candy. 'How are you today?'

I just have time to see her wrinkle her cute button nose before I move away to find a seat. I pick one with a good view of the counter. 'Oh, you know. Working, again. My feet are killing me and I'm only halfway through my shift.'

'Sorry to hear that. Hope you get to sit down soon. Thanks for the coffee.'

'No worries. See ya.'

He pops a pound in the tips jar as he turns and heads over towards me. I raise my eyebrows at him. 'Smooth.'

'Ah, you see. The old Irish charm comes in handy from time to time.'

'Are you going to ask her out?'

'No!' He looks horrified as he unwraps his baguette and takes a massive bite.

'Why not?'

'What's the point? I'm only here for a few more weeks. Besides, I'm not good at relationships. My attention is always focused on getting the next shot and wondering where the animals are going to be. Women don't like that, for some reason. And they get upset when I leave, as though it's a huge surprise when the reality is they've known what I do from the very beginning.'

'What about sex?'

'Oh, I'm an enthusiastic partaker when I can get it,' he says, taking another massive bite from his baguette. 'But it can be more hassle than it's worth. Especially at the moment when I'm studying animals that generally come out at night. Can't be bothered. By the way, that reminds me, you can do me a massive favour when your ankle's up to it.'

84

'What's that then?' I pull a piece of lettuce from my baguette and nibble it.

'There's a woman from the otter watch who's a bit keen, if you know what I mean. If you can pop by one day when she's due to come, can you pretend to be my girlfriend?'

'Will I have to kiss you? Or be naked?'

'No!' His shoulders shake with laughter. 'I'll just say, "this is my girlfriend, Orla", and that will be it.'

'Why don't you just talk about your girlfriend Orla when she comes by?'

'It's hard to slip in an anecdote about your girlfriend when you're discussing spraint. Believe me, I've tried.'

'How do you know she likes you if all you talk about is otter poop?'

'The way she looks at me and goes all red whenever I speak to her.'

'Maybe she's shy. And if she is, she's not likely to make a pass at you or ask you out. And even if she does, then you can just say you don't want a girlfriend.'

'No, no. I don't want it to get that far. If it does, I'll just end up in bed with her and it'll be a disaster. Best to put an end to it now before it gets to that.'

My jaw drops in disbelief. 'You don't have to go to bed with her! Why would you go to bed with someone you don't even like?'

Aiden looks up in surprise. 'I didn't say I didn't like her.'

'What?' I'm completely confused by him now. 'If you like her, then …' My voice trails off, fearing we're just going to go round in circles forever.

'I just don't like her like that.'

I blink at him. 'You like her but you don't fancy her?'

'Yeah, yeah.'

'Okay, good, well there's absolutely no need to sleep with her then, is there?'

'Yeah, but if she comes on to me, then I'd feel obliged.'

'You can't have sex with someone just because you feel obliged.'

'Yeah, but sometimes it just happens and then everything gets messy. I do my best to avoid all things like that.'

'So how does flirting with girls in coffee shops fit with that?'

'That's safe. She's at work and doesn't know where I live. It's just a bit of banter.' He takes another bite. 'So how about you and Mr Darkness over there? Are you going to ask him out, or wait until he makes his move?'

'Neither. I'm not interested in dating him. I just like to look at him.' I glance over to where he's still serving customers.

'But you fancy him?'

'Yeah but ...' I shrug. 'I'm just window shopping.'

Aiden frowns as though trying to work me out. 'You don't want to go in and try on the clothes?'

'Definitely not.'

Aiden rolls his eyes. 'Why?'

'I'm too busy for a boyfriend.'

'Rubbish!'

'It's not rubbish. Look, I've just landed my dream job and now it's time to concentrate on working my way up through the ranks. I work into the evening and some weekends. I don't have time.'

'You're sitting here with me now, aren't you?'

'Yes, it's lunch. I'm allowed lunch.'

'Well, that's a start.'

'I couldn't go for lunch with him, could I? He'd be working.'

Aiden laughs. 'So when was your last boyfriend?'

'I don't know. Couple of years? How about you?' Suddenly uncomfortable with the subject of my love life, I switch the subject back to him as fast as possible.

'About the same. So was your break-up particularly bad? Did something happen?'

'No.'

'Are you sure?'

86

'Yes! Why?' I ask, frowning.

'Because I thought girls your age are usually dreaming of wedding dresses and finding Prince Charming, aren't they?'

'Well, Katie certainly is, but not me.'

'You don't want to get married and have kids?'

'Not especially.'

'Never ever?'

'Not never ever, just not now.' I meet his gaze across the table, wondering why he's so interested. He's watching me intently, like he's some kind of psychologist or councillor or something. I laugh nervously. 'Wow, this got deep very quickly. How about you? I take it you're not looking to get married and have kids if you're travelling the world.'

'Absolutely not. Besides, this planet is full enough without me adding to it.'

'No kids, never ever?'

'Never ever ever.'

'Oh!' I nibble the end of my baguette, realising that I didn't think my choice of sandwich through properly. It's really hard to eat and far too phallic to sit at a table and devour. Aiden has had no such problem with his, but he's a bloke. He's already crunched his way through half of it, cheerfully oblivious to the crumb mountain that's formed on the table in front of him. 'That's quite a serious decision to make when you're still young. How old are you, by the way?'

'Twenty-eight.'

'Still plenty of time to meet the right woman and change your mind.'

His eyes meet mine, and just for a second I think I see a spark of something, but then it's gone, replaced by his usual humorous glint and I know I must have imagined it. 'Nah, I'm cursed to walk this earth alone.'

'Cursed?' I raise an eyebrow at him. 'Sounds like a choice to me.'

He nods slowly. 'Yep. Are you ever going to eat that baguette, or just pick it to death?'

'I'm not really hungry,' I lie.

'Do you want a knife and fork? And a plate?'

'No, I can't ...'

'Hold on, I'll get you one.' He's up out of his seat and across to the counter before I can protest. 'You can't let that baguette go to waste, Orla,' he says in a disapproving parental voice, returning to the table with a plate and the cutlery. 'You must eat it all! Come on now, eat up.' Reaching across, he slides the plate beneath my baguette and places the knife and fork into my hands.

'Yes, Mammy,' I say in my best Irish accent.

Aiden laughs. 'I should think so. There'll be no prunes and custard for pudding if that plate's not cleared.'

'Ugh! Good!'

'What? You don't like prunes and custard? It's lovely.'

'Gross.'

He tuts. 'Kids these days!'

I giggle and set about eating my sandwich with a knife and fork. I feel ridiculous, and it's not the easiest thing to cut through, but at least I'm not dropping the filling everywhere and gnawing at a massive phallic shaped loaf. It's not even because Sexy Coffee Guy is here. He's much too busy serving customers to notice me, and I realise I'm much too busy talking to Aiden to pay much attention to him.

'So back to you and your nonexistent love life,' Aiden says as soon as my mouth is full. 'Why do you think you can't have a job and a relationship? Surely that makes for a very lonely life.'

'No.' I cover my mouth to speak as I swallow the last of my mouthful. 'I have my friends, my family, my job. I don't need some guy coming in and messing with my head.'

'Is that what guys do? Mess with your head?'

'Eventually, yes. I've seen it loads of times with my friends. They're perfectly happy, independent women, and then suddenly

– bam! – some guy appears and they become moony-eyed love-sick fools, refusing to come out at weekends and changing their whole lives to fit around one guy who probably doesn't care that much anyway.'

'That's a bit cynical, isn't it?'

'It's the truth. I can't tell you the number of times I've sat up all night with friends who've been left brokenhearted by bastard men. I bet you've left a few women brokenhearted in your time, haven't you?'

'Like I said, they never understand that when I have to go, I have to go.'

'But presumably you could return to them?'

'Well …' He shrugs one shoulder. 'Where's the fun in that?'

'See, you're a bastard just like all the other men out there.'

He thinks for a moment. 'That's not entirely fair on me or the other men in this world, Orla.' Wiping his mouth on a paper napkin, he screws it up and places it on the saucer of his coffee cup. 'For one thing, I'm not a typical guy with a typical job, and I make that clear when I meet someone, but for some reason the girls I've dated in the past seem to take that as some kind of challenge or something, as though they're out to prove they'll be the one who'll finally change me and make me settle in one place. I don't know why, I really don't.' He looks away, out through the window, though I'm pretty sure it's not the shoppers in the street outside that he's seeing in his head. 'It's my job, my livelihood. What do they expect? For me to give up being a wildlife photographer? Don't they get that it's my passion? It's who I am. Why would they want to change that? If they really loved me as much as they claimed to, they wouldn't want to change that, would they?'

'I suppose that's how it works, doesn't it? People see love as a kind of ownership. They say that if you love someone, you'll set them free, but I don't think it really works like that in reality. Emotions seem to make people irrational.' I look at him for a moment. He seems disquieted by the ghosts of his past. 'It must be flattering to have these girls begging you to stay, though? How many are we talking about?'

'Not many, three or four. The last one ended really badly though. Put me right off getting involved with anyone ever again.' He shudders. 'Never again.'

'I take it you didn't love any of these girls as much as they loved you?'

'No.'

He sounds belligerent, and it makes me wonder if he resents these poor girls for changing the rules on him and turning what was supposed to be a casual affair into something more.

'Why?'

He shrugs. 'Different reasons for different girls. I liked them, but none of them were ever meant to be serious, and I always made that clear at the start. Besides, I don't think any of them really loved me for who I am. It was just the challenge of changing me into who they wanted me to be.'

'I'm sure it wasn't,' I say. 'I mean, look at you. You're kind, thoughtful and really great to talk to. Any woman would want a relationship with you.'

'Except you.' He laughs.

'Except me,' I confirm.

'And we still haven't got to the bottom of that, Orla.' Aiden wags a finger at me. 'So you're friends have been hurt, but that's part of life, surely? That's what happens. People come and go and that's just how it is.'

'Yes, but I like to keep my wits about me. I have my plan for where I want to be in five years' time, and it absolutely does not include a man.'

'So where will you be in five years' time?'

'I told you the other day: living in London, working on one of the big national newspapers.'

'Fair enough, and I'm sure that's attainable. But why would a boyfriend stop you doing that? If you went out with your sexy coffee guy over there, how would that affect your plan? You don't know he's going to stop you from doing anything. In fact, he could facilitate your path by being perfectly lovely in every way and doing all the chores and cooking your tea when you come in late from work. He could be a stay-at-home dad to your children while you power up the career ladder.'

I look across at the counter to where Sexy Coffee Guy's looking mean and moody again, stabbing the buttons of the till angrily as he takes yet another order from the never-ending queue.

'I doubt that would happen.'

Aiden follows my line of sight and chuckles. 'With him, yeah, me too. But the point is, you don't know until you take a chance on someone. You could date Sexy Coffee Guy and have great sex, but have nothing to say to each other, so it ends within a month. Or you could date Eric, the IT bloke from work and have great conversations, but really dull sex so it ends within a week. Or you could start sleeping with your boss, have great conversations, great sex, and rise up the ranks of the *Hawksley Gazette* faster than a rat up a drainpipe.'

'Oh God! Stop, stop!' I say, covering my ears with a shudder. 'You're grossing me out.'

Aiden laughs. 'Just don't be so closed off about things. Life is full of possibilities, and just because you date a guy doesn't mean that's it for the rest of your life. You don't have to get married and have kids. You don't have to stay with him forever. You don't even have to stay with him for the rest of the month if you don't want to. Just live your life and stop denying yourself opportunities to have fun.'

'And also,' I say, thinking back to what he was saying before, 'poor Eric from IT. Why would I dump him after a week just because he was bad in bed?'

'You don't think sex is important in a relationship?' He looks at me askance.

91

'I'm not saying it isn't important, it's just that other things are also important. Possibly more so, in fact. Especially in the beginning when you wouldn't be sleeping with them yet anyway.'

'Oh! Now this is interesting.' Aiden looks intrigued as he props his elbows on the table, crossing his arms in front of him. 'How long do you wait before sleeping with someone?'

'Oh, err, well …' I feel my cheeks flush and glance at the people sitting at the next table. They seem to have gone suspiciously quiet all of a sudden. 'Longer than a week, which is all you've given poor Eric from IT!'

'Poor Eric? Does Eric actually exist?'

'No! You made him up, not me.'

'So why are we suddenly feeling sorry for an imaginary man with erectile dysfunction? Is it because you're overthinking things again? Imagining how sad Eric will be if you leave him? How you could fix his little problem if you just give it time and work through his issues together?'

'No! I just … I don't … I'm …' I break off, flustered.

'See, that's the problem with women. You're always looking ahead. Five days, five weeks, five years. I haven't got a clue where I'll be in five years. I could be dead for all I know. Eaten by a lion or trampled by a hippopotamus.'

'Well, that's a cheery thought.'

'No point worrying about it though, is there? I can't change it.'

'You could if you settled down in Ireland with a nice wife and kids.' I smile mischievously.

'Not necessarily. I could get knocked down by a bus instead of a hippo. Makes no odds where you are. When you're number's up, it's up. Besides,' he goes on, ignoring my look of complete disbelief, 'even if it wasn't my job, I don't think I could stay in one place for very long anyway. I'm a nomad. I love travelling and moving from place to place. I hate being confined to four walls and I love sleeping under canvas, even under the stars if the weather permits.'

'You're a very strange man,' I say, shaking my head. 'You're a wild thing.'

He shrugs, unconcerned by my assessment.

'So what was your point again? I need to sleep with Phil to get promoted?'

'Would that make you happy?'

'No.'

'So no, then. Only do what makes you happy. Stop overthinking things. Live in the moment. Live your life for now, not for five years' time.'

'I think I'll stick to my plan, thanks,' I say primly, finishing half my sandwich and laying down my knife and fork.

'But what if you meet your ideal man in that time, but you say no, you're too busy with your Very Important Career, so he goes off and has babies with someone else.' He gasps dramatically and covers his mouth one hand while flapping the other at me in a rather camp way. 'Oh my God, what if it's your best friend or your sister that he has babies with and you have to live the rest of your life watching him play happy families with someone else, knowing he was your one true love?'

'Will you stop!' I gape at him for a moment. 'For God's sake, Aiden! We've literally just met. One week, that's all, and suddenly here I am, sitting opposite you in a café, talking about things that I don't discuss with anyone.'

Aiden laughs. 'Why not? Surely you discuss sex with your friends. What about that Katie from upstairs? Or is she one of the ones that are so wrapped up in their boyfriends they change their whole lives and have no time to talk to you anymore, until they're heartbroken and crying and you pick up the pieces?'

'No, not really. Katie gets obsessed very easily but loses interest just as quick. She just decides they weren't the right one and moves on to the next. She's your ideal woman, probably.'

'Doubtful.'

I smile and toy with the handle on my cup. It's only then that I realise the time. 'Oh my God! What time is it? I need to get back to work.'

'It's alright,' Aiden says easily, getting to his feet. 'Just blame it on your ankle.'

'No, no! I'm never late back from lunch.'

'Calm down.' He glances at his watch. 'Look, it's only five to two. What time are you meant to be back? Two?'

'Yes.'

'You'll make it. It's only up the road.'

'Not with this ankle.'

'Then they'll understand.' He takes my shoulders and makes me look at him. 'Breathe. It's going to be fine.'

I look into Aiden's eyes, and suddenly I do feel calmer and more grounded. He's right, Phil won't mind if I'm not back at my desk exactly at two. In fact, I have a feeling he's in a meeting this afternoon anyway, and won't even notice if I'm late or not.

'Okay.' I nod. 'Okay.'

'Good, come on then, let's go.'

We call goodbye to the staff behind the counter and Sexy Coffee Guy looks up and smiles. My stomach drops and I'm uncertain whether it's desire or fear or something else, but for the first time in a long, long while, Aiden's made me consider the possibility that I could date him or someone else, if I wanted to, and it wouldn't be that much of a big deal.

'What are you doing this weekend then?' Aiden asks as we walk up the road towards the camera shop.

'Resting my stupid ankle. What about you?'

'I'm out with my mate, Keaton, tonight. You know the sensory forest guy?'

'Oh yeah, you went to see him the other day, didn't you? How's it going?'

'It's looking good. Actually, you can help us out tomorrow, if you like? The path is now decked for wheelchair users, so you can come and try it out.'

'What? In a wheelchair?'

'Yeah, he's got one we can try.'

'Anyone can do that. Why do you need me?'

'You want to write an article about it, don't you? You may as well get the full sensory experience while you're still laid up with your ankle. I'll pick you up at eleven.'

'Oh, okay then!'

We pause next to the camera shop where Aiden's going to pick up his lens. Although I know I'm going to be late back to work, I find myself lingering next to him, searching for more to say. I know I'll be seeing him tomorrow, but I still don't want to leave him. He's watching me, smiling gently, his hair moving gently in the breeze. We stand for a moment, just looking at each other, both unwilling to leave.

'See you in the morning?' he says at last.

'Okay.' I smile brightly. 'Enjoy your evening.'

'You too.'

I start to move away, resisting the strange pull in my gut urging me to stay. I'll have to be careful else I might find myself starting to fancy him!

Chapter 8

Aiden picks me up the following morning and drives us through the bright spring sunshine to his friend's sensory woodland. My ankle is feeling much better this morning, and I can put more weight on it, so I feel a bit of a fraud when they force me into the wheelchair that's waiting at the end of the path, ready for me to get out of the truck. It's a good-sized woodland, situated next to a primary school and close to one of the new housing estates. Aiden introduces me to his friend, Keaton, who has long brown dreadlocks and several facial piercings, and is wearing a huge multi-coloured jumper. He greets me with a warm, patchouli-scented hug that makes me feel stupidly happy. I like him immediately.

'So, you're the girl that Aiden keeps talking about,' he says with a sly glance towards Aiden.

'What are you talking about? I've mentioned her, like, twice!' Aiden says as he pushes me slowly towards a large rainbow-shaped sign painted with the words 'Welcome to the Magical Woodland'. Carved wooden toadstools of various heights line the sides of the path, their flat tops designed so they can be used as stepping stones by the more adventurous children. The cool breeze whispers through the leaves of the sycamore and beech trees, and the

96

low notes of a bamboo windchime can be heard from somewhere inside.

'And the rest. You're all he talked about last night, you know.' Keaton grins down at me, the sun glinting off the gold hoop through his left eyebrow. I feel myself blushing and I don't know how to react, but luckily Aiden jumps in before I have to say anything.

'No, I didn't. Orla, ignore him. He's just stirring.'

I tip my head back to look at him and laugh.

'Oh yes you did,' Keaton continues. 'Orla this, Orla that. All night.'

'It would be odd if I didn't mention Orla, seeing as we'd had lunch together yesterday and were coming here today,' Aiden says crisply. 'All I can remember is you banging on about this place. Talking about the owl you've carved and the badger and the fox.'

'Hey! Banging on? That's rude.'

Aiden laughs. 'You're rude. Poor Orla. Think how she feels. She's only just met you and already you're making her uncomfortable.'

'No I'm not, am I, Orla? She just needs to be warned about your wily ways, that's all.'

'Wily ways? What wily ways?'

'You know!' Keaton winks at me. 'Tripping her up so you can take her to the hospital. You should be ashamed of yourself.'

'Oh yeah, sure I did.' Aiden huffs.

'I can assure you, Keaton, I really did step in a rabbit hole,' I say. 'And besides, I truly doubt that poor Aiden wanted to carry me up that hill to his truck. It was pretty hard going.'

Keaton laughs. 'Alright then. I'm only joking. This is my girlfriend, Mia, by the way,' he says, as we stop by the shadowy entrance to the woodland and a girl with short, cropped hair and a huge smile appears from between the trees.

'Hi, Mia.'

'Hello. Welcome to our Magical Woodland Experience,' she

says, waggling her fingers at the sign above our heads. 'You're our first visitor. Well, apart from Aiden, but he doesn't count.'

'I feel a bit of a fraud in this wheelchair. My ankle's much better now.'

'Yes, but you're doing us a big favour by going round our woods in it. We're hoping there'll be no issues, but if any of the corners are too sharp, or if it gets stuck anywhere, or bumpy, let us know so we can fix it before we get our first class in next week.'

'It's opening that soon?'

'Yes, we're really excited! Are you the reporter from the paper?'

'I am.'

'How exciting!' Mia giggles and clutches Keaton's hand. 'Everything's designed to be at eye-level for little people and people in wheelchairs, so hopefully that will work out.'

'Okay.'

I'm quite excited as Aiden pushes me into the shady tunnel of the woodland and we start our tour. The first thing we come to is a carved wooden fox family, with a wooden plaque with some facts about foxes.

'Wow! That's amazing. Did you do that, Keaton?'

'I did the mother fox. Mia did the two cubs.'

'Wow! You're both so clever!'

'I know, right?' Keaton flashes a cheeky grin at Aiden.

Aiden groans. 'Oh, please, Orla! Don't make his head any bigger than it already is.'

'Hey man, that's just the dreads. Aiden helped loads too. We couldn't have got it finished on time without him.'

'Ah, thank you.'

We move along the path, through a willow tunnel, emerging next to a bug hotel and a metallic bee sculpture surrounded by bee-friendly flowers and a plaque with facts about bees.

'We've done a fact-finder trail as well so it's more interactive for the older kids,' Mia tells me.

'I love the bee. Who did that?'

'Another artist friend of ours.'

'It's beautiful.'

'Yeah, she's really passionate about bees and how important it is for us to be saving them, so she was the obvious choice. We've been trying to set her up with Aiden, but he's having none of it.'

'Oh really?' I laugh. 'Have they met?'

'Once.' Aiden's voice is flat with disinterest. 'She was nice, but no, not for me.'

'Well, who is for you, dear Aiden?' Mia asks sweetly.

'No one. Like I said to Orla yesterday, I am destined to walk this world alone.'

'Cursed, you said,' I correct.

'Yeah, whatever.'

Mia and Keaton laugh as we continue on past a family of wooden badgers. Shiny spiral wind spinners hang from the trees, catching the light as they twirl in the breeze.

'Is the boardwalk okay, Orla? Not too bumpy?'

'Not at all. It's really smooth. Is that a hedgehog house?' I ask, bending to peer into the bushes where I spy a small domed wicker hide.

'Yes, well spotted.'

'I was tipped off by the hedgehog fact sign,' I admit.

'Ah, cheat.'

Laughing, we carry on through the woods, stopping to admire more carved wooden animals along the way. The trail is full of things for the children to explore and get involved in, things to see, feel and hear. There's even a scenting station where children have to identify things by their smell. Aiden tries to tell me it's different types of animal poo, but Mia assures me it will be flowers and herbs. As well as animal facts, they've provided information on how to identify the different types of trees and shrubs in the woods too.

'Wow, this is amazing,' I keep repeating as I'm wheeled through the wood. 'Will it be restricted to school visits, or can families come too?'

'Just school visits for now. As well as the sensory path, we're going to offer bushcraft and pond dipping sessions.'

'You have a pond?'

'Yes, quite a large one. It's fenced off at the back so the children can't fall in.'

'Oh, wait there,' Keaton says, rushing ahead. 'I'm just going to switch something on.'

'What is it?'

'Bubbles!' he cries as hundreds of bubbles start appearing out of bushes from either side of the pathway. He dances around joyfully, arms held aloft. 'Aren't they fabulous?'

'You're so embarrassing, Keaton!' Mia scolds. 'I'm sorry about him, Orla. He's supposed to be a grown man, but really he's just a big kid.'

'It's fine,' I say, laughing. 'I'd be dancing too if my stupid ankle was better.'

'It's improving though, isn't it?'

'Yes, I can put weight on it today. I don't think it's up to dancing though.'

Mia grabs hold of Keaton, pulling him into a hug.

'Alright, you two. Get a room!' Aiden says.

'Okay, Mr Grumpy! Just because you've sworn off women for the rest of your life, don't expect everyone else to do the same.'

'I don't! In fact, just yesterday I was trying to convince Orla to ask the guy she fancies in the coffee shop out on a date.'

'That's not what you said at all!' I protest. 'And no, I will not be asking him on a date.'

'Oh, come on, you can't be waiting for him to make his move. Women's lib and all that. How long have you been eyeing him up for now? Weeks? Months?'

'Few weeks,' I mutter, embarrassed by Keaton and Mia's sudden interest. 'He's probably got a girlfriend.'

100

'You don't know until you ask.' Aiden laughs, clearly enjoying my discomfort.

'Yeah, but what if he says no and I'm too embarrassed to go in there again? Where will I get my morning coffee from then?'

'Just brazen it out. No harm done.' Aiden looks at Keaton, who nods in agreement. Mia looks a little more sympathetic.

'Oh yeah! Besides, I told you, I just like looking at him. I don't actually want to go on a with date him. I'm too busy and it would be horribly awkward and embarrassing.'

'Oh, stop with the too busy!' Aiden says. 'And why would it be horribly awkward and embarrassing? Who or what have you dated before that's made you think that?'

'First dates always are, aren't they? Besides, I've heard enough horror stories from Katie to put me off for life.'

'It's never put her off, has it?'

'No.'

'And she's got a nice boyfriend now?'

'Allegedly.'

'Well then.'

I pull a face. 'I like being single. I like my own space. Do you miss being single, Mia?' I ask, when I catch her watching me curiously.

'I can't really remember being single,' she says, looking bewildered. 'Keaton and I've been together since we were 13.'

'Thirteen!' I gasp. 'My goodness. How old are you now?'

'Twenty-six.'

'Wow! That's amazing!'

'Well, when it's right, it's right,' Mia says simply. She smiles up at Keaton and he kisses her nose.

'Bleurgh!' Aiden makes puking noises from behind me before steering me round them and marching off through the bubbles. 'Hey, I want to go slowly through this bit!' I say, trying to catch some of the soft, iridescent spheres as they fall slowly around me.

Aiden breaks sharply and reverses back beneath the bubbles, almost tipping me out of the wheelchair as I'm flung forward.

'Hey!'

'You wanted bubbles, you've got bubbles!'

'I've got more bubbles than I need now,' I say as they start to land and pop, leaving wet marks on my top and dribbling down my cheeks. 'Move on.'

'No pleasing some people!' he mutters, pushing me forward. 'This corner's a bit sharp,' he shouts back to Keaton as we round a corner at the edge of the wood near the pond.

'This is the one I was worried about,' Keaton says, watching as Aiden reverses me back and tries the corner again.

'It's fine with me pushing it, but if it's a child in an electric wheelchair, or even a manual one, do you think they might struggle to get round? You don't want them tipping off.'

'No.' Keaton looks horrified at the thought and the pair of them spend a couple of minutes discussing how they could reduce the angle.

'Why can't you just make this bit wider?' I suggest, looking down at the boardwalk beneath the wheels. 'That way it will give them more room to manoeuvre without tipping off.'

'Hmm, that could work.'

'See, not just a pretty face,' Aiden says, tipping the wheelchair back suddenly so he can look at me. I scream and clutch the armrests.

'Oh my God, Aiden! Don't ever become a carer!'

Aiden laughs. 'Hey, don't be mean! I did a perfectly good job when you were properly laid up and I had to wheel you around the hospital.'

'Of course you did. I'm sorry.'

We make our way to the end of the woodland path, spotting more carved wooden animals and a willow deer looking out from beneath the tree trunks.

'Well, thank you for that,' I say, getting out of the wheelchair and standing on one foot. 'That was really lovely. I'm so impressed with it.'

'Make sure you give us a good write-up then!'

'Of course, I will. It's a wonderful place. I'm in awe of your talents.'

'Aww shucks, you'll make us blush,' Keaton says, not looking in the least embarrassed. He throws an arm around Mia's shoulders as they wave us off in Aiden's truck.

Chapter 9

'Mia and Keaton are lovely,' I say as we rumble off down the road in the direction of home. 'How long have you known them?'

'Six or seven years? They're great but they're always trying to fix me up with people.'

'You're trying to fix me up with Sexy Coffee Guy!' I splutter. He laughs. 'True.'

'I can't believe they've been together since they were 13. *Thirteen!* You'd think they'd have grown apart in that time.'

'I think they have split up a couple of times. I'm sure that when they left school they went their separate ways for a little while, then had a chance meeting a couple of years later and decided to give it a go again. They're both really easy-going people though so that helps.' He scratches his arm and stares out of the window at the passing fields. 'What do you want to do now?'

'I don't know. I just thought you'd take me home?'

'Well, I can do, or you can come down to my tent and check my camera traps with me?'

I laugh. 'Ooh, well who could refuse an offer like that?'

'You don't have to, of course,' Aiden says, looking embarrassed. 'I just thought …'

'No, I want to, it's just I'm not sure if my ankle will be alright down that hill.'

'Well, I've carried you once, I can do it again.'

'I'm sure it won't come to that,' I say with a confidence I don't entirely feel. After all, it's only my first day without a crutch. 'But you might need to support me.'

'Yeah, fine,' he says easily, switching on the radio. 'Oh, I love this song!' he adds, as a Beatles track comes on. Cranking up the volume, he dons his sunglasses before starting to sing along loudly. I'm laughing too hard to actually join in. And when that track ends, another one comes on that he knows, and he sings even louder.

'Come on, Orla! You must know this one!'

It's funny how you can meet someone and click straight away. I feel like that's how it is with us, though I suspect he's the type of person that clicks with lots of people on many different levels. I tell myself that though this kind of instant mateyness is unusual for me, it probably isn't for him. There's probably one of me everywhere he goes. I don't mind though. Instead of feeling resentful, I can only feel happy that I get to bask in the warm glow of Aiden Byrne's friendship too.

We drive the rest of the way, singing along to the radio along roads lined with blossom-laden trees. 'I love this time of the year,' I say dreamily as he pulls in through the gates of Lark Rise Farm and parks in the shade of a gnarled apple tree.

'Yeah, me too. It makes me miss Ireland though. It was always my favourite time growing up. Of course, in the winter I'm glad to be away.' Opening his door, he jumps down before coming round to help me out.

'Do you think you'll go back and live there? When you eventually do settle down.'

'Yeah, maybe. If I ever do settle.' He laughs mischievously, white teeth flashing against the darkness of his beard. Then he stops and looks at a small green car parked in the far corner of the yard. 'Oh! Looks like I've got a visitor.' He gives me a meaningful look before catching hold of my hand. 'Remember the otter girl I was telling you about? Jayne? She's here. So, if you wouldn't mind being my girlfriend for the afternoon, I'd be much obliged.'

'Oh blimey, really? Are you sure we can do that to her?'

'Oh yes.'

'I'm not sure I can. It feels mean.'

'Come on, Orla. It's just a little thing. A tiny, tiny little thing.' He measures a tiny space between his thumb and forefinger, giving me a pleading look. 'And it's not like we're breaking her heart or anything. She's just mildly interested, and this is just to nip that in the bud. This way she gets the message before she gets disappointed. Everyone's a winner.'

'Oh yeah, you keep telling yourself that.' I give him a look before pausing at the top of the hill. 'I really don't think this is wise, you know. I'm meant to be resting my ankle, not making it worse.'

'Coward.'

'What do you mean? How is it cowardly to not want to hurt my ankle more? I'm not even wearing the right shoes.'

'You've got trainers on, they're alright. And I'll help you. I said I would.' He wraps an arm around my waist and hooks my arm over his shoulder. 'Come on. Hop.'

'I can't hop downhill. What do you think I am? The Easter bunny?'

'I don't know. Do you poop candy?' He laughs as I try to push him away.

'Get off! I think I can manage.'

He lets go of me and I limp slowly down the hill. If I'm careful, I find it's alright.

Aiden walks ahead before turning and putting his hands on his hips, looking impatient. 'You're so slow.'

'Go on ahead then.'

'No, we have to have arrive together so Jayne sees you immediately.'

'Man up, Aiden! What do you think the poor girl's going to do? Throw herself at you?'

'Not if you're there.'

I roll my eyes at him. 'Sorry, Mr Irresistible, you'll just have to be patient.'

'Ah, come on. You're taking ages.'

'I'm not. I'm doing well. Tell me I'm doing well.'

He raises an eyebrow. 'You're doing well.'

'Thank you, now—' But before I can get my words out, I find myself thrown over his shoulder, head dangling as he starts marching downhill. I scream and grab his waist. 'Ow! Aiden! Put me down!'

'Relax, I won't drop you.'

'Please, Aiden. Please.'

'Oh, I love it when you beg.'

'Aiden!'

'Stop squawking. We're almost there now. Ouch! Watch what you're doing with your hands, you pinched me then.'

'I'll pinch you again if you don't put me down.'

'Pinch me again and I'll drop you.'

'Hey!'

'We're here now. Shh.'

'Don't shh me!'

'Oh, be quiet.' Bending, he sets me down on my own two feet and straightens up. I feel breathless and dizzy from being upside down and have to cling to him for a moment so I don't fall. He puts his hands on my hips and looks down at me.

'Sorry. But it got the job done.'

'I hate you,' I say weakly, and he laughs.

There's a noise to our right and a girl with long red hair appears through the trees. She stops when she sees me, the smile falling from her face, replaced by a scowl. She looks like a beautiful, unfriendly fox.

'Hi, Jayne,' Aiden says cheerfully, like he hasn't noticed her expression. 'I didn't realise you were coming today. This is my girlfriend, Orla. Orla, this is Jayne, a ranger from the local otter watch.'

'Hi, Jayne. Nice to meet you.'

She stares at me but says nothing back.

Oh.

'Have you seen any tracks today?' Aiden walks over to her, seemingly oblivious to her frostiness. She mutters something quietly to him, and together they disappear through the trees back along the river. I watch them go, feeling slightly disquieted by the girl's attitude. For some reason, I hadn't expected her to be so pretty or unfriendly. I'd had an image of her being homely and sweet. Perhaps being a bit put out by my presence, but too shy to show it. I don't know why I thought that. Maybe it was because Aiden said she went red every time he spoke to her. I really can't imagine that girl looking shy and embarrassed at all.

I stand alone among the trees, feeling really quite cross that he's gone off with her. He's carried me down here, and now he's just abandoned me. He's meant to be my friend, isn't he? Not Jayne's.

It's a childish thought and I feel immediately ashamed of myself. Looking to distract myself, I focus on the pain in my ankle, which now feels like it's swelling up. I hobble down to the river and take off my trainer so I can soak my foot in the cold water. It's so cold it makes me whimper, but after the initial shock, numbness sets in and I find it helps. Trying to push away the negative feelings stirring in my gut, I close my eyes and tip my face up to the dappled sunlight. Birds are singing and the water's bubbling and wind is whispering through the leaves. It's the most peaceful place, but still my stomach is knotted with ... *something*. I don't know what. Annoyance? Indignation? Jealousy? No, definitely not jealousy. Why would I be jealous? That's just stupid. No, I'm definitely annoyed with Aiden for using me like this. It's

Jayne that's jealous, not me, and she shouldn't be jealous either, because she has no reason to be.

It's unkind of Aiden to make her feel that way, and it's unkind of me to play along with it. Girls should support each other, not let men tear us down. Don't we have enough things to put up with in this world without competing with other girls over stupid men? These are the things I hoped to avoid in life by not getting involved with romantic relationships. Especially other people's.

Why did she look so unhappy and jealous if all she and Aiden had done was talk about otters? What if Aiden's already slept with her and is using me to dump her? How awful would that be? Poor girl.

Or what if he's using me to make her jealous so he can get with her? After all, I really don't understand why he wouldn't want to be with her when she's so hot. I know what he said about relationships and stuff, but he's spent so long trying to talk me into going out with Sexy Coffee Guy I'm not sure I believe him.

And all men want sex, don't they?

Hmm.

I feel sick with anger, and I really hate being this churned up and emotional. And over what? A guy I've known for about a week?

The thought shocks me and I tell myself no, it's about female solidarity, not letting the men get to us and use us. I take more deep breaths and gaze into the river. My feet look very white through the rippling clear water, and tiny silver fish are crowding around my toes.

'Watch out for the piranhas!'

'What?' I snatch my feet from the water in panic and Aiden laughs. 'There are no piranhas in this country, are there?'

'No, I'm kidding.'

I lean back and look behind him. 'Where's Jayne?'

'Gone. You scared her away. Good girl.'

Annoyed, I get my trainer and throw it at him. It misses and bounces off the trunk of the tree next to him.

'Hey, what was that for?' he says, looking surprised.

'Don't be mean! Poor girl. Did you see how unhappy she looked when she saw you were with me?'

'She was upset about a dead otter that's been found by the road, not about you.'

'Hmm.' I raise an eyebrow, sceptical. 'Well, she didn't look too friendly.'

'It takes her a while to warm to people.'

'Especially when they're with the bloke she fancies. Why wouldn't you want to go out with her, anyway? She's beautiful.'

He pulls a face. 'I already told you. It's more hassle than it's worth. This way, she might be a little bit annoyed now, but she's a lot less angry than she'd be a few months down the line.'

'You don't know that. She might be more than happy to see the back of you.'

'Not with my spectacular sexual prowess.'

'Oh really?' I scoff.

'Yes really!' His grin reaches from ear to ear as the breeze blows his hair across his face. 'What? Are you doubting my abilities?'

'No, no.' I hold up a hand to stop him from divulging further details. 'If you say so, Aiden. Anyway, what's up with the dead otter?'

'Someone phoned yesterday evening to say they'd found a dead otter beside the road near the lake. It's a male, and we don't know if it's our resident dog otter. It could be one passing though, searching for a new territory. They've brought it in for examination but I doubt it will tell them much.'

'Oh no. That's sad.'

'Yeah, it is sad. But you know, on the whole, otters are doing very well as a species at the moment, so we mustn't be too disheartened. Jayne's upset, of course, but we're optimistic we have cubs here so it's not like they're dying out as a species anymore. They've staged a massive comeback since we cleaned up the rivers.'

'Any sign of otter activity along this stretch of river yet?'

'We're not sure really. There was a flattened section of grass along the bank which could indicate an otter's been there, but it could have been something else. And no fresh spraint on the rock so … it looks unlikely.'

'Oh, the spraint rock. You were going to show me that.'

'Oh yeah, if you think you're up to it?'

'Is it easy to get to?'

He shrugs and turns to point along the river. 'It's just up there, along the bank. It's pretty easy, although you might want to put your shoes back on.'

'Can I paddle?'

Aiden looks uncertain. 'I'm not sure I'd recommend it.'

'It's only shallow, isn't it?'

'Well, yeah, I suppose. But what if you step on something sharp?'

'The stones look nice and flat.' I stand up and wade out a little way, pulling my cropped linen trousers up so they don't get wet at the bottom. The stones feel smooth and slightly slippery beneath my feet, but I think they'll be alright to walk on as long as it's not too far. 'Are you coming in?'

'No, I'll stay on the bank.' He shakes his head slightly. 'Orla, I really don't think this is a great idea. I don't want to take you to hospital again.'

'It will be fine!' I insist, wading upstream, the water sloshing around my shins. It makes me feel like a kid again, giggly and euphoric, but Aiden's looking terribly disapproving up on the bank. He runs a hand through his hair before placing them on his hips, shaking his head at me. 'I tell you what,' I say, wading towards him and holding out my hand. 'If you're staying on the bank, hold my hand. That way you can stop me falling.'

He rolls his eyes but takes my hand anyway. Now I feel even more like a child, my arm stretched upwards as though I'm a toddler holding the hand of a parent. I giggle.

'What are you laughing about?' he says as he ducks beneath a low branch.

'Nothing. It's just funny, that's all.'

'What's funny?'

'This. Holding your hand. It's like you're my dad or something.'

'Well, I certainly feel very disapproving right now.'

'Oh stop! It's fine. I like the water and it's soothing my ankle.'

'Or maybe making it so numb that you can't feel that you're damaging it more. And if you disturb my trail cam, I'll drown you.'

'Charming! Why, where's your trail cam?'

'Just tucked under this bank here.' He indicates a protruding segment of grassy bank with reeds growing beneath it. 'There's a few dotted around.'

'Well, I'll be careful not to tread on one.' I watch my feet, picking my way around the bigger stones, careful not to slip. Aiden stretches out his arm to accommodate my detour further into the river around the rock. The water's getting deeper and soaks into the bottom of my rolled-up trousers. I'm enjoying myself far too much to care though. I know I'm only paddling in a shallow river, but it feels like the most adventurous thing I've done in years. I'm completely focused on the here and now, with no thought in my head other than the sensation of the water around my calves and Aiden's hand in mine. He walks slowly, patiently, as I giggle and pant my way upstream towards the rock. 'Is it much further?'

'No, you can see it now. The large flat rock sticking up out of the water.'

'Oh yes.' I look ahead and see the rock he means. This section of river is far rockier and more treacherous, and I have to pick

112

my way around boulders and clamber over rocks, but before I know it we're there.

'Look, it's been used so much it's gone green.'

'Ugh! Does it smell?' I cover my nose in case it does.

'Otter spraint smells like jasmine tea, actually. It's not unpleasant.'

'Really? You'd think it'd smell fishy.'

'Not at all. Take a whiff.'

'No, you're alright.'

'Honestly, it doesn't smell bad.'

'I'll take your word for it.' I peer at the green layer on top of the stone. 'Did you see them on here when you saw them mating?'

'Once.'

'Do you think the holt is nearby?'

'I should think so. I don't know exactly where though.'

I look around at the river bank. Sunlight filters through the trees, making the water sparkle. Birds sing and a woodpecker drums. It's so pretty and peaceful, I can see why a shy otter would choose this as its home. With my feet planted firmly on the river bed and the water lapping around my calves, I feel suddenly connected to my surroundings in a way I've never experienced before. I think maybe this is how Aiden feels when he's down here, and why he chooses to camp out instead of staying in hotel rooms. I look up at him now, still holding my hand but looking downstream. He looks so relaxed and content, squinting slightly against the sunlight, and I get the impression that right now, in this moment, he can't imagine being anywhere other than here and that he is completely at peace with himself. It's fascinating to watch. Most people, especially at work, are thinking of the next thing they've got to do, the next place they want to be, the next person they've got to speak to, the next thing they want to say. Their minds are always busy, flitting from thing to thing, whereas Aiden seems to be still and rooted in the present. Though I know that he's constantly moving physically from place to place,

113

I get the feeling that when he is in one spot, he's truly in that spot, appreciating every aspect of it. Living it, absorbing it, recording it with his camera.

As though sensing the intensity of my gaze, Aiden turns his head, catching me staring. Embarrassed to be caught, I turn sharply away, letting go of his hand and starting to wade away.

'Hey, Orla …'

I only get a couple of paces before stepping on a particularly slimy rock. My feet disappear from beneath me, and suddenly the cold water is closing over my head, filling my ears and nose. Before I have time to panic, strong hands are pulling me upwards, and suddenly I'm on the river bank, gasping and coughing as I shiver and drip.

Aiden holds me upright, his hands digging into the top of my arms. 'You are such an idiot! Honestly, I've never met anyone as accident-prone as you. You should come with your own public health warning.'

'Oh God! I'm sorry!' I say, realising he's climbed into the river in his boots and they're now completely drenched. 'I just lost my footing.'

'I know. I saw. Christ almighty, why'd you let go of my hand?'

'I don't know. I'm sorry.'

He pulls me to him, crushing me against his chest in a rough hug so that his T-shirt and trousers are soaked as well as his boots. 'Are you alright?'

I nod. 'Yes, it was only about a foot deep.'

'I know but you went in so completely. I didn't think it was possible for you to go under like that. I thought you'd just slip on your arse or something, not go completely under. I'm mysti-fied as to how you managed it.'

I shrug and cough against his chest. 'Oh well, I'm wet now. At least you don't have to hold my hand on the way back to camp.'

He tuts. 'You know I'm not going to risk that with your dodgy ankle. I'll carry you, seeing as you've got no shoes.'

'Oh God, don't carry me again. It makes me feel so helpless and pathetic.'

'Too bad. You're meant to be resting your ankle, not wading around in rivers, trying to drown yourself.' Before I can protest further, he sweeps my legs up and carries me back to camp through the trees.

My humiliation is complete. Not least because I've just realised that my white T-shirt has turned completely transparent. I pull it away from my body and my mortifyingly lacy bra with one hand, while my other arm is wrapped tightly around his shoulders. His hair curls onto my forearm, sticking to my wet skin, and he strides through the trees as though eager to be rid of me. When we reach his tent, he deposits me into his camping chair so fast I think my skin must burn him.

He goes straight into his tent and I hear him crashing about, unzipping things and rustling in bags. Careful to keep my attention away from the tent in case he's getting undressed, I turn my full attention to my ankle. It's looking pretty good really. Most of the bruising has gone and it's not as puffy as it was before.

'At least the water's reduced the swelling on my ankle,' I call, cheerfully.

'Oh good,' he replies in a flat voice.

I wince and cast a sideways glance at the tent. He must be really pissed off with me and I don't blame him really.

'I'm not usually this accident-prone, I swear,' I say. 'I just seem to be having a bad week.'

'Yeah.' His voice is still flat, unhappy. Disbelieving, maybe. My chest feels hollow with disappointment and I feel almost tearful. He's not going to want to speak to me anymore. I've lost my new friend.

There's lots of rustling from the tent and suddenly he ducks out of the doorway wearing a fresh T-shirt and trousers. He passes me a towel and some clothes. 'Here, T-shirt and shorts. They'll be massive but it's better than sitting around in wet clothes.'

'Thanks,' I say, surprised he's not going to take me home straight away.

I go into his tent and he zips it up behind me to give me some privacy. I'm still dripping wet and I feel guilty about the wet patches I leave on his plastic groundsheet. I rub my hair vigorously with the towel before pulling off my wet clothes and changing into his T-shirt and shorts. It's a relief to be in something dry and warm, and I smile sheepishly at Aiden as I go back out. He glances up and then away, still obviously annoyed.

'I'll make a fire,' he says, getting up and going round the side of his tent.

'Oh no, you don't have to do that,' I protest. 'I'll just go home. I'm sure I've annoyed you enough.'

'You haven't annoyed me, Orla. Don't be silly,' he says, sounding annoyed. 'And I don't want to carry you up that hill yet, either. So you can sit here by the fire, and get warm.' He's arranging rocks in a circle and filling the inside with wood.

'You won't have to carry me. I bet it will be easier going uphill than down.'

'I doubt it.'

'And my trainers aren't wet. I can put them back on and walk. I don't want to put you to any more trouble.'

'Just sit down.'

He strikes a match and the flame catches on the kindling, curling and licking around the wood. Aiden leans forward and blows on it to spread the flame further. We're silent, just watching the orange flames and listening to the birds in the trees above. I'm still clutching my wet clothes, trying to hide my bra and pants inside my T-shirt and jeans.

'Do you want to spread those out on a rock in the sun or something?' he suggests.

'Oh yeah, okay.'

'Actually I'll do it. You've got not shoes on.'

'No, no, it's fine,' I say hurriedly, thinking of his big hands on

116

my small pants. The thought makes my stomach tighten with anxiety. 'It's just grass.'

And twigs, beech nuts and spiky holly leaves, but all the same, the ground is surprisingly soft as I go down to the river and lay out my clothes in the sun. As I'm bending to retrieve my trainers from the bank, I hear a faint splash and, from the corner of my eye, catch sight of movement in the water by the opposite bank.

It's probably just a big fish, gobbling up a fly. A frog, maybe. But still, I freeze and watch the water closely for signs of movement. Although the water's crystal clear, the combination of shade from the trees and sunlight glinting off the surface makes it hard to see anything from this angle at all.

But then I see the bubbles on the surface, made by the nostrils of whatever it is swimming underneath and know it's not a fish. I know I should run back to Aiden, but if I move now, whatever it is will disappear anyway. I can't believe it hasn't spotted me. I track the bubbles as they go down stream, and suddenly the flat top of a sleek brown head breaks the water then disappears from sight once more. That's definitely an otter.

Figuring it's far enough downstream for me not to disturb it now, I slip silently away through the trees and back to Aiden. I can barely speak when I get back to him, and stand pointing back towards the river, my mouth flapping uselessly.

'What have you done now?' He looks resigned, like he expects me to have walked into a tree or been bitten by something in the short time I've been away.

'I saw an otter.'

'You did not!'

'I did! Well, it was either an otter or a mink.'

He stands up in one fluid motion. 'Where?'

'Swimming downstream. It might have gone now. I heard a splash from the bank opposite, and I waited, wondering what it was, and then there were bubbles and then the flat top of a head.' I hurry after him back towards the river. 'I was standing here,' I say, indicating my clothes on the bank. 'And I saw it about level with that rock down there.'

'Just the one?'

'Yes.'

'Well, if it's the mother, where are the cubs?'

Obviously, I have no idea so I just shrug and stay silent.

'It could have been a mink, I suppose.'

'Maybe. I can't tell the difference.'

'Otters are bigger.'

I stay quiet, not wanting to point out that I'd only seen the top of its head and had nothing to compare it with anyway.

He puts his hands on his hips and makes a 'hmph' sound, staring downstream.

'And you say it entered the water directly opposite?'

'I think so. I didn't see it go in, I heard the splash and caught a movement from the corner of my eye.'

'Okay.' He paces up and down the bank, still staring off downstream, the wind stirring his dark hair. I'm starting to feel cold now and I wrap my arms around myself as moisture from my still-wet hair dribbles down my neck. 'Okay,' he repeats thoughtfully, more to himself than to me. 'If I set up the hide here tonight, maybe it will be back out later.' I step back as he circles the area, working out the best place to set up his equipment. Spotting bubbles in the water, I touch his arm and point. But there is no tell-tale flat brown head this time, just a trail in the water as it heads further downstream, away from us.

'I suppose we should keep our distance,' Aiden murmurs. 'Otherwise she might get spooked and not come back.'

He stoops and retrieves my clothes from the river bank before carrying them back to camp. I feel a bit sick as I follow him, knowing my bra and pants are somewhere inside the bundle of clothes in his hand. Back at the tent, he tosses them carelessly on to the camping chair and goes to poke the little fire with a stick. I assume he's brought my clothes back because he doesn't want the otter scenting them, so I fold them up, tucking my underwear inside the pockets of my trousers.

'Do you want to take me home now?' I ask.

'No,' he says. 'Can you stay a while? I want to concentrate on this.'

'Okay. I just thought you'd want me out of the way.'

'Not especially, and I can't leave now if the otter's out. Come and sit here by the fire and get warm. I'm going to set up my stuff.' He passes me the stick. 'If it starts to go out, give it a bit of a stir, but be careful not to set fire to the stick.' He looks worried suddenly, and casts an anxious look towards his tent and the surrounding trees as if he expects me to burn the whole lot down to the ground.

'Okay,' I say with more confidence than I feel.

'Maybe I'll get you a bucket of water, just in case,' he murmurs.

I roll my eyes at him. 'Don't worry, these things happen in threes, don't they? I've done my ankle, got stuck in the bath and fallen in the river, so I'm golden now. Safe.'

'Hmm.' He raises an eyebrow, a ghost of a smile playing around his lips. 'I'll still be keeping a close eye on you, Orla Kennedy. Just in case.'

He sets about collecting his equipment together, and I stare into the flickering flames of the fire. Despite the heat it's emitting, goose bumps line my arms and I rub my hands up and down them vigorously. Aiden obviously notices as he passes me a hooded sweatshirt to put on. It's the same one I wore to hospital, and still smells faintly of my perfume. The soft material makes me feel better immediately, and I pull the sleeves down over my hands, hugging it around me as I settle down to watch him work.

Chapter 10

I watch Aiden through the trees, erecting the hide. It's long and low, like a tunnel, so he can lie stretched out, watching the water. He's got another hide further along that's more upright, so he can sit on a chair inside it. I check my watch. It's already nearly three o'clock. I don't want to ask how long he'll be, knowing he's busy, but I haven't eaten anything since breakfast and I'm starving.

He's got some potatoes in his tent. I wonder if I should bake some in foil on the fire. I look for him, but he's setting up some kind of lighting thing near the hide, so I just go and get the potatoes and foil and set about baking them myself.

'Are you okay?' He comes back over after about half an hour. 'What are you cooking?'

'Just some potatoes. I hope you don't mind. I'm starving.'

'No of course not.' He sits down next to me and places a few more pieces of wood on the fire. 'I'm sorry, I forgot about food. Do you want something now? I think I've got some crisps and a can of Coke or something?'

'Yes please.'

He gets up and goes into his tent, returning a few moments later with the food. I'm so hungry I almost bite my fingers as I push the crisps into my mouth. Aiden sits down next to me, swigging from a can of Coke, and the fire crackles as smoke curls upwards. I find myself wishing it was dark already. A campfire is better in the dark.

'Is there any sign of anything out there now?'

'No, but it's still early. Good job you saw it.'

'Well, I hope it was an otter otherwise you'll be wasting your time.' I pull the ring on my can and take a good glug. The fizz stings the back of my throat, making me cough.

'It could have been a mink, but I doubt it.' He rubs my back as I continue to cough and splutter. 'I'm not saying for sure there aren't any around here, but I haven't seen any. And from what you said it's too big to be a water vole, but if it is that's pretty good anyway.' He scratches his arm and stares into the flames. 'I just hope it comes back. If it doesn't, hopefully it will have triggered some of the trail cams so I might get some shots on them, even if I don't see it later on.' I look up at him as he stands up, towering above me. From this angle, he's all legs and hair, but he has an intensity about him that I don't recognise. He's usually laid back, but now he's so focused on the task ahead of him that the air around him seems to crackle with energy. His excitement is contagious and I feel it stir inside of me too. Hurray! The otters are back! I feel giggly and oddly like clapping, but luckily I'm holding my Coke can so I don't, which is good because I've made enough of an idiot of myself already.

Aiden disappears back down to the river and I stay by the fire. It's strange but being down here has raked up old memories from when I was a child and camping with my mum and dad. We only went a couple of times. My mum didn't like it, and I remember her being cross and irritable all the time we were there, bickering with my dad and snapping at me. I can't even remember where-abouts in the country we went. The south coast, possibly. I just remember the grass and the sky and the sea in the distance. There were ponies in the next field, and they alone had made it feel magical. I so wanted a pony. I'd left Mum and Dad sniping at

121

each other and sat in front of the fence, talking to the ponies and feeding them long stems of grass that I picked from around the fence post.

It feels strange thinking about camping with my parents now. It's been so long since I pictured them together and it gives me a raw feeling in my stomach doing so now. I feel a wave of unhappiness remembering the arguments tempered with bouts of silent resentment from my mum. She doesn't argue with my stepdad that much. But then he takes her on holidays to Spain and Portugal.

I sit, lost in my memories, until it occurs to me that I should be checking the potatoes. I gather plates and utensils, and find a long-pronged fork to retrieve the potatoes from the fire. Cooking at such a basic level is oddly satisfying and I feel almost triumphant as I spear a potato and pull it from the flames. Aiden comes back over and sits down next to me.

'Do you have any butter?'

'No. But I have baked beans.'

'Ooh get them, get them!'

He gets back up and disappears into his tent before returning with a saucepan of beans. He holds it over the flames for a few minutes to warm them, and I wait, my mouth watering and stomach protesting at the hold-up. At last, they're ready, and I get to eat. I'm only small, so I wonder how hungry Aiden feels when he's so tall. There's a lot of him to fill.

He eats fast, done in minutes, and then he's back on his feet and setting up his equipment again. I eat slowly, savouring my food, mesmerised by the flames. Dusk creeps through the trees, silent and stealthy, and I'm surprised when I look up and everything is dark. How did it get so late when I'm just sitting here, staring into a fire? I have no idea how to clean the plates when I can't go near the river for fear of scaring the otters, so I stack them together and stow them behind the tent before going to find Aiden.

It's a bit lighter down by the river, the full moon rising in a navy-blue sky. I peer into Aiden's hide where he's lying stretched out, his face pressed up to his camera.

'Hello?' I whisper. 'What do you want me to do?'

'Nothing.' He shifts and lifts his head from his camera to look at me. 'I'm just checking this lens will focus properly. I'm still having trouble with it.'

'Where do you want me to be? Do you want me out of the way or in there with you or …?'

'You can get your head down in my bed, if you like. No need for you to be uncomfortable.' He crawls out of the hide and stands next to me. 'Do what you like. I'm not bothered.'

I raise an eyebrow. 'You're a crap date,' I joke.

'We're on a date? Jesus! Try dressing better next time, you look like Jimmy Krankie.' He tugs at the shorts I'm wearing and I grab his hand.

'Careful! They'll be around my ankles in a minute. I'm not even wearing any knickers.'

'Oh!' He backs up sharply, looking horrified. I'm surprised by how shocked he is. What did he think? That my knickers remained dry when all my other clothes were soaking wet? Although to be fair to him, he's probably not given much thought to my knickers, thank goodness.

'Maybe I should take you home.' He rakes his hand through his hair and glances back at the river. He looks cornered, as though he doesn't want to leave but doesn't want me there either.

'No need, I'm fine,' I say quickly. 'I've got my Kindle in my bag. I'll go in your tent and read until I fall asleep.'

'You sure?'

'Yep.' I smile and turn to go, wishing with all my heart I hadn't mentioned my knickers. 'What do I do if I need the loo?'

'Go behind a tree, unless you can struggle up to the farm.'

'Oh blimey, really?'

He shrugs as he bends to switch on one of his lights. Red light floods the river. 'Just keep out of the infrared and you'll be fine.'

'I'll try.'

'And do it away from the tent. I don't want to be lying there, smelling your wee for the rest of my time here.'

'Of course. I'm not stupid.' I'm glad it's dark, because my face is on fire. 'I'll wee in your sleeping bag if you're not careful.'

'You do that and you'll be buying me a new one.'

I'm laughing as I walk away, but I'm not looking forward to finding a place to wee in the dark. At least when we camped when I was a kid there was a toilet on site. And I had an airbed. Aiden's camp bed feels hard and it squeaks when I sit on it. I've already decided not to get into his sleeping bag. However much I like him, it just feels too intimate. Besides, who knows what he gets up to in it. I'm not going there.

So, I lie on his uncomfortable camp bed and read in the darkness of his tent, breathing in the cool night air and the smell of the canvas above me. It's kind of pleasant, but I still have no idea how he lives like this long-term. Does he not long for the softness of a mattress? A warm duvet? A carpet beneath his feet? I guess not.

He's such a different creature to me. It's bizarre that we get on so well.

I read until my eyelids grow heavy, but I'm really too cold to sleep. It's almost summer, but today's cloudless blue sky means tonight's temperature has fallen sharply. So I lie balled up beneath Aiden's crinkly sleeping bag, while the dark night presses in and the forest whispers around me. I can't stop my mind from wandering to every horror film I've ever seen. Every time the tent moves in the breeze, every time a twig cracks, every leaf that rustles, I think is a psychopath coming to get me. I tell myself that Aiden's not far away.

But what if they get him first?

I sit up and fumble for my phone to switch on the torch. The golden halo of light makes me feel better for about a minute and then I realise it's made the dark places even darker than before. I see shapes in the shadows and move the torchlight around, checking there's nothing there. That's when I hear it: a scratching, snuffling noise at the base of the tent. There may be nothing in here with me, but there's something outside, wanting to get in.

I don't recall camping being this scary.

But hold on. Let's be sensible here. The noise is coming from the back of the tent, where I stowed the dirty plates earlier, so it's likely just a fox having its supper. And as for Aiden, he'll still be in his hide, watching the water for otters.

There's no need to be scared.

There's no need to be scared.

But then the fox screams and I'm out of the tent faster than Usain Bolt. Skidding to a halt next to Aiden's hide, I find him shaking with silent laughter.

'Did the fox scare you?' he asks in a low voice.

I nod, my heart beating so fast I feel a bit faint. 'Can I come in here with you?' I whisper.

'If you like. It's only a fox though. It won't hurt you.'

'I know but I don't like it. It's too dark. I feel too alone.'

'Come on then.' He shifts over and I crawl into the dark tunnel and lie down next to him. He's got a blanket over him, and he moves it so that it covers me too.

'Thanks.' He's really warm. I feel the heat coming off him through his clothes and edge closer to him. He jumps as my bare feet touch his legs.

'Christ, you're cold!'

'I know. Why are you so warm?'

'I've got a T-shirt, a jumper and my camo jacket on over the top. Plus the blanket. Didn't you get into my sleeping bag?'

'No, it felt too personal.'

He laughs quietly. 'Yeah, well, you're wearing my shorts without knickers. That feels personal too.'

125

'Shhh, I'll wash them. And it's not like I've got any nasty diseases or anything.'

'Glad to hear it.'

We're silent for a few minutes, and I'm aware of how loud and fast I'm still breathing from my scare. Aiden peers through the lens of his camera towards the river, which is still bathed in red light from his infrared lights.

'Have you seen anything?'

'No, not yet.'

'Oh, I'm sorry.'

'Not your fault.' I feel him shrug, his shoulder pressed against mine.

'I got you all excited though.'

He laughs. 'And that was even before you mentioned your knickers.'

'Shut up about my knickers,' I hiss. 'They were wet. End of story.'

'Oh God, wet knickers. Now that's sparked all kinds of thoughts.'

'What? Aiden!' I squeak, outraged. 'This is me, remember. The girl who puked on your shoes.'

'Oh yeah, yeah okay.' He grimaces then chuckles some more. 'I'm just winding you up, Orla. Don't worry.'

'Good. You're a wicked man.' I shift closer and put my cold hands up his top. I don't really intend to touch his bare skin, especially as he's wearing three layers, but somehow I manage to burrow beneath his jacket, his jumper and his T-shirt and find smooth, hot flesh. He jumps and yelps a little.

'Jesus Christ, Orla. What the …' He tries to wriggle away, but there's nowhere for him to go.

'Shh, shhh, just give it a moment,' I giggle, keeping my hands on him.

'What do you mean, give it a moment? Your hands are like ice.'

'But you're so lovely and warm, and I'm so cold. Look, I'm warming up now. That's not so bad, is it?'

'That's because you've sucked all the heat out of me,' he squeaks. I didn't realise his voice could get that high-pitched. 'You're like a vampire.'

'That's not fair. I haven't even bitten you yet.'

'Yet?'

I laugh, low and evil, but Aiden suddenly stiffens and holds up a hand to silence me, his attention caught by movement on the river. Lowering his head to his camera, he looks through the lens. I hold my breath and try to see what he's seeing, but there's nothing obvious going on. Everything looks still and silent to me. The grass and trees and rocks all look exactly the same as they did a few minutes ago. And then I hear it. A whistle, followed by a splash. *Otters!* Aiden adjusts his focus and then presses a button on his camera.

'You're obviously my good luck charm,' he murmurs, leaning to one side and inviting me to look through the lens. It takes a second for my eyes to adjust, but then I see two dark shapes in the water, and another on the bank, seemingly hesitant to join its brothers and sisters in the water. There's another whistle that seems to make up its mind, and the cub slides into the river with a faint plop. 'She's teaching them to hunt,' Aiden whispers into my ear, his hot breath and stubble tickling the fine hairs surrounding it. It sets an army of goose bumps marching up my skin, and it occurs to me that this is the closest I've been to another human being for a very long time. The sensation is almost as fascinating as watching the otters' lithe shapes twist and turn in the water. 'This is probably the first time they've ever been in the water. She has to wait until their coats are fully waterproof.'

'I always assumed they were born in water and lived in water all the time.' I move away from the lens so Aiden can look. Now I know where to look, and if I strain my eyes, I find that I can see the dark shapes of the otters without the camera lens.

'No, they spend a lot of their time on land.'

'Doesn't your red light disturb them?'

'They don't seem to notice it.'

One of the otters climbs out of the water before sliding back in, and then the others follow, like children at a swimming pool. Aiden moves to one side again, inviting me to look once more and I see the otters in more detail. Their sleek heads and bright shiny eyes. Their bushy whiskers. I feel so privileged to be seeing them like this. It's magical.

They move downstream, out of shot, and I move out of Aiden's way so he can readjust the camera. Propping myself up on my elbows, I watch the dark shapes play in the water, hearing the occasional whistle and splash. I expect them to be gone within minutes, but they stay for a good thirty minutes, cavorting in the shallow water. Every so often, Aiden lets me look through the camera, and I'm amazed at how clearly I can see them.

'Have they gone?' I whisper when I can no longer see any dark shapes playing in the water.

'Think so.'

'Wow. That was amazing.' I roll onto my back, feeling the bobbles and bumps of the forest floor poking up through the mat we're lying on. Through the trees, I see stars glinting in the night sky.

'Yep. Told you. It's always worth the wait once you see something amazing.' He adjusts something on his camera and sets it to one side before crawling out of the hide. Standing up, he stretches and yawns, and from this angle he looks as tall as the trees around us. 'Be back in a minute,' he says, before disappearing into the trees. The instant he's gone, I feel lonely and vulnerable. The cool air nips at my skin, stealing away the warmth from my bones put there by Aiden. I could never live the life he does. Even with the highs of seeing such wonderful wildlife, the lonely moments in between would steal my joy.

Aiden comes back moments later, but to me it feels like hours.

I hate myself for being so pathetic and needy. He turns off the lights and then crawls back into the hide next me. 'We can go into the tent if you like?'

'I don't mind. I'm fine here.' Now he's back, I don't really want to move. The warmth of his body is already seeping into mine, and my limbs are growing heavy with the promise of sleep.

'You sure? You can have the camp bed.'

'No. I'm okay.'

'I'll drive you home if you want?'

'No, I'm too sleepy.'

'Okay.' He settles down, pulling the blanket over him and making sure it's covering me too. 'Are you alright with me sleeping here? Or do you want me to go somewhere else?'

'Stay there. I won't sleep without you next to me.' My eyelids are growing heavier, and I roll onto my side so I'm closer to him, my nose against his shoulder.

There's a pause, and then he asks, 'Do you want me to hold you or something?' in a voice loaded with fear.

'No!' I snigger and poke his side. 'Just be there to fight off foxes and psychopaths.'

'That's alright then.' He heaves a huge sigh of relief and I smile into the darkness. An owl hoots above us and Aiden lifts his head. 'I should get some photos of that.'

'It's already gone.'

'It'll be hunting. I should set up more camera traps.'

'Yes, you should. But not now. Tomorrow.'

'Hmmm.'

I have my eyes closed, but I sense his eyes darting, his mind whirring. His breathing is fast and shallow.

'What's the matter?' I ask, my mouth moving against the material of his jacket. It smells slightly dusty, but not unpleasantly so. I hear him swallow.

'I'm too excited to sleep.'

'Aw, like a little kid, excited about the otters?'

129

'Something like that.' He laughs, low and breathy.

'Practise some mindfulness techniques. Concentrate on your breathing. Count sheep.'

'Thanks for the advice.'

'You're welcome.' My nose itches and I rub it against his shoulder without thinking about what I'm doing.

'Are you wiping snot on me now?'

'No, sorry. Just an itch.'

'Likely story.'

I giggle. 'Go to sleep.'

'I can't. You'll have to tell me a bedtime story.'

'A bedtime stor … about what?'

'I don't know. Just something about yourself. Is this your first time camping?'

'No, I was thinking about this before. We went camping when I was about 8. I don't remember much other than my mum hated it. It was my dad's idea.'

'Was that the only time you went?'

'I have a feeling we went twice, but I don't remember much. Can't even remember where it was, only that it was near the sea and there was a pony in the next field. I'll have to ask my mum about it.'

'Are your parents still married?'

'No. They divorced when I was 14.'

'Amicably?'

'Not really.'

'You still see your dad?'

'Yes. Though I haven't for ages. He's living down south at the moment. I should arrange to go and see him.' Guilt tugs at my stomach and I open my eyes, blinking in the darkness. I phoned him last week, I remind myself. He's okay. He sounded happy.

'What's he like?'

The question takes me by surprise and I start a little then laugh. 'Why do you want to know what my dad's like?'

130

'I don't know. Just asking.'

'He's … he's a long-distance lorry driver.'

'That defines him, does it?'

'Oh! Er well, that's just what he does. He's okay.'

'He's okay? What's that mean?'

I frown into the darkness. 'It means he's okay. He's got somewhere to live. He's still got a job. He's found a new girlfriend.'

'Have you met her?'

'I didn't meet the last one. Or the one before that.'

'Does he have lots of girlfriends?'

I sigh. 'A steady stream of them. I used to hate it when I was younger and went to visit him and there was a woman there, but these days I feel relieved when he's with someone. It's when he's between partners I worry, because that's when he drinks too much and has nowhere to live.' I take a deep breath, trying to quell the rising anxiety. The guilt.

'It must be difficult to visit him if he's staying at random women's houses. How do you know where to send his birthday and Christmas cards?'

'I find him. Plus, I know the company he works for so I can send them there if I need to. He's okay.'

'Good.'

'Yeah. Good.'

'Why did your parents split up? Do you know or was it kept hidden from you?'

I laugh. 'It was hard to hide it when my mum had my stepdad's baby less than six months after my dad moved out.' I draw in a sharp breath, shocked by myself. I've never said that out loud before. Not to anyone. Not even my mother. Of course, all the family knew. My grandparents, my aunties and uncles. Even my schoolfriends must have known. What was most shocking was that no one seemed to mind. My stepdad moved in and was accepted as part of the family almost immediately. Even by me. I find it hard to forgive myself for that.

'What's your stepdad like?'

'Great.'

There's no arguing with it really. Ray's a good man. I just wish … I just wish … What? I have no idea what I wish. All I know is that I feel tense and anxious when I think about my parents' divorce. I don't like to think that my mum was having an affair behind my dad's back, but the facts are right there in front of my nose in the form of my sister. And I love my sister. It's very confusing.

'But?'

'But nothing. He moved in and … everything got better.' My voice thickens and I have to swallow hard. Naughty Orla. That's a bad thing to say. Disloyal to my father. But it's also true. The house felt brighter, happier, just like my mum. My sister was born, plump and gurgling and smiley. My bedroom was decorated, the broken window in the front porch fixed, the windows cleaned. Flowers grew in our garden and the lawn was mown. It felt like a cloud had passed over us, leaving only sunshine.

The fact that the cloud returned when I visited my dad in his miserable flat was something I didn't like to dwell on.

'But not your dad?'

'No. Not for my dad. Well, I suppose he's happy in his own way. I suppose what makes one person happy doesn't necessarily work for someone else. He likes his beer and his truck and he doesn't seem to care about where he lives so I suppose he does okay.' I sigh again. 'Looking at his life has made me want to work harder and achieve more, though. I heard my nan say he was a good-for-nothing layabout once, and it made me determined to work hard at school and make a success of my career.'

'Hence the five-year plan?'

'Yes.'

'Is your dad the real reason you don't date, either?'

I inhale sharply. 'I don't want you to think he's a bad man,

132

you know,' I say, my voice brittle. 'He never mistreated my mum or anything. He's just a bit … too laid back. He lacks ambition. Drive, I suppose. He's just happy to drift. And that's okay if it works for him. I just feel bad that my mum couldn't accept him for what he was and moved on to someone else. She should have worked harder to keep us together. He'd have stayed with us then, not moved around the country, living in horrible flats that I hated visiting. He was a right state sometimes. Stinking of booze, his clothes dirty. I hate that we did that to him. We abandoned him. Traded him in for someone new. Someone better.'

'*You* didn't.' Aiden rolls on his side so he's facing me. 'Your mum did. You were a child, Orla.'

'I was 14.'

'A child. Have you ever spoken to your mum about this? Your dad?'

'No.'

'Don't you think you should? You're not responsible for your parents' relationship.'

'Yes, but I just accepted Ray. I just accepted my sister. I love them both.'

'And that's a good thing. If your parents' relationship wasn't working, then that's down to both of them, not just your mum. You can't blame her for everything.'

'I don't blame her, I just wish … I don't know what I wish.' I'm back to the wishing again. I need to stop that.

'Maybe you wish that your dad was a bit more together? That he'd found the happiness your mum has?'

'Maybe. Yes.' That's as good a wish as any, I suppose.

'Maybe he's not wired that way. Maybe he wasn't cut out for family life. Maybe your mum kept it going for as long as possible and then couldn't go on anymore.'

'Hmmm.' I roll onto my back and stare upwards, into the darkness. Aiden puts a hand on my stomach, above the blanket so it doesn't feel weird or intrusive, just warm and comforting.

I close my eyes and say the thing that scares me the most. 'She told me once that I was just like him.'

'Did you stink of booze? Were your clothes all dirty?'

'No!' I laugh, despite the well of sadness inside me. 'No. I think I hadn't cleaned my room or something.'

'Ah, mothers say all kinds of things when they're cross. You should hear my mother yelling at me, sometimes.'

'What if I am like him though? What if I can never be happy?'

'No! You said he lacked ambition. You don't, do you? You have your plan, remember. Your qualifications. And you're happy and bubbly and bright. You bring happiness. And otters. I'd have never found the otters if it wasn't for you.'

'Yes, you would! Don't be silly.'

'No, I wouldn't. Not tonight. I was all for having a beer and going to sleep.'

'And here we are still awake at what time – 3 a.m.? Talking about my parents' divorce.' I wipe away a tear that's somehow escaped to roll down the side of my face, towards my ear. I don't know what it's doing there. I'm not crying. 'I'm sure I must have bored you enough for you to be feeling sleepy by now.'

'You haven't bored me at all.' He presses his lips to my temple and I close my eyes, comforted by his touch. 'Your parents made their own mistakes, their own decisions. You're not responsible for your father's happiness nor your mother's affair.'

'I know, but …'

'There is no but, Orla. It sounds like you made the best of things. What else could you have done? Rebelled against your mum and stepdad, rejected your baby sister, made everyone's life a misery? What good would that have done? It wouldn't have saved your mum and dad's marriage, would it? That was already over.'

'I know, but by just accepting everything that happened … it's like … well, like something my dad would have done. He just accepted it. Allowed it to happen. Moved out. Rolled over.'

'What else could he do? He and your mum couldn't have been getting on very well, could they? Maybe he was glad to go. You don't know because you were just a kid. The only thing you can know is that you made the best of a bad situation, and there's nothing wrong with that. It doesn't mean you abandoned your dad. It doesn't mean that you're destined to be like him either. And for what it's worth, I really can't see you becoming a long-distance lorry driver.' I laugh and try to shove him with my shoulder, but he pulls me against him, his arm wrapped around my stomach. It seems like the most natural thing in the world to roll onto my side so he can curl around me.

'Christ, does this count as holding you?' Aiden says. 'I never hold women after sex.'

'Just as well we haven't had sex then.'

'Hmm. Maybe that makes it alright then.'

'Hold on, why don't you hold women after sex?'

'Because after a while it's just annoying, and you want to let go and be in your own space, but you know they're going to be like "hey what's wrong?" if you turn away, and act all hurt and offended. So you just lie there, all hot and sticky, wishing you could go to the bathroom but you're too scared to move.'

'Really?' I lift my head and look back at him.

'Yeah, so I don't hold anyone anymore. I don't want to get into all that holding business. It's just sex. Let's just fall asleep straight after and be done with it.'

'You're talking figuratively, I take it?'

'What?'

'You said, let's just fall asleep straight after. You're not having sex with me.'

'Oh no, I'm talking figuratively, of course,' he says hurriedly. 'Besides, I'm not having sex with anyone right now. Even sex without holding people is too much hassle these days.'

'Huh.' I lay my head back down, blinking in the darkness. For someone so kind and generous and understanding, he's sure got a lot of issues about relationships. 'Christ, Aiden, you've just given me a whole new reason never to date anyone ever again. Seriously, feel free to move whenever you want.'

'Okay, good.'

'And don't feel like you have to hold me at all. I'm not asking to be held.'

'No, no, this is actually quite comfortable.'

'Oh okay.'

'You feel nice. Warm. Soft.'

'Oh, good.'

'Are you okay? Would you rather I didn't have my arm around you?'

'No, it's fine. I was cold and now you're keeping me warm.'

'Good. And protecting you from foxes of course.'

'And psychopaths.'

Sleep is tugging at my eyelids, and Aiden's breathing is becoming slow and even. Slowly, the tension leaves my body and I slide gently into a dreamless sleep.

Chapter 11

The birds are so loud. I can't believe how loud they are. Have they got their own PA system or something?

Aiden is obviously so used to it that it doesn't even wake him. His body is still curled around mine, his arm thrown across me. So much for not holding anyone. I need a wee, so I extract myself from his arm and limp off into the trees to find a suitably private spot. My ankle is protesting and I regret running on it last night, but hopefully it will ease off as the day goes on.

What day is it again? Sunday?

I choose a secluded spot and relieve myself in the bushes. It makes me feel dirty to be squatting against a tree like this. Once again, I wonder how Aiden can live like this. He's an alien species as far as I'm concerned. I can't even wash my hands. I go to the stream and rinse them in the cold water. It sparkles in the early morning sunlight, so pretty it hurts my eyes, and I sit on the bank and look around me, taking in the beauty of the new day, the green trees, the blue sky, the sound of the river and the birds and realise that this is exactly the reason why Aiden lives this way. Maybe it's worth forgoing simple luxuries to feel this free and connected to nature.

I lean back on my arms and just watch, reimagining the otters playing here from last night. I still can't believe I got to see them. I feel so lucky.

There's a noise behind me, and I turn to see Aiden emerging from the hide.

'Hey!' he says. 'Did you sleep okay?'

'Surprisingly, yes. Must have been because you held me all night.'

'Eh?' He barks a surprised laugh. 'Must have been because I was absolutely knackered. And you can keep that to yourself. I don't want that getting out and spoiling my bad boy reputation.'

'You have a bad boy reputation?' I laugh in disbelief. 'With whom? Baby rabbits?'

'Oh no, all the baby rabbits love me.'

'I bet they do, along with everyone else in this world. You're just about the nicest guy I've ever met.' He comes over and sits down on the bank next to me, his long curly hair glowing chestnut in the sunlight.

'I'm not sure everyone thinks that, but thank you.' He smiles at me, squinting against the sun, then reaches up and plucks a leaf from my hair.

'I bet I've got earwigs and all sorts in there.' I scratch my scalp vigorously.

He laughs softly and leans back on his elbows, looking up through the leaves at the sky. 'Beautiful day.'

'Mmm, yeah. Beautiful place too.' I tip my face up to the sun and close my eyes, and we just sit together, listening to the river and the trees and the birds. I don't think I've ever felt so peaceful and content. Aiden touches my arm softly.

'I'll make us some coffee.'

'Mm, thank you.' I squint through my eyelids to see him looming over me, and for a second I think he's going to kiss me and my heart lurches, but he's just getting clumsily to his feet. I sit back up straight and glance backwards over my shoulder as

138

he walks away through the trees. My heart is still banging and I feel slightly breathless.

What if he had kissed me? Would I have minded? Of course I would! I don't like him like that. And, more to the point, he doesn't like me like that either. I don't even know why I thought he was going to kiss me, when he was just getting up to make a drink. It must have been the angle he was at when he got to his feet, and the way I'd tipped back my head combined with the sun glinting through the trees. I feel guilty, like I've just accused him of doing something wrong.

But when I go over and join him next to his tent, Aiden is cheerfully oblivious to my errant thoughts.

'I thought you were going to stay over there,' he says, looking up from where he's knelt beside his gas stove. 'I'd have brought it over.'

'I thought I'd save you the trouble.' I smile and sit down on the camping chair, which is still slightly damp from the soaking it got from me sitting on it yesterday in my wet clothes. I'm surprised by how long ago that feels. 'I'd better be going home soon. Are you okay to give me a lift or shall I get a taxi?'

He looks up, shaking his hair back from his face. 'No, I'll take you. Don't be silly.'

'Thank you.'

The kettle starts to hiss and Aiden spoons coffee granules from a metal tin into two metal cups.

'I hope you like black coffee. I haven't got any milk.'

'That's fine.' I reach for my trainers and slip them on, ready to go. Even though I'm looking forward to a hot shower and being able to sit on a comfortable sofa, I feel a little sad to be leaving this beautiful, peaceful place. And Aiden, I suppose, too.

He pours the boiling water into the metal cups and hands one to me. It's not the nicest thing, it's too hot and too bitter, but the caffeine hits the spot and I feel better for drinking it. Aiden watches my reaction from the floor, one arm propped on his knee.

'Go on, say it. It's not a patch on your brooding sexy coffee man's coffee.'

'I suppose not. But then he doesn't even make the coffee. He just takes my money.'

'The scoundrel!'

I laugh. 'Yes, the scoundrel. Yet another reason to look and not touch.'

'What are you doing for the rest of the day?'

'Nothing much. You?'

'Just going through footage of the otters.'

'Do you think they'll be back out later?'

'I don't know. Maybe I need you to lure them out. They only seem to come when you appear.'

'Don't be daft. Are you going to tell your pretty otter girl that you saw them?'

He pulls a face. 'Yeah, I suppose I should.'

'Maybe she'll keep you company in your hide tonight?' I raise my eyebrows suggestively.

He smiles and shakes his head before draining the rest of his coffee. 'Right, come on, let's get you home.'

Sensing I've hit a nerve, I get up and gather my wet clothes from yesterday together.

'Do you think you'll be able to walk up the hill?'

'Yes, I think so.'

'Let me know if you're struggling.'

'Okay.' I follow him up the hill and can't help noticing how grubby and creased his clothes look. Bits of bark and dried mud fall off him as he walks tiredly up the hill, and his hair is halfway to being matted. But I'm pretty sure I don't look much better, and I try and dust myself off as I duck past the overgrown hedgerow and low hanging branches. My ankle hurts but I keep going, aware of a weird subtext between us that didn't exist before.

140

We reach the top and Aiden calls hello to a man walking across the farmyard. He raises a hand in greeting and I wave back before climbing into the truck.

It's still early. Only just past six. Aiden looks half asleep as he drives out of the yard and takes the road towards home. I yawn, making him yawn too. He laughs. 'Thanks for that.'

'You're welcome.'

'Do you want me to drop you off at your café, so you can get some real coffee from your guy?'

'Er, no, it's a Sunday morning. It won't even be open, and even if it was, I doubt he'd be working. Besides, I look awful.'

Aiden smiles across at me. 'I think you look beautiful. Very au naturel.'

'Ha ha very funny.' I laugh.

'What?' He laughs too, his eyes back on the road. 'I'm not joking.'

I turn my face to the window, embarrassed now. The grass verges and hedgerows are lush with thick green vegetation that billow and sway as the truck passes by. I wind down my window a little, feeling the fresh air on my face, blowing back my hair. Aiden does the same, and suddenly it feels like we're on a road trip to somewhere new and exciting. Maybe on some American highway, Route 66, with the sun on our faces and the wind in our hair, endless possibilities ahead of us. It's disappointing when we get closer to my flat and I can't pretend anymore. The truck swings into the car park and I unbuckle my seat belt and look across at Aiden.

'Coffee? Breakfast?'

For one stomach-dipping moment, I think he's going to refuse, but then he shrugs and unbuckles his belt too. 'Okay. Thanks.'

I slide from his truck, careful to land on my good foot.

'Hey, you forgot something,' Aiden calls, pointing to the seat I've just left. 'Are those Mr Men knickers?'

'What? Oh!' To my horror, my knickers have somehow slipped

141

from the trouser pocket I tucked them into yesterday and are lying on the seat. I roll my eyes and snatch them up.

'Mr Men knickers? With the days of the week on them?'

'Yes! Christ. How closely did you look at them?'

'I just saw the word Saturday, which means you were even wearing them on the correct day!'

'So? When do you expect me to wear Saturday's pants? On Monday?'

Aiden doubles up with laughter. 'I expect you not to be wearing pants with the days of the week on them! And if you do, not care what day they have written on them.'

'Why? My mum bought them for me. They were like fifty pence in the bargain bin or something.'

'I can't believe they actually make days of the week knickers for women?'

'Well, no, actually, but they're aged 15–16 years and on the big side so they still fit. Anyway, how about you keep your eyes and your thoughts off my underwear else you won't get any breakfast.'

'Okay, sorry, sorry,' he says, still laughing and shaking his head. I walk ahead of him slightly, trying to appear dignified and not like someone who wears children's knickers. It's a hard thing to pull off when I'm wearing his baggy shorts and huge hooded sweatshirt. 'I'm sorry,' he says, as I let us into my flat and go into the kitchen to make us breakfast. It's just occurred to me that I might not have any food to feed him so I'm distracted as I fill the kettle and check the contents of the fridge. 'But I have to check, do you always wear the correct pants on the correct day?' He leans on the counter, his eyes sparkling with mirth as his shaggy hair hangs around his face.

I consider the question for a moment, still holding the fridge door open. 'Yes.'

'Oh God!' Aiden puts his head on the counter, his shoulders shaking with laughter.

'Of course that would be funny to you! You, who doesn't even

142

know what day it is half the time. If you had days of the week underpants, no doubt you'd be wearing Tuesday on Friday and Wednesday on Monday.'

'Who cares? They're hardly a point of reference, are they? Er, what day is it? Let me just check my underpants …' He dissolves into laughter once more, his dark unruly hair falling forwards onto the counter.

'I was thinking that might be quite useful for you, so you don't miss your next appointment with the next reporter that comes to interview you,' I say sarcastically.

'Oh, don't worry about that,' Aiden says, straightening up and wiping a tear from his eye. 'I won't be doing any more interviews in future.'

'Why?' I take out some eggs and cheese from the fridge, thinking an omelette might be the best way forward. My stomach growls hungrily. 'Because I've taken up so much of your time?'

'I don't really do interviews anyway. I only agreed to this one because I thought the locals needed the heads-up about the otter population and being respectful around the rivers.'

'Do you often get asked to do interviews?' I get out a bowl and start cracking eggs into it.

'Well' – he turns towards the lounge, pushing his hair back, then turns back to me – 'you probably don't know this, but a few years ago I went missing.'

'What? Where?' I glance up, startled.

'Ah, it was nothing. In Canada, in the Rockies. I just got lost. It was very undramatic and really quite embarrassing. My mum and my family made this whole big fuss, and when I finally found my way back to civilisation, this whole media circus was waiting for me. It was … awful, honestly. I hated it. I just wanted to get home and see my mum, but there were all these reporters sticking microphones in my face and asking me what happened. I kept telling them nothing happened, I'm still alive, for God's sake, but still they kept mithering me, and in the end I just refused all

143

interviews. Since then I've gained a bit of a cult following. Just in the photography community, of course.'

'You mean you've got fans?' I laugh as I whip up the eggs. 'Is there a fan club I can join?'

'No! And don't you dare get posting things about me online or telling people where I am. People can know after I leave, but not when I'm there.'

'I've already written the article in the paper.'

'Yeah, that's alright. And you didn't put exactly where I am anyway, did you?'

'No. Have you had people coming down to see you work?'

He shakes his head, and I think he's saying no, but then he says, 'People are weird. Like, really weird. I appreciate their support, but …' He shakes his head again, staring at the countertop.

I laugh. 'What kind of thing do they do? Do you have a stalker? Someone who sends you knickers in the post?'

'No, just someone who leaves her knickers in my truck.'

'Hey! That's not fair. It was an accident.'

'Yeah, you're very accident-prone, aren't you?'

'Around you, I am. You're obviously a bad influence.'

He laughs. 'I'd like to be a bad influence. I'd like to be such a bad influence that you forget which day of the week it is, and you wear your Friday pants on a Monday.'

'Ho! That will never happen! I'll have you know that I'm highly organised and efficient and not even you and your crazy ways will change that.'

'My crazy ways? Maybe it's your ways that are crazy, not mine.'

'Maybe so.' I look up and smile at him before turning to pour the eggs into the sizzling pan. I tuck my hair behind my ear and for one fleeting moment, I feel as pretty and as feminine as if I'm standing barefoot in a summer dress, wearing make-up with my hair pinned up. I give myself a mental shake, wondering how that's possible when I'm wearing Aiden's clothes and my hair is

144

a matted mess. I'm having a very strange morning. Perhaps I need more sleep.

We eat in relative silence, but it's a comfortable silence. Aiden has two cups of coffee then gets to his feet to go. My heart drops like a stone.

'You sure you don't want to shower here?' Suppressing a strong urge to wrap my arms around his legs to prevent him from leaving, I stand up with him, sucking ketchup from my finger, and following him to the door.

He hesitates then shakes his head. 'No, all my stuff's at the farm.'

'Okay. Well, I'll wash your clothes and bring them back in the week.'

He nods then bends to hug me. It's a long, proper hug that fills me with warmth and happiness. I wrap my arms around him, my face against his chest, and I don't want to let go. It feels like a long time since I've been hugged so well.

'I'll see you soon,' I say, as he lets me go.

'Sooner,' he says, catching my hand and squeezing it.

'Let me know if the otters come back.'

'Will do. Enjoy your shower.'

'I intend to.'

He opens the door, then turns and smiles as he lets go of my hand, my fingertips catching on his before our hands part and fall, and then he's walking away from me, down the path towards his truck. I don't want him to go, but I don't understand why. I close the door softly behind him and lean back against it.

Chapter 12

It's great to be back driving again and not have to rely on taxis to and from work. I've been able to resume my morning visits to the coffee shop to get my tall skinny latte with a side of sexy man, and I've been able to visit Aiden and walk down the hill to his camp without his help.

I've been visiting him to watch the otters most evenings this week, and it's lovely to see them playing together on the bank. I'm surprised by how bold they are. We keep our distance, obviously, watching them through Aiden's camera lens in the infrared lights when darkness falls.

I was worried that Aiden wouldn't want me to come down anymore once the otters appeared, in case I disturbed them, but he's been actively encouraging me to come and see them, even phoning me at work to check I'm coming. Phil overheard one conversation and jumped to the conclusion that something was going on between us. I laughed at him before assuring him that Aiden and I were just friends. Phil gave me a cynical look and said even if I felt like that, he bet Aiden didn't, which annoyed me because Aiden's made it clear that he's not looking for a relationship with anyone, and especially not with me, the girl who puked on his boots! He knows I'm a walking disaster area. There's no way he fancies me, and I don't fancy him either.

And yet, there are times when I think that I might fancy him a little bit. I don't know. Maybe I'm just confusing friendship with something more. I hope so. Aiden's friendship means a lot to me, and I don't want to jeopardise that by developing feelings for him. I'm enjoying just being with him and spending time watching the wildlife by the river. It's so calming to just sit and watch and take notice of everything that's going on around me.

Like now, for instance. I'm lying on my back on the grass outside Aiden's tent, staring up at the blue sky through the tree-top canopy of green leaves. The evening sun lends a golden tinge to the light, and the burbling river and the sweet rising notes of a blackbird are the only sounds. Aiden's inside the tent, examining footage from one of his trail cams. He's been inside for about half an hour already, completely absorbed in his work. Ordinarily I might be bored, but right now I'm feeling dreamy and relaxed. I've got one hand on my stomach and the other drawing lazy circles in my hair. My eyelids are growing heavier and heavier …

'Hey …' I feel a soft hand stroking back my hair from my forehead and as my eyes flutter open, I see the light's beginning to fade.

'Did I fall asleep?'

'Yeah, sorry, I shouldn't have left you for so long.'

'No, it's fine.' I sit up with a yawn. 'I didn't realise I was so tired.'

'Maybe I'm just boring.'

'Don't be silly.' I wipe my face with my forearm, hoping I haven't been snoring or dribbling. 'Have the otters come out yet?'

'I don't think so, but I'm going down to my hide so I'll be ready for them when they do.'

'Okay.' I get to my feet, brushing bits of leaf and stick and dust from my trousers. 'I'll get going then.'

'You don't have to go,' he says, catching my wrist in his big hand. I look up at him in surprise, caught up in his green eyes. He looks uncertain for a moment, his eyes flicking between mine, and then he smiles. 'Stay a while. I feel like I've hardly seen you tonight.'

'Are you sure I won't disturb the otters when I leave?'

'No, you'll be fine.'

'Okay then,' I say, keeping my voice light even though my heart has started to beat harder and my wrist is tingling from his touch. 'I can stay for an hour or so.'

He nods and lets go of my wrist. 'I'll get you a blanket. The temperature drops pretty fast when the sun goes down.'

Ducking back into his tent, he grabs a brown fleecy blanket and we walk through the trees towards the hide. The smell of the fresh river water mingles with the woody evening scents of the trees and surrounding fauna. Crawling into the hide, I lie on my front and cover my legs with the blanket, making myself comfortable while Aiden fiddles about repositioning his tripod and adjusting his camera lens before settling down next to me. His arm presses against mine, and I can smell the dusty scent of his jacket and the apple shampoo he's used on his hair. This isn't the first time I've been in this hide since Saturday night, but for some reason it feels more intimate than the other times I've been here. Maybe it's because I'm tired, or because he woke me by stroking my hair, or the fact it was written so plain on his face that he wanted me to stay, but I'm acutely aware of the warmth of his body next to mine.

It's almost too intense. My heart takes up a slow deliberate thump.

Is it just me feeling like this, or does Aiden feel it too? I look at him from the corner of my eye, but he gives no sign he's feeling anything at all. He's just looking through his view finder and adjusting the focus. Maybe if I move my arm away from him slightly and put some space between us, it will make things easier ...

I move my arm, but within moments Aiden moves his too and we're right back where we started. Well, I suppose if he's not bothered …

Lowering my chin onto my forearms, I look through the grass towards the river and glimpse the black shape of an otter slipping silently into the rippling water. My head jerks upwards to alert Aiden, but I see immediately that he's already spotted it as he's aiming his camera that way. There's another plop as a cub enters the water.

'You're definitely my good luck charm,' Aiden murmurs. 'They always seem to come out much earlier when you're here.'

'Must be my perfume,' I say drily.

'Must be,' Aiden chuckles, before removing his eye from the lens and briefly burying his face in my neck. 'You always smell nice.'

I freeze, heat flooding my body as my heart pounds, but if Aiden notices my strange reaction he doesn't let on. He's already got his eye back to the lens, watching the otters, while I'm struggling to control my breathing. Christ, what's wrong with me? It's only Aiden. Maybe I should go home now. It might be the safest option.

But the truth is, I don't want to go home yet. The otters are out, and I'm enjoying being so close to Aiden. I just need to get a grip of my hormones and keep my head together. I mean, it's not that I really fancy Aiden. It's just been a long time since I was in such close proximity to a man. It's only natural my body should react like this when it's been so long since my last boyfriend.

Not that I miss having a boyfriend, of course. It was just hassle and the one I had was pretty useless as boyfriends go. But I do still like boys. I'm a woman, and I have needs just like anyone else does. Just look at how I've been eyeing up Fabio in the coffee shop for months. These feelings aren't specific to Aiden at all.

Maybe I should arrange a night out with Katie, see if I can

meet someone for an uncomplicated hook-up that wouldn't jeopardise my new friendship.

Still, the thought doesn't fill me with any great joy. I'm not great at tolerating idiots, and most of the men I meet on nights out tend to be idiots.

Without thinking, I let out a sigh and Aiden turns his head to look at me. 'Are you alright?'

'Yes. Fine.'

'Are you bored?'

'Not at all, I was just thinking about something at work, that's all.'

'Hey! You come down here to forget about work.' Aiden turns the camera towards me, nudging me with his shoulder. 'Have a look through here, that will cheer you up.'

Accepting, I look through the lens and see the dark shape of one of the otter cubs appear on our side of the bank. It's quite a surprise to see it, seeing as they tend to stay over the other side of the river, where the undergrowth is tangled and wild. I indicate to Aiden, who takes back the camera. I can still see the otter in the fading evening light, and it takes my breath away to see its sinewy body this close. The mother whistles, but the youngster ignores her and continues scurrying around on the grassy bank. Aiden and I stay as silent and as still as possible in the hide. I haven't moved too far away from Aiden's shoulder, and my cheek brushes against the coarse material of his jacket. It occurs to me, even while absorbed by the otter, that I could turn my head and press my lips to his arm. It's a strange invasive thought that fills me with wonder at myself. Why would I think that?

But still, I don't withdraw. I don't kiss him either though. I stay where I am, not moving away, not moving closer, just savouring the thought that I could kiss him if I wanted to. If I wanted to destroy our friendship, that is.

How did this happen? How did I get here without realising?

The otter pup plops back into the water and Aiden exhales in a sigh.

'Did you get some good shots?' I murmur.

'Yeah, I think so.' His voice is barely a whisper as puts his eye back to the lens. I withdraw slightly, putting some space between us. I can't see or hear the otters anymore and I suspect they must have moved downstream to continue their hunting in deeper water.

Aiden obviously thinks so too, because he takes his eye away from the lens and turns to look at me. His face is very close as his eyes settle on mine. 'Okay?'

'Yeah. I was thinking I should probably get going actually.'

'Really? That's a shame. It's still quite early.'

'It's gone ten, and I'm tired,' I say, starting to crawl out of the hide. Standing up, I look round at the surrounding trees, their trunks bathed in red light from the infrared. I feel bad about leaving. Not least because I don't want to leave, but also because I know I'm disturbing his work. But I need to put some distance between us. I can't be thinking about Aiden like this.

But even when I get home, I can't stop thinking about him. I can still smell him on my skin and my hair, which is unhelpful, so I shower and change into my pyjamas, then watch TV hoping that will help drive him from my mind. But it's no use, he stays in my head. I think about the way his mouth stretches into that slow, easy smile and think about his bright green eyes with gold flecks.

It's when I find myself seeking out someone Irish on TV just to hear their accent that I think I really need to go to bed. Maybe I should keep my distance over the next few days. Spend time with some other friends and see if I can get him out of my head. I need to nip it in the bud before it turns into a full-blown crush.

But there's already a text from him the following morning when I wake up. It just an update about the otters and what a crap night's sleep he's had, but it makes me smile before I remember I'm meant to be keeping my distance. So I don't reply and go and shower instead. By lunchtime, I'm itching to reply, but I don't, leaving it until it's time to go home before I allow myself to look at his message again.

Jesus, why am I looking at it again? I'll just text him, and tell him I'm visiting my mum tonight, which is Friday. Then I can arrange to go out with Katie on Saturday night, say I'm too tired on Sunday, which takes us back to Monday again when I can say I'm tired from work. Perfect.

But as soon as I send the text, my phone rings in my hand and Aiden's number flashes up on my screen.

'You're not coming down tonight?'

'No, sorry, I'm going to visit my mum.' I make my voice sound casual, even though my throat is tight. Grey clouds are gathering in the sky and a chilly breeze sends a crisp packet rustling along the pavement.

'Shame, I had some great footage of the otters to show you. They came back later, and one of the cubs came right up to the hide.'

'Really?' I smile as I head round the back of the building towards the car park. 'What did you do?'

'I stayed as still as possible so as not to frighten it. It came right up to the camera lens. You can see droplets of water on its fur and whiskers. I couldn't believe my luck. I can't wait to show you the picture. Are you sure you can't pop in on your way home?'

'Oh … err well …' I feel my resolve weakening. I haven't actually told my mum I'm coming yet, so I suppose I could go and see Aiden quickly then pay Mum a quick visit a little later on. It's not what I was intending to do, and I know it will possibly feed my new-found attraction to Aiden, but … 'Okay then,' I say quickly. 'I'll come now if that's okay?'

'Perfect. See you soon.'

'Bye.'

Aiden's waiting at the top of the path when I arrive. He's grinning from ear to ear, looking like an excited kid on Christmas Eve. His joy is infectious, and despite the gathering clouds and the fine rain that's misting in the air, I can't help smiling as I climb out my car.

'What are you doing up here?' I call as I lock up my car.

'Waiting for you, of course! What took you so long?'

'What are you talking about?' I laugh. 'I came straight here!'

'You seemed to take ages!' He nudges me playfully as we turn to go down the path together. 'I've been waiting to show you my photo all day.'

'Aw sorry, but I couldn't get here any faster than I did. I came straight from work. Look, I'm still in my work clothes.' I indicate the white linen trousers I'm wearing, which are wholly inappropriate for visiting Aiden at his camp.

'I know. I'm just an impatient sod, that's all. But I know you'll want to see this. You're going to be so impressed.'

'I'm sure I will.'

We go inside Aiden's tent. I sit on his camp bed and Aiden switches on a lamp, though it does little to dispel the gloom. Wind rustles the trees and flaps the canvas, and there's a splatter of rain as it drips from the leaves above.

'I think there's going to be a storm tonight,' Aiden says as he opens up his laptop and presses a few buttons. The screen bursts into light to display the most adorable close-up photo of the otter pup's face.

'That's amazing! I can't believe how close he came!'

'I know. He's so bold. Or she, I don't know if it's male or female.'

I sit and stare at the otter's face, each individual whisker glistening in stark relief against its dark fur. Its huge chocolate brown eyes stare down the camera lens as though it's taking a selfie. It's absolutely adorable.

'Did you get any others?'

153

'Yes, but I think that one's the best. Here, let's see ...' The camp bed protests as he sits down next to me and brings up another image. 'This one's cute too. And this one. He only came over for about thirty seconds and then he was off. It's a miracle I managed to capture what I did.'

'That's amazing. Well done you.'

'Well, that's why I sit up all night, waiting. Imagine if I'd fallen asleep and missed it.'

'I'm glad you didn't. Are you sitting up again tonight?'

'Yeah, I think so.'

'Well, good luck.' I get to my feet, feeling awkward about leaving so soon after getting there. 'I guess I should be going then. Thanks for letting me see the photos.'

'Ah, you don't have to go yet, do you?' He looks crestfallen, the corners of his mouth drooping as he gazes up at me with big sad eyes. 'Come on, I've been on my own all day.'

'You like being alone.' There's a long spiralling piece of hair sticking up on his head, and I have to fight the urge not to stroke it down.

'I like being with you more.'

'Really?' I'm surprised. He likes his own company. Loves it, even. Why does he like being with someone he's only known a few weeks?

'Of course! You're really easy company and you make me laugh.' He smiles up at me. 'Go on, stay for a bit longer.'

'Well, alright then.' I sit back down on the camp bed. 'I will need to go soon though.'

'What time did you tell your mum you'd be round?'

'I didn't say a time,' I say, trying to avoid admitting I haven't told her I'm coming tonight. 'I'll just text her before I leave.'

'Okay. How was work today?'

'You don't want to hear about that.'

'Yes I do. I bang on about my work all the time, it's only fair I listen to you too.'

154

So I tell him about my day. It's nice to talk to someone that really listens. Katie's great and she listens to a point, but she's easily distracted and doesn't really want to know about work stuff unless it's some kind of juicy gossip. Aiden listens to me talk, asks me questions and suggests things that might help. For instance, today, Martin the photographer refused to come on a job with me because he considered it a waste of his time, so he went on another job with a more senior reporter. I understand that I'm just the trainee, but it still hurts not to be taken seriously. Though I doubt Aiden's suggestion of kneeing him in the balls would go down too well.

Rain is pattering on the tent roof and the dull glow of the lamp makes the tent feel cosy and safe.

'Well, I guess I should be going,' I say, after we've been talking for a good while.

'Are you sure? The weather's awful.'

'It's not too bad,' I say, getting up and going to the tent door to look out. Rain is dripping from the trees and pattering on the tent, but it doesn't seem too heavy yet.

'Yeah but we're sheltered by the trees here. It'll be worse on that path up to the farm.'

'I'd better go before it gets any worse then.'

'Why don't you stay? You don't have work tomorrow so you could see your mum then instead.'

I laugh. 'No, I can't stay! I'm in my work clothes. And besides, you need to work.'

'I can work with you here.'

'No, I'd distract you.'

'You can sleep in here and I can sleep in the hide.'

'That didn't work out too well last Saturday, did it?' I say, thinking of the fox scream.

'Well, I'll stay in here with you then.'

'But that stops you working.'

'Not necessarily. I have all the camera traps and I got some great shots already.' He's smiling up at me hopefully, but I shake my head.

'No, I have to go. It's only a bit of rain. I'll be okay.'

'Oh, come on, Orla. Stay.'

'No, Aiden, I can't.' I look away from him, back out into the dim woods. An owl hoots from a nearby tree. Aiden reaches out and catches my hand.

'Please?'

I look at him curiously. 'Why do you want me to stay so badly?'

He laughs, white teeth flashing against the dark of his beard. 'I told you, I like your company.'

'You want to sleep with me?'

'No!' He looks surprised and releases my hand. 'We're just friends, aren't we?'

'Of course!' Damn, why did I say that? He's offended, I can see. 'Sorry, I didn't mean ... I just ... I was just making sure you weren't expecting anything.'

'Expecting? Of course not!' He looks appalled as he rakes his hand back through his hair, and I feel awkward and embarrassed, like I've just ruined everything. 'Did I really give you that impression?'

'Not at all! I'm sorry,' I say, flustered. 'You just seemed a little bit eager for me to stay and I thought ... never mind. I'll go. I'll see ...'

'No, don't go.' He grabs my wrist again, drawing me back inside the tent. 'The weather's really bad. I don't want you driving on those narrow winding country lanes in this.'

'It's not that bad, Aiden. It's not even properly dark yet.'

'It will be by the time you get home though.' As soon he's finished speaking, there's a flash of lightning followed by a loud crash of thunder. 'Come on, I just need a bit of company. I'm going a bit stir crazy living down here all by myself.' He scratches his head as he admits this, looking embarrassed.

'But I thought you liked being alone.'

'I do, ordinarily. But it's good to share stuff with people too. I haven't seen Ivy and Bill for days, and I know you were here last night, but it seemed like you were only here for a few minutes before you had to leave. I know I sound like a needy loser, and ordinarily I'd make arrangements to meet Keaton or get on a train and visit someone else, but I need to stick around for the otters right now. So, if you wouldn't mind staying for a while longer, I'd really appreciate it.'

I look from his worried face to his hand on my wrist, then smile. See, he doesn't fancy me at all. It's all in my head, not his. 'Okay then.'

'I promise I won't try it on.'

I shake my head at him, starting to laugh. 'I'm sorry I even thought that.'

'Ah don't worry. I'm a bloke begging you to stay, aren't I? What else are you going to think?' He smiles reassuringly. 'Shall I make us some hot chocolate?'

'Yes, please. Thank you.' I sit back down on the camp bed and look around at the spartan interior of the tent. I still don't understand how he lives like this. No wonder he needs some company, poor man. I'm mortified that I just accused him of wanting to sleep with me, and more than a little disappointed that he definitely doesn't. God, how humiliating.

I really need to shake off this crush I'm developing, but how can I do that when he's telling me what great company I am and making me hot chocolate on his tiny stove. So much for my plan of putting some distance between us.

While Aiden is making the drinks, I send a text to my mum telling her I'll be round to visit her tomorrow. That way, I won't be tempted to spend the whole day with Aiden.

The rain is getting heavier now, and despite the shelter provided by the leafy trees above us, it's drumming on the tent roof with the odd blast of wind flapping the loose doorway. There's another crash of thunder, and I give an involuntary shiver. Aren't you supposed to keep away from trees in a thunderstorm? What if one gets hit and it falls on the tent? What if the tent poles get hit and we both get electrocuted?

I ask Aiden if he's worried, but he just shrugs and shakes his head. He tells me about other storms he's camped through, and one where he was camping on the side of a cliff when a storm blew in and all but destroyed his tent. I'm horrified but he seems to find it funny.

We drink hot chocolate and chat, and Aiden seems completely unbothered by my earlier accusations. In contrast, I've got an achy feeling inside, which I suspect is hurt pride and disappointment, but I know I'm just being silly. I'm lucky that Aiden is so laid back. He's more amused than anything else.

I get cold so I climb inside his sleeping bag and lie down on this camp bed. I feel I know him well enough now to not mind how personal it feels to be in the space he sleeps in, and as my limbs grow warm, my eyelids grow heavy.

'I'm going to go out to the hide,' he says, getting to his feet and putting a warm hand on my shoulder. 'I'll be back soon.'

'Okay,' I murmur, though I can barely be bothered to speak.

I'm dimly aware of him zipping up the entrance before I drift off to sleep.

When I wake up the following morning, I find him asleep on the floor next to me, with a blanket wrapped around him. The sun is already up and the trees are dripping from last night's rain. I feel bad that he's slept on the floor, until I remember how he begged me to stay. Strange, strange man. Propping myself up on one elbow, I watch him fondly. His eyelids flutter slightly, as though he's in the middle of a dream, but otherwise he's completely still.

He looks younger when he's asleep, his dark hair falling back from his face, and his long eyelashes brushing his sharp cheek bones. Feeling bad for watching him sleep, I lie back down on the camp bed, but I still watch the rise and fall of his shoulder with each deep steady breath. Oh dear. I think I definitely fancy him. And I know it's not just because I haven't had a boyfriend for ages, or because Phil suggested that I did. It's because Aiden's the most interesting man I've ever met, and the fact he's so kind and funny. And even though long hair on men isn't really my thing, I do like it on Aiden.

Aiden stirs and I turn my head away, in case he realises I've been watching him.

'Hey,' he says, sitting up. 'Shall I make coffee?'

'Yeah, okay.' I smile at him. 'Did you sleep okay on the floor?'

'Yes, I'm used to it. Did you sleep okay on that camp bed?'

'Like a log. Must be all the fresh air! I didn't even hear you come into the tent. Were the otters out last night?'

'They made a brief appearance, but nothing as spectacular as the night before. You can't even say it's because of the weather because what difference does a bit of rain make to an animal that spends so much time in water?' He sighs as he gets up and sets about making the coffee. 'Never mind. They'll probably be back out tonight. Are you coming down again?'

'Oh errr …' I should tell him I can't, but somehow the words won't come out. All my good intentions of staying away from him have dissolved overnight and there's no question I won't come down. 'Yes, okay. I need to go home and change, and I'm going to my mum's this afternoon, but I can come back after?'

'Yep, great.' He smiles over his shoulder at me. 'Like I said, you're my lucky charm. I need you to bring out the otters.'

As it happens, I don't bring out the otters later that evening. Aiden and I lie in his hide, waiting patiently but they don't make an appearance. Aiden's not too worried, and thinks the mother otter is perhaps taking her cubs to hunt in one of the fishponds in the farmer's fields instead tonight. He's convinced they'll be back tomorrow or the next day.

We chat idly about various things. Nonsense mostly, but it's easy conversation and we make each other giggle. It's not raining

159

as heavily as yesterday, but there's a misty drizzle in the air and everything feels damp and chilly. I'm wearing tracksuit bottoms and a sweatshirt, but I'm still cold, so I'm pressed up close to Aiden, trying to get warm.

'You're always so warm,' I say, snuggling closer so I'm practically lying on top of him. 'How come you never feel the cold?'

'I don't know. Just used to it, I guess.'

'I'm freezing!' My teeth are starting to chatter, and I press my cold nose into his shoulder. 'I'm going to have to go home to warm up.'

'Aw come here, I'll warm you up.' Rolling onto his side to face me, he pulls me against his chest. 'I can't believe you're this cold when you're wearing a sweatshirt and sweatpants.'

'I know. I've got a T-shirt underneath too.'

'Wear a thermal vest next time.'

'I think I will.'

He's rubbing my back vigorously, his hands moving around and around, over my shoulder blades then back down my spine to my waist. It feels good and I'm already starting to feel warmer. 'Ooh, that's good,' I groan.

'Eh steady on!' he says, starting to laugh. 'No sex noises, please. You'll turn me on.'

'Sorry!' I laugh too.

'Don't be sorry.' He stops rubbing up and down my back and instead rubs up and down my arm. 'Is the blood flowing better now?'

'Yes. Thank you.'

'Good.' He's still laughing as he props himself up on his elbow and looks down on me. 'I still feel bad about yesterday. I'm sorry if I upset you.'

'Upset me, how?'

'Saying I don't want to have sex with you.'

'Oh no, don't be silly.'

'You looked a bit offended.'

160

'Of course I wasn't. I know we're just friends.' I roll away to rearrange the blanket so it's covering me better.

'Exactly. It's better not to complicate that, isn't it?'

'Of course.' I fuss about with the blanket some more, though I'm feeling a whole lot warmer all of a sudden, more from embarrassment than anything else. 'Don't worry, you didn't offend me at all.'

'Are you sure? I didn't mean to insult you. It's not like I don't find you attractive.'

'Don't worry about it. I wasn't offended, honestly.' I give a nervous, slightly breathless laugh. Why is he talking about this now?

'I didn't want you to think that was the reason I wanted you to stay. To have sex with you. I want you to feel safe around me. To trust me.'

'I do trust you.'

'But when you asked me if I wanted to have sex with you, you seemed like you didn't.'

'I'm sorry. I don't know where that came from.' I swallow uncomfortably. 'I think it was just because my boss, Phil, said there must be more to it than us just being friends.'

'He did? Why?'

'I don't know. He heard me talking to you on the phone and then he said that. I told him we were just friends, but then he snorted and walked away.'

'Oh. Well, what does he know?'

'Exactly. He knows nothing. But I suppose he threw me for a minute, so I'm sorry I said that to you, but you don't need to worry, because I do trust you.'

'Good.'

'And I'm not offended that you don't want to sleep with me, so please stop apologising for that too.'

'Okay.' He's quiet for a moment, just watching me, and then he says, 'Only you did look quite disappointed.'

'Oh, for goodness' sake, Aiden! Drop it, will you!' I smack his arm, then roll over so my back's to him.

'No, but, if you ever did want to have sex—'

'I don't,' I lie.

'Then we could—'

'Stop! Stop talking.'

'—come to some arrangement.'

For goodness' sake, what is he talking about? I stare wide-eyed into the darkness, wondering how to react. What would he say if I said okay then? Would we have sex now, in this hide? Would we go into his tent? Back to mine? It would all be too awkward though. Too premeditated and it would definitely affect our friendship.

'Aiden,' I say, eventually.

'Yes?'

'We're just going to be friends.'

'Okay then.' He rolls over, as if to punctuate our conversation. 'I've got to tell you though, you're missing out.'

'Really? Why's that then?' I say drily.

'I'm pretty good in bed.'

I can't help laughing at him. 'I'm sure you are, Aiden. I'm sure you are.'

Chapter 13

I thought our conversation about sex might put a strain on my friendship with Aiden, but it hasn't at all. If anything, we're closer than ever, and because I know he doesn't find me physically repulsive, I feel able to touch him and hug him and basically lie all over him whenever I feel like it. And for his part, he seems completely unconcerned by anything. He still asks me about Fabio, Sexy Coffee Guy, and I'm happy to fill him in, knowing it will make him laugh. In truth, I'm more interested in Aiden than Fabio these days. Ironically, since I realised this, Fabio's started making smouldering eye contact and trying to make conversation with me whenever he sees me lately. I much preferred it when I was just another anonymous customer, watching him brooding behind the counter. It doesn't hold the same appeal now as it used to. In fact, it makes me a little bit uncomfortable. Like right now, I'm standing in the queue watching him serve the customers in front of me without so much as a smile. It's weird when he switches on the charm for me.

My phone rings and I fumble in my bag to answer it.

'Hello?'

'Hey, it's me,' says Aiden. 'Do you want to come to a party tonight?'

'Whereabouts?' The queue moves forward and I step forward, getting my cup ready to hand to Fabio.

'Beach party with some old friends of mine. There'll be a barbeque. I'm going to have a drink so we'll have to sleep in the truck.'

I wince. 'Is that meant to tempt me?'

'I've got an old mattress. I'll just sling it in the back.'

'What if it rains?'

'It's not going to rain. Have you seen the forecast? It's going to be scorching all weekend. The sun's blazing already.'

'Can I think about it?'

'No, just say yes.'

I laugh. 'I'll think about it. Let you know this afternoon.'

He sighs. 'Well, don't leave it too long or I'll ask someone else.'

'Who?'

'Jayne.'

'Ask Jayne then. I'm sure she'd love to sleep in your truck with you.'

'Oh, come on, Orla. I want to go with you. We'll have a laugh.'

'I won't know anyone.'

'You'll know me.'

'Hold on, I'm at the front of the queue.' I take the phone away from my ear and smile as I pass my cup to Fabio, who grins at me, showing practically his whole set of sparkling white teeth. Everything about him is perfect. His teeth, his hair, his skin, his beautiful brown eyes.

'Hey, Orla, how are you this morning?' He asked me my name earlier this week and since then he's managed to use it every time he speaks to me. It's kind of cute and kind of creepy, all at once.

'Good, thanks. How are you?'

'My day's just got a lot better, thanks to you, Orla.' He smoulders at me across the counter, and I find myself blushing more from embarrassment than flattery. The person behind me clears

164

their throat pointedly and I hear Aiden laugh from the other end of the phone. 'What can I get for you? The usual?'

'Yes please.'

I hand over a five-pound note, and when he hands me the change, his hand closes around mine. 'Are you out this weekend, Orla?'

My heart plummets. 'I'm, er, I'm out of town, actually. I'm going to a beach party.'

'Beach party? Wow, Orla, that's cool. Really cool.'

'Yeah. Well, have a good weekend.' I extract my hand from his and start to move away.

'Thanks. Will do. Bye, Orla.'

'Bye, Fabio.' My throat closes over his name and I gulp halfway through. God, I'm an idiot. I can still hear Aiden chuckling from the other end of the phone and I raise it to my ear.

'What are you laughing at?'

'You! I guess you are coming tonight then.'

'Well, maybe …'

'Ah, you can't back out now. I'll heard you tell the Italian Stallion, and you know he'll want to know about the really cool beach party on Monday morning.'

'Oh yeah, sure.'

The girl behind the counter hands me my coffee and I thank her and go back out into the sunshine. It's not eight o'clock yet and the heat is already building. I take a sip of my coffee, still holding the phone against my ear.

'Are you drinking your coffee now?'

'Yep. Mmm.'

'I'm drinking mine too.'

'Wow. Synchronicity.'

'Yeah, mine's not as good as yours though.'

'No, yours is foul. What'll I wear tonight then?'

'Whatever you want. It's just casual. No big deal.'

'Should I bring some food?'

'We'll stop off somewhere on the way, stock up then. It'll be vegetarian, by the way, so there'll be none of your murdered animals.'

'Okay. That's fine.'

'I'll pick you up about six?'

'Okay, see you later.'

The party is in a secluded cove, in a popular surfing spot. All the families, surfers and sun-worshipers have gone home for the day, so there's just Aiden's friends on the beach, setting up the barbeque. There's a good quota of men with long hair and beards, and the girls all have long wind-swept hair and denim shorts. I feel a little out of place in the long floaty skirt and crocheted top I've put on, but everyone seems friendly when Aiden introduces me. I sit on a log, next to a campfire which isn't really needed considering the sun's still up, but it adds to the romance of it all. A girl with long red hair, called Reanna, comes to sit next to me and tells me there's been a pod of dolphins sighted in the bay today.

'It's so cool you're here with Aiden,' she says after she's finished telling me about the dolphins. 'Has he mentioned his ex-girl-friend?'

'Oh, er, a couple of times, maybe?'

'Really. What's he said about her?'

'Not much. Just that she wasn't happy when he had to go away.'

'Ha! Understatement of the year. He broke her heart, is what he did. I expect he told you that to prepare you for when he ditches you.'

I shrug. 'He's a wildlife photographer. He has to travel.'

Reanna snorts. 'That's what he'd have you believe. He doesn't have to travel the sodding world for months at a time to do it. He could specialise in UK wildlife if he wanted to.'

'Well, I expect he doesn't want to.' I look at her, taking in the long red hair and freckles. There's a bitterness in her tone that makes me wonder if she's actually the ex-girlfriend she's talking about. I watch her watching Aiden through narrowed green eyes, her long silky hair blowing around her face.

'Wow! He's got you well trained, hasn't he?'

I open my mouth to tell her Aiden and I are just friends, but then shut it again. It's none of her business what we are.

'Anyway,' she says, finally dragging her eyes away from Aiden, 'you have my sympathy for being with him. I mean, he's funny and sweet when he remembers you're there, but let's face it, he's crap in bed. And then he'll leave and expect you to understand that's his job and there's no other alternative in the universe.'

'If you thought he was crap in bed, why did you care when he left?' I say, unable to keep the irritation from my voice. 'And also, hasn't it been like two years since you split up? Maybe you need to let this go now.'

She looks at me sharply and for a second I think she's going to go mad, but then she just laughs. 'Let's just see how you feel when he leaves you,' she says. 'And for the record, I'm not pining for him anymore. I'm with Luke now.' She nods towards the barbeque where a thick-set guy with a black beard is drinking beer with the rest of the guys that Aiden's talking to. 'He's lovely.'

'Good.'

'So, you needn't worry. I'm not competition. I'm not about to try and take Aiden back.'

I swallow, my throat tight from an unexpected surge of jealousy. 'Glad to hear it.'

'I'm just warning you, that's all. He's not like other men. He's like a cloud or something. He just drifts about, not really caring about anything other than the planet and his camera.'

I want to point out that the planet is a fairly big thing to care about but the bitterness seems to be leaving her, and it would be counterintuitive to upset her further.

'Hmm, well from what I've seen, he barely knows what day it is,' I say.

167

'Yep. That's Aiden. Although, don't be fooled. He'll know exactly what day and time his plane leaves to wherever he's going next.'

I shrug. 'That's who he is, I guess. I suppose we just have to enjoy him while we've got him.' Just saying it brings a lump to my throat, and I take a swig from my bottle of beer and look away towards the sea. When I turn back to her, she's watching me, smiling.

'You know what, I like you, Orla.' She points her bottle at me. 'That's a lovely way to look at it. I wish I'd been able to see things like that.'

We clink bottles in a show of solidarity, and I ask her how she got together with Luke.

'He's one of Aiden's friends and he looked after me when Aiden left.' She smiles sadly and takes another sip of her beer. 'I was in a bit of a state for a while. He's put up with a lot, bless him, but he's really kind and sweet and patient. We didn't get properly together until about six months ago, but he's always been there for me.'

Another group of people arrive carrying more beer and a guitar. There's lots of cheering and laughter and more introductions to people I like immediately but whose names I forget. Reanna gets up and goes to slide her arms around Luke's waist while I make polite conversation with a few of the guys that have just arrived.

'Hey, are you alright?' Aiden squats behind me, a knee on either side of my waist, and puts a hand on my shoulder. My heart speeds up and I feel a hot flush of pleasure that he's so close.

'Yeah, fine,' I turn my head and find his face surprisingly close. 'Are you?'

'Yeah.' He leans over to shake hands with the guys next to me, and there's a fair bit of back slapping before he turns back to me. 'Did I see you talking to Reanna before? Was she okay?'

168

'She was fine.'

'I didn't realise she was going to be here.'

I smile and shrug. 'She was nice. She was telling me about Luke.'

'Good. Did you say we were … you know, together or anything?'

I shake my head. 'No, but she assumed we were and I didn't correct her. I didn't know what to say really.'

'Oh okay, that's fine.'

'You sure? I can enlighten her if you want?'

'No need.' Sliding his arm around my chest, he pulls me back against him and kisses my temple. 'Keep that going. That works for me.'

My stomach flips and I draw in a deep, shaking breath as heat floods my entire body. I feel slightly breathless as I sit in the cage of his embrace, his voice rumbling through me as he chats to the guys next to us.

The food is ready so we line up to eat. I collect my paper plate and wait for my veggie burger while Aiden stands behind me, chatting away to his friends. Occasionally, he places a hand on my shoulder, or my arm, or my waist as though checking I'm still there. Being touchy-feely is nothing new for us, but this feels different. It's not being crammed into a tiny hide together, snuggled up for warmth. It's not leaning up against him when I'm bored or sleepy. It's not our matey hugs or playful shoves. This is more than that. It feels like something might happen between us and it's sending my blood pressure sky high.

But I've misread his signals before. I'd hate to do that again. I know he said he doesn't find me unattractive, but I still don't want to make things weird between us.

I need some space to gather my thoughts. I gaze longingly towards the sea where the sun is dipping towards the horizon, and once I've collected a plate of food, I leave Aiden talking and slip away towards the shoreline, where the cold waves lap at my toes and the sea breeze blows my hair back from my face. I feel calmer here, away from the sound of voices and the smell of the smoke. Away from Aiden. I eat and feel better, the food soaking up some of the alcohol. I've never been a big drinker, though feeling drunk after just one bottle of beer is lame even for me.

The sun drops lower, its bottom just touching the top of the horizon. The sea shimmers red and gold beneath it, reflecting the fiery sky. I stand entranced, watching the colours change as the sun slides lower and the sky darkens.

'Hey.'

Aiden's voice makes me jump and I turn to see him standing a few feet behind me. He's watching me warily.

'Are you okay?'

'Me? Yeah. I'm just watching the sunset.'

He nods and steps a little closer, his arms behind his back. 'Everyone thinks I've upset you.'

'Oh? Sorry!' I laugh. 'No, I just wanted to be by the sea.'

'You fancy a swim?'

I shake my head. 'No swimming costume.'

His eyes gleam as he raises his eyebrows suggestively.

'No!' I say, before he can say the words skinny-dipping and he laughs, turning half away from me as he throws his head back.

'Are you going to come back and sit with everyone? Before Reanna accuses me of treating you badly. Again.'

'Again?'

'Yeah, she's had a couple of digs already. Says I've brainwashed you. What the hell did you talk about?'

I laugh. 'Oh, she was saying you would just up and leave one day, and I said it was who you were and that we should just try appreciate the time we had with you.'

'Oh.' He grimaces slightly and looks out across the sea. 'That does sound a bit like I've brainwashed you.'

'Yeah, I suppose. It helps that I'm not actually your girlfriend.' I turn to face him, my arms crossed over my body. 'Or in love with you,' I add, then wish I hadn't when his eyes flick to mine, sharp and calculating instead of his usual warm humour. What does that mean? My stomach tightens and I drop my head and step backwards, turning back towards the sea. There are probably fewer dangerous currents beneath the waves than between Aiden and I right now.

'Neither was Reanna. Not really,' he says, after a moment's pause. He's still facing me. Watching me. I keep my eyes on the sunset so I don't have to look at him. I'm afraid of what I'll see in his eyes. Does he want me or does he just want to be friends? I want more, but I'm afraid things will change and I'll lose his friendship altogether. I don't want that. I don't want to end up like Reanna.

'She seems to think she was.'

He wrinkles his nose, shakes his head. 'She was just miffed I left when she said I couldn't. She thought she owned me. We couldn't agree on anything. We were always arguing.' He steps closer and turns to watch the sea. 'Anyway, I think we're being watched, so I need us to look like we're not fighting, otherwise she'll have a field day slagging me off to anyone that will listen.'

'She didn't seem that bad really. Though she did say one thing.'

'What?'

'She said you were crap in bed.'

He looks shocked for a moment, but then laughs good-naturedly and shrugs. 'See, she makes stuff up. That's just what she's like. Anyway, if she really thought that she should have been glad to see the back of me, shouldn't she?' The wind lifts his hair and blows it across his face.

'I suppose. Though maybe she thought you'd improve with time.'

'Hey! Whose side are you on? Never mind laughing!' He nudges me with his shoulder, making me step to the side. 'Honey, any time you want to find out what I'm like in bed, just say the word.'

'Aiden!' I laugh in surprise. 'We're friends.'

171

'So? Why can't we be friends that have sex?'

I laugh for a little while longer, then stop when I realise he's not joking. 'Because I don't want to lose you as a friend.'

'Why would you lose me as a friend? And besides, that's not saying you don't want to have sex with me, is it, Orla?'

'No, I suppose it isn't.' I look down on my bare feet, sinking into the wet sand. I'm not sure I'm comfortable with the turn this conversation has taken. I've just wandered out of safe, familiar territory into uncharted water, and it's exciting and terrifying in equal measure.

'Why are you looking like that for?' he asks gently.

'Like what?'

'Terrified.'

I glance up and find him watching me with an amused glint in his eyes. 'Aren't you?'

'What, terrified? No! Why would I be? Why would you be, for that matter?'

'Because this changes everything.'

'No, it doesn't. Don't take things so seriously! It's not a big deal. It's just sex, Orla. It's meant to be fun.'

'It is?' I give him a sceptical look. None of the fumbling encounters I've had so far have been much fun, that's for sure.

'Of course!' Laughing, he drapes an arm around my shoulders. 'Why does it have to be complicated? Why can't we just have some fun together? After all, neither of us wants a relationship. I'll be moving on in a few weeks' time, and you have your five-year plan. I don't see what the problem is so long as we both know what we're getting into. We'd still be mates, wouldn't we?' He takes a swig from his bottle of beer and stares off out to sea. 'And anyway, this is just a conversation we're having here. It's not like we're signing a pact or anything. If you don't want to do anything, we won't do anything. It's as simple as that. No pressure, okay?'

'Okay.' I feel a bit disorientated. It's weird to be standing here

172

discussing it so dispassionately, but I suppose if Aiden can be casual about it, then so can I. And he's certainly casual. He's already turning to look back towards his friends, as though this conversation is over.

'Anyway, come back to the fire,' he says, taking my hand and threading his fingers through mine. 'There's music and dancing to be had. And more beer. Come on, let's go and party!'

We turn back towards his friends. The light's faded so much that fire flickers brightly in the dusky pink light. Everyone's still sitting around in a circle, talking or listening to the guy playing his guitar, so I don't know why Aiden was going on about dancing. As soon as we get near, Reanna calls me over. Aiden glances at me, but releases my hands so I go and sit with her on the log with a few other girls.

'Are you okay?' she asks with a fierce look in Aiden's direction. 'What's he done now?'

'Oh nothing. It's fine.' I smile reassuringly but they're all still staring at me, wanting to know what's gone on. 'Everything's fine, honestly. I just went to watch the sunset. It's so beautiful out here.'

The girls look disappointed I'm not going to divulge any gossip, but they grudgingly agree. Aiden's my friend. I don't want to talk about him with these strangers. Luckily, one of the girls starts talking about her boyfriend, taking the attention away from me.

I look through the flames of the fire to where Aiden is sitting, laughing at something one of his friend's has said. His eyes shine in the glow of the fire, and shadows flicker across his face. I want to be sitting next to him. I want to be laughing with him. I want … him.

The guy with the guitar starts to strum and sing, and people join in. I stretch out my feet, digging my toes into the sand, feeling the warmth of the crackling fire on my legs. Reanna drapes an arm around my shoulders as she sings, using her beer bottle as a microphone and making me laugh. I feel Aiden's eyes on me, and looking up, I meet his gaze head on. He smiles, and heat that has nothing to do with the fire courses through my veins.

Someone passes me another bottle of beer and soon I'm singing along with the songs and feeling much happier and relaxed. I keep looking at Aiden, and every time I do, I find him looking back.

I get up and go to him. He's sitting on the sand, his back against the log as though he's slid off and can't be bothered to get up. I wonder how drunk he is, but his eyes are intense and focused as he watches my approach. I sit cross-legged on the sand next to him, my arm pressed up against his.

Someone says, 'Are you two going to kiss and make up now?' and Aiden laughs and shrugs then drapes a lazy arm around my shoulders.

'We're fine,' he says. 'Aren't we, Orla?'

'Or course we are.' I smile as I lay my head on his shoulder.

'Come on, this is meant to be a party,' the guy with the guitar says suddenly. 'Get up and dance, will you!'

There's a lot of groaning from around the circle and some of the girls announce they're going to the toilet over the road. Regretfully, I realise I need to join them and get to my feet to find the sandals I kicked off earlier. It takes me a while to locate them, and by the time I'm ready, the girls have already gone. I see them queuing by the little wooden hut and arrive in time to hear the tail end of a whispered conversation.

'He's obviously not that into her. I haven't even seen him kiss her.'

'Are you kidding, have you seen the way he looks at her?'

'No way. He'll be gone again within the month.'

There's a bit of nudging and a hush as they realise I'm behind them, but I pretend not to have heard, and stare up at the night sky instead. I'm amazed by how bright the stars are out here. Someone comes out of the loo and Reanna goes in and the girl in front of me turns and whispers, 'I think you and Aiden make a lovely couple. Don't let Reanna poison you against him. Aiden's lovely.'

I smile gratefully at her. 'Thank you.'

It's a relief when everyone's gone and I'm left on my own to use the loo. I didn't realise how much I needed a wee until I sit down. Bizarrely, I feel quite upset by hearing Reanna say Aiden's not that into me. I put my hot flushed face in my hands and close my eyes for a moment. All I see is Aiden and his dark-lashed green eyes looking back at me. I'm drunk. So drunk.

I splash water on my face, then realise there's no towel to dry myself, so I take my cardigan off and use that instead. My make-up's disappeared over the course of the night, so I look about 12 again. I shake out my hair with a sigh, wishing once more that I'd never had it cut and slap my cheeks a little to try to sober myself up. Maybe I should just go to bed. It's probably the most sensible option.

When I get back, Aiden's getting another beer from the ice bucket next to the barbeque. Someone's got a wireless speaker and there's music playing. 'Hey,' I say, going over to him. 'I think I'm going to go to bed.'

'What?' He laughs and slips his arm around my waist, pulling me against his body. 'No, you're not. There's still beer. There's still dancing.' He gestures with his beer bottle to the girls dancing by the fire and then starts to sway against me. 'Come on, Orla.'

'I still think it's, erm …' I lose my train of thought as he starts to kiss my neck, still swaying against me, holding the lower half of my body close to his. My body's a mass of goose bumps as his lips move down my neck to my shoulder and then back to my throat. I arch against him, and the hand I originally put on his shoulder to push him away slides round his neck and into his hair as his mouth finds mine. Soft lips, soft beard, soft tongue. My head spins and I want the kiss to last forever, but he pulls away and instead presses his forehead to mine.

'Okay?' His voice is thick and husky.

I nod and smooth my hands over his wide shoulders, down to his chest. We're just swaying to the music, looking into each other's eyes, and it feels like we're a million miles away, floating on our own cloud. The songs keep playing, changing tracks, some old, some new. I lay my head on Aiden's chest, and he kisses my forehead. His hand is on my back, beneath my top, and his thumb stroking my bare skin sends sparks of electricity zinging through my body.

'Do you know what you do to me, Orla?' he whispers, making all the hairs on the back of my neck lift. 'You drive me crazy.' He presses his cheek to the side of my face, traces his nose along the outside of my ear. 'I think about you all the time. And I mean every minute of every day since the moment I met you.'

I raise my head to look at him, thinking, *Christ, he's really drunk*, but I find his eyes are deep and steady and deadly serious. My lips part to say something, but he kisses me and all sensible thought leaves my mind.

'Shall we go to bed?'

Taking my hand, he leads me up the beach, calling goodbye to the three guys still sitting next to the campfire as we pass. I'm surprised by how deserted the beach has suddenly become. How didn't I notice everyone leaving?

The sand is cool as it fills my sandals, gritty between my toes. We climb the steps back up to the road, and Aiden helps me climb up into the back of the truck, his hand on my bum as he pushes me up. We collapse giggling onto the mattress together, the sky spinning above us, a kaleidoscope of stars.

'We don't have to do anything you don't want to, you know,' he murmurs, kissing the edge of my mouth, my chin, my throat. 'We can just sleep if you like?'

'No, I want to,' I whisper, already undoing the buttons on his paisley shirt.

'You're sure?'

In answer, I kiss him, rubbing my hands over the soft hair on

176

his chest. He groans against my mouth, pulling me on top of him and kissing me so fiercely that he leaves me breathless. I thought I'd feel shy and awkward, but right now I want to get as naked as possible with him. Straddling him, I rip off my top, arching as his mouth closes over my nipple, sucking it through the pale pink lace of my bra. His hand is burrowing under my skirt, pushing up the layers of material so it sits at the top of my thighs.

'What day are you wearing today?' he asks, rubbing circles around my hips, down my buttocks and back up my thighs. It feels nice but is nowhere near where I want his hands right now. 'I'll be very disappointed in you if you're not wearing Friday.'

'What do you mean?' I can't think what he means for a minute, but aah, my days of the week pants. 'I'm not wearing them … look … here.' I know he's trying to be funny, but I don't want to be distracted right now. Unzipping my skirt, I pull it up over my head so he can see my pink lace thong by the light of the moon. 'There you see, not a Mr Man in sight.'

Aiden looks entranced as he gently trails a finger over the front seam of my pants. I writhe slightly, pressing against him, craving his touch. I want him so badly right now, but he takes his time, exploring me slowly, all the while dropping butterfly kisses on the soft skin of my stomach. I feel like I might go mad with desire if he doesn't get a move on, but with one hand on my hip, he holds me firmly in place as his kisses get lower and his probing gets deeper. My legs are trembling so much I'm not sure they can support me for much longer.

'Aiden,' I beg, as the tension builds to an almost unbearable level. 'Aiden.'

He looks up at me, his eyes gleaming in the moonlight. I'm quivering all over as he lays me down on the mattress. I hear the rustle of a condom packet and then he enters me, slowly and carefully.

'Open your eyes,' he whispers, as he starts to move inside me.

But my eyes are already starting to roll as my orgasm builds with each thrust. He moves faster and harder, and suddenly I'm over the edge and falling, my fingers entwined in his hair as I experience the most powerful orgasm of my life.

It takes me a few minutes to come down, and even then I can still feel the odd flutter between my legs. Aiden's still breathing hard, his face buried in my neck.

'Reanna really was lying, wasn't she?' I say, after a few moments of lying there, staring up at the stars. 'Wow! That was pretty good.'

'Pretty good?' Aiden laughs in disbelief as he props himself up on his elbow to look at me. 'Did you expect it to be bad or something?'

'Well, from past experience, sex is usually pretty disappointing.'

He blinks at me, his brow creased with concern. 'But that was okay?'

'More than okay.' I smile up at him. 'Do you want to go again?'

'Christ, Orla.' He laughs as he reaches for the bottle of water again. 'I'm older than you, remember. Give me five minutes.'

'That's okay, I can wait.' I give him a cheeky smile and he chuckles before taking another good glug of the water.

'Have you really only had crap sex?' he asks, passing me the bottle.

'Yeah, pretty much.'

'Oh no! Well, I feel it's my moral duty as your friend to show you that sex should be fun.'

'Okay, you're on.'

'Excellent!' Taking back the bottle from me, he screws on the lid and places it back down next to the mattress. 'Well, to begin with, I think we'd better remove this bra, don't you?' he says. 'I can't think what I was doing letting you keep it on.' His hands slide under my back as he undoes the catch on my bra, then he slowly peels it away to reveal my breasts. My nipples harden in the cool night air and he gently blows on one before circling it with his tongue. I'm fascinated by how erotic it feels to be watching

178

his tongue flick back and forward over its dark pink point, and without even realising it, my legs open wider and my breathing quickens.

We make love again while the pale moon watches over us, and once again I'm astounded that sex can feel this good. If Aiden wants to teach me how fun sex can be, then I figure I'm more than happy to let him.

'They don't call me Aiden the Sex God for nothing,' he says afterwards as he lies back on the mattress.

'Oh really? Who calls you that?' I scoff.

'Well, no one, but you could start if you wanted.'

'I'll think about it.' I smile as I rest my head on his chest and close my eyes.

'I'll be your own personal sex guru. How's that?'

'Sounds good to me,' I murmur as I drift off to sleep.

Chapter 14

I awake early, blinking in the pale morning light as gulls circle and scream overhead. Aiden is still fast asleep, his arm thrown across me. Reaching for the water bottle, I prop myself up on my elbows and gulp it down. My head is throbbing and I'm so thirsty I feel as if I could drink a river dry. There's no one else around, so I take the opportunity to put my clothes back on, just in case we get early morning visitors.

Aiden looks so peaceful. His hair is all ruffled and falling over his face, and his thick black lashes are resting on his cheek bone. I readjust the blanket so it's covering his shoulder and lie back down next to him. To my relief, I have no regrets, though he might have been right about the truck. In the cold light of day, it looks a bit like a skip and I don't dare look at the state of the mattress. Instead I keep my eyes on Aiden. At least the man was right. Always a silver lining.

I must fall asleep again, because the next thing I know Aiden is up and making coffee by the side of the road on his tiny gas stove. He's surrounded by three of his friends, and they're talking in low voices so as not to wake me.

'Morning,' I say, peering over the edge of the truck at them. 'How are your heads?'

'Oh, don't ask,' one groans, rubbing his forehead with a pained look on his face. 'We slept by the fire and carried on until the early hours.'

Aiden looks up at me, and I can tell he's wondering if I'm regretting last night. I smile at him. 'Can I have a coffee?'

'Sure.' His eyes crinkle at the corners as he smiles back, and I feel myself blush. It's embarrassing to feel this giggly and girly, especially with his three friends looking on. As if realising they're intruding, they step away and turn to look out to sea, talking among themselves. Aiden makes the coffee and stands up to give it to me, kissing my nose as he does so. 'How are you feeling this morning?'

'Fine. I woke up earlier with a headache but I feel okay now. You?'

'I'm good.' He leans his forearms on the side of the truck and watches me take a sip from the coffee. 'Still not as good as your sexy coffee man's?'

I wrinkle my nose. 'It's better, because you made it.'

'Now I know you're lying.' He nods to the back of the truck with the bare mattress on the floor. 'How d'you like your chariot this morning?'

'It felt a whole lot more romantic last night.'

'Yeah, sorry about that. Maybe you should get out and sit in the cab before you realise just how horrible it is.'

'It's fine.'

A shout goes up from the men, and they're pointing out to sea. 'Dolphins!'

And there are. About three of them, joyfully leaping out of the water, the spray glinting silver in the morning sun. I've never seen dolphins in the wild before and the sight of them brings tears to my eyes. Aiden helps me down from the truck and we stand with the others by the wall, watching them play. 'I should have my camera,' Aiden sighs.

'They're too far away to get anything decent. You need to go out in a boat.'

181

'I don't know. I've got a pretty decent zoom.'

'Still doubt it would be good enough. Not from this distance.'

Aiden hesitates, and I see him open his mouth to argue, but then he just shrugs and laughs, as if he doesn't want an argument. 'Ah, maybe you're right.' He puts his arm around me, rubbing the goose bumps that have appeared on my arms from the cool morning breeze. 'I suppose we'd better get going before all the holidaymakers arrive. Shall we help clean up?'

The other guys clear away the barbeque while Aiden and I fill bin bags with beer bottles and cans. Aiden throws the bags in the back of the truck to take to the recycling centre, then we say our goodbyes and start on our journey home.

'Do you want me to share the driving?'

'No.' He smiles across at me, rubbing a hand up his arm.

'You sure you're not tired?'

'I'll stop if I feel tired. I can always get in the back for a nap.'

'Among the bin bags?'

'Yeah. Classy.' He laughs, deep and throaty, making my stomach clench. The sun is already hot and burning my arm where it rests on the edge of the window. I watch the landscape rise and fall, the green fields dotted with sheep, the yellow fields of rapeseed that make my nose itch. The radio plays songs, but we don't sing along. We don't even talk. But Aiden smiles his smile and I smile mine and the truck eats up the miles to home. He calls in at a recycling centre and we dispose of the bottles and cans, and Aiden slings the old mattress into a skip, explaining it was just an old one that Bill and Ivy had asked him to get rid of.

'So what happens now?' I say, when we finally reach my flat. I don't want to get out and go inside, back to my normal life. I want to stay here in this truck with Aiden, watching the countryside fly past, with endless possibilities ahead of us.

'What do you mean?' He reaches over and tucks a strand of hair behind my ear.

'Are you coming inside?'

He shrugs. 'Sure.'

'Have you got otter things to do today?' I ask as I open my flat door and go inside. The window blinds are still drawn and everywhere's in shadow. Crossing to the window, I open them and let the light flood in.

'Yeah, I'll have to go through a ton of trail cam footage.' He sits down heavily on the sofa and groans, pushing his hair back from his forehead. 'Will you help me?'

'If you want me to?'

'Of course I want you to.' Reaching for my hand, he pulls me down onto his lap and starts kissing me. 'But we don't have to go straight away. We could hang around here for a bit.'

'Oh no, let me go,' I laugh, between kisses. 'I need a shower. And so do you.'

'Well, that's rude. Can I take one with you? Save water?'

'No, you cannot!' Giggling, I struggle out of his hold and head for the bathroom. 'You can have one after me, if you want?'

'I'll wait 'til I get back to the farm. All my stuff's there and I need to change out of these clothes. They stink of the fire smoke.'

'Okay, I won't be long.'

I shower quickly, then we head back to the farm. It's such a beautiful day, I can't think of anywhere more perfect to spend it than next to the river with Aiden. I sit on the river bank while he showers up at the farm. The water sparkles almost as much as my mood. I keep smiling at nothing in particular. A dragonfly darts across the water, and a school of silver fish crowd around my bare feet as they dangle in the water. Aiden comes back and squats next to me.

'See the kingfisher?' He points across the water and I squint, following Aiden's line of vision until I see it sitting on a branch of the tree. It's smaller than I expected, but I'm still startled I didn't see it before.

'How did you see that?'

He sits behind me, and pulls me back against his chest, pressing a toothpaste-scented kiss to the side of my face. 'Just used to looking for things, I guess. Plus, I know that's where it sits, so I cheated a bit.'

His warm breathy laughter in my hair sends chills down my spine and when he kisses my ear, he makes my skin tingle.

'Right,' he says, after a few minutes of relaxing in the sun. 'These trail cams aren't going to check themselves. Come on, let's get on with it.' He stands up, pulling me with him, and we head over to the tent to watch his camera footage.

I'm glad it doesn't feel awkward today. Really, it feels like nothing's changed at all. We're still laughing at each other and joking around. We're still talking about the otters and the surrounding wildlife. We're still friends, and for that I'm so grateful. It's just a bit of fun, that's all. How funny to think I was so worried about it affecting everything. Imagine if I'd said no; I'd be missing out on all this joy.

It's great that we can do this without labelling what we have as anything more than being friends. It takes the pressure off. I don't have to feel guilty about putting my work first, and he doesn't have to feel bad about leaving soon. It's a win-win situation. We both know where we stand, and everything's honest and open.

The first couple of weeks after we slept together pass in a rose-tinted haze where I believe we've found the answer to the universe. Being with Aiden feels so, so good, and we have so much fun that I don't need anyone or anything else.

And then I realise I'm in love with him.

It shouldn't come as a shock, but it does. It feels like the sky is falling. Literally. The three-week heat wave we've had expires in a spectacular thunderstorm, with the wind thrashing the trees and the rain cascading down on a biblical scale. The river is tumultuous as it rushes by and Aiden's standing in the middle of it, stripped to his waist with his arms held out, laughing up at the sky. He looks like a mad man, with his long dark hair plastered to his head, his eyes closed, and the rain running in rivulets down his naked torso. I was about to call out to him, to laughingly demand that he come inside out of the rain, but something stops me and instead I just stand and watch him, getting soaked to the skin myself in the process.

He's so beautiful and so, so wild. Love slams into me, leaving me winded and furious to realise I've fallen so hard and so fast without realising. Apparently, my heart wasn't listening when we'd agreed to be just friends that slept together.

Aiden opens his eyes and catches me watching.

'Come in,' he shouts, holding out his hand to me. 'It's wonderful.'

I'm already drenched, so I take his hand and step into the raging water that rushes and bubbles past my thighs. The rocks are slippery beneath my feet, but he holds me steady as he pulls me against him, smoothing back my hair as he looks down at me. I'm almost afraid to meet his eye, fearing he'll see the emotion that lurks there, but he just smiles and kisses me while the rain continues to hammer down around us.

Chapter 15

'Shall we go for a swim?' After last week's storm, the hot weather has returned with a vengeance and I'm lying on the river bank in a heat-induced haze.

'Where?' Lifting my head, I look doubtfully at the shallow river, its stony bed clearly visible through the clear, rippling water. 'It's a bit shallow.'

'Not here. There's a deeper pool further up.'

'Won't it be cold?'

'That's the idea. Aren't you too hot now?'

'True.' I peer up at him. He's been off in the woods looking for wildlife to photograph while I've just been lying here for hours, so I feel like I owe it to him to do something. 'Where is it?'

'Just up there. It's only a short walk.'

I slip my trainers back on, but Aiden walks barefoot through the grass, his hair lifting in the breeze. He's a true hippy – a Seventies throwback. He fascinates me. I try to commit this moment to memory so I'll remember it forever. The glint of sunlight on water, the sound of the birds singing, the smell of the forest. And Aiden. Always Aiden. We pass the spraint rock where I fell and carry on to where the river runs deeper, curling round past a row of shady willow trees, their leaves brushing the surface of the water. A little further on, the river splits, and through the trees I see a disused water mill, its wheel still and silent, frozen for eternity.

'Wow, look at that!' I say, bending to get a better look through the trees. Its windows look black and empty against its soft sandstone walls. 'Such a shame it's fallen into disrepair.'

'Yeah, it's beautiful. Bit spooky though. I've had a good look round it.' He peels off his T-shirt. 'Come on, get your clothes off.'

'I'm looking at the mill.'

'You want to live there? We can do it up. You, me, four kids.' There's a splash as he leaps into the river and I squeal as a tide of cold water soaks me. 'How about it?'

I laugh. 'Yeah, right, like you want four kids!'

He's doing a lazy kind of backstroke away from me, just his head poking out of the water, watching to make sure I get in the water with him. I take my clothes off slowly, making him laugh as I treat him to a silly striptease, and then I jump into the water. It's freezing and I give a little squeal as I resurface, gasping for breath. Aiden laughs as he paddles over to me.

'Is this a good time to tell you I can't swim?'

His expression falters and I see real fear in his eyes. 'Oh, please no!'

Laughing, I splash him and swim away. He follows, pulling me back against him and biting my earlobe. We laugh and swim and play, much like the otters did the other night. We float on our backs beneath the willow trees, watching the sapphire sky through the emerald leaves, and then when we're cold, we lie on the bank in the sun to dry off.

'It's a good job I'm not allergic to grass,' I murmur. Aiden lies on his front, propped on his elbows while he makes a daisy chain. It makes me laugh. He's so masculine and hairy, and yet he's plucking sweet little flowers from the grass and carefully joining them together. When he's finished, he places it on my head like a crown. 'There you go. Now you're a queen. The queen of my heart.'

I laugh at him. 'Could you say that with a bit less sarcasm, do you think?'

'What do you mean?' He laughs and kisses my collar bone. 'Did you know your name means golden princess?' He readjusts my daisy headdress and runs his fingers through my blonde hair. 'You're my golden princess.'

'Have I been downgraded? I thought I was your queen a moment ago.'

'You are. That too. But that's what Orla means.'

'Oh, I see.' Supporting my chin on my hand, I watch him with amusement.

'Didn't you know that's what Orla means?'

I shake my head. 'Maybe I did once, but if I did, I've forgotten.'

'Well, never forget again.'

I giggle. 'What does Aiden mean, then?'

'Little fiery one, I think. Something to do with a Celtic sun god.'

'Ah, makes sense.'

'What does?' He looks amused as he plucks at the grass with his long fingers.

'You being named after a god.' Taking off my daisy crown, I place it on his head instead.

'A god? Steady on.' He laughs and rolls over onto his back so the daisy crown slips back onto the grass. 'I think that might be stretching it a bit.'

Settling down next to him, I kiss his shoulder and stare up at the blue sky above us. I think the silly conversation is over, but then he says, 'If I was a god, I'd be able to control my feelings for a start.'

There's a pause while I process his words. 'What do you mean?'

'I messed up, Orla. We messed up.' He raises his hand before letting it fall back onto his stomach in a hopeless gesture. 'This is no good. Or rather it's too good, depending on whichever way you look at it.'

I frown. 'What are you saying?'

'I'm saying you mean a lot to me. I'm saying you're going to be difficult to leave behind.'

I go cold all over. This is it, I think. This is where he tells me he's leaving. 'You're going away?' I say eventually.

'I got the call this morning.'

I sit up and reach for my T-shirt, pulling it on over my head. I don't want to be naked while we're having this conversation. 'You didn't say straight away?'

'I didn't know how.'

I swallow hard, reminding myself I have no right to feel this angry and betrayed. It's not like I didn't know Aiden would be leaving. What was it I'd said to Reanna? *That's who he is*, I'd said, *we have to enjoy him while we can*. I have to live by those words. I have to be brave. And in my heart of hearts, I knew our time was coming to an end. Aiden's been here all summer, and it's nearly September now. I know he has enough footage of the otters. He has no reason to stay here longer.

I pick a daisy and roll it through my fingers, watching the green juice from its stem stain my fingertips. 'Where are you going?'

'India.'

I nod, gathering myself together in order to be as positive possible. 'Well, that's amazing. When do you go?'

He jolts slightly, as though he felt my question as a physical blow. 'Next week. Tuesday, probably.'

Next week? But that's so soon! I feel like I'm in freefall as I struggle to keep my emotions from showing on my face. I know he has to go. I've always known. It's who he is. It's what he does.

'I'm sorry,' he says, eventually.

'Don't be sorry,' I whisper. 'You've always wanted to go to India, haven't you? It'll be wonderful. You'll love it.' My tone is light, but my throat aches. 'An excellent opportunity.'

He nods, but he can't meet my eye. 'I don't want to leave you though. Will you come with me?'

I stare at him. He can't be serious, surely?

'I'm serious, Orla,' he says, sitting up and putting his hand on my shoulder. 'I've never felt like this about anyone before. Ever. I don't think I can go without you.'

I can't speak for a moment. My heart stutters to a stop then starts beating again at a million miles per hour. Could I go with him? Could I really? My head fills with possibilities, a road trip movie filled with sunny days and endless kisses. We could travel the world together, see incredible places and animals that most people never get to see. It would be the adventure of a lifetime, and most importantly of all, I'd be with Aiden.

I really want to be with Aiden.

But …

What if Aiden and I don't work out? What if we get halfway round the world and decide we can't stand to be in each other's company for a moment longer? Looking at him now, I can't ever imagine that happening, but that's what every couple thinks when they first start out. I'm sure that's what my mum and dad thought when they got married, and look what happened there. What if I gave up my job, my flat, my five-year plan and find I did it for nothing?

Plus, I'm not that keen on camping. I love staying with Aiden in his tent, but I'm just visiting. I can go home to my comfortable bed whenever I feel like it, but if I went with him, I wouldn't be able to do that. I'm pretty sure the novelty of sleeping under canvas would wear off after a while if it was full-time, even if I was wrapped in Aiden's arms. Plus, at the end of the day, I'm a woman. How would I cope with having periods if we're camping in the middle of nowhere, miles away from civilisation and a proper toilet? I know there are bound to be ways around it, but I'm not sure I want to know what they are. I'm too used to my creature comforts. It's alright Aiden digging a hole and declaring it a latrine, but I like a nice clean porcelain bowl and double-ply toilet tissue. I like showers. And soap.

But I'll miss Aiden. How will I get through the day without seeing him, or hearing his voice. We've become inseparable these last few weeks.

Aiden's watching me closely, a troubled expression in his eyes. 'What are you thinking?' he asks softly.

I blink once. Twice. Three times. 'I'm thinking everything. All at once.'

'You don't have to decide now.'

'But you go in a week! I couldn't just leave in a week. I'd have to give notice on my job and my flat. Put my stuff in storage.'

'You could pack up in a week. Tell your landlord you've left and let your lease lapse. And at the end of the day, your job is just a job. They can't stop you leaving if you want to. You can just walk out.'

'I can't just walk out.' I'm appalled by the thought. 'Besides, what would I do for money?'

'Go freelance. Start a travel blog. Or even a vlog on YouTube. Write for magazines and newspapers. There're loads of things you could do. I have contacts that would give you freelance work. People would love to read about the places we'd go and the things we'd see. You'd never be short of material. And it would be amazing to go travelling with you. We'd have the best time. It'd be just you and me, seeing the world together.'

My initial spark of excitement is tempered immediately by black, sticky fear. I've never considered being a travel writer before. The farthest place I've been is Spain on a package holiday. There's so much to think about. I'd need injections against malaria and all sorts to go to the more tropical places. I'm not even sure how

191

long my passport has until it expires. It might even have expired already.

'Talk to me, Orla.'

I look at him and the fear and the doubt must show on my face because he sighs and strokes my hair back before kissing my forehead.

'You don't have to decide now. Think about it.'

'I haven't got long though, have I? Not if you're going in a week.' I can't keep the tremor of panic from my voice.

He shakes his head and sighs. 'A week or so. Nothing's definite yet. I need to sort out flights and I should go home to see my parents first.'

I nod, feeling numb. It's hard to believe that I woke up this morning so happy, and now I feel like the world is ending.

'And, you know, you could always come out and join me later on. You don't have to give everything up immediately. And even if you don't come, it doesn't have to mean the end of us.'

I give a silent laugh that's more pain than humour. How long would he be away for? Where would he go after India? There's no guarantee he'd come back to England. He's not even from England. He's Irish. All his family live in Ireland. Why would he come back here to see me when he doesn't need to be here?

There's too much against us.

'I need time to think.'

'Okay.' Aiden's voice is calm, soothing. He wraps his arms around me and holds me tight, his chin resting on the top of my head. 'Whatever you decide is okay, you know that, don't you? No pressure. I'd love you to come, but I know it's a massive thing for you.'

'I'm not sure I can live in a tent indefinitely.' My voice is muffled from where my face is pressed into his chest.

'We can stay in hotels. Rent apartments. We don't have to sleep in a tent all the time.'

'But you like living like that. You said that's what connects you to nature.' I lift my head and look at him reproachfully.

'I do like living like that. Like this' – he waves his hand at the river and the trees and the cornflower blue sky above us – 'but I like you more.' He smiles at me, his eyes soft and full of love. Full of hope. I drop my head back onto his chest, unable to look at him.

I don't think I can go with him.

I don't think I can live without him.

I want him to stay here with me forever. I want to go back to the minute before he took that phone call and make that last forever. Now there is life before the call, and life after the call. But I've always known that he will leave. I have no excuse for feeling this way. I've always known that Aiden is one of life's wanderers. A free spirit. The only surprising thing about this moment is that he's asking me to go with him.

I'm so confused.

'I should go home and think this through,' I say softly, making no attempt to leave the safety of his arms, which tighten around me.

'Don't go. Don't—' He tuts and tips his chin, staring up at the sky. 'If you don't come, we only have a week left. Let's not waste time.'

'But I don't know what to do. What am I supposed to do?'

He shakes his head slightly and shrugs. 'You don't have to go back to your flat and sit there alone to do decide what to do.' He strokes my hair and kisses my head. 'Stay with me.'

We hold each other like we won't ever let go. But we know we will. Deep down, I know I won't be going with him, and I think he knows it too. I feel it in every tremulous thud of his heartbeat, every deep shaking breath he draws into his lungs.

And though I wrap my arms around him like I'm frightened he will float up and away in the afternoon breeze, I know I'll let him go when the time comes. I'll let him go because I have to. I can't go and he can't stay. But I also know that some part of me will be forever sitting here on this river bank, wrapped in his arms, and that when he goes, he'll take a part of me with him. Because no matter what happens, he'll always have my heart.

Chapter 16

Present day – London, UK

The train starts to sway and I take hold of the metal pole next to me to keep myself upright. Aiden and I stare at each other across the carriage. He looks as shocked as I am that he's on this train.

'What are you doing?' I can't breathe properly. I think I must be hallucinating. A woman sitting in the centre of the carriage looks between us with interest, but otherwise it's just us, staring at each other in the yellow light of the train. 'You have to go back. You can't just leave your own exhibition!'

'I couldn't just let you leave!' He strides up the carriage towards me, holding on to the metal bars as he goes. 'I hadn't even spoken to you properly.'

For a second I think he's going to kiss me and my heart jerks, but his determined expression falters as he reaches me and is replaced by an uncertain frown. 'Why did you leave?'

'It's late, Aiden. I have work tomorrow.' I'm pleased that my voice sounds strong, even though my knees are weak and trembling.

'We haven't seen each other for five years.' He sits down on the seat next to where I'm standing. 'You could have waited.'

'You were busy. I didn't want to disturb you. I could tell you had lots of important people to see.'

'None more important than you. Have you been crying?'

'What? No!' Self-consciously, I wipe my face on my sleeve then sit down opposite him. 'It's just the wind and the rain. It made my eyes water.'

He seems to accept my answer, though he still looks troubled as he watches me. I stare back at him, almost afraid. 'Shouldn't you be back at the gallery with your friends and family.'

He shrugs. 'I've done my speech and thanked everyone for coming. What else do I need to do?'

'I don't know, but …'

'Nah.' He pulls at his tie until it hangs loose around his neck, then unbuttons the top two buttons of his shirt. At once, he looks more like the old Aiden than he has done all night. 'Everyone was leaving anyway. How are you? What have you been up to?'

'Just work and stuff.' I shrug. 'I live in London now, obviously.'

'Yeah, so your five-year plan worked out then?'

'Yes, I suppose it did.' I smile at him, though it feels stiff and not quite natural. 'And you? You're doing well, I see.'

'Ah well, you know.' He shrugs modestly. 'So, did you get married or anything?'

He eyes my naked left hand speculatively and I shake my head. 'I'm seeing someone.'

'Yeah? Lucky man. Who is he? What's he like?'

My insides recoil in surprise. The last thing I'd want to hear about is who he's seeing.

'His name's James and he's nice.'

'Nice?'

'Mm, nice,' I say with a firm nod.

'What's he do? Where does he come from? Do you live together?'

'Oh, err no, we don't live together. It's very early days.' I look at my shoes, uncomfortable talking to Aiden about James. 'He's

196

a business analyst, and he's originally from Manchester, but he's living down here in London.'

He tips his chin and looks at me searchingly. 'When you say early days, how early is early?'

'Two months or so.'

'How did you meet?'

'Oh God, is this the third degree, or something?' I laugh awkwardly. 'On the tube, going into work. I dropped my glove and he picked it up.'

'Oh, very romantic.'

'Well, not really.' I clear my throat. 'So how about you? Are you married, engaged, seeing anyone?'

'Me? Nope. Don't do relationships, remember.'

'Ah.' I frown slightly and nod. 'All the travel. Where are you off to next?'

'Home.'

'Home?'

'Ireland. I'm not going to be going anywhere further afield for a good while. To tell you the truth, I'm a bit fed up of travelling constantly.'

'I never thought I'd hear you say that!' I gaze at him, amazed.

'No, well, it's time to spend a bit of time at home, I think. I'm sticking around in London for a couple of weeks though, if you want to meet up?'

'Yes, I'd like that,' I reply, carefully, though inside I'm telling myself that I'll cancel. I can do without stirring up old memories.

'Great! Can I have your number then?' He digs his mobile out of the inside pocket of his suit and I fish mine out of my bag. I reel off my number as he inputs it into his phone, then mine beeps as he sends a text message.

'Ah and there's yours.' My stomach fills with butterflies as I see his message pop up on my screen. Aiden's number. After all this time. 'What are you going to be doing in London for two weeks? Stuff for your exhibition?'

'A bit, perhaps. I'm meeting up with someone who has a fox family living in their back garden, and there are some birds I'd like to photograph. It's not a great time of the year to do it, but we'll see.' He turns to look out the window as we pull into another station. I expect him to say he'll get off here and catch the next train back to Waterloo, but he makes no attempt to get up when the doors slide open. A couple of people get on and sit a little further down the carriage, then the doors shut and the train speeds away. 'Are you happy living here?' he asks, turning back to me.

'Yes.' I'm surprised by the question. Why wouldn't I be happy? I'm living in London, where I always wanted to be. I've got my dream job and …

Well, that's about it, really. I've got my job and I love it, but my flat's crap and London itself is exhausting. All the noise, all the people, the constant rush, rush, rush. Not that I'll admit that to anyone though. My stock answer is that I love the buzz. It's exciting and makes me feel alive. It certainly did at first, but the longer I stay here, the more drained I feel.

'And you? You're happy?'

'Of course! You know me, Orla. I'm always happy.'

I smile. Yes, I suppose that's true. I can't imagine he spent days crying over me, like I did him. I bet he just got on with his life and quietly lost himself in the nature he was photographing. 'But you're enjoying making the documentaries? You seem to be a bit of a celebrity these days.'

'Ah, no, not really,' he says dismissively. 'But yeah, I enjoy the documentaries. I work with a great team. It's busy though, and I'm not so used to having to work to someone else's schedule, but it's going okay so far.' He shrugs. 'We'll see. So what's the plan for the next five years then?'

'Pardon?'

'Your plan? What's next for you?'

'Oh, I don't know. I don't really have one.'

'What? You don't have another five-year plan? Orla!'

'What? You thought my plan was stupid anyway.'

'Yeah, I did, but I still expected you to have one.'

'Oh well, you know. Things change.'

'But no plan? Come on!' He raises his hands before letting them fall back to his knees and I laugh. 'I thought you'd be wanting to move to New York next, or planning world domination.'

'Because those two things go hand in hand? Moving to New York and world domination?'

He laughs. 'Or even just meeting someone and getting married and having children. Or is that still not for you?'

'What do you mean, *still not for me*?'

'You were always dead against it in the past.'

'I was?' I frown, puzzled. Was I really not interested in marriage and children back then?

'You were, yeah.'

'I'm sure I said maybe someday, whereas you said never ever.'

'Oh well, maybe I'm tarring you with the same brush as me then. I'm sure you said something about relationships getting in the way of your career though.'

'Well, maybe back then.' I shrug again. 'And I've met James, so, we'll see.'

'Early days though?'

'Yes.' Clearing my throat, I look away from him and realise we're approaching my stop. 'I get off here,' I say, gathering my bag to me. 'Are you getting off and catching the train back to Waterloo, or …?'

The *or* hangs between us, heavy and loaded, and Aiden gets up with a lopsided smile. 'May as well walk you home. See where you live.'

'Are you sure you have time?' I check my watch as I get to my feet, nerves making my heart thump in anticipation of the walk home. 'Do you not have an afterparty to go to?'

'No, it was just going to be after-drinks in the hotel reception with my family, but I think they've all had enough of me anyway.'

'I'm sure that's not true.'

He laughs good-naturedly as the doors ping back with a rapid beep-beep-beep-beep and then we step off onto the platform and head towards the exit.

I live in a small one-bedroom flat above a hardware shop, which lies in a long parade of shops including a grocery store, launderette, betting shop and several takeaways. It's not the most salubrious of areas and is a far cry from our woodland paradise of five years ago. Chip papers litter the pavement and the air smells of garlic and diesel fumes. We cross the road at the traffic lights, and Aiden catches hold of my hand as we break into a run at the sound of an approaching police siren.

How is it his hand still feels so familiar after all this time?

How is it my hand feels like it belongs there?

We don't speak as we make our way round to the back of the shops to the metal fire escape that leads up to my flat. Our feet clang as we make our way up, and I get my keys ready to let us in.

'Jesus Christ, Orla! They could provide you with some light.' Aiden leans against the thin metal railing and peers around into the darkness.

'Don't lean on that, it might give way!' I tell him, taking his arm and pulling him away like he's a child. 'There used to be a security light, but it stopped working.'

'You could kill yourself on these steps. And what if someone was waiting round here for you? It's not exactly safe.'

I glance back at him then down at the dark courtyard below. Apart from the hulking shapes of the wheelie bins and refuse skips, it's completely empty. There's a CCTV camera attached to the back of the betting shop, but that's about all.

'Thank you for that comforting thought, Aiden.'

'Have you got a rape alarm?'

'Yes, I got one after I went to interview some guy in the woods once and got trapped in some weird love spell.'

'Ha ha, very funny. Still taking risks after all these years, I see.'

'I can't exactly help it. I do live here. Besides, I can get to my flat through the shop below, and I rarely come back after the shop's closed.' I stop talking, aware that I've just exposed too much information about my very boring life. Dates with James aside, it's rare that I go out these days. I didn't even realise the light wasn't working until I came home after my first date with James. Before that, it had been ages since I'd stayed out late. A glass of wine and Netflix was about the most exciting my life got. Aiden needn't know that though.

I slip my key in the lock and shove the door with my shoulder to open it. The wood is swollen from the damp winter weather and catches on the bottom of the doorframe. Ushering Aiden into the dark hallway, I lock the door behind us and switch on the fluorescent strip light, which flickers and buzzes as it illuminates the bleak white walls with their black scuff marks and fluffy cobwebs. I try not to look at Aiden as I squeeze past him and unlock the white door on the left.

'Here we are,' I say, with unnecessary brightness as the door swings back to reveal more stark white walls and shabby furniture.

I rarely bring anyone back to my flat. In fact, I'm not sure anyone's been here since my mum, stepdad and sister when I first moved in. Maybe Katie when she visited a few months after, and possibly a short-lived boyfriend who was so dull he was easy to forget.

'Geeez,' Aiden whispers as he looks around, and I get the impression it's not in awe. 'Orla! What the hell is this place?'

'My flat! And you're being very rude right now!'

'But it's tiny. And shit. And there's a big patch of damp in the corner.' He points at the dark patch of mould that's been spreading

201

across the ceiling for a few months. I've told the landlord and he said he would come and sort it out, but he never has. Besides, I've got to the point when I don't see it anymore. I don't see any of it, in fact. Not the shabby carpet, the black leather sofa that's seen better days, nor the tired little kitchenette with the missing cupboard door.

'It's all I can afford.' I say, slightly belligerently. 'Besides, you saw how close it is to the tube station. It's pretty central and I can get to work easily. And anyway, you live in a tent, so you can shut up!'

He laughs. 'I think I'd rather live a few miles out of London in my tent and commute in than live here.'

'It's not so bad,' I say, trying to shrug off his comments. 'Anyway, what do you want to drink? I think I've got some beer in the fridge, or red wine? Or something softer? Tea? Coffee?'

'I'll have a beer, thank you.'

He sits down on the battered sofa, still looking around him like he can't believe his eyes.

'The guy that owns the hardware shop downstairs owns this,' I say as I pass him a bottle of beer. 'He's lovely. I get all my dish-cloths and scrubbers and stuff for free.'

Aiden gives me a look that suggests he thinks I've gone mad. 'And how much are dishcloths? A pound? Two pounds? Think how much that damp patch is costing your health!'

'He says he's coming to fix it.'

'He could do with decorating while he's here too. Is this your sofa or was it already furnished when you got here?'

'Oh no, it's all the landlord's. It saved a lot of bother when I was moving down.'

'But your flat in Hawksley was so nice! How can you be living here in this?'

I sigh and look around at the plain white walls. I'm glad the blinds are drawn so that he can't see the bars on the windows. 'I can't afford anything else. Seriously, have you seen the price of rent in London? I want to actually have some money left after I get paid at the end of each month. And like I said, it's convenient and I stopped seeing everything but the TV, the fridge and my bed a long time ago.'

'Christ, Orla, it's the pits.'

'Thanks!' I give him a look, annoyed he's being so judgemental when he doesn't even live under a roof half the time. 'I take it you won't want to stay then! You know where the door is.'

'Oh no, I'll stay, if you're offering. Thanks, Orla.' He sniffs and looks about him before taking another swig from his bottle.

I stare at him. Stay? He means stay for a drink, obviously. Not *stay*. He can't *stay* here. The sofa's really uncomfortable and I only have a single bed.

Besides, what would James think?

'So how come you didn't watch my documentaries?' he asks, throwing me completely off my train of thought.

'How do you know I haven't watched them?' I sit down next to him on the sofa, tucking my leg beneath me.

'Because you didn't know I'd cut my hair.'

'I thought you'd tied it back!'

'Bollocks. You haven't watched them, have you? Why? If you'd been in anything, I'd have watched it. Even if it was a programme for pre-schoolers or an advert for sanitary products.'

My face feels hot with guilt, but how do I explain I didn't watch them because I knew seeing him again would be too painful? I'd been excited to watch them at first, but the trailer I'd seen had made me feel so desolate that I'd realised it wasn't a good idea. To see him on screen and know he wasn't in my life anymore would renew my sense of loss and make me miss him more than ever.

I can't tell him that though. It's much too pathetic.

'I just never got round to it.' I shrug, trying to pretend it's not a big deal. 'You know how it is. Life gets so busy.'

'Really?' he says sardonically, clearly not impressed by my

answer. He takes another swig from his bottle of beer, eyeing me over its base.

'I am intending to watch them though,' I tell him. 'They're still available on catch-up.'

'My mum bought the DVD,' he says pointedly.

'Ah, well there's loyalty. Who has DVDs now, though? I don't even own a DVD player!'

'You don't?'

'No, I just stream everything. It's the future, baby.'

He rolls his eyes and looks back up at the damp patch.

'Stop looking at it!' I snap.

'Sorry.' He laughs as he turns his attention back to me, and I relax slightly, sensing I'm already forgiven for not watching his documentaries. 'Did you get my postcards?'

'Oh, those were from you? I didn't know,' I say teasingly. Of course I knew they were from him. Who else would I know that had been to locations as exotic as Kuala Lumpur, Tokyo, Ecuador and the Galapagos? I must have received about fifty over the past five years. He never writes anything on them though, just my name, work address and a heart in the space where the 'wish you were here' comment should be.

He gives me a look and I laugh. 'Yes, of course I got them. Thank you. Everyone at work asks me about who I know that goes to such amazing places and I just say it's a mystery. You've been to so many different countries. It makes my head spin.'

'You should have been with me.' Leaning forward, he places his bottle firmly on the table with a dull *thunk*.

'Oh, Aiden! It would never have worked,' I say with a forced laugh, scratching my head uncomfortably. 'I'd have got on your nerves and you'd have sent me home after a couple of weeks, I'm sure of it.'

'I don't think so.'

'Or I'd have run home. I'd never have coped without hot water and a proper toilet. Living wild like you do is not for me.'

'At least we would have been together.' He turns sideways to face me, his eyes serious, but I brush his comment off with a laugh.

'Is that supposed to comfort me? Anyway, why has it taken you five years to come back? I bet you've been back to the UK before now.'

'Yeah, but not to London.' He looks annoyed as he takes a deep breath and looks away. 'I missed you.'

'I missed you too.' The words are out before I can stop them, and butterflies swirl in my stomach. I can't do this, though. I can't let him back in. It was so painful when he left last time, and he's sure to leave again. Besides, he can't really mean it, can he? It's been five years. He'd have been back before now if he really missed me.

'Did you? Or are you just saying that?' He looks back at me, and I'm shocked by the accusation in his eyes.

'Of course I missed you! It was horrible when you went away.' I can't believe he'd think I didn't miss him. Did he not know how much I loved him?

'You practically pushed me onto that plane.'

'I did not!'

'You were very cheerful. Almost excited, in fact. I felt like you'd have a party when you got home.'

'Aiden! How could you think that?' I gape at him. 'I didn't want you to see how sad I was. What good would crying all over you have done? It would have made it ten times worse.'

'It didn't exactly do my ego much good.'

'You knew I didn't want you to go!'

'You never said. All I knew was you didn't want to come with me. Even after I practically begged you.'

'You did not. You asked, I said no, we moved on. You never begged. If I didn't say I didn't want you to go, it was because I knew you had to. Come on, Aiden, it was India! It was an amazing opportunity, and I knew you wanted to go. I didn't want to put

205

a dampener on your excitement, and I didn't want you to remember me as clingy or controlling, or as someone that was stopping you from chasing your dreams.'

'You knew I'd never think that about you. You were always more. We always had a great time when we were together. There was no one I'd have rather travelled to India with.'

'But I couldn't *go*!'

'Why? Because of your five-year plan?'

For a moment, I'm lost for words. Did he really not understand that I had my own dreams? That I wanted to pursue my career for myself? If I'd gone with him and we'd fallen out, I'd have returned to England brokenhearted and without a job. It would have meant starting as a trainee again, and it would have put everything back years. Because I stayed, I'm right on track. I work on a well-read paper with a big distribution network, and I live in London, just like I always wanted.

Does he really not see that? I stare at him and he stares right back, his jaw rigid. His green eyes are dark in this light, and I can't see the golden flecks in the iris, nor the amber ring around the outside.

'Aiden,' I say, when the standoff becomes too much to bear. 'How can you think I was glad you left?'

He looks away, and I can see he's unconvinced. 'Hmm. Anyway, I'd better go if you've got work in the morning.'

My heart stutters and I'm suddenly awash with disappointment that he's leaving. I have an urge to tell him about how I cried for weeks after he left and that my eyes were sore for a month. I want to tell him how worried my mum and friends were about me when I stopped eating. But instead, I say, 'Will you be alright getting back to your hotel? Do you know where you're going?'

'I'll call a cab.'

'You can sleep on the sofa if you want?' My heart goes mad, flapping about in my chest, desperate for him to say yes.

'No, I'd better go,' he says, stiffly, already tapping the number

206

of a cab company into his phone. A lock of hair falls forward over his forehead and I have to stop myself from reaching out to stroke it back into place. 'What's your address?'

I tell him, even though I don't want to, even though I'm desperate for him to stay. I don't want to leave it like this, with him angry with me, and me unable to express how much I missed him. He gets to his feet as soon as he calls the cab. 'Five minutes, he said, so I'll wait out front.'

'Okay.' My breath hitches as I follow him to the door. *Please don't go, please don't go.*

'Do you need to lock the outer door behind me?'

'No, it locks on its own.' I hope he doesn't hear the tremor in my voice.

'Okay, well …' He hesitates in the doorway then turns to look at me. 'See you soon, Orla.'

'Okay.' I smile awkwardly, not knowing what to do. Should we kiss or hug? Or just simply say goodbye? I can't remember it ever being this awkward between us. Aiden checks his pockets as though he thinks he's left something, and I grip the doorframe, my knuckles whitening. *Please don't go, please don't go.*

'Right,' Aiden says when he's apparently satisfied he's got everything. 'Bye then.'

'Bye.' My voice is so small it's barely more than a whisper.

He goes to walk away, then changes his mind and turns back towards me with his arm out, ready for a hug. Without hesitation, I slip my arms around his waist and squeeze him tight. He feels warm and solid, his shirt smooth against my cheek, and I don't want to let go, but I have to and before I know it the door's swinging shut behind him and he's gone, leaving an empty corridor and me, bewildered and sad.

Chapter 17

I can't believe Aiden thought I was glad to see him go. I toss and turn all night thinking about it, then think about it some more on my tube journey to work. At least it takes my mind off the packed train carriage I'm standing in. My nose is about two centimetres away from the man in front's puffer jacket, and a woman behind has her bag wedged against my hip. Just the same as any other day, really.

Why would he think I was happy he was going away? It just doesn't make sense.

I'm so distracted I barely register the ticket barrier or the walk to work. Instead, I see the bright airy interior of Manchester city airport, and Aiden's back as it disappears through security. It was a horrible feeling watching him disappear like that. It was only then that I allowed myself to fall apart. I remember sitting in my car afterwards and crying so hard and for so long that I had to pay for extra time in the short stay car park.

I never want to go through that again. I can't let Aiden in this time.

'Someone looks tired!' Belinda, the editor in chief, stops by my desk on her way into her office. 'How did last night go? Did Emma enjoy the exhibition?'

'Yes, I think so. It was good. Really powerful stuff.'

'Did Emma get to speak to him?'

'She did. He was very busy but she got a few words.' My stomach dips and I feel a little breathless as I wait for my computer to boot up. He really had been busy last night. Far too busy to just up and leave and come racing after me.

Belinda runs through a couple of things with me before going back into her office to take a call. Emma appears at the side of my desk, brandishing her piece from Aiden's exhibition.

'Morning!' she says perkily as she perches her bottom on the edge of my desk. 'Did anything happen after I left last night?'

'No! No, nothing at all.' I say, innocently, focusing my attention on the printout of the review. 'I saw some people that I knew so I just chatted to them for a while and then left. This is good. Well done.'

'Thanks.' She beams as she takes back the review, then turns to look at the postcard that's pinned to my notice board on my wall. 'Cool postcard. Who do you know who's been to Kuala Lumpur?'

'Oh, err …' I narrow my eyes at her. That card's been there for months yet she's never asked about it before. Emma's not daft; she knows it's from Aiden and is trying to stir things up. My cheeks flush as she unpins it from the wall to read the back, though she won't find the answer there. It's just my name, work address, and a heart.

'Just a heart, eh?' Emma gives me a knowing look and pins it back up. 'I bet that's from Aiden Byrne, isn't it? He's so in love with you. I hope you took him home and gave him a good seeing to?'

'*Emma!*' I splutter.

'Well, I would!'

'What's that?' Belinda appears out of her office like an apparition. I swear she has special senses that tell her when her staff are talking about anything other than work. 'Who did Orla take home and give a good seeing to?'

'Aiden Byrne,' Emma says helpfully. Or rather, unhelpfully.

'*The* Aiden Byrne?'

'No! I didn't give anyone a good seeing to.'

'Oh, Orla!' Belinda says, looking disappointed. 'For about two seconds there you got a whole lot more interesting.'

'Thanks!' I say crossly.

'So why are you suggesting Orla went home with Aiden Byrne, Emma?'

'You should have seen the way he was looking at her!'

'He wasn't …' I break off, shaking my head. 'He's just … an old friend, that's all.'

'What? *The* Aiden Byrne's an old friend?' Belinda's eyebrows shoot up in surprise.

'Yes. And why do you keep saying *The* Aiden Byrne like he's George Clooney or something? He's not a celebrity. He's just a wildlife photographer.'

'But he's done all those documentaries now. He's becoming quite a household name. Wasn't he voted fiftieth sexiest man in a recent magazine poll?' Belinda looks from me to Emma and back to me again.

'What? No!' I start to laugh. 'Fiftieth? I'm not sure that's that great.'

'Hey, at least he made the list.'

I put my head in my hands, still laughing. There's no way Aiden is on a sexiest man list! I really should have watched those documentaries. 'What did he do in these documentaries? Take all his clothes off?'

'There was one where he stripped off and waded out into a crocodile-infested river.'

'What the hell!?' A crocodile-infested river? I'm appalled.

'You couldn't see his dong or anything. Just a back view.'

'Glad to hear it.' I feel an irrational stab of jealousy. 'But why would he go into a crocodile-infested river? I thought these documentaries were on climate change?'

210

'Can't remember.'

'No, no one does. We just remember that arse.' Emma and Belinda cackle and I roll my eyes at them. I have a sudden urge to watch every documentary he's ever done, right here, right now. 'Seriously though,' Emma sniffs when she's finished laughing. 'He's done quite a few different ones. I think that one was about deforestation in the Amazon or something, and they were probably alligators not crocodiles. He had to go in because they'd dropped a bit of film kit in there.'

'He risked his life for a bit of kit?'

Emma shrugs. 'Made good telly. I think the ratings went through the roof on that one. I'm surprised you don't know about it.'

I shake my head, annoyed. So not only does he take close-up photographs of forest fires like the one in his exhibition last night, but he also goes swimming in dangerous rivers and swamps just to up his TV ratings.

Not that I care, of course. I can't let him wheedle his way into my affections again. Besides, he seemed so angry with me last night I doubt I'll see him again.

'Did you get his number last night?'

'Maybe.' I cast a warning glance towards Emma and Belinda. 'We said we might meet for a drink before he leaves for Ireland, talk about old times and that sort of thing. I doubt it will actually happen though. Besides, I don't know if you two remember, but I'm seeing someone already.' I turn back to my computer, stabbing at a few keys though I have no idea what I'm typing.

'Oh yeah, the pickle guy?' Emma and Belinda exchange looks and snigger.

'James. And I don't know why you two are laughing.'

'He's just got a funny name, that's all. James Pickles. You'd be Orla Pickles.'

'No, I wouldn't, because I'm not about to marry him, am I? I've only just met the guy!'

'I much prefer Orla Byrne.'

'Yeah well that's never going to happen, sorry.'

'Never say never, Orla.'

'In this case, I really think we can because in a couple of weeks he's going back to live in Ireland.'

'Ireland's only across the water. You can be there in an hour or so.'

I roll my eyes at them. 'Look, how did we get on to this? Aiden is a friend, that's all.' I focus my attention back on my computer screen, but Belinda and Emma continue to stand by my desk, staring at me.

'Did you think he was interested in Orla, Emma?' Belinda asks.

'Definitely. He kept gazing at her, and then she'd gaze back, and it was like a scene from some romantic film or something.'

'Hardly!' I scoff. Though I think about the way he appeared on that train. If he'd kissed me then … I swoon a little and have to blink to clear my vision as I push the thought away.

'Ooh, look at her face!' Belinda says, peering closer at me. 'Something did happen last night. I can tell.'

'No, it didn't!' I protest. 'Like I said, we just talked that's all. Then he left and I went to bed.'

'Wait, he left? As in, left your flat? How did he get in your flat?'

Realising my mistake, I get all flustered and panic. 'Oh, he … err, he followed me onto the train.'

'He followed you onto the train? What, from the gallery?'

'Why did he do that?'

'Did he kiss you?'

'Is he some kind of stalker?'

'No! I left early and he wanted to speak to me, that's all. He ran after me and jumped on the train just as it was leaving.'

'Aww, that's so romantic!'

'Will you two stop! We just talked!'

'What about?'

'Just stuff. Like what we've been up to in the past few years. He didn't stay long. Anyway, why are you two being like this?'

'Like what?'

'All gooey and romantic. You didn't want to know when I told you about James finding my glove. This is just the celebrity thing, isn't it? You're only interested because Aiden's semi-famous.'

'No, it's because James sounds a bit creepy, if you want to know the truth.'

'Creepy? What are you talking about? How is he creepy?'

'That whole glove thing … weird.'

'It was sweet. He found my glove and handed it to me. How is that creepy?'

'Because, Orla, it wasn't even your glove.'

'Oh, no it wasn't in the end!' I laugh, remembering the moment I discovered both of my gloves safely in my coat pocket.

'Yeah, exactly,' Belinda gives me a knowing look. 'Why did he think it was yours? I bet he carries a supply of women's gloves around so he has a reason to chat up girls on public transport.'

'He's not like that at all!' I protest. 'He's sweet.' The thought of sweet, affable James using tricks like that is unthinkable.

'What does he look like?' Emma asks.

'Oh, er …' I stop and think for a moment, trying to push the image of Aiden aside and picture James instead. It's pathetic that Aiden has this hold on me after all this time. To alleviate my guilt, I go a bit overboard on my description of James. 'He's cute. Short, tight, curly blond hair. It's sort of fuzzy. And he's got blue eyes and a round face. He always looks smart and smells nice.'

'Not being funny but he sounds like Fozzie Bear. Does he wear a pork pie hat and tell bad jokes?'

'Emma! That's really rude!' I say, laughing despite myself. 'Anyway, Fozzie Bear is my favourite muppet so it's all good.'

'Really? I prefer Animal. Aiden would be Animal.'

'Aiden would not be Animal!' I scoff. 'Aiden would be … who would Aiden be?' I muse as Emma and Belinda slip away from my desk and go back to their own. I'm so busy thinking about Aiden and which muppet he'd suit best that I don't even notice Malcolm, the big boss, walking through the office. 'Rowlf!' I shout triumphantly. 'Aiden would be Rowlf. Even if he doesn't have hair like Rowlf's ears anymore, he's still laid back and affable.'

I look across at Emma, but she sinks down in her seat and shakes her head at me just as Malcolm sweeps past, casting a disapproving look my way before entering Belinda's office.

I wince. Oh well, he's not to know what we were talking about is he. Deciding I haven't got time to worry about Malcom, I set about my work, determined not to think about Aiden until the end of the day.

But as soon as Malcolm leaves Belinda's office, she's back over to my desk with Emma slinking behind her.

'Rowlf?' Belinda says. 'You're comparing *The* Aiden Byrne to Rowlf?'

I shrug. 'Well, the Aiden I knew, anyway.'

'So, tell us how well you used to know him then.'

I shrug. 'I spent a summer with him five years ago, sleeping in his tent and watching otters.'

'Watching otters? Well, that's a new one!'

'Ha ha, very funny. Anyway, the point is, that was five years ago.'

'Five years?' Emma whispers. 'And you still look at each other like you did last night? And he still sends you postcards from all around the world?' She points the postcard that she pinned back to my wall out to Belinda.

'Yes, but I live in London, and he lives in Ireland. Or more likely a tent, in whatever country he happens to take his fancy next.'

'So, he comes to visit you in London. And you go on holiday to his tent.' Emma shrugs, like it's the simplest thing in the world.

'Sounds like the ideal relationship,' Belinda says. 'You wouldn't even get sick of each other because you'd spend all that time

214

missing each other and being overjoyed when you actually did see each other.'

'I'd live in a tent if it was with a guy as sexy as Aiden Byrne,' Emma chips in.

I shake my head. 'Look, which part of it's over and I'm seeing James now don't you two understand? You'll have to meet James. I'll bring him to the Christmas party if we're allowed partners.'

'We'd rather you brought Aiden Byrne!' Belinda says sourly.

I roll my eyes at her. 'What did Malcolm want anyway?'

'Oh, just trying to blame us for a slump in sales figures, that's all.' Her shoulders drop. 'So, we need more salacious gossip. More sex. More scandal. If you fancy doing a kiss-and-tell exposé on Aiden Byrne or have any naked photos of him, now's your time to get them out.'

'I don't think so.'

'Oh, well, failing that, do you think he'd write a column for us? Something environmental?'

'Maybe.' I shrug, and then realise she'll be expecting me to ring him.

'Great. And that gives you a good reason to talk to him too, doesn't it!' She winks at me before spinning on her heel and heading back to her office.

Chapter 18

I'm so tired by the end of the day, I'm struggling to keep my eyes open. My mobile rings just as I'm about to leave the office and I snatch it up, my first thought being that it's Aiden. I feel a wave of guilt when I see James's name on the caller display.

'Hi, James!' I say, cheerfully. 'How are you?'

'Good thanks! Listen, Orla, I'm really sorry but I'm going to have to cancel our date tonight. I'm so behind at work I'm going to have to stay late.'

'Oh!' Guilt and surprise roll through me. I'd completely forgotten we had a date tonight. 'That's okay. I'm really tired anyway so I could do with an early night.'

'You are lovely, Orla. Thank you for being so understanding. Ordinarily, I'd catch up tomorrow instead but I'm going up to Manchester in the morning for my grandmother's birthday.'

'Yes, of course. Honestly, it's no problem.'

'Well, for the record, I'm disappointed not to be seeing you.'

I laugh slightly breathlessly. 'Me too,' I say, then realise it's a lie. I'm so relieved not to have to go out tonight I feel like thanking him. 'Shall we rearrange for one evening next week?'

'I can do Tuesday?'

'Yes, Tuesday's good for me too. Shall we meet in our usual place?'

'Sounds good. Eight o'clock?'

'Yes, great.'

We say goodbye and I hang up, my heart thudding guiltily. I'm shocked I'd forgotten about our date. So shocked in fact that I'm seriously starting to doubt we'd made arrangements in the first place. I suppose we must have done though. My head has been so full of Aiden and his exhibition all week that I shouldn't be surprised things have slipped. Still, I feel bad about it. What if he hadn't cancelled? I'd have gone home to sleep and stood him up.

I'm doubly glad James cancelled when I get outside into the wind and the rain. Another storm is forecast for this weekend, so it's bound to get worse. I put up my umbrella, but it instantly gets blown inside out, so I give up and hurry to the tube station without it. I'm drenched by the time I get home. My flat feels cold and damp, so I crank up the heating and change into my pyjamas.

I wonder what Aiden's doing now.

Pushing the thought away, I phone my landlord and leave a message about the damp patch and the broken cupboard, then make a start on making my dinner. It's only stir fry, but at least the smell of sizzling vegetables and soy sauce eradicates the pervasive smell of fried chicken from the takeaway next door. It's always worse on Friday and Saturday evenings. I settle down to eat in front of the TV, and realise that this could be a good time to watch Aiden's documentaries. It takes me just a moment to find them, and I stare at the thumbnail for a moment, trying to work out if it's a good idea or not. Belinda and Emma have got me curious though, and I really do want to see the river scene.

It's strange to see him on the TV. I finish my dinner then sit on the floor in front of the TV so I can be closer. He's surprisingly natural on camera. I'm on the second episode when there's

217

a knock on the door. Thinking it's the landlord, I pause the TV and get up to answer the door. I'm a bit annoyed because Aiden's just taking his shirt off ready to jump into the Amazon river, but I need to get this damp sorted.

'Hello!' I say, as the door swings open.

'Hi!' Aiden's standing the other side holding a black suit carrier in one hand and a massive holdall at his feet. 'Am I too late for dinner?'

My jaw drops. Oh Christ, and I've got him paused topless on my TV screen too. I'm going to look a right pervert!

'How did you get in?'

'I came up the fire escape and the door was unlocked.'

'It was?' I stick my head out and peer down the corridor in surprise. 'Really? It must have been open all day. I came up through the shop.'

'Oh well, I've locked it now. You going to let me in or what?' Picking up his holdall, he steps towards me.

'Sorry!' Flustered, I step aside to let him in. 'I was expecting the landlord actually. I phoned him before.'

'Good. Do you think he'll come?'

I don't answer immediately. I'm too busy staring at his bags. Why has he got all his stuff with him?

His holdall lands with a thud behind my sofa and he lays his suit carrier over the back of the cushions. I scratch my head with the TV remote. 'Oh!' he says with a grin, stopping to stare at my TV screen. 'Are you watching my documentaries?'

My heart jerks and I laugh, going red. 'Yes! Trust you to walk in at this bit. I can't believe you're actually going to jump into a river with alligators in it!'

'Nah, it was pretty safe really.'

I shut the door and go into the kitchen to hide my hot cheeks. 'I've got some stir fry left if you want to finish it off?'

'Yes please, I'm starving! I just got back from seeing my family off at the airport.'

'Oh, that's nice.'

'Yeah, Mum cried as usual but I think that was more fear of flying than anything else.'

'Aww. Was she there last night? I didn't see anyone I thought could be your mum.'

'Yes, she was there, and my dad. They were lurking at the back somewhere with my brother and his family.'

'I didn't even know you had a brother.'

'Yeah, you did.' He sits down on my sofa and points again at the TV. 'I can't watch myself, by the way. Hate it. Do you mind if I switch it off?'

'Okay.' I carry his plate over, still confused about him having a brother. 'You're very good on camera. Very natural. I can see why you made number fifty on the sexiest men list.'

He goes bright red, making me laugh. 'Oh God, *that*! It's so ridiculous. I wanted to die with embarrassment when I heard about that.'

'Why? It's great. And quite right too. Obviously, I think you're sexy. Well, used to anyway,' I add hastily as he raises an eyebrow at me. Now it's my turn to blush. He laughs as he takes the plate and cutlery I'm holding out to him.

'Thank you for this. I was only joking about dinner. I'd have gone to the chippy or somewhere.'

'No, it's no problem. It'll only go to waste if you don't eat it.' I sit down next to him, my eyes drawn to the suit carrier resting on the back of the sofa.

'So, you brought your stuff …?'

'Yeah, thanks for letting me stay. It's really kind of you.' He points the fork at the food as he chews. 'Wow, this is really good.'

'It was only thrown together quickly.'

'Well, it's lovely. Thanks. I was starving. I got a cab back from the airport and got stuck in traffic for ages.'

'Oh dear.'

'Mmm,' he nods, chewing another mouthful.

'About you staying,' I start, falteringly. 'I don't recall you actually saying you were coming to stay?'

'Oh? Really?' He swallows the mouthful he's chewing and wipes the side of his mouth with his hand. 'It was when I was moaning about your flat last night. You said "you won't want to stay then" and I said "yes, I would, thank you".'

'And you thought that was me inviting you to stay?' I blink at him.

'Well, yeah.' He shrugs. 'We haven't seen each other in five years, I thought it would be nice for us to spend some time together.'

I hesitate, recognising this as my chance to tell him that I don't think it's a good idea for us to spend time together. But now he's here, all long-limbed and gorgeous with his dark floppy hair and big green eyes, I realise the temptation to keep him here is too great. 'Of course, you can stay, but I'm not sure where you'll actually sleep?' I look around my little flat as my heart flutters like a bird in the cage of my chest. 'I suppose you could sleep on the sofa but it's not very comfortable.'

'I don't care. I'll sleep on the floor. I've brought my sleeping bag.'

'You have?'

'Sure. I always have my sleeping bag.'

'But weren't you booked into a hotel?'

'For a few days, yeah, but I knew I was staying for a bit after so I thought I'd be able to crash at my mates. I still can if you don't want me here?'

'It's not that I don't *want* you here, it's just I don't know how it will look to James …'

'Ah, your new boyfriend.' Realisation dawns on his face. 'Is he coming tonight?'

'No, not tonight. He's never actually been here before so him finding you here isn't really a problem.'

'So, what is the problem?'

'I don't know. It's just, how's it going to look if he finds out you're staying here?'

'Why? I'm just an old friend crashing on your floor for a few days. What's wrong with that?'

'Well, nothing when you put it like that, but …' My voice trails off.

'You still fancy me?' He laughs wickedly.

'Aiden!' My heart bungees to my feet and back up.

'Well, what's a guy to think? I am number fifty on a list of the world's sexiest men. And I just found you watching me shirtless on TV!' He runs his tongue round his cheek, obviously enjoying himself.

'Hey!' I splutter. 'You turned up at the wrong time, that's all. It's the first time I've seen it.'

'Likely story. You could have been watching it over and over again for months for all I know!' Aiden laughs as he forks up the last of his dinner.

'Oh ha ha! Very funny,' I say, resorting to sarcasm in the absence of any other sort of defence. I can't believe how different he seems from last night. Did I imagine his anger and resentment? 'Besides, *you're* the one who chased me onto a train.'

'That's true,' he concedes, leaning forward to slide his empty plate onto the coffee table. 'And I just turned up at your flat and invited myself to stay.' He shrugs and stands up. 'You know me, always chancing my hand. Well, thanks for dinner. I'll go to Ben's. He said I could stay with him.'

'Oh! No! You don't have to go!' I stand up with him, suddenly so terrified at the thought of him leaving that I almost put my hands on him and drag him back down onto the sofa. 'You can stay. It's no problem.'

'Yeah?' His eyebrows lift. 'What about James?'

I shrug. 'Like you say, you're just an old friend crashing at my place for a few days. Besides, he doesn't need to know.'

Aiden pauses, considering. 'Well, if you're sure?'

'Of course, I'm sure. It will be good to spend some time together. Besides, the weather's awful. You don't want to have to go back out in that.'

He shrugs and sits back down. 'Okay, thanks.'

'I didn't get you a drink. What do you want? Beer? Water? Tea?'

'I'll have tea, please.'

I go to make it, wondering what the hell I'm doing. My heart is hammering and I feel sweaty with panic. I should have let him go to his friend's. I can't afford to let him back in. But I felt bad about not making him feel welcome, and now he's here, I don't want him to go. My stomach's full of butterflies and my hands tremble as I fill the kettle from the tap. I wash up while I'm waiting for it to boil, relieved to have something to distract me from Aiden's disturbing presence. I glance at him every now and again, but he's texting on his phone, a slight frown on his face as he taps out his message with his thumb. I want to ask who he's texting, but it's none of my business, so I turn my back and get on with making the tea.

'Shall I hang your suit up in my wardrobe?' I say, placing a steaming mug down in front of him. 'Save it getting crumpled?'

'Sure, if you have room?'

'I'll make room. It's fine. Do you have anything else in your bag that needs hanging?'

'Nah, it's fine. I need to wash most of it anyway. Did I see a launderette up the road?'

'Yes, that's the one I use.'

'I might go tomorrow morning.' He presses Send on his text message and leans forward for his tea. 'Thanks for the tea.'

'You're welcome.' Picking up the black suit carrier, I take it into my bedroom and hang it in my wardrobe. It gives me a funny feeling in the pit of my stomach to see something of Aiden's hanging next to my clothes. I stare at it for a moment before

222

closing the wardrobe door. Rain runs in rivulets down my tiny bedroom window, and I shut my curtains to block it out.

'So did your landlord say he'd come to look at your damp?' Aiden asks when I go back into the lounge.

'Oh, I didn't get to speak to him. I just left a message.' I go back and sit next to him, tucking my feet beneath me. 'Was it sad saying goodbye to your family?'

'A bit, but I know I'll be seeing them again in a couple of weeks.' He scratches his head and yawns. 'When are you seeing James next? Tomorrow night?'

'No, he's in Manchester this weekend. I'm meeting him for a drink on Tuesday night. We were supposed to be going out tonight but he had to work late.'

Aiden frowns. 'Are you sure he's not married?'

'Why do you say that?'

'Well, he's never been here, you've never been to his, he's cancelling dates then away all weekend.'

'We're taking it slow. Nothing wrong with that.'

'No, of course not.'

'Not everyone's like you, you know?'

'What's that supposed to mean?' He looks at me sharply and I feel a stab of alarm. *Let's not have another argument, please.*

'After I met you, you just kept turning up at my flat, and then after that we spent every spare minute together.'

'Well, I was interested in your welfare at first. You had just injured yourself. And then you wanted to see the otters, so …' He shrugs. 'It's not like we had sex straight away.'

'No, I know.' I feel my cheeks grow hot and I shift uncomfortably on the sofa, pulling my pyjama sleeves down over my hands. 'But we were always together.'

'Well, we were mates,' he says, as he reads a message that's just pinged onto his phone. 'I liked your company.'

I hide my smile behind my mug, remembering all the hours

we spent together, laughing and talking until late into the night. 'Who's your message from?'

'Mum. They've landed safe and are waiting to be picked up from the airport. She's glad to get her feet on firm ground.'

'She must be terrified to think of you flying all around the world.'

'Yes, she is, bless her. I don't usually tell her when I'm flying though. I just let her know where I am when I land.'

'Via a postcard?'

'Usually email, actually.'

'No, well, I don't suppose she'd find out very much from one of your postcards. It's not like you write anything on them.'

'What do you want me to say?' He chuckles.

'I don't know, tell me how you are and what you've been doing, that kind of thing?'

'But you didn't want any of that, remember? No contact, you said.'

'You still sent the cards. You may as well have made use of the space.'

He shrugs. 'They were just to let you know I was thinking of you.'

My stomach tightens and I push my hand into my hair, gripping it firmly at the roots to relieve some of the tension I'm feeling. 'That's sweet. Thank you.'

'And to make sure you didn't forget me.'

I laugh. 'How could I forget the man dressed in full camouflage who scared me so much I fell and twisted my ankle?'

Aiden chuckles as he sips his tea. 'Not my finest hour.'

'Oh, I don't know. You looked after me pretty well.'

'It was the least I could do.'

'You were great. You did more than most men would.'

He shrugs and then looks directly into my eyes, making my stomach lurch. 'We had a pretty good time, didn't we?'

'Yep. Pretty good.' I smile at him, then look away as I lean over

224

to place my mug on the coffee table. 'You'll have to tell me all about your travels.'

He laughs and puts his head back. 'That'll take a while.'

'Well, how long are you staying for? We might have a few evenings to fill.'

He shrugs. 'I don't expect you to put me up for the whole two weeks. I'll be at my friend's house photographing foxes for some of the time anyway.'

'You can stay as long as you like,' I hear myself say. 'I'll get you the spare key, so you can let yourself in.'

He smiles. 'Thanks, Orla. I really appreciate you letting me stay, you know.'

'It's no problem. I just hope you'll be comfortable, that's all.'

'Don't worry about me.' He settles back against the sofa, looking up at the ceiling. Tucking my legs beneath me, I turn to face him, studying his profile. He looks older, more manly than he used to. His skin's tanned from the sun and there's a fan of fine lines around his eyes. His shoulders are broader, his body harder. I want to touch him, but I know I can't. He's out of my reach now.

He turns his head and looks at me. 'What are you thinking about?'

'You look different.'

'Me? How?'

'Just older. Harder. More together. More like a man, I suppose.'

He narrows his eyes and laughs. 'I was 28 when you met me. I should have looked like a man then.'

'Yeah, I know, but you still had something of a boy about you back then. And you were so wild-looking. You were all over the place. It was quite a shock when I first saw you at your exhibition, in your suit and with your hair all tidy.'

He laughs softly. 'Those things are just an illusion. I can still look just as scruffy and wild, believe me. I'm still the same guy that doesn't know what day of the week it is half the time.'

'Should have got yourself some days of the week underpants like me,' I say, then blush as I realise I shouldn't be talking about my knickers with him these days.

Aiden laughs. 'They were funny. I still can't believe you had them.' Pushing up the sleeve of his top, he scratches his sinewy forearm. His nails ruffle the dark hairs and leave white streaks on his tanned skin. 'How are your family?'

My stomach drops slightly and I tense. My father died last year, and I'm not sure I want to discuss it with Aiden. It's still too raw. 'Mum and Ray are fine. Keeley, my sister, is 15 now and is getting a bit of a handful so Mum just moans about her when I speak to her. She's fine though. Just a typical teenager. Do you remember Katie who lived upstairs?'

'Of course.'

'Yes, well, she's married with a baby now.'

'Did she marry the lad she was with when I was around?'

'Yeah, that's the one. They live on one of the new-build housing estates on the outskirts of Hawksley. She's really happy, bless her.'

'Good. Has she got a boy or a girl?'

'A girl. Amy. She's so gorgeous. I want to cry when I hold her. She's all warm and soft and perfect and has tiny hands with tiny, tiny fingers.'

'As babies generally do.'

'Well, yes, but she is exceptionally cute. She's coming up to six months now. I'll have to go and see her soon to get my cuddles.'

Aiden cocks an eyebrow. 'Somebody's broody.'

'Who, me? No! I like to be able to give her back,' I lie, then wonder why I'm even bothering.

'So, you're still all about your career?'

His words sting, and I'm momentarily thrown. I suppose he's right though, so I just nod. Aiden tilts his head, watching me curiously.

'You don't look too sure about that,' he says.

'Don't I?' I laugh and lean forward to get my tea again.

'Could you be starting to see a future that's not just about your career?'

I frown. 'I don't think I ever saw a future that was just about my career.' I say, crossly. 'It was only a five-year plan I made, remember. You were the one who said you don't do relationships and never, ever want children.'

'Did I say that?' He blinks like he's surprised.

'Yes, you did.'

'Oh.'

'Have you changed your mind?'

'Maybe.'

'On what? A relationship or the children? Or both?'

He pulls a face. 'Both, I suppose. If I met the right woman.'

'Wow! You'd change your stance on not having children?' I gaze at him in wonder. 'But you said the world was full enough without you adding to it. What's changed your mind?'

He shrugs. 'Just getting older, I guess. Besides, my brother and his wife are going through IVF at the moment. Hearing them talk about it and seeing how much it means to them, and my parents too, has kind of changed my perspective. I don't know why really. We'll see, I guess. It's not like it's on the cards, is it? I'm not even with anyone. And I'm not thinking *yes, I want kids*, I'm just a bit more open to the possibility to having kids one day in the future. Maybe. If the circumstances are right.' He shrugs again and laughs.

I'm reeling from this revelation that he might consider having children. Not that it makes any difference to me, of course. Why should it? We're not together anymore and he's only here for a measly two weeks. He's not going to be having babies with me, is he?

I think about Katie, in her neat little house with its neat little garden and feel a pang in my stomach. She must spend her life cleaning because everything seems to sparkle. The taps, the worktop, the bathroom. The scent of new carpets and paint still

227

linger in the air, mingling with the fragrance of baby lotion and nappies. It's a world away from my dark mouldy flat; it's a sunshine-filled home, full of love and hope and happiness. I love visiting her. Love seeing her so happy. It's the life she always dreamed of and I'm so glad it worked out for her. It's funny, but I used to feel a little bit sorry for her. All those boyfriends seemed like such hard work and it exhausted me just watching her go off on her dates. But looking at how happy she is now, I wonder if I should have spent more time searching for Mr Right, instead of focusing all my attention on my career.

Of course, it could be argued that I did find my Mr Right. That summer I spent with Aiden was pretty much perfect. I wonder where we'd be now if I had have gone with him to India. Would we have made it? I tell myself we wouldn't, but who knows what could have been.

'What are you thinking?' Aiden asks.

'Oh, nothing.' I laugh as I brush the question off. 'Just Katie and how happy she is now.'

'You're clucking about that baby, aren't you?'

'No!' I laugh. 'Well, maybe a little. To be honest, it's surprising how long it's taken me to feel this broody. I was 12 when my sister was born and I was obsessed by her. She made everything better. I couldn't wait to get home from school so I could hold her and give her a bottle. My mum was even worried I'd go off and get pregnant so I could have my own baby. I had to sit through so many lectures about teenage pregnancy and how it could affect my education and job prospects.' I shake my head, remembering. 'She needn't have worried though. The love triangle between her, my dad and my stepdad was enough to put me off men for life!' I look at him and laugh. 'Well, not quite for life, but you know, until I met you.' I suddenly realise what I've said and go bright red. 'Anyway, would you like another drink?'

'Yes, please. But surely James isn't your first boyfriend since me?'

'No, no, I've had a couple,' I say, going into the kitchen and rinsing the mugs. 'No one serious though.'

'No? How come?'

'Oh, err, I don't know, really.' I squirm, uncomfortable to be discussing this with Aiden. 'I just haven't met anyone I've really clicked with. James is nice though. Anyway, I'm not sure I want to discuss this with you, Aiden.'

'Why not? We're adults, aren't we? I haven't seen you for five years, I want to know what's going on in your life. I've had sex with women since you, I don't see why you shouldn't have.'

I go hot then cold as I turn away to boil the kettle. I'm filled with sick, impotent jealousy, which I know I have no business to be feeling. Of course, he's had sex in the past five years. He's a guy. He's on TV. He's on a list of the world's sexiest men! Everyone wants to sleep with him now. Even Emma.

'Not many, of course. There's a limit to how many women you meet on top of a mountain or in the middle of a rainforest. But I've had the odd hook-up.'

I struggle to control my emotions as I noisily get the teabags out of the cupboard. 'I bet you're getting more offers since you've been on TV!' I say, pleased that my voice sounds reasonable and steady, even though I'm screaming internally. 'I bet you're fighting them off. Actually, I'd have thought you'd have met someone working in the same field as you, by now.'

'Nah.' He picks up a magazine from the coffee table and starts flicking through it. 'Just crap one-night stands, mostly. Waking up feeling awful the next morning.' He exhales long and deep. 'I'm surprised no one's snapped you up though.'

'Snapped me up?' I force a laugh. 'Like I'm on offer in a supermarket or something?'

'No, I just mean you're gorgeous and lovely and any man would be lucky to have you.'

I blush, feeling a bit better, but then he adds, 'Or are you still hung up on your mum and dad's divorce?'

229

'Hung up?' I say, surprised. 'Is hung up really the right term?' The kettle comes to the boil and I pour it into the mugs.

'I'd say so, yes.'

'I wouldn't.' I frown as I stir the teabags round, watching the water turn amber. 'It made me careful, that's all, and there's nothing wrong with careful.'

He laughs, and I hear a note of sarcasm in there. 'Maybe.'

I pour the milk before carrying the mugs over to the sofa and sitting back down. Aiden's flicking through an old issue of *Woman and Home* magazine, which I buy so I can look at the nice homely interiors and dream about what my life could have been like if I'd been less careful. I'm surprised Aiden's interested in it, although from the speed he's flicking through I doubt he's taking anything in. His hands are shaking slightly, and I wonder if our conversation is making him as uncomfortable as it is me.

'So, has there really been no one?'

I shrug. 'Well, I'm seeing James.'

'Ah yes, the guy who you've been dating for a couple of months but who you haven't brought back to your flat? I'm guessing you haven't had sex with him yet?'

I blow the steam rising from my mug of tea. 'I could have been back to his.'

'True. Though from the way you said it's very early days I'm guessing you haven't.'

'We could have been having sex in other places, you know. Public toilets and car parks and bus shelters. That kind of thing.'

Aiden visibly flinches. 'I don't see you doing that kind of thing, Orla. Although, thinking about it, you did have sex with me in the back of a truck so …'

'Hey!' I slap his thigh, almost spilling my tea, and he laughs. 'It was beautiful and romantic, beneath a star-studded sky with the sound of the ocean in the background.'

Aiden's laughing and I feel like it's the most genuine laugh

I've heard from him since he's been back. 'Well, I'm glad you remember it like that.'

'It's important that I do, thank you.'

'Okay, sorry.' He stops laughing, but his grin still stretches from ear to ear. 'So, the, err, bus shelters and public toilets?'

I wrinkle my nose. 'No. You're right, I haven't slept with James yet. We're not anywhere near that stage to be honest.'

'Really? Wow, the guy doesn't move fast, does he?'

'No, but he's sweet and he's nice to have a drink with.'

'Christ! Sounds like you've friend-zoned him already.'

'Friend-zoned?'

'Yeah, maybe I should have a word with him, give him some pointers on how to escape the friend-zone.'

'Don't be naughty! I haven't friend-zoned him at all. *We* were friends. You were definitely friend-zoned at the beginning.'

'No, I'm not having that! You always fancied me.'

'I did not!'

'Yeah you did. Admit it.'

'I did not!' I laugh, incredulously. 'I thought you were scruffy and … you lived in a tent, for goodness' sake!'

'What's wrong with that? I'm an outdoorsy kind of guy. An adventurer. I'd rather sleep under the stars any day than sleep under a mouldy roof.' He casts a disapproving eye towards my damp patch.

'Feel free to go and sleep outside,' I say, as a particularly vicious gust of wind splatters rain against the window. 'It's lovely and quiet in the yard behind the shops, and I'm sure there'll be a handy cardboard box around.'

'Oh no, Orla,' he says, innocently with a glance towards the window. 'I'd love to but I've said I'll stay with you now and I know how fond of me you are. I don't want to disappoint you.'

'No, no, Aiden. You must do what's best for you. If you'd rather sleep under the stars, then that's what you must do.'

'No, Orla.' He puts his arm around my shoulder, drawing me

231

against him. 'It'll be hard, but I've said I'll spend this time with you, and that's what I'll do.'

'You're so selfless, Aiden!' I flutter my eyelashes and clutch my heart. 'I can't thank you enough for coming to stay in my flat with me.'

'I know. That's just the kind of guy I am!' He laughs and ruffles my hair, and I sit back up straight, laughing. 'Seriously, though, do you think you should call your landlord again?'

'No, I left a message. I don't want to hassle him on a Friday evening.'

'What the hell, Orla! Are you a newspaper reporter or what? I thought you guys were meant to be like a pack of rabid hounds!'

'Ah, I am when it's a story, but less so when it comes to hounding my landlord. Besides, I know it's going to be a nuisance when he actually comes to fix it. I'll have workmen in and I won't be able to sit down and relax.'

'You could always visit someone. Your mum, perhaps, or me?'

'You?'

'Yeah, why not?'

'And stay where? In your tent?'

'You loved my tent!'

'In the summer, perhaps.'

'Well, maybe sweet James will have escaped from the friend-zone by then and you'll be able to stay at his.'

'Hmmm.'

'You don't sound very thrilled by that?' He tips his head to one side. 'You don't seem very thrilled by anything, in fact. What's the matter? It's like you've given up on life.'

'I have not given up on life!' I elbow him in the side. 'Cheeky sod! I just don't want the hassle of having my flat invaded by workmen.'

'You'd rather live with the mould?'

'Yes.'

'Well, if it's here to stay, maybe you should name it like a pet, or something.' He closes one eyes as he peers up at the dark, spreading stain. 'What do you reckon? Maurice?'

'Maurice? Why Maurice?'

'Mouldy Maurice?'

'Damp Dwayne?' I wrinkle my nose. 'No, it's no good. I'm not naming it. It's too depressing.'

'Well, if you're going to live with it you may as well make a friend out of it.'

'You're such a strange man.' I give him a sidelong look. 'You've not even been drinking.'

'No, I know. But at least you've acknowledged that the damp is depressing. Especially when you've got this, showing you how lovely your home could be.' He flaps the magazine at me.

'If I had the money, time or inclination.'

'Why did you buy the magazine then? Did you think a few scatter cushions and a scented candle would make the damp magically disappear?'

I sigh. 'No. I realised that a long time ago. I just like looking at the pictures of other people's cosy homes.'

'That's sad, Orla.'

'I know. I'm a sad case, it seems. But, you know, it's all fine. I'm in London and I love my job.'

Aiden curls his lip. 'But where you live is rubbish!'

'No, it's fine. I'll just work my way up and get more money somehow, then I can get a better place.'

'And what about all those babies you want?'

I puff out my cheeks and shrug. 'I'll just play with Katie's. All my friends seem to be getting married and settling down these days so there'll be plenty to go round soon, I should think. Maybe Keeley will have one, then I can be Auntie Orla.'

'Would that be enough?'

'Yes, I suppose so.'

'Really? Jesus Christ, Orla. How about we draw up a plan for you that includes getting a life?'

'Thanks very much! I have a life already, I'll have you know. Just because it's not how you thought my life would be doesn't make it any less good or rewarding. Besides, having babies is very much dependent on finding a decent man that wants to have babies with me. I have yet to find such a man.'

Aiden laughs. 'But you have James now. Your plan could be to seduce James and get pregnant, then trap him into marrying you. Does he earn a lot of money?'

'I think so. Maybe.'

'There you go then. You could have a nice house too.'

'And what if I don't love James or he doesn't love me?'

'Bah well, we'll worry about the fine details later.'

'This is all very devious, Aiden. I really can't approve. And I can't believe you'd suggest I'd get pregnant just to trap a man into marriage. Besides, this isn't the early twentieth century, you know. He wouldn't have to marry me. It's more likely I'd end up raising the child on my own, stuck in this flat with mouldy Maurice for the rest of my life.'

'Bloody hell, that's a depressing thought. God, I hate that James! Fancy getting you pregnant and not marrying you? That *bastard*! I'll kill him when I get my hands on him.'

'Aiden!' I laugh.

'Hey, I'm just being a good friend here. I'll always have your back, you know that, right? I'll come and visit you and the baby. Bring you food parcels and give you money for when you can't afford the electricity. And I'll get my mum to knit you woolly jumpers to keep you warm when mouldy Maurice spreads all over the ceiling and all over the walls.'

'Stop, Aiden!' I groan. 'It's too depressing!'

'Yeah, it is.' He looks grimly up at the corner of the room again. 'You need to find somewhere else to live.'

'I know.'

'I mean it.' He looks at me, and even though he's trying to be disapproving, my stomach tightens with desire. I want to feel his arms around me, to feel him kissing me and holding me tight. I want …

'Another cup of tea?' I offer, getting up to go to the kitchen.

'Jesus, Orla, I'm still drinking the last one. I'll have a beer if you have one though.'

'Okay.'

'I'll go to the shop and replace what I drink.'

'No need. I mostly drink wine or gin these days, and they've been in there for ages. I'm glad to be rid of them.'

'Do I need to check the expiry date?'

'Maybe.' I laugh as I go to get one from the fridge. 'Oh no, they're still in date. You're okay. So, what have you got planned while you're here then?' I ask when I sit back down next to him. 'I know you said about your friend and his fox family, but is there anything else?'

'I've got an interview on a radio station, a meeting with my producer about a documentary on recycling, and I want to look around some of the local parks for birds.'

'Will there be any in winter? I thought they'd have all flown south.'

'No, some birds come to us to winter. I'm hoping to see a waxwing or fieldfare. Do you want to come with me tomorrow?'

'Yes, I'll come with you,' I say, excited in spite of the wind howling outside and the rain hammering on the roof. I'm not even sure I've got a coat waterproof enough to be out in a park all day. Maybe I could buy one from somewhere on the way. 'When are you going fox watching?'

'Tomorrow night, probably.'

'So you come and stay with me, but leave me all alone on a Saturday night?'

'I thought you'd be out with James,' he says apologetically. 'I didn't want to make a nuisance of myself.'

I hide my smile behind my hand, amused by the irony of him not wanting to be a nuisance, even after he's invited himself to stay in my flat.

'I can cancel if you prefer?'

'No, it's fine. I'm used to spending Saturday nights alone.'

'Don't you usually go out on a Saturday?'

'Not really. Not often, anyway.'

'What does James do?'

'Like I said, I've only known him a few weeks, and he's actually had things on the past few weekends. He's had stag weekends and family birthday parties and he's been away with work.'

'Well, for the record, when I was with you, I never wanted to be anywhere else other than by your side.'

'Aww, Aiden. That's sweet.' I want to add something sarcastic about when he went off to India, but I know it's true, we really did want to spend every minute of every day together. I've never felt that way about anybody since. For one horrible moment, I think I'm going to cry, but I manage to hold it together as I give him a rather wobbly smile. 'I still can't believe you're here, you know. It feels like a dream.'

'A dream or a nightmare?' he laughs lightly. 'It's really good to see you again, Orla.'

'It's good to see you, too.'

We smile at each other, and suddenly the air feels electric. I see the amber flecks in his eyes and have a strong urge to push back the hair that's fallen over his brow. His gaze drops to my mouth and the butterflies in my stomach take flight.

'I'm just going to the loo,' I say, not trusting myself to sit next to him any longer. My legs feel rubbery as I cross the room to the bathroom and lock the door behind me. I lean against the door for a moment, my eyes screwed tightly shut. I wanted him to kiss me. I wanted to feel his lips on mine. But what if he had? Two weeks and he'd be gone again, and I'd be right back to square one.

Not to mention the fact I'm seeing James.

I try to summon up an image of James in an effort to ward off my feelings for Aiden, but I can't even picture him. I can only visualise pieces of him, like some kind of jigsaw puzzle I can't fit together. Blond hair, blue eyes, round face. How does he smile? What are his teeth like? Aiden's smile floats into my mind and I draw in a deep shaking breath. This isn't helping.

Giving myself a shake, I use the toilet and wash my hands.

'Is it really eleven o'clock?' I say, when I go back out and catch a glimpse of the time on the oven clock. 'How did it get so late?'

'Eleven o'clock! Oh no! Is that way past your bedtime?' Aiden laughs as he puts the bottle of beer to his lips. 'It is a Friday, you know.'

'I know. I just meant that it feels like you've only been here a few minutes, that's all.'

'Well, time flies when you're having fun.'

He smiles, and the butterflies take flight again. Do I trust myself to sit back next to him?

'I am quite tired, though,' I hear myself say. 'I really ought to go to bed.'

'Okay, I suppose we had a pretty late one last night. I'm tired too, actually.'

Getting to his feet, he stretches and I can't help my eyes wandering over his body. The side of his top lifts slightly, exposing a couple of inches of the smooth, taut flesh above his hip.

'Will you be okay?' I say, trying to ignore the rush of heat between my legs. 'Do you need a pillow or blanket?'

'No, I'm good.'

'Well, help yourself to anything.'

'Thanks.' He raises an eyebrow and sniggers slightly. I don't know what he's laughing at, and I'm not sure I want to, so I go back into the bathroom to brush my teeth. When I get back out, he's laid his sleeping bag out on the floor behind the sofa, and is finishing off his beer.

'Goodnight then!' I call as I go into my bedroom.

'Goodnight, Orla. See you in the morning.'

Once the door is shut between us, I stand for a moment, listening to the sounds of him moving around in the lounge. The kitchen tap gushes as he runs himself a glass of water, then the bathroom door closes. It's strange having someone else's noises in my flat. I'm used to the sounds of traffic, sirens, and occasional rowdiness from the street below, but not the sound of the toilet flushing or footsteps crossing the lounge.

And it's even stranger that it's Aiden.

What the hell am I doing letting him stay? My heart flutters in panic. I should be distancing myself from him so I don't get hurt, not inviting him back into my life. What happens when he leaves again? Will it hurt just as much as last time?

Climbing into bed, I pull the covers up to my chin and stare up into the darkness. The one good thing about having him here in my flat, with all his stuff all over the place, is that he's likely to get on my nerves. Who knows, maybe I'll be glad to see the back of him when he leaves in two weeks. Having him here might be the antidote I need to get over him at last. He's bound to have changed over the years, and so am I. We're sure to be different. So different, perhaps, that we might not get on at all these days. It's different already, isn't it? Look at us, settling down to sleep in different rooms. Five years ago, we'd never have had this much space between us. We were always together. Even before we *slept* together, we slept together. I was always touching him or leaning against him or hugging him. Now I get the sense that we're circling each other, scared to get too close. Or maybe that's just me. Whichever, I'm comforted by the notion that this might be the nudge I need to let go of Aiden. I don't have to let go of the lovely memories, but it might mean that I can finally move on.

Chapter 19

The next morning, we go to the park. The rain has stopped, but the sky is still steely-grey and the wind blows cold. Everything is dripping: the bare trees, the bushes, the metal fence, the wooden benches. I'm surprised to see other people out and about so early on such a damp, dismal Saturday morning. There's a couple of people jogging, a woman walking a basset hound, and an old couple walking hand in hand along the path.

It's nice to be outside in the fresh air though. Taking a walk in the park isn't something I'd usually do. It occurs to me that most of my life is spent indoors these days, either in my flat, at the office, or stuck on a crowded tube. I even exercise inside a gym. The summer I spent with Aiden was probably the most time I've ever spent outdoors. I loved it too. Once Aiden left, it all stopped, which is sad really. He'd taught me so much about the local birds and wildlife, but apart from hanging a birdfeeder and a bug hotel in the communal garden of my block of flats, I didn't really do anything with my newly acquired knowledge. Spending so much time with him had influenced me in other ways though. He'd made me more environmentally conscious about the amount of energy I use and waste I produce, and I'd switched to being vegetarian, with a view to becoming vegan eventually.

'I can't believe you haven't got a waterproof coat,' Aiden says, grinning at my navy-blue duffel coat.

'Why? This is fine! It's not even raining that much anymore.' I stuff my hands deep into its pockets and tuck my chin into the yellow scarf tied around my neck.

'What happened to that yellow one you used to have?'

'I lost it, somehow. Besides, it was only a thin summer coat. It wouldn't have done today.'

It gives me a warm feeling that he remembers what I used to wear five years ago.

'You look like Paddington Bear in that,' he says, and snaps a photo of me.

'Hey! No photos, please.'

'Why not? I don't have enough photos of you!'

'You don't need any photos of me. Just look for your birds.'

Laughing, he returns to scanning the trees. He's wearing a black jacket and blue jeans and his camera hangs around his neck. Dark stubble lines his jaw, and I think how much it suits him, adding definition to his face and making him look older and sexier. I remember how his stubble used to feel when he kissed me, and …

Okay, let's just backtrack here and focus on how messy my lounge was this morning after he'd upended his bag to sort through his clothes. And his sleeping bag is still unfurled behind the sofa. Not to mention the amount of washing up he produces. Although, to be fair, he did offer to do that himself.

'See anything?' I ask, stifling a yawn.

'Not yet.' He gives me a look. 'Are you bored already? We've only just got here.'

'I know! I'm tired, that's all, but I'm enjoying the fresh air.' I tip my head back, just as the branch above me drips water directly into my eye. Glad he didn't see, I wipe it away with a gloved

240

finger. 'I was just thinking that I don't spend enough time outdoors these days.'

'You should get out more. It's good for you.'

'I know. But since you left, I've not really spent any time with nature at all.'

'That's a shame.' Aiden frowns down at his camera, fiddling with a dial on the top.

'I know. It is really.' Despite the grey sky and skeleton trees, the park is still beautiful. The neatly trimmed grass and shrubbery is pleasing, and though the branches appear to be devoid of birds this morning, there's always the squirrels. One scampers towards us, obviously used to people bringing food. Squatting down, Aiden produces a monkey nut from his pocket and holds it out so the squirrel comes closer. It reaches out with its two front paws to take the nut. I expect it to run off immediately, but it stays on the path to eat while Aiden snaps a few photos. I'd forgotten how still Aiden can be. How deeply calm he is. He has an intensity about him when he works – the ability to focus his entire attention on that one thing he's trying to photograph.

Finishing the nut, the squirrel's bushy tail twitches as it sniffs the air, eager for more food.

'Do you want to feed it, Orla?'

'No thanks. It might bite me.'

'It won't bite! Look how tame it is!'

'It's lulling you into a false sense of security. It'll go in a rage in a minute and rip your face off.'

Lowering his camera, he smiles at the squirrel. 'You wouldn't do that, would you?' he says, passing it another nut.

My knees go weak. Who can resist a man that's kind to animals?

'Here,' he says to me, reaching into his pockets again, this time bringing out a handful of sunflower seeds. 'See if it will take these.'

'Oh great,' I say nervously, holding out my palm so he can fill it with seeds. 'So, I don't just get to pass it a nut, I actually have it eating out of my hand, do I?'

'Yep.'

The squirrel eyes me beadily as I squat down with my handful of seeds. Its whiskers quiver as it sniffs the air, then it moves towards me, placing its paws on my thumb as it eats the seeds from my hand. I close my eyes briefly at the sensation, forcing myself to focus on how cute it is, rather than considering how many fleas it might have, or how sharp its teeth and claws look.

'Perfect,' Aiden says, as he refocuses his camera lens and starts clicking away.

'You better not be getting me in any of these photographs,' I mutter.

'Just the squirrel.'

'Good.'

He laughs as he takes his eye away from the camera, then deliberately focuses on me and takes another photo.

'Oi!' I say, and the squirrel takes fright and races off up the nearest tree. Straightening up, I brush the last of the sunflower seeds onto the floor. 'You better not get any ideas about standing me in the centre of Trafalgar Square with a handful of sunflower seeds. I don't want a pigeon on my head.'

Aiden chuckles as he stares down at his camera, checking out the photographs. 'Now there's an idea,' he murmurs. His hair's fallen forward over his forehead again, and he flicks it back with a jerk of his head. I walk on to stop myself from staring.

'Hey, where are you going?' he says, catching up with me.

'Nowhere, just walking. Enjoying the cool damp air.'

'At least it's not pouring with rain.'

'True. You used to say that you tried to go to warmer places in the winter. You obviously timed your exhibition wrong, having to come back here in November.'

He shrugs. 'I'm moving back to Ireland, so I may as well get used to the cold and the damp. Besides, last winter I was in the Arctic so there's no comparison really.'

'Wow!' I glance up at him then away again. 'I can't imagine all the places you've been to and all the things you've seen.'

'No? Well, that's because you didn't come with me.'

'True.' I wince slightly, not wanting to return to our conversation after his exhibition, when he accused me of not being bothered when he left. An uncomfortable silence hangs between us for a moment, then he sighs.

'I'll have to take you through my photos some time.'

'Yes, definitely. I'd love to see them,' I say, sounding almost too eager. 'Where was your favourite place? India?'

As soon as I say it, I regret it. Why did I have to mention India? It's like I'm deliberately trying to take the conversation back to him leaving.

'No,' he says, sounding annoyed. 'I hated every moment of India.'

'Oh.' I feel oddly put out. Part of the reason I let him go without a fuss was because I knew India was a place he really wanted to see. I didn't want to stand in the way of that. It's a slap in the face to find he didn't really enjoy it.

Why didn't you come back then?

I can't really say that though. It was me who banned all contact. And if he thought I was glad to see the back of him at the airport, then maybe he didn't feel like he could. My stomach turns over at the thought.

'Is the pond this way?' Aiden's voice jolts me out of my reverie as we come to a fork in the path.

'Huh? Oh yeah.' We take the left-hand path and walk down to the large pond. Aside from a robin, a pigeon and a couple of blackbirds, we've seen nothing out of the ordinary as far as bird-life is concerned. And when we reach the pond, there's nothing more exotic than a group of swans. They are beautiful though.

Aiden photographs them as they sail gracefully towards us through the still water.

'I bet you've got hundreds of photographs of swans,' I say, as he kneels, clicking away.

'I feel like I've got hundreds of photographs of everything. But there's always that one special one that could be waiting. The light's not great today, but you never know.'

I stay silent as he works, not wanting to distract him. The clouds thin a little, allowing the pale winter sun to glow through and the flat grey water instantly looks more attractive, its surface sparkling as it ripples in the wake of the swans. I step back as they approach, but Aiden stays put as the large white birds crowd around him, expecting some bread or seed to come their way. He doesn't even move when they peck at his boots and tug at his trousers. I move further away to sit on a nearby bench.

One pecks at Aiden's camera lens and he stands up quickly. I laugh, and he turns to look at me, laughing too.

'It could've been worse,' I say. 'It could have been your nose.'

'Yeah, true.' He digs into another one of his pockets and sprinkles some seed on the ground before coming to sit next to me.

'What have you got?' I ask, shuffling closer so I can see his camera.

'Meh, nothing much,' he says, scrolling through.

'Did you get it pecking the lens?'

'No. Self-preservation took over.' He laughs then leans forward to look past me, towards a small wooden hut in the distance. 'Do you think they sell coffee in there?'

'Maybe. If they're open.'

'Shall I go and see?'

'Go on then.'

I smile as he gets up and walks along the path to the booth. I can't imagine it will be open, but you never know. He disappears around the corner, and to my surprise, reappears a few minutes later carrying two cups of coffee.

'Hurray!' I cheer, as he gets closer. He grins and sits down next to me on the bench.

'So, weren't you invited to whatever your boyfriend's doing tonight?'

'No.' Hearing Aiden refer to James as my boyfriend causes a pang deep down in my stomach. I duck my head and blow on the steam rising from my coffee. 'He's gone to Manchester for his grandmother's birthday party.'

'Why weren't you invited?'

'Me? No, why would I be invited?'

He pulls a face, puzzled. 'Well, usually if you're dating someone, you take them to family events, don't you? Even I know that, and I don't date.'

'Oh!' I shrug. 'It didn't even occur to me, to be honest. I probably wouldn't have gone anyway.'

'Why not?'

'It's too soon for that kind of thing. If it was local, I might have minded not being invited, but it's in Manchester so would have involved a weekend away.'

'Oh no! Not a *whole* weekend! I'd have thought you'd be glad to get out of your flat for a weekend at least.'

'Well, it's a good job I didn't go, isn't it?' I say, ignoring the jibe about my flat. 'I wouldn't have been here for you if I'd have gone.'

Aiden smiles and looks away. The swans have finished their seed and are floating back out across the pond.

'We were meant to be going out last night, actually,' I say, after a few moments have passed. 'But he had too much on so he cancelled.'

Aiden frowns at the swans, then turns to frown at me some more. 'He cancelled you?'

245

I shrug. 'It's no big deal. I was pleased actually because I was so tired and the weather was so bad. And then you showed up, so …' I leave the rest of the sentence hanging and sip my coffee instead.

'Wow, obviously you two are mad for each other,' Aiden says sarcastically.

'Says the man who doesn't date.'

'Says the man who couldn't keep his hands off you.'

'Says the man who went to India and didn't even like it!'

'Oh!' His eyebrows shoot up and he laughs in surprise. 'Well, do you know why I didn't like India?' he says, his voice rising with indignation. 'Because you didn't come with me, that's why. I spent the whole time I was there pining for you.'

'Why didn't you come back then?' I say, annoyed.

'Come back? What to? The girl who didn't even cry when we said goodbye? The girl who didn't want to keep in touch with me?'

'Don't be ridiculous! You know why I didn't want you to write! I knew it would be too painful. Just like crying all over you at the airport would have made it ten times worse!'

'No, it wouldn't have!' He stares off across the water, his jaw tense. 'If you miss someone, you contact them and you draw comfort from that. If you care, you tell them so.'

I sit back, bewildered. 'Well, I'm sorry, Aiden, but I can't change the past. You didn't cry either!'

Aiden says nothing, just continues to watch the swans' steady progress across to the reedbeds on the other side of the pond. I can't believe he's playing the injured party when it was him who left. *He* left me, not the other way round! Doesn't he know how sad I was when he left? How I cried for weeks? How I stopped eating? No, I don't suppose he does.

I open my mouth to tell him how much I hurt, but then shut it again. To admit it, feels weak. Instead, I reach for the hand that's resting on his leg and cover it with my own. He looks down,

246

and for a moment I think he might shake me off, but then he turns his hand and slips his fingers through mine, squeezing gently.

I still don't understand why it feels so right when he holds my hand.

'If you'd come back …' My voice trails away, thinking of all that could have been if he had. All that we lost. It's hard to express how I feel when I don't want to open up too much to him. 'I kept hoping you would.'

He looks at me. 'Why didn't you ask me to?'

'What?' I can't help laughing. 'Why would I stop you from doing your job? I just wanted what was best for you, and living with me in Hawksley, or even here, in London, would never have made you happy.'

Aiden looks away again, the expression on his face almost anguished. 'You knew how I felt about you, Orla. What we had was special. Surely you know that?'

'Yes, but I wanted to keep it that way. I was sure you'd have moved on and found someone better.'

'There is no one better than you, Orla,' he says in a low voice. 'Trust me, I've been all around the world, and I've never met anyone that I connect with like I do with you.'

My heart kicks in my chest, and I struggle to process what he's just said. More sun penetrates the cloud and the world brightens suddenly. I should tell him I've never met anyone better than him either, but that would reveal more than I'm ready to yet. I flounder for a moment, then laugh gently, making a joke out of it: 'Oh, come on, Aiden. You can't possibly have met *everyone* in the world!' I bump my shoulder against his. 'There'll be someone out there who's much better than me. She'll love camping and trekking up mountains and sleeping under the stars just as much as you, and she'll cry and sob at airports and she won't live in London with a dirty great damp patch in the corner of her sitting room.'

247

'Really?' He looks at me, eyebrow raised, and I'm relieved when a slow smile spreads across his face. 'Somehow, I doubt that.'

I open my mouth to reply, but he gets up from the bench, pulling me up with him. 'Come on, let's go. I've got to get my stuff ready to go to Ben's.'

'Why are you going to Ben's again?'

'He's the guy with the fox family in his back garden. I said I'd go this afternoon and we'd make a night of it.'

'Oh!' I'm winded by disappointment. A whole night without Aiden? I can't even …

But then I catch myself. He's been back two days. *Two days*! I can't feel like this after just two days. It's good he's out tonight. He should go out every night. In fact, I should ask him to leave. I can't become reliant on him being around when he's leaving in two weeks. My thoughts are muddled as we walk along the path, back towards the gate. I wish he hadn't said that about there being no one better than me. Even after laughing it off, I can't get it out of my head and I know his words are going to play over and over in my head all night.

We catch the tube back to my flat and he packs up his stuff, ready to go to his friend's house for some fox watching. I watch him from the kitchen as I fix our lunch.

'Are you alright?' he asks, when we've finished eating. 'You're very quiet.'

'Am I?' I shrug. 'Just tired, I guess.' Gathering our plates together, I take them to the sink to wash. 'I'll go to the gym in a bit. That'll perk me up.'

Aiden comes over and stands in the kitchen, watching me. 'I could cancel tonight if you like? Stay in with you?'

I look over my shoulder at him. 'No! You don't have to do that!' I laugh, though my heart is crying out for him to stay. 'No, you go. I'm going to the gym, then I'll have a bath and an early night.'

Aiden frowns slightly and looks down at his boots. 'Okay.'

Shrugging on his coat, he grabs his bag and hoists it onto his shoulder. 'Right, see you.'

'Oh! Bye!' I say, as the door slams shut behind him.

I stare round at my suddenly empty flat, bewildered by the creeping coldness that's stealing through my bones. It's like he's taken a piece of me with him. My heart, perhaps, or my lungs. My liver even. I feel completely hollow. And as I stare and stare, I realise he's taken all of his stuff, not just some.

Is he coming back?

Chapter 20

There's still no sign of Aiden the following morning. Not that I was expecting him back or anything, but still, I was kind of hoping he might roll in in the early hours of the morning. I check my phone for messages, but there's nothing. Resolving to do my own thing, I go to the gym, then shower and change before catching the tube to Oxford Street to do some Christmas shopping. It will be good to get organised and start wrapping. Then I can relax and enjoy the run-up to Christmas without stressing as much as I usually do.

I could get Aiden something too, then he could take it back to Ireland with him. It's a good job he's not with me, I tell myself, before realising the chances of Aiden coming shopping down Oxford Street are slim to none. I'm sure he'd be horrified by the thought.

I glance at my phone to see if he's called. There's nothing, of course. I don't know why I keep checking. He didn't say he would call and there's no reason why he should. The only reason would be to get back into my flat, and he has his own key.

Even so, I'm disappointed every time I find he hasn't called. Maybe I just want reassurance that he is actually coming back. After he left yesterday, I checked in my wardrobe and found his suit still hanging there, so I'm pretty sure he will be back. But still, I'd like to know when.

Ha! So much for not letting him back in. I can't stop thinking about him. I can't get the sound of his voice out of my head. The way he laughs. The way he touches me. I already know it's going to hurt just as much when he leaves this time. I sigh heavily, and the woman sitting next to me on the tube shuffles further away.

Oxford Street is teeming with people, but I manage to get my shopping done in good time. It helps that I know what I'm looking for and everything I buy is small and easy to carry. I buy my mum earrings, my sister make-up, Katie perfume, and Ray a jumper. The hustle and bustle of the city street helps take my mind off Aiden, and the afternoon passes pleasingly quickly. I give up looking for a present for him in the end, but I reason I've still got time to get him something before he leaves. It's only on the train home that I realise I haven't bought anything for James. I haven't even thought about him, in fact. Not once.

What does that mean?

Well, I know what it means, but I don't feel like acknowledging it just yet.

I'm convinced Aiden will be back by the time I get home, but when my flat door swings open to reveal nothing but empty space and shadows, my heart plummets to the floor. I'm so disappointed I could cry. The thought of spending another night alone in my flat makes my bones itch.

There's nothing I can do about it though. I need to be practical and keep my head together. Closing the door behind me, I kick off my shoes and carry the shopping bags through to my bedroom.

At least I can spend the evening wrapping them.

At least I can watch one of Aiden's documentaries on the TV.

At least I can eat my dinner in my pyjamas.

Always a silver lining.

But by eight o'clock, I've done all of those things and I'm

bored and lonely. The jumper Aiden wore yesterday is flung over the back of the sofa, so I pull it on over my pyjama top, inhaling his scent. Somehow, it makes me feel closer to him and reminds me of how I used to wear his clothes all the time. I suddenly have an overwhelming desire to hear his voice, and before I can talk myself out of it, I pick up my phone and ring his number.

'Ssup?' He answers on the second ring and my heart leaps.

It takes a moment for my heart to settle, and then I can't think of anything to say. 'Ssup? What kind of greeting is that? I could have been your producer or someone else important.'

'Well, my producer's number's is stored under the name Alan, while yours is stored under the name Orla, so I figured it was a pretty safe bet that you were Orla and not Alan.'

'Oh, of course.' I clear my throat, embarrassed by my stupidity.

'What can I do for you?' he asks after a moment's pause.

'Nothing really,' I say, keeping my voice breezy. 'It just occurred to me I never checked you found your friend's house okay.'

'Really? You're checking now?' He laughs in disbelief. 'I've been here over twenty-four hours already, Orla.'

'Well … exactly. I just thought I'd check you weren't dead in a ditch somewhere.' I wince at the stony silence coming from the other end. 'Well, as long as you're okay. When are you coming back?'

'Don't know. Tomorrow or the next day. Sometime. Why? Is it a problem?' He sounds annoyed, and I wonder if he thinks I'm mithering him or being a nuisance.

'Not at all, you've got a key, haven't you in case I'm at work or out or something?'

'Yep.'

'Right, well …' My voice trails off, and I don't know what to say to him next, but I'm not ready to end the call yet. Silence stretches between us, and I flounder around for something to say. 'Are the foxes okay?' I venture at last.

He doesn't answer immediately, and for a horrible moment I

think he might have hung up already, but then he sighs and says, 'Yeah, they're good. Got some good shots.'

'Great!'

He sniffs and I hear the sound of him scratching his stubble. I close my eyes, imagining it rough beneath my fingers as I stroke his face, or grazing my chin as we kiss like we used to.

'Well, you'll be glad you weren't with me today, because I went Christmas shopping,' I say, wrenching my mind back to reality.

'Sounds awful.' He couldn't sound less interested if he tried.

'Yes, I'm tired now.'

'Best go to bed then.'

'Yep, I may as well.' There's a raw pain in my gut that's shooting pins and needles down my arms and legs. 'I'll see you tomorrow or the next day or sometime whenever then.'

'Yeah. Sometime whenever. Nice one.' He sounds so pissed off it takes my breath away and I freeze, wondering what I said to upset him so much.

'Bye then,' I say, in a tiny voice.

'Bye,' he says, in a hard voice that I've never heard before. 'Oh, and Orla?'

'Yes?'

'Ring me back when you've worked up the courage to say what you actually phoned to say in the first place.'

The phone goes dead and I go cold. Then hot. Then cold again. What does he mean? I didn't want to say anything in particular. I just needed to hear his voice.

I don't ring him back. Instead I go to bed feeling bruised and sad, hugging his jumper close to me.

'Blimey, Orla, you look rough!' Belinda stops by my desk and peers at me. 'Are you ill?'

'Maybe. I think I might be coming down with something,' I say, throwing a balled-up piece of paper into my wastepaper basket.

253

'Christ! Well, don't give me the flu. Go home if you don't feel well. You can work from there instead.'

'Thanks, Belinda, you're all heart,' I mutter as she stalks away from my desk. I don't want to go home and I know I haven't got the flu. I'm just miserable and cranky because of Aiden sodding Byrne.

I keep replaying last night's phone conversation over and over in my head. I'm still so confused about it. Why was he angry with me? The only thing I can think of is that I was disturbing him, and he resented me checking up on him. After all that stuff he said about how he wished we'd kept in touch and never thinking of me as an annoying possessive ex-girlfriend too!

Well, he needn't worry, because I won't be phoning him again.

As if on cue, my phone rings and his name appears on the caller display. Snatching it up, I answer immediately, my heart pumping hard.

'Hello?'

'Hi, have you seen my jumper?'

'Which one?' I say, even though I know exactly which one he means. I screw my eyes shut, realising I'm going to have to admit to wearing it last night.

'I left it on the back of the sofa?'

'Oh, I think I wore it last night because I was cold,' I say, making my voice as breezy as possible to show it's not a big deal. 'It's probably in my bedroom. I'll wash it with my stuff if you like?'

'No need, I've got it. It's tangled up with your pyjamas.'

'Sorry!' I cringe.

'It's okay. You always used to wear my clothes back in the day. You used to say you liked my smell.'

'Did I?' I force a laugh. 'It was just handy, that's all, and I was—'

'Cold, yeah you said, I get it. I'm going to the launderette now so I'll see you later, okay?'

254

'Okay, bye.'

Well, at least he sounded happier than last night. And he said he'd see me later, so hopefully he'll be at my flat tonight. My mood lifts slightly. I hate myself for wanting to see him so badly when he was so off with me last night, but I can't help looking forward to going home.

But when I get home that evening, Aiden isn't there after all. It feels like Groundhog Day when my door swings open to reveal the dark lonely flat. A wave of loneliness envelops me as I click on the light and drop my bag by the door.

I don't want to be here on my own.

I don't want to be alone anymore.

I sit on my sofa with my coat and shoes still on, wondering if I've always felt this lonely and just never noticed. Maybe it took someone else being here to show me I need company. Or maybe I just miss Aiden because I'm still in love with him.

The thought irritates me so much I kick off my shoes and hang up my coat. I get some pasta out of the cupboard and pour a glass of wine. Then I phone Aiden. If he gets angry with me again I'll just tell him to leave.

'Hello?' He answers straight away, his voice friendly and warm.

'Hi,' I say, surprised. 'Are you coming back for dinner? I just wondered if I should make you some pasta?'

'No, sorry, I'm out for dinner with some guys from the production company this evening.' In the background, I hear laughter and the chink of glasses.

'Oh okay, no problem. Have fun!'

'I'll be back later though.'

'Will you?'

'Yeah, I shouldn't be too late.'

'Okay. You've got your key, haven't you? It's no bother whatever time you're back.'

There's a pause, and then he says, 'I want to see you, though.'

'What?' My heart kicks and I think I must have misheard him.

255

'Doesn't matter. I'll see you later.'

The phone goes dead and I stare at it in my hand, trying to ignore the storm of butterflies that have taken flight in my stomach. Well, that phone call has left me more confused than ever. If he's annoyed with me for phoning to check he's safe, why is he telling me he wants to see me later?

As soon as I put the phone down and turn away to make the pasta, it buzzes with a message, and I rush to it, thinking it might be from Aiden. My heart drops when I realise it's from James, asking if we're still on for our date tomorrow. I reply that we are, but I'm uneasy about it. Mostly because I know I don't want to go. But I can't cancel James because I want to see Aiden. Aiden will be gone soon, and I'll be left to pick up the pieces of my life afterwards. If Aiden's taught me anything these last few days, it's that I'm lonely. Pushing James away isn't going to remedy that once Aiden's gone.

Still, it's not great that I'm not enthusiastic about seeing James. Maybe I'll see how I feel about him when I see him tomorrow night. There's no point carrying on dating James if I don't feel anything for him, no matter how lonely I am.

Aiden gets back just after eleven. I'm in the bathroom, brushing my teeth when I hear the door go.

'Hello!' I call from the bathroom, spitting white foam into the sink and rinsing my brush. 'Did you have a good night?'

'Yes, it was good.'

Drying my face on a towel, I go out to see him. I'm in a blue stripy nightshirt, and he's wearing his suit. The sight of him gives me a jolt and I have to avert my eyes so I don't stare.

'Where did you go?'

'The Ivy.'

'The Ivy? Wow! Can you take me as your plus one next time?' I laugh as I duck back into the bathroom to hang up the towel.

'If you like.'

256

I laugh, thinking he's joking, but he looks serious as he collapses heavily on the sofa and pulls off his tie.

'You look tired,' I say, hovering by the kitchen counter.

'I am, I'm knackered.'

'You can sleep in my bed, if you like? I'll sleep on the sofa.'

Aiden sits back and looks at me as though he thinks I'm mad. 'No, it's okay.'

'Are you sure? It's no problem. I feel bad about you sleeping on the floor. Especially now you're this big star who's used to dining at The Ivy. It must be a bit of a come down to come back here to my miserable hovel and sleep on the floor.'

'If it was a problem, I'd stay in a hotel, wouldn't I? Besides, all that bullshit isn't me, you know that. And I meant what I said, you can come with me next time if you like.'

'Really?' I flit from the kitchen to the lounge and sit on the floor with the coffee table between us. I'm aware I'm behaving quite strangely, but I can't sit on the sofa next to him right now. I'm so pleased to see him I don't trust myself not to stroke him or hug him or randomly run my fingers through his hair.

'Yes, I've got something tomorrow as it happens. Not at The Ivy though. Some other restaurant. Can't remember where. I'll have to check.'

My heart drops. 'I can't tomorrow. Sorry.' I wrinkle my nose apologetically, hugging my knees.

'Why? What's tomorrow?'

'I'm seeing James.'

'Oh.' His eyes flicker. 'Where are you going with him?'

'Just a pub in Covent Garden.'

He scratches his chest, frowning. 'Cancel him and come out with me.'

'I can't, I've just confirmed I can make it.'

'Say you made a mistake and you have the dentist or something.'

'Dentist?' I raise my eyebrows at him. How late does he think dentists work?

'Yeah, tooth extraction. You won't feel like going out drinking after a tooth extraction.'

'But that would be a lie, Aiden.'

'Okay, well tell him your ex-boyfriend's back in town and you'd rather go out for a meal with him instead.'

I feel my cheeks flame. 'Erm, I'm not sure that would go down so well!'

'Go to the pub with James then. I'll go and have my lovely meal in my lovely posh restaurant.'

I smile, trying to cover my disappointment. 'Who are you eating with tomorrow?'

'Just my agent. He wants to discuss a few details. We could have done it tonight really, but I get the impression he likes to wine and dine his clients as much as possible.' Leaning forward, he slips off his jacket and unbuttons the top of his shirt. 'You couldn't give my neck a rub, could you? It's really sore.' He undoes a couple more buttons and then slips his hand beneath the collar to squeeze the left side of his neck.

'Okay.' I get up from the floor and go to the sofa to sit next to him. He shifts forward so I can sit behind him, and I think he's going to sit on the floor but as soon as I'm in position he shuffles back against me. My senses are suddenly full of him. I can feel the heat of his body and my nose is full of his scent. It takes all my willpower to only touch the shoulder he's indicated, and not run my hands down his back like I would have done five years ago. I focus on the smooth material of his shirt instead of the heat of the skin beneath it, and it helps me keep my head when he groans and bends his neck to the side.

'There?' I dig the pad of my thumb into the knotted muscle.

'Yeah. Ooh, down a bit. There. Yeah, yeah, yeah.'

There's a ridge of muscle beneath my finger and I find myself

258

holding onto his other shoulder to exert enough pressure to make a difference. 'I'm not hurting you, am I?'

'No, it feels good.'

'How have you done this? Where have you been sleeping the last two nights?'

'In Ben's spare bed. The pillow's really high and hard though.'

'It's kind of ironic that you do your neck in when you've slept in a bed instead of a floor.'

'Yeah, it's what you're used to, I suppose.'

I carry on massaging his shoulder. My fingers are hurting, but I'm enjoying it too much to complain. Aiden unbuttons more of his shirt then pulls it down his arm, and suddenly my hands are directly on his warm skin. There are three moles running in a line down his shoulder, and the urge to kiss them is almost overwhelming. I can't help wondering what would happen if I did. Would he freak out? Would he kiss me back?

Maybe I should try it and see what happens.

I feel myself leaning closer to him, as if drawn by an invisible force.

'I'd really like to meet James, you know.'

'*What!?*' Did I hear him correctly? Why would he want to meet James?

'You heard.'

'But why?'

He shrugs the shoulder I'm not massaging. 'I don't know. I just figured it might be nice to meet the man you're seeing. Check he's good enough for you.'

'Aiden!' I roll my eyes at the back of his head. 'You meeting James just feels weird. Besides, you're out tomorrow so you can't.'

'I could come after.'

'You won't have time.'

'I might. It depends where the restaurant is.' Picking up his phone, he scrolls through his text messages. 'Here you go. Where's that?' he asks, showing me the name of a restaurant on a message.

'No idea.'

'Well, it's bound to be central, isn't it? The table's booked for seven so I bet we'll be done before nine. You'd still be out then, wouldn't you?'

'I suppose.'

'What time are you meeting?'

'Eight.'

'There you go then. I could come and meet you.'

'Don't you think meeting my new boyfriend might feel a little bit strange?'

'No, why should it?'

'Well, I wouldn't want to meet your new girlfriend.'

'Why?'

'Because …' My voice trails off. Because I'd be jealous, that's why. But I can't say that out loud. 'Anyway, what's James going to think if I say, "Hi, this is my ex-boyfriend Aiden"?'

'Just introduce me as an old friend. You don't even have to admit we arranged it. It could be a chance meeting. I'll be all like "Wow fancy seeing you here!" and you'll be all like "Amazing! Come and join us!"'

I snigger and resume kneading his shoulder, making him hiss in pain. 'Too hard?'

'A bit.'

'Sorry, I'll be more gentle.' I ease off with the kneading and instead smooth the heel of my hand over his skin.

'Why wouldn't you want to meet my girlfriend?' he asks, after a moment's silence.

'You have a girlfriend?' I ask in a bewildered voice, sick jealousy churning my gut.

'No, but I don't know why you'd have a problem with it, if we're just friends?'

'I don't have a problem with it. I just wouldn't want to meet her.'

'Why?'

'Because … I don't know why, I just wouldn't. It would be weird.'

'Because you'd be jealous? Ouch!' He winces as I dig my fingers into his muscle again.

'No!' I scoff, easing off the pressure a little. 'Well, yes, maybe, I don't know.' I start kneading his shoulder again and he grabs my hand to still it.

'Why would you be jealous?' he asks.

'It would just be weird, seeing you with someone new!'

'New? It's been five years, Orla.' He laughs.

'I know, but … I don't know. Anyway, you just said you don't have a girlfriend, so why are we even talking about this?'

'Because I'd like to stay in touch with you.'

'You would?'

'Of course.'

'But you're not going to be here. You're going to Ireland.'

'And? It's not a million miles away, you know.'

'It's not exactly down the road, either. I'd have to catch a plane or take a ferry.'

'Oh no, not a plane or a ferry!' Aiden mocks.

'Well, you know what I mean. If you go back to Ireland and settle down with a girl then I doubt I'll ever see you again.' Just saying the words makes my heart squeeze.

'Well, I doubt that's going to happen.'

'You don't know that.' I rub his shoulder with the palm of my hand. 'Love can strike at any time.'

'Oooh, like a lightning bolt?'

'Exactly.'

'Is that how it was for you and James? He handed you the glove and you were zapped from above?'

'Hardly!' I laugh, thinking about the Orla Pickles thing.

'So why did you agree to meet him then?'

'I don't know really. He just seemed like a nice guy.'

'Is he handsome?'

261

'Yes. He has a kind face.' I try to conjure up an image of him in my head, but I can't seem to remember what he looks like. Somewhere along the line, and this is probably down to Emma, he turned into Fozzie Bear, and now that's all I see when I try to picture him.

'Do you think he's The One?'

'Not really.'

'What's the point in dating him then? You may as well cancel and come out with me.'

Laughing, I give his shoulder a gentle shove, and in response he leans back against me, trapping me against the back of the sofa.

'Hey!' I protest. I've got one leg either side of him and this feels alarmingly intimate. His shirt is all the way down his arms, and my chin is trapped against his naked shoulder. 'You can't trap me when I'm giving you a massage!'

'Don't push me off the sofa then!'

'I hardly pushed you off! You didn't move.'

'I thought I was going to, though. It was very upsetting.'

'Oh dear, poor Aiden.' I chuckle as he sits back up and for some reason, I lean forward and plant a kiss on one of his moles without even thinking about it. He stills, and my heart lurches. 'Sorry!' I say, flustered.

'What for?' He sounds surprised.

'Kissing you.'

He half laughs. 'Don't be sorry for kissing me, Orla. I don't mind you kissing me at all. In fact, you can kiss me any time you like.'

Heat floods through my body, and the air feels charged with electricity. I still have my hands on Aiden's bare shoulders, and the temptation to kiss my way down his spine is overwhelming. Giving myself a shake, I start to massage both of his shoulders at the same time, concentrating on the way his skin moves beneath my hands. He groans, and I feel a pull in my groin.

'Ooh, you're good at this, Orla.'

'Maybe I should give up being a reporter and become a masseur instead.'

'I'll hire you. You can be my personal masseuse.'

'Oh yeah? That sounds a bit dodgy.'

He tips his head to one side, stretching out his neck. 'It probably would be, to be honest.'

'Aiden!'

'Well, come on, I know what you can do, remember.'

'What do you mean, *do*? I didn't *do* anything.'

'Oh, you did. You just didn't realise at the time.'

'I think you might be mistaking me for someone else,' I say drily.

'Well, let's see? Were you the girl who treated me to a striptease on the side of a river bank?'

'Oh, shut up!' I feel my cheeks flame.

'Were you the girl that—'

'No, no, no! Stop it now, Aiden. We're just friends now, remember.'

'We were always just friends, remember. We just happened to have quite a lot of sex while we were about it.'

'That was a long time ago.' I go to scramble out from behind him, but he grabs my leg to stop me.

'It doesn't feel that long ago.' His eyes seer into mine, as he twists to look at me. 'Especially not now, with you here like this.' We stare at each other, and for a moment I think he's going to kiss me. My eyes flick to his mouth and then back up to his eyes, but he doesn't move towards me. Instead he gently strokes my hair back from my face. 'We still have that same connection we always had.'

My blood thrums in my veins as I stare at him, trapped in his gaze. I can't deny it because it's true, we do have that same connection. But I can't let myself agree either.

'I should go to bed,' I say at last.

He looks disappointed, but he nods and stands up so I can get up too. I feel bad about not responding to him, and I hover next to him for a moment while he stretches out his back and moves his head from side to side. 'That's much better. Thank you for the massage.'

'You're welcome.' Collecting a couple of empty glasses from the coffee table, I take them through to the kitchen and leave them on the side to wash tomorrow morning. 'Goodnight then.' Glancing back, I see he's taken off his shirt and my heart skips a beat at the sight of his broad shoulders and hard, flat stomach.

'Goodnight, Orla.'

Chapter 21

I'm too worked up to sleep. My blood is thrumming through my veins and my limbs feel jittery and restless. I lie in bed, staring up into the darkness, going over and over everything Aiden said to me tonight. He seemed so different to yesterday on the phone. I still need to ask him what that was all about. Should I go back out now? Sleep feels a long way off.

I lie in bed for a bit longer, then get up and go back out into the lounge. Everything is dark and still and I pause, listening for any sound that might indicate he's still awake. Thinking he must be asleep already, I tiptoe into the kitchen and run myself a glass of water instead.

'Are you alright?'

His voice makes me jump. 'Oh! I thought you were asleep! Would you like a glass of water?'

'I've got one, thanks.'

I hover in the kitchen for a moment, deliberating whether to ask him or not. I don't want an argument, or to upset him again, but I know I won't sleep if I don't talk it through with him.

'Are you alright?' he repeats.

'Yes.' I take a sip of cool water. 'Can I talk to you a minute?'

'Sure.'

Tonight, he's laid his sleeping bag on the floor between the sofa and coffee table, so I hop onto the sofa over the arm and curl my legs beneath me. He's just a dark lump on the floor. I don't know what to say to start this conversation, and the silence stretches out into the darkness.

'What do you want to talk about then?' he asks, but not impatiently. I hear him sniff and scratch his head.

'The other night, on the phone. You were angry with me. I want to know why. It wasn't like you at all. What did I do to upset you?'

He's silent for a moment. 'Why did you phone me?'

'Because I wanted to know you were okay. I wasn't checking up on you or anything like that. You know you're free to come and go as you please.'

'I wasn't annoyed because I thought you were checking up on me, Orla. Did I sound pissed off when I first answered the phone?'

'No.'

'So, what do you think could have annoyed me then?'

I blink in the darkness. 'I don't know, that's why I'm asking.'

He tuts. 'Well, how about you have a good think and come back to me when you've come up with something?' His sleeping back rustles as he turns on his side, away from me.

'How about you tell me so it's one less thing I'm confused about?'

'What else are you confused about?'

I pick at my nail miserably and stay quiet. I think again that I should just ask him to leave, but I don't want him to. The problem is I don't think I ever want him to leave.

'Doesn't matter,' I mutter.

'Well, if you don't tell me, I can't help you.'

'You sound like my mother,' I say accusingly, climbing back over the arm of the sofa so I don't step on him. I feel tearful, suddenly, the thought of him leaving tugging at my emotions.

266

'And I phoned you because I missed you, if you really want to know. I needed to hear your voice.'

'Why didn't you just say that then?' I hear the rustle of his sleeping bag as he sits up. 'Orla, come back.'

'No, I'm going to bed.'

'*Orla!*'

Shutting my bedroom door, I curl up in a ball beneath the covers, trying to get warm again. The heating went off an hour ago, and my flat is cold. I wish I hadn't gone out to talk to him just now. I shouldn't have admitted to missing him and I definitely shouldn't have said I wanted to hear his voice. Talk about revealing too much.

There's a knock on my door and then it opens. 'Orla? Can I come in?'

Turning over, I sit up and look towards the dark shadow in the doorway. 'Okay.'

The bed dips as he sits down on the edge of the mattress. 'That's why I was mad at you.'

My heart stills. 'Because you knew I missed you?'

'No, because you wouldn't say it.'

I frown into the darkness. 'Isn't checking you're okay a little bit like saying I miss you?'

'I suppose. But it's the way you dress it up as something else that annoys me. Why didn't you just say you missed me?'

'Because I shouldn't be missing you, Aiden. You've been back just a few days, yet I'm phoning you up to hear your voice? That's pathetic. I can't be missing you after twenty-four hours when you're going to live in Ireland in just over a week's time. What's going to happen then?'

'We'll keep in touch this time.'

'But that's even worse! Talk about prolonging the agony.'

'Don't be ridiculous. Come on, budge up.'

'Why, what are you doing?'

'I'm getting into bed with you.'

'You can't get into bed with me! I have a boyfriend.'

'I'm not going to do anything. Just let me hold you for a little while.'

My heart thuds as I shift over to make room for him, and he slides in next to me. I've only got a single bed so there's not much room, and little choice but to hold on to each other so we don't fall out. Every cell in my body is on red alert, and I try to control my breathing so he doesn't realise how fast and shallow it's become.

I can't believe he's got into bed with me. I want to resent the space he's taking up, but it feels nice to be pressed up against a warm body and despite my reservations, I start to relax. He always did feel like home.

'Before we were lovers, we were friends, weren't we?'

'Even when we were lovers we were friends, yeah.'

'Exactly. And why was that?'

'What do you mean?'

He sighs. 'Why did you want to spend time with me?'

'Because you're kind and funny and interesting and I always felt comfortable with you.'

'Yes, and I felt the same about you. I could say anything to you, and you could say anything to me, right? So why has that changed? Why should that change?'

'Because of sex.'

'But we were still friends when we were having sex. Why aren't we friends now when we're not having sex?'

'We are friends. You're here in my flat, aren't you? Here in my bed?'

'But you don't talk to me. I feel like you're holding back from me all the time. Why can't you tell me how you feel?'

'Because it's more complicated now. We were friends, then lovers, then you went away. What are we going to do? Repeat that cycle again? Go through all that pain again? I don't want to tell you how I feel because it opens us up to all that pain again. And not just me, you too.' My heart is hammering. This conversation feels dangerous, my feelings too close to the surface, shining through.

'So, you're saying you're still in love with me?'

I sigh and close my eyes. 'I'm saying we hurt each other last time, and we stand to hurt each other again this time. And no matter what you think I did or didn't feel when you went away, I cried for months over you.' I swallow hard. 'I really can't afford to do that again, Aiden. And I don't think you can either.'

He's quiet for what seems like a long a time, and then he says, 'But do we even have a choice?'

'There's always a choice.'

'I don't think there is though.' He tightens his arm around me. 'Not for me, anyway.'

'What do you mean?'

'I've spent the last five years thinking about you and missing you. I don't see that changing any time soon. Even if you tell me to leave. Even if I go to Ireland and never see you again, you're always going to be there, Orla. In my head. In my heart.'

I blink into the darkness. 'But we can't be together.'

'What if we can?'

'But we can't, Aiden. It's not practical.'

'Practical?'

'We're going to be living in different countries. I don't see how it could work.'

'Friends or lovers?'

'Pardon?'

'I'll take either just to have you back in my life.'

Drawing in a long, slow breath, I close my eyes. It would be so easy to turn to him and kiss him. I want him back in my life too, but I don't want to have to live some miserable half-life where I spend all my time pining for him.

Plus, there's James to think about. It's really early days, but he seems steady and solid and sensible, and not like someone who's

269

going to live in a different country any time soon. Should I really give up on that?

'Look, I don't mean to put you under pressure or confuse you any more than I have done already. I'll leave if you want me to, and you'll never hear from me again. If that's what you want.' He starts to withdraw, but I catch his arm and pull it back round me.

'I don't want that,' I say. 'I don't know what I do want yet, but I definitely don't want that.'

'Okay.' He settles back down, and I hear him swallow. 'Do you want me to stay here with you? Or go back to the lounge?'

'Stay with me.'

We lie quietly together, drawing comfort from each other's warmth. I can tell from the way he's breathing that he's not asleep yet.

'I never told you that my dad died last year,' I say, without even realising I'm going to say it. The words just spill from my lips.

'Oh no, I'm so sorry.' His arm tightens around me. 'What happened?'

'He had cancer.'

'Were you with him at the end?'

'Yeah.' A huge lump has appeared in my throat, and tears are stinging my nose as they do every time I picture my father lying in his hospital bed, with tubes going in and out of his body.

'On your own? Or with one of his girlfriends?'

I shake my head. 'Mum came. It was strange because they hadn't spoken in years. I didn't really know if he'd want to see her, but he did.' A tear escapes from my eye and rolls down my face into my ear. I clamp my jaw shut. Why am I talking about this now? It's still too raw. Aiden stays quiet, and I can tell he's waiting for me to go on. When I eventually do, I whisper, 'They held hands and it was like they made peace with each other. My dad said he was sorry, which I thought was weird because I always

270

blamed my mum and her affair with Ray for the breakdown of their marriage.'

'I suppose there must have been more going on than what you saw as a child.'

'I suppose. It was just strange because I always thought they hated each other. When I talked to my mum after, she said she never really stopped loving him. Not completely. She said he just wasn't cut out for marriage or family life, and she couldn't stay married to him.'

'Have you made peace with that part of your childhood now? You don't still feel guilty, do you?'

I sigh, deeply. 'No, not really. I wish I'd been a better daughter though. Maybe visited him more.'

'It sounds like you were there when it mattered. That's what counts.'

'There was hardly anyone there at his funeral. Just a few work-mates and me and Mum.'

'No other family?'

'He didn't have anyone. My grandparents died when I was young, and he was an only child. No cousins, either.' I close my eyes, feeling suddenly tired. Aiden presses a kiss to my shoulder.

'Thank you for telling me,' he whispers.

Chapter 22

The following morning, I wake up to find I'm still in Aiden's arms. I feel such a rush of love for him that I kiss his cheek, waking him up too.

'Morning, sleepy head,' I say, clambering over him to go to the bathroom. 'I've got work so I need to get up.'

'Okay. I'll make coffee.' He yawns and stretches.

I smell more like him than myself, I think as I get into the shower. I sniff my shoulder and my arm, then grab a handful of hair and smell that too. It makes me happy that I smell of him, and I'm a little sad that I'm about to wash. It's weird to think we slept in the same bed though. What happens now? Is he going to expect to sleep with me again tonight, and tomorrow and the night after that? Or was it just a one-off?

Aiden showers after me, while I change and make breakfast. He's left the bathroom door open, and fingers of steam curl out into the kitchen where I'm pouring the milk onto my cereal. I don't know why he has to leave the door open like that. I've already caught a glimpse of his naked backside through the shower screen, and though it wasn't altogether unpleasant, I resent the fact he's provided yet another image that will haunt my thoughts all day.

Aiden comes out of the shower before I've finished eating my breakfast, and stands in the bathroom doorway with a tiny towel wrapped around his waist, dripping water.

'Aiden! You're dripping wet!' I say, pointing my spoon at the puddle he's making on the floor.

'I'll dry it, don't worry. Have you remembered the name of that pub yet?'

'What pub?'

'The one you're meeting James in tonight.'

My stomach drops and I almost choke on my cereal. 'You're not coming!' I say. 'It would be too awkward.'

'I don't know what your problem is! It's not like I'm going to challenge him to a duel or anything.'

'I don't want you there.'

'Why?'

'We slept in the same bed last night! I won't be able to cope with you and him in the same room together.'

'We didn't have sex. It's fine. Besides, I'm great with people! We're sure to get on like a house on fire.'

Rolling my eyes, I turn away to rinse my bowl under the tap. 'Right, well, I'm going to work now.'

'Come on, just tell me the name of the pub.'

'No.'

'I'll just try every pub in Covent Garden until I find you then.'

'No, you won't! *Aiden*!' I cover my eyes as his towel slips south.

'What?' Laughing, he whips it up and uses it to rub his hair dry. 'You've seen it all before, anyway.'

'Yes, but … that was then and now I'm going to work.' My cheeks are flaming hot as I grab my coat and bag and head out of the door.

'I'll find you in the pub later,' he calls.

'No, you won't!' I shout back as the door slams behind me.

*

273

Bloody hell! I'm so flustered, all I can think about all day is Aiden and what I'll do if he turns up. I toy with the idea of phoning James and changing where we meet, but Emma and I are in court all day, following the trial of a gang of jewel thieves, and I don't get a chance. I'm glad Emma's with me because I keep drifting off into my own thoughts and I'm bound to have missed something important. Aiden's really got under my skin though. I keep getting flashbacks to the moment his towel slipped, and sigh. Emma looks at me from the corner of her eye before turning her attention back to the defence barrister.

'Is it hot in here?' I ask Emma when there's a break in proceedings.

'No, I'm freezing,' she says, pulling her suit jacket closer around her body.

'Really?' I fan myself with my hand. 'Maybe I'm coming down with something.'

'Maybe you are. You do look very red.'

At the end of the day, I check my phone and find a text from Aiden saying he might not make tonight after all. I almost sag with relief and then feel annoyed when I realise he must have only said he'd come to mess with my head. What kind of game is he playing? I hurry down the steps of the court with Emma at my heels and hail a cab. Emma chats about how interesting the day's been and I find I can actually have a sensible conversation about it without worrying about tonight. Now that Aiden says he won't come, I feel like a weight's been lifted off my shoulders and I can finally look forward to seeing James.

It comes as a shock to realise, when it comes to getting ready, that I really don't want to go out anymore. I sit on my bed, holding the clothes I'd planned to wear, wondering what to do. Should I cancel? There's still time, and it's not like James didn't do it to me on Friday. But I tell myself I should go. I'll feel better when I go. Who knows, seeing James again might just take my mind off Aiden. At the end of the day, I've been there, done that, and I know he's just going to leave. James, on the other hand, is uncharted territory and that's exciting. Plus, he lives in London, and his sensible, steady job means he's not about to leave any time soon. Always a bonus in a boyfriend.

Decision made, I take a deep breath and go for a shower.

Two hours later, I'm sitting at a small round table in the pub, waiting for James to arrive. He's ten minutes late, which is unusual for James, and the pint of mild I've bought for him and placed carefully on the beer mat opposite my gin cocktail makes me feel like I'm having drinks with an imaginary friend.

My phone screen lights up with a message and I smile when I see it's from James. *Hi! Sorry, got held up! Be with you in ten!*

At least he's coming. I sip my drink and look around me. The bar is dimly lit and populated with professional-looking people chatting in groups by the bar, or sitting at little round tables. Tracing my finger down the condensation on my glass, I try in vain to keep my thoughts from wandering to Aiden again. I didn't reply to his earlier message, and I haven't heard from him since either. Idly, I wonder if he will turn up. I wouldn't put it past him.

James enters the pub with his beige mac flapping and makes a bee line for me, looking flustered and apologetic. 'Sorry, sorry, sorry, sorry!' he says, leaning down and kissing me on both cheeks. 'I've come straight from work! It's been absolutely mad today! Everything's gone wrong!'

'Oh no! You should have said. We could have done this another night.'

'No, I already let you down on Friday, I didn't want to do that again.' Slipping off his mac, he drapes it over the back of his chair and stows his briefcase beneath the table. He's still wearing his grey pinstripe work suit, and looks very smart, if a little red in the face. 'You look beautiful, by the way. As you always do, of course. So what are you drinking?'

'I've got one already, and so have you!' I indicate the glasses on the table.

'So you have!' he laughs as he sits down opposite me. 'Silly me!'

'I got you a pint of mild? That's your usual, isn't it?'

'Yes, fantastic! Thanks so much! I really needed this.' His blue eyes close as he takes a good few gulps, and I watch his throat move as he swallows.

Oh God, I don't fancy him at all.

'How was Manchester?' I ask. 'Did you have fun at your grandmother's birthday party?'

'Yes, she turned 90. Still as fit as a fiddle and giving out orders. She's always been a bit of a force to be reckoned with.'

'Does she still live in her own home?'

'Oh yes, goodness, she wouldn't go in a home, and my dad certainly wouldn't have her in his!' He laughs loudly before taking another gulp of his beer. 'No, she's amazingly active for her age.'

'Where did you have the party?'

He tells me about the party, and I smile as I listen, trying to find what I saw in him when I first agreed to meet him for a drink. He's handsome enough, and sweet and jolly in a bumbling self-depreciating way, but the truth is I wish I was sitting here talking to Aiden. James's rambling story about this grandmother's party is quite dull, and shows no sign of ending any time soon. I only have myself to blame, I remind myself as I down the last of my drink. I did ask him about it, after all.

'I'll get you another drink,' he says, getting to his feet as he notices my empty glass. 'Same again?'

'Yes, please.'

I look over at him while he's at the bar ordering the drinks. His suit jacket strains across his shoulders as he braces himself on the bar, leaning forward to ask what crisps they have. He's a nice man. The nicest man I've met for ages, in fact. Why don't I fancy him? I could blame Aiden, of course, but I'm not sure that's entirely true. I'm not sure I ever truly fancied James. It just took Aiden coming back to make me remember what it feels like to really desire someone.

I sigh and run a finger around the rim of my glass. I don't want to hurt James, but I suppose it's better to do it sooner than later. It's not like I've known him long, after all.

Arriving back at the table with our drinks, he drops a packet of nuts into the centre of the table from between his clenched teeth.

'Hope you don't mind,' he says, ripping open the bag. 'I'm starving.'

'Have you not eaten dinner?'

'No time.'

'Do you want to order something from the bar?'

'Food's finished. I just asked.'

'We could go somewhere else?'

'No, it's okay, I'll just get a kebab on the way home. Good excuse.' He beams at me. 'So how has your day been?'

'Good. I've been in court all day. It's been interesting.'

'Really? What's the case? Would I have heard of it?'

'Possibly. It's the one about the jewel thieves? They've been on the run for years. It's fascinating stuff.'

'Oh yes, I heard about that.'

We chat about the court case for a while, and then out of the corner of my eye I spot Aiden at the bar. He's wearing a black shirt and dark jeans, and looks lean and dark and dangerous. My heart jolts to see him there and I draw in a sharp breath.

'Are you alright?' James asks.

'Huh? Yes, I just spotted someone I know, that's all.'

'Oh really?' He turns and peers around us. 'Who's that then?'

'Just an old friend. Never mind. Carry on with what you were saying.'

'I can't remember what I was saying now.' He scratches his

head, looking confused, and I battle to keep my attention on him instead of Aiden, who's now heading over towards us.

'Orla!' he says, jovially, his Irish accent seeming much more pronounced surrounded by London accents as he is now. 'How the devil are you?'

I hesitate before offering a tight smile. My hands are already shaking. 'Hello, Aiden,' I say, before introducing him to James.

'Hold on a minute,' James says, pointing his finger at Aiden and looking from me to Aiden and back to me again. 'That's not … you're not … *The* Aiden Byrne are you? From the television?'

'The one and the same,' I say drily.

'My goodness!' James grabs Aiden's hand and pumps it vigorously, despite having shaken it just moments ago. 'How wonderful to meet you! You know, I was terribly impressed when you dived into the Amazon river to retrieve your camera. So brave, so brave.'

'So stupid, more like,' I mutter.

'Please, won't you join us?'

'Are you sure?' Aiden looks surprised to be invited, despite the fact that's what he intended all along. 'Well, if you're sure I'm not intruding, thank you so much.'

Dragging a chair over from the next table, he sits down and smiles at us both. His hair, so short by his previous standards, now looks long and unruly compared to James's closely cropped fuzzy blond curls.

'So how do you two know each other?' James asks, eagerly. 'You never said you knew Aiden Byrne, Orla!'

'Didn't I? Well, I haven't seen him for years.' I shrug, trying not to betray the extent of my panic. 'We met in my hometown of Hawksley when I was sent to interview him for the local paper I worked on.'

'Really? What were you doing in a backwater place like Hawksley, Aiden?' James laughs.

'Studying otters in the local river. It was a magical place really. So quiet that I managed to get shots of the otters in the daytime as well as at night. Orla used to come and watch them with me, didn't you, Orla?' He looks at me and I look quickly away, swirling my drink round in my glass so the ice cubes clink on the sides.

'Yeah, they were lovely,' I say, vaguely.

James blinks. 'Were you two together as a couple then?'

'No, just friends,' Aiden says, picking up his pint and taking a long slow sip. 'I was only there a few weeks then I went to India.'

'Wow! India! You must have been to some amazing places,' James says, his face aglow as he gazes at Aiden. He's certainly never looked at me like that. Maybe I don't need to feel bad about ending it after all.

'I have.'

'Where's the best place you've ever been?'

Aiden opens his mouth to answer then hesitates, looking at me. He's got a glint in his eye that makes my stomach drop, and I swear if he says Hawksley I'll pass out.

'Erm, well, it's hard to pick any one particular place. There's beauty to be found everywhere, and I've seen amazing wildlife and amazing landscapes all over the world. India was amazing. South Africa was absolutely beautiful. Borneo, too, was really wonderful. I feel so privileged to have been to those places and seen the things I've seen.'

'Is there anywhere you still want to go?'

'Not at the moment.' Aiden folds his arms, resting his elbows on the table. 'I want to spend some time at home in Ireland for a while. I've been travelling since I left university, and I'm pretty worn out.'

'Really? Gosh! Is that it for you then?'

Aiden shrugs. 'I still might travel in the future, but not like I have been doing. Not for months and months on end, going from one country to another. I want to spend some time with my family. My parents aren't getting any younger and my brother's hoping to start a family. I don't want to be a stranger. Plus, I have a project in Ireland coming up that will keep me busy for the next year at least.'

'You never know when those itchy feet will set in though.' James laughs and slaps Aiden on the arm. 'You're a nomad. Can a nomad ever settle down?'

Aiden shrugs. 'I think so. Why not? I love Ireland. I've really missed it these past couple of years. It'll be a relief to get back there.'

A relief? I feel an unreasonable stab of disappointment that he can't wait to leave me and get back there.

'So, what are you doing in London then?'

'Didn't Orla tell you?' Aiden's eyebrows shoot up as he glances at me. 'I've got an exhibition running at the Hayward Gallery.'

'It's the one I went to last week,' I say, stiffly. 'This is the first time I've seen you since.'

'Oh of course, my bad, I had to cancel, didn't I?' James guffaws heartily. 'We should go though, Orla. You can show me around if you've already seen it.'

'Yes, we should,' I say, feigning enthusiasm.

'Maybe at the weekend?'

'Okay.'

'Oh, actually no, I've got something on this weekend. It'll have to be the following week. Sorry.' James looks flustered, patting down his pockets as though he's looking for something.

'It's okay. You can go whenever. You could go on your own, if it's more convenient for you,' I say, brightly. 'It runs for a month, doesn't it, Aiden?'

'Yep. Plenty of time.' He smiles and drains the last of his pint. 'Can I get you both another drink?'

'No, I'll get these.' I get to my feet and squeeze his arm without thinking. He looks at my hand and then up into my eyes, and I get a swirling sensation in the pit of my stomach. 'Same again?' I say to James. He nods, and I go to the bar, relieved to put some distance between us all.

There's a tight knot in my stomach and I feel queasy and tense. Seeing Aiden and James together like this feels all kind of wrong, and I can't help comparing them. James looks doughy and soft in comparison to Aiden's strong, straight outline, and he's so dull in comparison. Although to be fair anybody would be really. It's hard to compete with someone who's been around the world and starred in his own documentary series. But still, I thought James's solidity and dependability would be a greater pull than Aiden's here-today-gone-tomorrow routine. Clearly, I was wrong.

I don't want James, I want Aiden. And though it's not exactly news, it's frustrating because I know we want different things from life. My job is here, and Aiden's is in Ireland. Well, for now, anyway. Goodness knows where he'll head off to after that. I tend to agree with James that Aiden will get itchy feet and be off travelling after a few months. Even if we do the long-distance thing and keep in touch, it's not ideal. Not if I want marriage and babies and a man that lives in the same country as me.

Plus, he keeps blowing hot and cold on me. I still haven't got to the bottom of why he's been so angry and distant with me. And yet, last night he was quite flirty saying I could accompany him to dinner and kiss him whenever. I don't know what he wants.

I glance over my shoulder to where Aiden and James are still deep in conversation. I'm surprised they get on so well, but I suppose Aiden gets on with everyone. He'd talk to a rock if there was no one around to listen to him. James throws his head back and laughs at something Aiden's said, and Aiden's shoulders shake as he laughs too. I smile, but my insides feel raw and uncomfortable as I pay for the drinks. Just as I'm trying to figure out how to carry back two pints and a large gin glass, Aiden appears next to me and takes the pint glasses from the bar.

'Thought you might need some help,' he says, standing so

close I can feel the heat from his body. He's taken his jacket off and is wearing a black long-sleeved T-shirt that fits snugly over his pecs.

'Thanks.'

As Aiden turns back towards the table, I get a waft of his scent and it makes my head spin. It's not even that strong, but it starts a gnawing sensation in my stomach – a sort of hunger that won't be satisfied by food.

I sit back at the table and busy myself by putting my purse back in my bag. The conversation seems to flow perfectly well without me anyway. James can't stop laughing at Aiden's story of a disastrous train ride across India, and I find myself smiling at the way Aiden's recounting it.

'James seems like a nice guy,' Aiden says when James goes the toilet.

'He is,' I say, avoiding his eye even though he's doing his best to catch mine. Leaning both elbows on the table, he dips his head to try and make me look at him. I sigh and shake my head at him. 'Why are you here, Aiden?' I ask.

'What do you mean? I wanted to meet him. I don't think he minds, does he?'

'Obviously not, but I do.'

'Why?'

'You know why?' I hiss.

'Say it.'

'Say what?'

'Say you love me. Come on, admit it.'

'*Aiden!*' I hiss, looking around us to check no one heard. 'I'm out on a date. With my boyfriend.'

'Come off it! I'm more your boyfriend than he is. He's a nice guy, but he's not for you.'

'And you've just decided that, have you?'

'Yeah, why not?'

'Oh, just go, Aiden! Please.'

He stares at me for a moment, then shakes his head. 'Okay, if that's what you really want.' He scrapes back his chair, and my hand comes down on his before I even register what I'm doing. Both of us stare at it before looking at each other.

'Don't,' I say in a low voice. 'Don't go.'

He looks thoughtful as he moves his chair back into place. I withdraw my hand but he catches it and holds it gently.

'Ooh this looks a bit serious!' James booms as he comes back to his seat. My heart drops into my stomach and I snatch my hand away from Aiden. 'What's going on here? Should I be worried?'

'Not at all,' Aiden says, cheerfully. 'I was just telling Orla about some family problem, that's all. Orla says you're from Manchester. What are you doing all the way down here then?'

James doesn't look totally convinced as he settles into his chair. I'm not sure what my expression betrays about my emotions, but James is looking at me curiously, and I feel so guilty I can't meet his eye.

'You know what,' I say. 'I think I ought to call it a night. I've got another long day in court tomorrow and I'm absolutely exhausted.'

'Oh, okay!' James looks dismayed as he gets back to his feet. 'That's a shame, but I suppose I ought to go too.' His eyes flick to Aiden. 'It was great to meet you, Aiden. I had no idea Orla had such famous friends. No one's going to believe it when I go into work tomorrow and tell them I met you.'

Laughing self-consciously, Aiden shakes his head and gets to his feet to shake his hand. 'It was good to meet you, too, James. Take care of yourself.'

'You too, Aiden.'

'Bye, Orla.' Aiden presses a kiss to my cheek before turning to go. I'm about to ask where he's going, but I suppose he doesn't want to be around when I say goodbye to James. Besides, it will look suspicious if Aiden and I leave together. Not that it really matters now. I've already decided what I need to say to James. But when it comes to it, I don't need to say anything at all.

'I don't suppose I'm going to see you again, am I?' James says regretfully as we say goodbye on the street outside the pub. The rain mists around his head as he smiles sadly down at me, and though regretful, I get the impression he's not particularly heart-broken.

I shake my head. 'I'm sorry, James. I don't think it's going to work out for us.'

'No. I suppose not. It's been an absolute pleasure though.'

'It has, James. Thank you so much.'

We embrace in the cold damp drizzle as the traffic splashes past, and then I set off in the direction of the tube station, leaving James to wait for his cab. My heart is heavy as I make my way down to the underground station, but I know it's for the best. I just don't know what happens next.

Aiden is waiting on the platform. I stop when I see him and watch him for a moment, taking in his sharp nose, and those large, expressive eyes. As if sensing me there, he turns and catches me watching, then jerks his head for me to join him.

'Well?' he asks. 'Are you seeing him again?'

My throat feels too tight to answer him immediately, so I shake my head. Aiden nods slowly, approvingly.

'What happens now then?' I say, when I feel like I can speak again.

He looks at me. 'What do *you* want to happen now?'

I want to say that I want him to stay in London with me, and we'll live together, happily ever after. I want to say that I don't want him to go to Ireland. I want to say that I love him and think I will always love him. But I don't. Instead, I say, 'I'm scared.'

'What of?'

'Getting hurt again.'

He shrugs. 'There are no guarantees against that, whatever happens. That's just part of life, I guess.'

284

The train pulls into the station, and the rush of air swirls around us, lifting my hair from my head. The doors beep as they slide open, and Aiden takes my hand as we board the train. We sit close together, our arms and legs touching despite there being plenty of empty seats around us. He keeps hold of my hand, and I can't help thinking of that day he held my hand in the hospital, despite the fact we were near strangers. It felt right then, and it feels right now. I rest my cheek on his shoulder and close my eyes.

'I love you,' I hear myself say, and instead of feeling scared, I feel calm and peaceful, like it was the right thing to say.

'There now, that wasn't so hard, was it?' Aiden kisses the top of my head. 'I love you too, Orla. I never stopped loving you, and never will stop loving you.'

He runs a finger from my cheek bone to my jaw, and I look up into his eyes.

'But what do we do? You're leaving.'

'I'm only in Ireland. It's not exactly the end of the earth. You can be there in just over an hour.'

'Yes, but …' My voice trails away and I lay my cheek against his shoulder again.

'It's not ideal, but it's better than nothing.' He slips his arm around my shoulders and kisses my head again. 'Unless you want to come with me?'

'I can't. I have work.' I fiddle with the hem of his shirt.

He's silent for a moment. 'Okay, but the offer's there if you change your mind. I'm serious when I say I want you in my life, Orla. I know we can make this work.'

I swallow. I want to believe him but I'm full of fear. Admitting I love him after so long felt like jumping off a cliff, and now I'm in the sea with the waves rising above me. Will I swim or be dashed against the rocks? I fear it's the rocks for me, but I don't say that. Instead I nod and squeeze his hand.

We're quiet for the rest of the journey. Aiden sits deep in

thought, his fingers entwined with mine. I can almost hear the whir of the cogs in his brain, and I'm dying to ask what he's thinking about, but I don't. Instead I keep my head on his shoulder, breathing in his warm, woody scent and wondering if we really can make this work.

My flat feels cold. Colder than outside, in fact. Crossing to the boiler, I press the button to start the heating and peer worriedly at the pilot light to make sure it's lit. Last winter the boiler stopped working and I had to wear my coat in bed. It had better not do that this year.

'It stinks in here!' Aiden wrinkles his nose as he sits down on the sofa, arms stretched out along the back of the cushions.

'I know, it's the takeaway next door,' I say, pushing my hair behind my ears. Now we're home, I feel nervous and skittish. 'Some days are worse than others. I'm always paranoid my hair and clothes are going to smell of it. I'd open a window but I'm freezing.'

Aiden glances towards the small window at the end of the room and raises his eyebrows. 'I'm surprised it opens with those bars on it.'

'Well, at least I feel safe.'

I expect him to laugh, but he just rolls his eyes. 'Do you mind if I have a quick shower?'

'Of course not. Go ahead,' I say. 'Would you like me to fix you a drink?'

'Yeah, go on then.' He's already removing his clothes in the doorway to the bathroom. He drops his T-shirt on the floor before pulling off his socks. I'm not sure why he wants a shower when it's so cold in here, but maybe he thinks the water will warm him up.

I'm also slightly disappointed that we're not going to sit and talk things through. For someone who's just got back together with the love of her life, I'm feeling a bit flat. Maybe it's because of James, or maybe I'm just scared about all the things that could go wrong with Aiden. I know he doesn't have all the answers and it's a case of working it through together, but still …

'Orla?' I hear him shout from the bathroom.

'Yes?' I shout back.

'Come here.'

'What? Why?' I go in anyway. I can see him through the steamy glass, rinsing white foam from his hair. 'Are you okay?'

'No, I need something.' He draws back the cubicle door and peers out at me.

'What?'

'You.' He grabs my wrist and I squeal as he drags me into the cubicle with him.

'Aiden! My clothes!'

'It's only water.' His hand closes round my jaw and he kisses me, his tongue sliding into my mouth as he presses me up against the wall. The hot water soaks through my shirt into my bra, and it's oddly sensual.

'I see you're pleased to see me,' I say, laughing between his kisses.

'I missed you so much, Orla.' His eyes burn into mine and their intensity makes a white-hot kick of lust seer through me. I'm no longer laughing, just kissing him back with ferocious, desperate need.

He pulls my blouse off over my head and I arch against him as I unhook my bra, all the while kissing him hungrily. He undoes my trousers and pushes my pants down, his fingers exploring between my legs, making me groan against his mouth. Lifting my leg, I hook it around his hip, inviting him in. He doesn't need asking twice and I find myself lifted and pressed against the slippery tiles before he thrusts inside me. Pleasure radiates up through my stomach and down to my fingers and toes. His mouth's on my mouth, my jaw, my throat and I tip my face up to the shower spray as the tension builds inside me.

I'd almost forgotten how it felt to be loved by Aiden. We fit together so well. I cling to him, my fingers digging into his shoulders as my orgasm liquidises my muscles and I feel him convulse as he climaxes, groaning into my neck.

He sets me down and we kiss, deep and slow beneath the spray of the shower. He takes the shower gel and squirts some into the palm of his hand before gently soaping my body.

Taking the shower gel, I wash his body too. His sinewy back and his hairy chest and his flat, hard stomach. Even his buttocks are hard. His body is so different to mine, and yet at the same time so familiar. It's hard to believe he's been back just a few days. How have I lived without him all this time? And how will I survive when he leaves again next week? It's a worrying thought, but one I can't let myself dwell on. Any time we have together is too precious to waste with worrying about what comes next. I know we need to talk about it properly, but for now I want to enjoy being with him again.

Chapter 23

'If you're staying in London, do you think we should look for a better flat for you while I'm here?' Aiden calls from the bedroom. It's Saturday morning, and I'm looking forward to spending the whole weekend with him.

'Before Christmas? No, not a good time.'

'Why not?'

'I can't afford it. Besides, I've still got goodness knows how many months' lease left on this place.'

'You could at least start looking. No point leaving it until just before your lease expires. And you need to check when it does expire, otherwise it will roll over and you'll be stuck here for another year or whatever. Or, they could throw you out and you wouldn't have anywhere to live.'

'Hmm. Yeah, I know.' I frown at him, pretending to be cross about how practical he's being, even though a little bit of me is quite cross for him to be asking such serious questions when we have so little time together. 'Since when does the guy who doesn't know what day of the week it is give me advice on organising my life?'

He laughs. 'I got some days of the week underpants, and now there's no stopping me. Do you still have those knickers?'

'No!' I laugh, embarrassed. 'I have grown-up knickers now that match my bra and everything.'

'Yeah, I noticed that. Do you want to show me them again?'

'No! Behave yourself!'

'Oh, come on. What else are we going to do in this tiny flat?'

'We could go for a walk somewhere.'

'We could, or we could go to bed.'

'Or we could go out for lunch.'

'Or we could go to bed.'

'Or we could go to the cinema. Or the theatre. Or ice skating. Or …'

'Ice skating? What are we? Thirteen?'

'Don't be silly! Lots of people go ice skating. It's a lovely romantic thing to do.'

'Is it though? Really? Can you imagine me on skates? I'd be like Bambi. And you'd be even worse. Remember how accident-prone you are?'

'I haven't hurt myself in years! In fact, that summer I spent with you is the only time I ever sprained my ankle or fell in a river or anything.'

'Yeah, well, maybe it was my influence then. In which case, best not go skating with me.'

'We'll do something else then. Something touristy and special seeing as you're not here very often.'

'Yeah, you know why I'm not here very often? I hate the place. I hate London. All the noise, all the smells, all the people.' He tips his head back and closes his eyes. 'Why are there so many people? It's exhausting.'

'Oh no, poor you. Anyway, you've been to some of the busiest cities in the world. You left me to go to Mumbai. You sent me a postcard from Tokyo! I'm sure there are plenty of people in those places.'

'True, but I knew I was only passing through. I feel like I've been here too long already.'

'Charming! Well, we don't have to go shopping in Oxford Street, you know. We could go back to the park. Look for some of that urban wildlife you're here to photograph.'

'The weather's awful.'

I look towards the rain spattered window. 'Oh yeah! Well, good weather for ducks. Tufted ducks, even?'

'Nooo.'

'So what do you want to do with me?' I pass him a cup of tea and sit down on the end of my bed.

'I'll give you two guesses.' He reaches for me, pulling me towards him so I'm straddling him.

'Aiden!' I protest weakly, white-hot flames of desire are already licking my insides as his hand slides up my nightshirt. 'We can't just have sex all the time.'

'Why not?'

His mouth finds mine, and I forget all the reasons why. I forget everything but the feel of his warm hands sliding into places they have no business being. Maybe this is the best way to spend time with Aiden after all. The parks and the restaurants and the theatres can wait for another day.

We spend all weekend making love. The day runs into night and night into day and by the time Monday morning comes around I can barely believe I have to go outside and join the thousands of other people making their way into work on the packed tube train. To make matters worse, the weather's still awful. Cold, sleety rain slants sideways as the bitter wind blasts down the street. I've wrapped my big scarf around the bottom half of my face, but the top half is still exposed. My eyes are streaming as I hurry towards the underground station, already dreading the sea of bodies waiting on the platform below.

Aiden was going to meet some MP this morning to ask about the government's commitment to tackling climate change. He wouldn't give me any details, just a mischievous smile, and said he'd fill me in later. If he could keep his hands off me long enough to tell me about it, that is.

Belinda and Emma can't wait to find out what I've been doing with Aiden all weekend. They flock to my desk, eager for gossip, but of course, all we've been doing is reacquainting ourselves with each other's bodies and I'm not going to give them the details of that. They've noticed how happy I am though. Pity it's not going to last long.

'How long is he here for?' Belinda asks, after I've gone bright red and refused to answer their rather personal questions.

'Just until Friday,' I say, my smile fading slightly. 'But he's only going to be in Ireland. It's not too far away at all.' I've rehearsed this part well and even I'm starting to believe it now.

'Well, that's shit, isn't it?' Belinda looks appalled. 'Has he asked you to go with him?'

'Sort of.'

'What does sort of mean?'

'Well he suggested the other night I could work for him as his personal masseuse,' I say, going slightly pink at the memory.

'You lucky bitch!' Emma spits.

'Emma!' I say, shocked. 'Can I just remind you you're only a trainee?'

'Until you go off to be Aiden Byrne's personal masseuse and I get your job,' she retorts cheekily.

'Well, actually, I said no to his tempting offer on account of my very important job on this newspaper.'

'Nobody's irreplaceable, Orla,' Belinda says tartly.

'Thanks!' I roll my eyes at her.

'Is Aiden going to be part of this protest march outside the Houses of Parliament this afternoon?' Emma asks.

'What protest march?'

'It's a climate change protest march. Some of my friends are going.'

'Oh God!' Belinda snorts. 'It's not going to be a big one, is it?

They're not going to affect the tube service or anything? I need to get home tonight.'

'I don't know much about it, to be honest.'

'Do you think we should go down and see what's going on?'

'Of course you should!' Belinda clicks her fingers. 'Both of you. Go. Get. Let me know if the tube's running.'

'Okay, okay!'

Emma and I catch a cab to the Houses of Parliament where a large crowd of climate change protesters have gathered. There's a buzz in the air and I can't help but feel excited when I catch sight of all the people holding banners. It's only when I get closer I see Aiden standing on a wall, talking to the crowd and praising them for their commitment to environmental issues.

'Oh look, it's Aiden!' Emma says excitedly. 'How cool is that?'

The hairs on the back of my neck lift just watching him, and I'm filled with admiration for his bravery. Emma waves to a girl near the back of the crowd, and she comes over to talk to us.

'Hey! This is Jemma. Jemma, this is Orla. What's the plan today, Jemma?'

'Yet another peaceful protest. We'll stand outside here for an hour or so, then we'll march through the streets, trying to get our message out there.'

'What kind of reaction do you get from the general public?'

'Very positive, in the main. Of course, you always get a few people annoyed with us, but you have to factor in ignorance. The government have declared a climate emergency, and this is just putting the pressure on, saying we want to see action with real results.'

'Do you live in London, or have you come from further afield to join in this protest?'

'I'm only in Surrey. But I've spoken to people from all over. Freddie over there has come down from York, and Jenny's from Scotland. I can't believe Aiden Byrne has joined us!' She pulls an excited face. 'He's such a legend!'

'Did you know he was supposed to be here?' I ask, curious to know if Aiden knew about this but just hadn't told me.

'No! He just appeared and joined us! It's a complete surprise.'

We talk to a few more people about how far they've come to join this protest. Aiden's in the crowd somewhere, and I stand on my tiptoes to try and catch sight of him. After a while, I see him talking and laughing with a group of people.

'Hey!' he says, coming over after he sees me waving to him. 'What are you doing here?'

'Oh, you know, just a bit of reporting.' I roll my eyes at him. 'Did you know about this?'

He looks shifty. 'Maybe.'

'You could have told me! What's the point in having you as a boyfriend if I don't get the inside scoop on these protests? Emma knew more than me.'

'Sorry. I really was coming to meet with an MP. I didn't know if I'd miss it.'

'Okay. Can I get a quote from you then?'

'If you like, this is just a peaceful gathering to remind the government of their commitment to the Paris Agreement on climate change, and to say we want real action after they declared a climate emergency in the wake of the extinction rebellion protests.'

'Can I just ask,' Emma pipes up from beside me, 'you've been all around the world, right? So your carbon footprint is probably much higher than the average person's. How can you campaign for zero emissions when you spend so much time travelling on aeroplanes?'

Aiden smiles, not the least bit offended by Emma's question. 'You're quite right. I have travelled an awful lot and my carbon footprint is high. But, when I get to where I'm going, I try to travel within that country by more carbon-efficient means, like train or bicycle or on foot, wherever possible. And you know, the media needs more people reporting on important environmental matters to bring about more change. Unbelievably, there are still climate change deniers out there, and the media attention in the past has often been about the debate between scientists and those that do not want to recognise what's going on, so I feel it's important that that changes. People need to know what's happening in the world. People need to understand that climate change is already happening and other parts of the world are already suffering irreversible effects. And they need to understand that it's not something that's happening somewhere else, but it's coming for them too. It's happening here, right now, and we need to stand up and take action today, not tomorrow.'

'Okay, thanks,' Emma says, scribbling away in her pad.

'There's something you can do, too, Emma,' Aiden adds, and I brace myself for him to start lecturing her on veganism.

'Oh yeah, what's that then?'

'You need to convince Orla to move to Ireland with me. Otherwise she's going to rack my carbon footprint up even higher with our visits to see each other.'

'Oh, that's cool. We were talking about that this morning, weren't we, Orla? Belinda already told her she's not irreplaceable.'

'Hey!' I squawk, going red. I hate to think Aiden thinks I've been talking about moving to Ireland with him. Aiden laughs and wraps his arm around my shoulder, pulling me against him.

'There you go then. What's for tea tonight? I'm starving.'

'I don't know. Whatever you fancy.'

The crowd of protesters is starting to move off down the road in a flurry of banging drums and whistles. Aiden looks behind him, clearly thinking he should go with them.

'Are you coming with us? Go on, you can do a live stream to your Twitter or whatever.'

'I don't know. We should get back to the office really.'

'Come on, you can walk with us for a bit, can't you? This is history in action. You can't miss this to go and sit in an office and write about yet another stabbing or some other equally depressing piece of news.'

Emma and I join the protest march. One of Emma's friends hands her a sign with 'Save the Bees!' on it and we follow the seething mass of people through the streets. It's uplifting to be part of a movement like this, and though I'm sceptical it will change the minds of those in power, it's encouraging to see the support of the people watching us pass by. Shopkeepers come out to clap us and taxi drivers beep their support. I'm sorry when we leave to go back to the office.

Chapter 24

The thought of Aiden going away on Friday makes me want to scream. I love him so much. Life is going to be so hard when he leaves, even with keeping in touch, like we've promised to.

'Are you okay?' he asks later that evening when we're eating our dinner in my flat. 'You're very quiet tonight.'

'I know, I keep thinking about you going away on Friday.' I put my fork down on my plate, my appetite gone. 'I'm going to miss you, that's all.'

He smiles. 'You don't have to miss me. Come with me.'

'You *know* I can't.'

'No. I know that you *can*.'

'No, I can't, Aiden! Listen, we could argue about this all night, but we both know it's not practical. I can't just walk out on my job and my flat. Even if I said yes, I'd still have a lot of things to sort out. I couldn't just come on Friday and that'd be it.'

'Well, just come with me on Friday for the weekend.'

'No, Aiden! We've been through this already. You know I can't.' Picking up my plate, I take it into the kitchen to wash. 'I do love you, and you know I want to be with you. God knows I'll miss you when you've gone. Part of me wants to say yes and just leave with you, but the sensible parts says it would be madness to give everything up and follow you to Ireland.'

'So, you're happy to have a long-distance relationship?'

I sigh and shrug. 'It's not so long distance, is it? Like you say, it's just an hour away.' My tone is upbeat, but I can feel the anxiety building at the thought of not seeing him for weeks on end. 'Maybe, if things are going well for us, and we find somewhere to live, and I find work, we could think about it again.'

'How very sensible!'

'Well, we have to be, don't we? You've only been back a short time. What if I went with you and you got the opportunity to go to Australia to report on the Great Barrier Reef or something? I'd be stuck in Ireland, living with your parents, while you're the other side of the world.'

He frowns. 'Why wouldn't you come with me? Besides, that wouldn't happen, because I've already agreed to a project based in Ireland, so that's where I'm going to be.'

'But what about my job?'

He thinks for a moment. 'You could work for me.'

'Doing what?'

'My personal assistant. God knows I need one. I've got stuff coming out of my ears at the moment, and you know what I'm like. I've got better but I'm still really disorganised and forgetful.'

'But that's not what I do,' I protest. 'I'm a reporter.' It's not that I'm averse to being his PA, I just don't believe he's thought it through.

'So, freelance. Or get a job on a paper in Dublin. Do whatever you like, I don't care as long as we're together.'

'Oh, Aiden, it's just not practical.' I lean my head back against the cupboard door, and close my eyes. 'I haven't even met your parents. I couldn't just agree to live with them. They might not like me. I might not like them.'

'Sure, you'd all love each other. But if you want to meet them, you should come with me this weekend. Even if it's just until Sunday.'

I shake my head. 'I can't.'

'Why can't you?' he laughs in disbelief.

'Because we may as well get used to being apart. It's just prolonging the agony, isn't it? You may as well go alone and spend some quality time with your family after being away so long. You don't need me getting in the way of that.'

'You wouldn't get in the way of that. My parents would love to meet you, and besides I only saw them the other week at the exhibition so it's not like they'll be desperate to spend time with me.'

'Do they even know about me?'

'Of course they do.'

'Really?' I'm surprised he would have told them about me, and it must show on my face because he laughs at my disbelieving expression and comes round the counter, wrapping his arms around me.

'Yes, really! What, do you think I don't talk to them? Of course I told them about you. Don't you know how happy I am that we're back together? Now, stop being so negative.' He smiles down at me, and I see the love shining in his eyes. My resolve starts to slip, but I know I can't just up and leave everything behind.

'I'm not being negative, I'm being practical. It's too soon for me to give everything up and just follow you to Ireland.'

'But we spent all that time apart. Don't you feel it's time for us to be together now?'

'Yes, I do, but you've only been here just over a week.'

'Long enough to know how we feel. Long enough to know we should be together.'

'Do we though?' I look up at him, my arms around his neck. 'You know I love you, but how does that translate to a future together? I know it's too soon to think about marriage and babies, but if you're asking me to move to Ireland, I'd like to know how you feel about having those things in the future. Maybe.'

His eyebrows shoot up. 'You want to marry me?'

'Well …' I falter. 'I'm not saying right now. Maybe not even marriage if you don't believe in that, but some kind of commitment would be nice. Some kind of security. And I know you said the other day that you're not totally against having kids anymore, but is that really true? Because I'd really like a baby. I'm not saying now, but one day.'

He blinks, as if thinking hard. 'Well, what would you do if I said no? Find someone you don't love, just so you can get married and have children.'

'I'm not saying that at all. I'm just saying that if we're not thinking along those lines now, then it's too soon to give up my life in London and follow you to Ireland.'

'Oh.' Aiden looks bemused as he mulls this over. He stares at the extractor fan above my head, frowning hard. 'All I'm thinking is we've been apart for five years already and why should we waste another minute being apart? Life's too short for that.'

I inhale deeply, before letting it out as a sigh. 'I don't know, Aiden. Maybe you're right. I just don't feel brave enough to make the leap right now.'

He looks disappointed for a moment, but then his arms tighten around me and he smiles. 'Okay, that's fine. You know I'll wait for as long as it takes. Whenever you're ready is fine by me.'

Smiling back at him, I lay my head against his chest. I know that I'm right. It would be foolish to rush this without any idea of what the future holds for us. But still, each hour that passes is one step closer to me saying goodbye to him again, and that thought fills me with dread.

300

Chapter 25

The week passes quicker than a week has ever passed before, and before I know it, it's time to say goodbye to Aiden. We keep the mood cheerful as we take a cab to the airport, but I can't help the panic-stricken butterflies in my stomach as I remember the last time we travelled to an airport together, and I said goodbye to him for what I thought would be forever. Last time I held my smile in place, and even though I now know it must have seemed like I didn't care, I'm still hoping I can do so again. I don't want to embarrass myself in the middle of a busy airport by howling, and also, I know I'll be seeing him again soon so I really don't need to.

This is just the beginning of our journey, I reassure myself, not the end.

My legs are shaking as we climb out the cab and make our way into the brightly lit building. The evening has taken on a surreal quality. I can't believe I'm about to wave Aiden off again. I can't believe I'm not going to wake up with him beside me tomorrow morning. I can't believe it. I can't believe it.

Aiden still doesn't understand why I won't go with him just for the weekend, and as I stand there, watching him check in his luggage, I start to question why too. Why have I been so stubborn and awkward about it? Why am I waving him off again when I could go with him and spend another couple of days in his company?

He reckons he'll come back again either next weekend or the weekend after. He's been deliberately vague about when he'll be back, and I'm pretty sure it's to force me to say I'll visit him in Ireland. To be honest, I've been feeling a bit resentful about it, thinking that if he's the one that's going, he the one who should be coming back. But as I stand there, watching people hurry past with their baggage, passports in hand, I start to think maybe I should be more flexible. I can't have things all my own way, and if I want a future with him, it stands to reason I should go to Ireland and meet his family.

Aiden comes back over with his backpack and coat over his arm. Dropping them onto the floor, he pulls me against his chest.

'Are you okay?' he asks.

'Fine,' I lie, smiling up at him.

The corners of his mouth pull down and a crinkle appears above his nose. 'You've not changed your mind then?'

I wrinkle my nose at him, full of regret. 'Bit late now.'

He shakes his head. 'It's not too late.'

'I haven't got any of my stuff with me,' I say, laughing to cover the fact I want to cry.

'So?' he shrugs. 'It's one weekend. Two nights. You could buy or borrow everything you need.'

With a shake of my head, I look down at the floor, but he tips my chin up so I'm looking at him.

'I love you,' he says. 'Even if you are a coward.'

I close my eyes, smiling at his words. 'It's true. I am a coward.'

'Never mind, we can work on that.' He bends to kiss me and I squeeze him tight. I don't want to let him go. He belongs with me. I don't want to see him walk away. I have a flashback to him disappearing the last time he left, and my heart drops into my hollow stomach. I don't want to experience all the fear and despair I felt back then. This isn't fair. This isn't how it's supposed to be. Burying my face into his neck, I breathe him in, trying to memorise his smell and the feel of his body against mine. I don't want to let go. I don't want him to go.

'I'd better go,' he says gently. Though I can't think why. He's got plenty of time, hasn't he?

'Can't you stay a little longer?'

He shakes his head. 'I'd better get the security check over and done with.'

Giving him one last squeeze, I let him go and step away, crossing my arms across my body as if to protect myself from the onslaught of despair I know I'm about to experience.

'It's not for long. Two weeks? Maybe three?' He smiles apologetically as he lifts up his coat and backpack, shifting it up to his shoulder.

I smile bravely and nod.

Three weeks and then I'll have one measly weekend with him. It's not enough. It's not fair.

'And then its Christmas, so we'll sort something out for then, okay?' He reaches for my hand and squeezes it.

'Okay.' My chest feels tight and it's getting harder to breathe. He's still holding my hand as he steps away and I'm reluctant to let go of his fingers, so I walk with him to the security checkpoint, until I can't go any further.

'Well, this is it,' he says, turning to me. He stares at me, and for a moment I think he's going to say something, but then he kisses me firmly on the lips and releases my hand. 'See you soon, Orla. I'll phone you when I get there.'

'Okay. Have a safe journey.'

'Thanks. Will do.'

I cover my mouth so no one can see it wobbling as he turns

303

and puts his bag, phone and coat into a tray on the conveyer belt. Then before I know it, he's through the human scanner and collecting his stuff on the other side.

I can't bear that he's the other side of the barrier to me.

I can't bear that we're separated like this.

I get a flashback to the last time I said goodbye to him at the airport, watching him stride away from me for what I thought would be forever. It was so painful. Even now it gives me chills to remember seeing his back disappearing through to the departure lounge. I can't bear to watch him disappear again.

'*Aiden!*'

The sound that comes from my mouth is so desperate and guttural that I'm as shocked to have made it as everyone else around me seems to be. People are looking, wondering what's wrong with me, but I can't hold it together anymore. I'm covering my face and crying, shaking all over.

Aiden stops, his back still to me, and for a moment I think he's just going to carry on walking. But then he turns and looks at me, then returns to the barrier.

'Look in your bag,' he calls, pointing.

'What?'

'Look in your bag.'

Wondering what he means, I open my bag and peer inside. I'm half-expecting a love letter or postcard or something, but what I see makes my heart leap with joy. Nestled next to my purse is my passport and a printed boarding pass for the flight Aiden's about to board. I look up at him in amazement.

'Go and check in,' he says, pointing towards the desks at the end of the hall.

'But …'

'No buts. Just go. We'll sort it, don't worry.'

I practically run down to the check-in desk, so excited I can hardly breathe. People are staring, but I don't care. I don't care about anything but the fact I'm going to be with Aiden for another two days. Check-in doesn't take long, and within minutes I'm through the security check and back in Aiden's arms.

'Thank God for that!' he says, lifting me off the floor and hugging me tight. 'You're shaking like a leaf.'

'I know. I just couldn't stand to see you walk away again.' I bury my face in his neck. 'Will your parents mind?'

'Of course not. I told them to expect you.'

'You did? What if I hadn't come?'

'Then my mum would have hated you forever.'

'Hey!'

'I'm only joking,' he laughs. 'I mentioned you might come, that's all. It's not a problem either way.'

There are shops in the departure lounge, so I'm able to buy toiletries and underwear and a change of T-shirt. Sparks of happiness are exploding in my stomach, and I'm still trembling, but now it's with relief rather than distress. All the same, I experience the odd stab of anxiety about exposing my feelings like that, in front of everyone around too. It feels undignified and weak, though Aiden doesn't seem to mind. He holds my hand tightly as we wait for our flight to be called, and I press my body against his side, seeking reassurance that he's still there and won't disappear any minute.

I'm nervous and excited as we board the plane and take our seats together. Aiden shoves our bags in the overhead storage compartment and sits down next to me, muttering about the lack of leg room. He fidgets about, trying to get comfortable, before taking my hand and entwining his fingers through mine.

'Excuse me,' says a woman appearing next to Aiden's seat. 'Are you Aiden Byrne, from that documentary series?'

Aiden hesitates before smiling at her. 'I am.'

'Oh wonderful! My daughter loves you! Would you mind

305

signing this napkin for her? She'll never believe I saw you on this flight.'

'Of course! I'd be happy to. What's her name?'

'Linda.' The lady looks on, pink-cheeked and happy as Aiden takes the pen and napkin she offers him and writes *To Linda, best wishes, Aiden Byrne x* in his lovely cursive script.

'Well, I feel like I'm travelling with a celebrity now,' I murmur, once she's gone back to her seat, satisfied with her autograph. 'Do you get that a lot?'

'Not really.'

I stare at him, noting how embarrassed he looks.

'That means yes, doesn't it?'

'No!' He pulls the air safety instructions from the pocket of the seat in front of him and busies himself reading them.

'Wow. You'll have to get your own private jet if this continues.'

'I doubt that. Although, I wish we were somewhere private right now so I could ...' Leaning across, he whispers into my ear exactly what he'd like to do to me if we were alone.

'Aiden!' My cheeks go red and he laughs and kisses me.

'Mind you,' he says, 'my parents are quite, erm, traditional in their values so I doubt we'll be sharing a room while we're staying with them.'

I blink at him in disbelief. 'Really? You tell me this after you whisper that in my ear? That's really cruel, you know.'

He laughs. 'We'll find a way round it, don't worry.'

'No, if that's their rules, that's their rules. I don't want to upset them the first time I meet them.'

'Don't worry about it.'

'Do you think they'll like me?'

'Of course, they'll like you. They'll adore you. You'll meet my dad at the airport when he picks us up.'

'I'm really nervous now, you know.'

'Why?'

'Because I'm meeting your family for the first time!'

He laughs. 'It's me that should be nervous, not you. They're all a bit full-on. I'm worried you'll take one look at them and turn and run.'

'I'm sure I won't.'

He winces. 'You haven't met them yet.'

Chapter 26

Aiden's dad is waiting in the airport car park, with his engine running and the heating up full blast. 'Great, glad to see he's not left his engine running to curb his pollution level,' Aiden says sarcastically as we approach the beige Land Rover Discovery.

'Jesus Christ, Dad,' Aiden turns down the heater as soon as he gets into the front passenger seat. 'It's hotter than hell, in here! How can you stand it?'

'What do you mean? It's feckin' freezing outside! I like to be warm.' He cranks up the dial again and the hot air blasts out. 'You're lucky I've come to pick you up! The bloody traffic's been murder tonight. What are they all doing out on a Friday night, tell me that, eh? You couldn't have picked a worse time to fly home! Pick a better time next time.'

Aiden glances at his watch. 'Dad, it's ten o'clock! How can the roads be busy at this time of night?'

'I don't know, do I? Bloody cars all over the place. People indicating left then turning right. And every bloody traffic light was against me.'

'Oh well, you're here now. Thank you for picking us up. We'd have got a taxi if y—'

'No, no, no need for any bloody taxis! I'm here now. Who's

this in the back then?' He peers into the rear-view mirror at me, and I see that his eyes twinkle kindly below bushy white eyebrows and wiry white curly hair. 'You didn't tell us you were bringing anyone, son.'

'Yes, I did! Dad! This is my girlfriend, Orla. Orla, this is my dad, Donald.'

'Hello, Donald. Lovely to meet you.'

'Lovely to meet you, too. Orla's a fine Irish name!'

'She's not Irish, Dad,' Aiden mutters.

'Did I say she was? I just said it was an Irish name, that's all.'

'You said the same when you first met me, Aiden,' I remind him.

'Hey, whose side are you on?' He peers around the back of his seat at me and winks, making me laugh.

'Well, Aiden's mum is looking forward to meeting you, Orla. He's never brought a girl home before, so there's much excitement in the Byrne household tonight.'

'Oh! That's sweet.'

'Da-ad!'

'What, son? What? The girl needs to know that she's a big deal. You should tell her how big a deal she is before she meets some other guy who does tell her and leaves you stone cold dead in the ground.'

Aiden groans.

'Come on, lad. You must have known how delighted your mum would be to meet your girlfriend at long last.'

'Jesus Christ, Dad. I'm 33 years old, and you're embarrassing me like I'm a teenager.'

Donald throws his head back to laugh loudly, and the Land Rover swerves alarmingly towards the side of the road. Aiden goes to grab the steering wheel in panic, but his dad slaps him away and quickly corrects his steering. Laughing, I settle back against the dusty seats. There's a strong smell of dog in the car, and a mud-covered hairy blanket lies on the seat next to me. It strikes me that I don't know much about Aiden's family. I have a vague notion they live on a farm, and looking round the vehicle that seems likely. I can't see much of Aiden's dad from the back seat, but I can see he has broad shoulders encased in a green woolly jumper and a bone structure like Aiden's from the side. They have the same ears, slightly on the long side with rounded lobes. But it's not until we reach Aiden's home and I get out of the Land Rover that I'm struck by the similarities between the two of them. Aiden's dad is tall, like Aiden, and the only real difference between the two of them is his dad's white hair and the craggy lines around his face. He's got the same laughing green eyes and wide smile.

'Christ, I'm glad to be outside in the cold after your heating!' Aiden says, climbing out and inhaling the cool night air deep into his lungs. 'It's about time you got rid of this old thing.' Aiden slams the door of the Land Rover. 'I'm amazed it's passed its emissions test.'

'You leave the old girl alone! She's served me well.'

'It's about time you retired her then, isn't it?'

'Shut up and go and see your mother!'

Aiden holds out his hand to me and we walk up to the front door. It's a wide, white bungalow and from what I can see in the darkness, it stands on its own, surrounded by tall fir trees swaying gently in the breeze. A lamp is glowing from the front porch and the door handle squeaks as Donald opens the door and leads us into a dark hallway.

'Where's Mum?' Aiden asks, sounding slightly miffed.

'She's here, somewhere.'

Donald opens a door on the right and flicks on the light, and suddenly there's a roar of 'Surprise!' and about twenty people appear, laughing and blowing hooters and firing party poppers.

'Jesus Christ!' Aiden looks flabbergasted as he stares around at his friends and relatives. 'I was just expecting to see my mum! What are you lot doing here?'

'Well, that's charming, isn't it? Aren't you glad to see everyone?' A small woman comes towards him and takes his face in her hands before kissing him as everyone else laughs. 'No one was around last time you came back so I thought we'd get everyone together this time. Why do you think I was asking if you could get an earlier flight?'

'Oh! Sorry, I didn't realise.'

'Doesn't matter. Now who's this then?' she asks, turning her twinkling blue eyes onto me.

'This is Orla. Orla, this is my mum, Mary.'

'Hello, Mary.' I smile as she comes towards me and envelops me in a warm hug.

'Hello, Orla. Lovely to meet you. Everybody, this is Orla, Aiden's girlfriend,' she announces to the rest of the room before turning back to me. 'Come in and make yourself at home. Did you have a good journey?'

'We did, thank you.'

'Can I get you a drink? Wine? Beer? Gin? Or something soft if you prefer?'

'I'd love a glass of wine. Thank you.'

Mary squeezes my hand as she crosses the room to a long table loaded with buffet food and drinks of all kinds. Aiden's busy greeting his friends and family, but he reaches back and grabs my hand, drawing me closer to introduce me. They're a lovely, friendly bunch. I recognise a couple of faces from the exhibition last week. They look at me curiously, and I feel my cheeks flush self-consciously. I'm not wearing a scrap of make-up and my hair is loose and curly, so I know I probably look about 17, not 27.

'So, this is Orla, huh?' says a man who look just like Aiden and his dad. I definitely remember seeing him at the exhibition.

'Yes. Orla, this is my brother, David, and his wife, Siobhan.'

'Hello, hello,' I say shaking hands with them both. Siobhan has a soft happy look about her and laughing blue eyes. I like her immediately.

'Hi, Orla. Pleased to meet you,' she says, shaking my hand.

'You too.'

'So, you're the girl Aiden dashed after at the exhibition last week.' David's looking me up and down, obviously checking my suitability for his younger brother.

I feel my cheeks flush. 'Yes.'

'Alright, alright,' Aiden says, shaking his head. 'Don't rub it in.'

'Leaving us to deal with the organisers and all the questions about where you went.' David punches Aiden playfully on the shoulder.

'I'd spoken to everyone by then, anyway. There was nothing else I needed to do.' Aiden rolls his eyes.

'You could have said goodbye. Mum thought you'd spontaneously combusted. I had no idea what you were up to. It was only after Mia and Keaton filled us in on your obsession with Orla that we started to piece it together.'

'Hey! It's not an obsession. I'm not obsessed with Orla. That makes me sound like a creepy stalker. I just wanted to speak to her, that's all. I hadn't seen her in five years and then she just left.'

'And now you've brought her home, to our parents' house?'

'What's wrong with that?'

'Nothing's wrong. You just seem a bit … *obsessed*, that's all.' David winks at me.

'I'm not obsessed.' Aiden glances down at me as he slips his arm around my shoulders. 'We're not obsessed, are we, Orla?'

'Well, maybe a little.' I laugh and wrap my arms around his waist, making him blush.

'Well, yeah. I suppose. Just a little.' He laughs, embarrassed. 'Anyway, David, it wasn't a problem that I left. I sent you a text explaining. And the organisers wrapped it all up. It's not like you actually had to do anything.'

'I know. I just like making you feel bad. What are big brothers for?'

I'm introduced to more people whose names I have no chance of remembering, but all of whom seem lovely. Aiden's family home is alive with chatter and laughter, and there's a real feeling of love and warmth. Someone starts to play a fiddle and Aiden groans.

'Oh no! I'm sorry about this,' he says, as his dad appears with an accordion. 'Every flaming family gathering we have turns into a flaming ceilidh!'

'What's that?'

He shakes his head. 'Just Irish music and dancing. You'll see.'

Standing to the side, I watch in amazement as the furniture's pushed to the sides of the room and the food table is taken away. People are singing and clapping and dancing arm in arm, spinning round in joyful circles. The most exciting thing that happens at my mum's house is when she breaks out the biscuits!

'It's all a bit crazy, isn't it?' Aiden says, cringing slightly. 'You're going to think we're all crazy Irish people and run away screaming.'

'Not at all. I think it's lovely. I'm loving it and your family are amazing.'

'Really?'

'Yes.'

He tips his head to one side, considering. 'You may as well join in then. Come on.'

'What? No, Aiden!' I protest as he takes my hands and pulls me into the centre of the room.

'Come on!' His eyes sparkle with laughter and suddenly I'm dancing with everyone else, or rather skipping round in circles, arm in arm with Aiden, and then David, and then Siobhan, and then another lovely lady whose name I've already forgotten. By the end of it, I'm red in the face and breathless from exertion.

The party goes on until the early hours, and people start leaving to go home. I begin to help clean up, but Mary stops me.

'Stop that now, darling, and go on up to bed. You've had a

long journey, and this will all still be here in the morning. We can do it then. Aiden will show you to your room. I've put her in David's old room, honey.'

Aiden rolls his eyes, but he kisses his mother goodnight and leads me across the hallway and down a corridor towards the end bedroom. 'You're in here,' he says, opening a door and switching on the light. 'Mother's orders.'

'That's okay.'

'Is it?' He grunts and pulls me into the room, shutting the door behind us. 'David's right, you know. I am obsessed with you.' He strokes my hair back from my face and kisses me, walking me backwards towards the bed.

'Aiden!' I start to laugh as he pushes me down onto the mattress then lowers himself on top of me. 'Your mum!'

'Oh God, Orla!' He draws back his head and looks at me in disappointment. 'I doubt there are any other two words in the universe that can douse the flames of desire faster than *your mum*!'

'Good! Get off me. I don't want her thinking I'm a slut!'

'She won't think you're a slut.' He starts to kiss my throat, and I close my eyes, laughing as it tickles. 'She'll just think I'm a slut.'

There's a knock on the door, and Aiden gets off me faster than I've ever seen him move before. I gasp out a laugh and cover my mouth with my hands as Mary's voice floats through the door, surprisingly sharp. 'Aiden? Are you in there?'

'Yes, I'm just showing Orla where we keep the towels.'

'Oh, good boy! Go to bed now, there's a good lad.'

'You do know I'm 33, right?' Aiden snatches the door open and disappears into the hallway.

'I do, as a matter of fact, but while you're under my roof, you'll abide by my rules. Now, leave that lovely girl alone and get to your own room. Good night, son.'

'Good night, Mum.'

I can't help laughing as I get into my newly purchased pyjamas and go across the hallway to the bathroom to brush my teeth. As much as I'd like to spend the night in Aiden's arms, I'm happy to be here, meeting his family and friends. He's waiting for me when I come out of the bathroom.

'Give them twenty minutes to fall asleep, then I'll be in,' he whispers.

'No, you won't! You heard what your mum said.'

'She won't know.'

I laugh as I slip my arms around his waist. 'No, Aiden! This is her house. What she says, goes. Besides, I'm exhausted and I bet you are too.'

'I know but I just want a cuddle.' He squeezes me tightly, rubbing my back in soothing circles.

'Huh, likely story.' I lay my head against his chest before kissing him and letting him go. 'I'll see you in the morning. Wake me up when you wake up.'

'Okay. Good night.' He steals another kiss before moving aside to let me go into the bedroom.

I fall asleep almost immediately, only waking at nine o'clock the next morning when Aiden brings me breakfast in bed. He's already dressed in jeans and a black jumper, and from the voices I hear floating from the kitchen, I assume everyone else is up too.

'I told you to wake me up when you woke up!' I protest as he carries in the tray and sits down on the end of the bed.

'No one's been up that long anyway. Mum's still in her dressing gown. Did you sleep alright?'

'Like a log!' I yawn and take a sip from the mug of tea. 'Did you?'

'Yeah. Strange being back in my old bed though.'

'You weren't here long ago though, were you?'

'No, not really. Just a few weeks.' He shrugs and scratches his arm.

'It was so sweet last night when they all jumped out. They were all so happy to see you.'

He rolls his eyes. 'Yeah. They're a good bunch. And they all loved you.' Leaning forward, he kisses me as I clutch the tray in case the toast and cereal slide off.

'Everyone was so nice. It was a really great night.' I take a bite of the toast. 'What's the plan for today then?'

'I thought we'd go for a walk. There's something I want to show you.'

'What's that then?'

'It's a surprise.'

'What is it? Tell me!'

'If I told you, it wouldn't be a surprise, would it!' He catches my foot through the duvet and shakes it gently.

'Okay. Will it be a long walk?' I look towards the window where the rain clouds hang low and grey.

'Not really. But you might have to borrow a pair of my mum's wellies.'

After I shower and change, we venture out into the damp morning air and walk down his parent's driveway and turn left onto a country lane. I couldn't see much last night because it was so dark, but we're surrounded by trees and fields and countryside. The weather's cold and damp, with a thick drizzle that patters on my raincoat and dribbles down my sleeves.

'I can smell the sea,' I say, drawing in deep lungfuls of cold damp air. 'Are we even near the sea?'

'Yes, not far. You'll see it when you get to the top of the hill.'

He takes my hand and we walk on. I'm excited to see what he's got to show me, and I realise I'm perfectly content in this moment, just walking along this lane with Aiden, not worrying about what comes next. I have a vague notion that tomorrow, when it comes to flying back to London and leaving Aiden behind, I'll feel rather different. But for today, at least, I'm happy.

We reach the top of the hill and through the trees I glimpse the grey sea ahead. We're quite high up above it, on top of a cliff. 'There it is!' I say excitedly. And even though it's a dull day and the sea looks angry and grey, I'm happy to see it because I can imagine how beautiful this view would be on a lovely sunny day, with a blue sky and sunshine glinting on the waves. 'Wow! What a place to grow up.'

Aiden looks pleased. 'Yeah, it's a great place to grow up. We were forever at the beach or playing in the hills or pond dipping or making dens. It was idyllic really.'

'It's a wonder you ever wanted to leave.'

'Yeah, well … you go where life takes you. Besides, it's a good job I did or I'd never have met you.' He wraps an arm around my shoulder and kisses my head. 'It's funny though, my desire to keep moving from place to place isn't as strong as it was. I want a base. Somewhere to call home that isn't just my parents' house. And I love it around here, so, I thought …' He opens a gate into a field bordered by trees and overgrown shrubs. It looks like nature's trying to reclaim it for its own. 'I'd buy this.'

'Oh!' Blinking in surprise, I step into the field, my wellies squelching in the muddy puddle that's formed in a rut next to the gate. 'Are you going to build on this? Please tell me you're not just going to erect your tent and live in that!'

He laughs. 'No, no, I am going to build on it.' He squelches forward in his wellies and stands, looking around him with a satisfied look on his face. 'But it's going to be a cob house.'

'A what?'

'A cob house. Made from a combination of mud and straw. It's environmentally friendly and really cheap to make. There are various ones in existence all over the world, and there are eco villages where people live in as eco-friendly and sustainable way as possible. People call them hobbit houses.'

'Are you serious?' I'm completely bewildered and just a little bit disappointed. And he had the cheek to moan about my flat

317

when all the time he was planning to build a house from mud! I can just imagine what Belinda will say when I tell her.

'Sure I am. The documentary team are going to film the building process and hopefully it will inspire lots of other people to build their own eco-friendly homes from recycled and sustainable materials.'

'So, you'll get a TV series out of it?'

'Yes. I get filmed doing this, and I'll also be exploring other eco-friendly building projects and houses that are already in existence in and around the UK.'

'Wow!' I try to dredge up some enthusiasm as I let this new information sink into my brain. So, this is what he's going to be doing in Ireland, and when he's not in Ireland, he's just going to be in and around the UK. This is good news, I think. No more swimming in alligator-infested rivers or getting too close to forest fires. And like he says, Ireland's not so far from London. It took little more than an hour to get here. I'd be up for visiting him in his mud hut when it's done, and his family and friends are lovely so I know they'd make me welcome. It's not a house in the conventional sense, but at least it's a house. 'That's really cool. Why didn't you tell me about this before?'

'I wanted all this to be a surprise.' He spreads his arms to indicate the dripping greenery.

All this? I turn a slow circle, looking at the trees and the bushes and the long, long grass. There's literally nothing here. He really is a crazy wild man.

'But you'll be living in your parents' house while you're building it, won't you? When do you start it, anyway?'

'Filming's scheduled to start early March.'

'So that's like four months away?' I wince. 'So you'll be at your parents' for how long, do you think?'

Aiden shrugs. 'I don't know. Not too long really. It probably won't be as long as you're thinking.' He puts an arm around my shoulder. 'You'll come and stay with me, won't you?'

'Yes!' I say brightly. There is no question that I won't. 'So how big is this cob house going to be? One room? Two rooms?'

'It needs to be quite an ambitious project for us to make a programme out of it. It'll be on a scale of a small house, so it's going to have two rooms downstairs and two rooms upstairs. I've still got to finalise the plans with the producers, but that's what we're looking at right now.'

'It'll have stairs? Will it have windows?'

'Of course! There are some amazing cob houses out there, you know. You should have a look online at them.'

'Sounds like it'll take a while?'

'Probably not as long as you think.'

I raise my eyebrows, trying to absorb this new information. So, he invited me to come and live over here in Ireland when he knew he only had a field and his parents' house? I suppose that's the joy of being someone who lives so utterly in the moment; you forget the practicalities of everyday life. He appears to be completely oblivious to any problems this may present.

'So, you'll be living with your parents until then? Oh well, I guess you'll just have to keep visiting me in London.'

'Yeah, I suppose.' He looks crestfallen. 'Still not tempted to move over here then?'

'I'll come and stay in your tent from time to time.'

'Yeah?'

'Yeah!' I smile and slip my arms around his waist. 'It'll be like old times.'

He laughs and ducks his head to kiss me. The sound of our anoraks rustling is loud in my ears. 'Well, we could stay in my tent,' he says, taking my hand and leading me through a gap in the thicket, 'or we could stay here.'

I gasp as we push through the shrubbery and find a pretty white cottage with a gabled roof and wisteria clinging to a trellis on the wall next to the doorway.

'Who does this belong to?'

Aiden laughs and pulls a set of keys from his pocket. 'Me!'

'Really?' I gape at him before playfully smacking him on the arm. 'Don't you think you should have shown me this first?'

'Now where's the fun in that? Do you want to look inside or shall we stand outside in the rain all day?'

'Get the door open!'

He unlocks the front door then turns and lifts me off my feet so he can carry me over the threshold. Shrieking with laughter, I say, 'I think you're supposed to do this after we're married?'

Married? Christ, did I just mention the 'm' word? My heart jolts and I expect him to drop me in horror, but he just laughs as he steps into the hallway. I expect him to put me straight down, but he keeps holding me for a moment longer as he smiles into my eyes. 'I'll do it every day for the rest of our lives, if you'll let me.'

I want to make a sarcastic comment about him probably being off filming somewhere most days, but it dies on my tongue as I gaze back at him and all I can think is that I'd really like that to be true. Hope and happiness swell inside me as he lowers me gently to the tiled floor.

The cottage smells cold but clean. Its rooms are empty of all furniture and our voices and footsteps echo on the floorboards as we walk from room to room.

'When did you buy this?' I ask, as we walk into the kitchen. A large window looks across to cows grazing in a field.

'A couple of months ago. It went up for auction and my dad put a bid in for me. I came to see it just before the exhibition.'

'You bought it without seeing it?'

'Kind of.' He laughs as he opens a cupboard door and peers inside. 'I've been in here before though. I was friends with the boy that lived here when I was younger. He'll laugh when he finds out I bought it.'

'Wow!' I stand in the kitchen, looking round. It's quite old-fashioned, with worn farmhouse-style pine units and a peeling

Formica worktop with a singed looking blister where someone's left a hot pan, but it's a great space with an amazing view across fields to the hills beyond. 'I'm amazed you stayed in London so long when you had this waiting for you over here.'

'Ah yes, but I had you in London, so it really wasn't that difficult at all.' He crosses to the sink and turns on the tap. Clear water gushes out into the white Belfast sink.

'When are you going to move in?'

'Soon. It needs a rewire and some other bits and bobs doing, but that shouldn't take long. My dad's been onto an electrician so work should start soon.'

'Great!'

I can't believe Aiden's bought a house. A proper house! This is big news. It means he's actually planning on staying in one place. I know he'd told me that was what he was planning on doing, but I didn't completely believe him. Is the wanderer really ready to settle down?

'My mum's been in cleaning it all up.'

'She's done a great job. The place is spotless.'

'Yeah. It's only going to get messed up when the work begins though. Shall we look upstairs?'

The rooms upstairs are big and airy, and there's a sweeping view of the sea from the master bedroom.

'I've always loved the view from this room,' Aiden puts his arm around me as we stand looking out towards the sea. Below us, the front garden is full of overgrown vegetation and long grasses that sway in the wind.

'Wow! It's amazing!' I look around the room again. Aiden has plans, real, solid plans that appear to involve him staying in Ireland for the foreseeable future. If this doesn't make our relationship viable, I don't know what will. 'So, I'll be able to come and stay with you here when it's done up?'

'Yep. That's the plan.'

I beam at him. 'Brilliant!'

321

'You can move in, if you like?'

I laugh, not taking him seriously. 'Well, we'll see about that, Aiden. But this is great. I'll definitely come and visit.'

'Oh, come on!' Aiden turns me to face him, his hands on my shoulders. His eyes are almost pleading as they burn into mine. 'Move in with me. I know I'm asking a lot, and I know your career's just as important as mine, but you could get a job on a newspaper over here, or even stay on your own paper and work remotely. I know you had your five-year plan, and I understand that's why you couldn't come with me last time. But you've achieved all that now. You've left Hawksley, you're living in London and you're working on a big newspaper. What's next for you? Where do you see yourself in the next five years? What's your plan for then?'

'I don't really have one.' I feel bewildered by this turn in our conversation and start to feel a bit panicky. He's right, I should have made another five-year plan by now.

'Well, do you see yourself with me in those five years? Because I see myself with you, Orla. In fact, I can't picture a future without you in it.'

'Really?' I blink up at him. As his words sink in, joy swells in my heart and I feel it shining from my eyes. Aiden really feels like that? He's such an 'in the moment' kind of guy, it's quite a shock to hear that he visualises a future with me in it.

'Of course, Orla. I love you. I'm in love with you and I think I have been since you fell into my life when you came to interview me all those years ago! Come on, make *me* your five-year plan. In fact, no, make me your *forever* plan. I want you to be my forever plan, because I can't see myself with anyone else, ever. There's no one else like you, Orla.'

I stare at him, completely overwhelmed. I never expected to hear these words from his mouth. It's like all my dreams have come true, opening up the possibility of a future I've never let myself believe in before.

'And I'm not saying you must move in immediately,' he continues. 'You'll need time to sort out your job and your flat, of course. But when you do, please know I'll be here, waiting for you, and I always will be.'

'Aw, Aiden,' I say, stepping into his embrace. 'Thank you. That's so sweet.'

'You're all I want, Orla,' he says. 'I've been all around the world, and I've never met anyone like you.'

I can't speak I'm so choked up. I can't think of anything I'd like more than to spend the rest of my life living in this gorgeous cottage with Aiden.

'And if you want kids, we'll have kids,' Aiden adds. 'I'm no longer "I'm never having kids" man, okay?'

'Okay.' I laugh against his chest.

'If you want kids with me,' he says, anxiously. 'I'm not saying we must have kids if that's not what you want. It's not my intention to turn you into a baby machine or something.'

'I know, Aiden. And I do want kids, you know I do. I can't imagine anything cuter than a little baby Aiden running around the place.'

'Or a little baby Orla.' He kisses my nose before squeezing me tight and lifting me off the floor. 'Oh, and I'll need your help decorating, if that's alright. You know what I'm like. I'm used to living under canvas and spending my time in bird hides. If it's left up to me, everything will be khaki.'

'Khaki?' I splutter with laughter.

'Yeah, it's a great colour for camouflage. Especially useful for hiding from beautiful reporters who come to interview you when you're bird-watching in the woods.'

'Well, I suppose I'd better supervise you then, hadn't I?' I laugh as he kisses me. 'I can't have you painting your walls khaki!'

'I think you better had.' He rests his forehead against mine, and we stand for a few moments, wrapped in each other's arms.

I could stand like this for hours without registering how much time has passed.

'I love you, Aiden Byrne,' I say softly.

'I love you too, Orla Kennedy.'

And just like that, the promise of a future opens up. And though there's a lot to sort out, I believe that Aiden and I can make this work. I can no longer say that our lives are incompatible. I can no longer dismiss Ireland as somewhere that's out of reach. Aiden and I stand a chance, and with a bit of compromise and flexibility, I'm convinced we can make this work.

Epilogue

Five years later

'Mummy, look at all my shells?'

'Wow, Daisy! You've found so many!' I smile down at my 3-year-old daughter. Her curly blonde hair spirals around her head in the sea breeze as she bends to tip her prized shells out onto the wet sand.

'Nanny helped.'

'Good old Nanny.' I bend with some difficulty, my huge pregnant belly getting in the way as I poke through the shells with my finger. The baby's due any day now and I feel heavy and cumbersome.

'Are you okay, Orla?' Mum walks slowly towards us, her bare feet leaving prints in the wet sand. I can't believe she's taken her shoes off to walk in the surf. The September sea is freezing! 'I'll take Daisy if you want to go back and lie down. You must be exhausted.'

'Well …' I shrug; it's true, I am exhausted, but I'm also enjoying the fresh air. I woke up this morning feeling not too good, and the salt air is reviving me a little. 'I might go back in a minute.'

Mum smoothes back Daisy's hair as she bends with us to

inspect the shell haul. 'We did well, didn't we?' she says in a bright voice. 'Shall we see if we can find some crabs in the rock pools?'

'Yes!' Daisy begins scooping her shells back into her pink sparkly bucket, before taking Mum's hand and heading off up the beach. 'Bye, Mummy!'

'Bye, darling.'

Mum turns to look over her shoulder. 'We won't be long. Go back home and have a lie-down.'

I watch them walk up the beach, hand in hand, and feel a wave of love. It's so lovely that my mum is getting to spend time with my daughter. Keeley is away at university now, and I get the feeling Mum is suffering empty-nest syndrome.

'Orla!' I hear my name carried on the wind, and turn to see my husband coming towards me. 'What are you doing down here?' he asks, as he gets closer, his eyes full of concern. 'I thought you weren't feeling well.' As soon as he reaches me, his arms go round me, and he kisses my forehead.

'I needed some fresh air,' I say, covering his hand with my own as he rubs my stomach. 'Mum's taken Daisy to look in the rock pools.'

Aiden turns to look down the beach to where two figures are small now.

'Right, well, let's get you home then.'

'I'm fine, Aiden. You don't need to worry.'

'I do need to worry. You know how fast Daisy came! I don't want you giving birth on the beach.'

It's true, Daisy did come fast. The midwives at the hospital couldn't believe it when I delivered twenty minutes after arriving on the ward. As she was my first, they'd expected me to be in labour for hours. This time, we're going for a home birth and Aiden's got the midwife on speed dial.

'Okay, I'll come home now.'

Dry sand is always difficult to walk on but, but today it's harder than ever. I'm seriously regretting my decision to come down to the beach as I stop for the third time to catch my breath. Aiden waits patiently as I cling to his big warm hand with both of mine and lay my head against his arm. My stomach tightens ominously, painfully, and suddenly I know our new baby will be born today.

'It's starting, isn't it?' Aiden says in a voice that betrays his nerves.

I nod as the contraction passes. 'It wasn't a bad one. It will be a while yet.'

Aiden gives me a look that says he doesn't believe me, then takes out his phone to ring the midwife. Gulls wheel and circle in the grey sky and the waves crash behind us as we reach the top of the beach. It's a relief to be back on firm ground, but then I remember the steep hill we have to climb to get home. Aiden obviously thinks the same thing.

'Shall I run and get the car?'

'No, don't leave me!' I gasp, holding onto his hand as tight as I can.

'Okay, okay.'

We wait for the contraction to pass before starting the ascent up the hill. The leaves on the trees are taking on the copper and gold hues of autumn, and they're suddenly illuminated by the sun poking through the clouds.

'There you go!' Aiden says, forcing himself to sound joyful. 'The sun's come out to welcome our new baby.'

'Yay,' I say, forcing myself to sound equally joyful, despite the fact I've got to walk up a massive hill to get home and am terrified of the impending labour.

I've done this before, I remind myself, I can do it again.

'This is probably a good thing to do,' I pant. 'It's good to be active in labour. It makes it easier, apparently.'

Aiden's brow is creased with worry, but he tries to smile. 'Yeah, let's hope it doesn't make it faster than last time. Christ, I'm so glad I came to get you when I did.'

'Me too.' I stop walking as another contraction wracks my body. Aiden holds me, rubbing the small of my back in circular motions. I'm so grateful he's here, so solid and warm beside me. Even if I have this baby right here, right now on the side of this narrow country lane, at least Aiden will be here with me.

The contraction passes and we start walking again. The baby feels low in my pelvis, pressing downwards. I feel a sort of popping sensation, and a trickle that turns to a flood of warm liquid. 'Oh! My waters just broke.'

'Oh God!' Aiden starts to panic. 'That midwife better be on her way! What if she gets held up? What if I have to deliver the baby myself? I don't know what to do!'

'Aiden, shh, shh.' I reach up and put my hand on the side of his face. 'We've done this before, remember. We can do it again. I know what I'm doing.'

He holds my gaze, and I see the panic dying in his eyes, though he still looks frightened, especially when another contraction takes over and I lean into him, breathing through the pain.

'I'm supposed to be timing these,' he says, looking at his watch. 'How long was that? They seemed really close together. We're only halfway up the hill!'

There's a beep and a red Toyota pulls up alongside us. 'Looks like I was just in time,' says a cheerful Irish voice.

'Oh my God, am I glad to see you!' Aiden says, sagging with relief when he sees its Raine, our midwife. 'I thought I was going to have to deliver this baby myself by the side of the road.'

'No need for that. I'm here now. Jump in and I'll whizz you up the hill to your house.'

'My waters just broke,' I tell her. 'I don't want to get your seat wet.'

'No matter, there's a plastic sheet in the back, just sit on that.'

Aiden opens the rear door and lays out the sheet for me to sit on. Two minutes later we're back at home.

'Now what were you doing down that beach?' Raine scolds as

she gets all her stuff ready for me to deliver. The contractions are coming so fast now they almost run into each other.

'I just needed some air.'

'Open a window next time! Come on, let's examine you and see how far you're dilated.'

I lie on our bed, while Aiden crosses to the window. 'Yes, it's a bit of a recurring theme, really. Orla denying she needs help.'

'Hey! That's not fair. I'm not denying anything, I just wanted a walk on the beach.'

'What if I hadn't come and got you?'

'Mum was there. She would have phoned you.'

'She was about half a mile away when I got there.'

'Oh, you're nine centimetres already!' Raine says, interrupting our bickering. 'This baby will soon be here.'

I hold my hand out to Aiden, and he crosses over and takes it.

Half an hour later, Poppy Anne Byrne enters the world, red faced and screaming, and Aiden cries when he holds his second child in his arms.

'Another girl!' he says, looking at her in wonder. 'We'll have to keep trying for a boy.'

'No chance! I'm never letting you near me again, Aiden!' But we're both laughing as he leans across and kisses me.

'Well done, Mrs Byrne,' he whispers. 'You're a goddess. I love you so much.'

'I love you too.'

'I suppose I'd better phone everyone and let them know the news,' he says, getting up from the bed and passing Poppy back to me. I gaze down at my new daughter's soft round cheeks and half-closed eyes and feel so much love I'm almost knocked sideways. Her tiny perfect fingers wrap around my thumb as I latch her on to my breast for a feed. Raine watches to make sure she's feeding well before she leaves.

'I'll call in tomorrow, just to check in on you,' she says, gathering all her stuff together, ready to leave. 'Just call if you need anything.'

'Thank you.'

She goes downstairs and I hear Aiden letting her out and thanking her profusely for arriving so quickly. Soon after, the door opens again, and Daisy's high-pitched excited voice floats up the stairs.

'Well, Poppy, it looks like you're about to meet your big sister,' I murmur. She's fallen asleep feeding, so I unlatch her from my breast and prepare for the onslaught of three-year-old enthusiasm.

'I'm sorry!' Mum opens the bedroom door and peers round as Daisy pushes her way past. 'I tried to keep her away as long as possible but she overheard me on the phone and twigged the baby had arrived. Not much gets past her, does it?'

'No, it doesn't.' I laugh as Daisy clambers onto the bed with me. 'It's fine. Daisy, say hello to your baby sister, Poppy.'

'Hello, Poppy,' Daisy says in a hushed voice. With her little knees on either side of my legs, she peers down at the baby intently. 'She's very red!' she observes.

'So were you when you were first born!'

'Was I? Was I cute?'

'You were very cute. And you're still cute now,' I say, kissing her nose. 'Here, Mum,' I say, tipping Poppy so my mum can see her better. 'Would you like a hold?'

'Oh yes, please.' Mum's eyes fill with tears as she takes Poppy and sits on the end of my bed. Daisy follows her with her eyes, but then throws her arms around my neck, nestling closer for a cuddle. Gathering her warm body to me, I kiss her rosy cheeks, inhaling the smell of the wind and the sea in her soft golden hair. 'I can't believe you had her so quickly!' Mum says. 'You were only on the beach an hour ago!'

'I know. It's a good job Aiden came when he did. And the midwife, for that matter. I thought I was going to give birth by the side of the road.'

Mum shakes her head, clearly overwhelmed. 'I've phoned Keeley. She wants to come at the weekend, if that's okay?'

'Of course. She can sleep in the cob house like last time.'

The cob house is finished now and resembles the kind of cottage you'd expect to see in a fairy tale. It's got a thatched roof and warm butterscotch walls, and round windows that twinkle in the sunlight. We use it as a guest house, and Aiden's documentary was such a resounding success that we've had people from all over the world asking if they can come and stay in it. Aiden's in talks for another series.

With hindsight, it's easy to see that I should have given up my manky flat and moved to Ireland immediately. I've never been happier than I am now, and life just keeps getting better. I was sad to leave my job and my friends in London, but I got another job on a newspaper in Dublin and still write a regular column about moving to Ireland and setting up home with Aiden Byrne in the countryside. People have loved where my life has taken me over the years, and I even get the odd message from readers telling me I've inspired them to make a leap they might not have made if they hadn't have read my column. Sometimes, the responsibility weighs heavy on my shoulders. What if they've made the wrong choice? What if they've got the wrong man? There aren't many as good as Aiden Byrne in this world.

For me, I knew all along I had the right man. I just needed to be sure he was willing to stay in one place and lay down roots.

The bedroom door opens and Aiden appears with two mugs of tea and a beaker of juice for Daisy.

'Err, do you want the bad news?' Aiden says, looking shifty as he puts the mugs down on the bedside cabinet and passes the juice to Daisy. My heart stills.

'You're going away?'

'No!' He looks appalled that I could even think such a thing. 'Orla, we've just had a baby. Why would I go away now? No! My family's on its way round. The whole bloody lot of them!'

331

'Daddy!' Daisy says. 'Daddy said a bad word!'

'I'm sorry, sweetheart!' Aiden picks Daisy up and kisses her. 'Naughty Daddy! Yeah, so they're coming round now, even though I told them not to.'

'That's okay,' I say easily. 'You're on tea duty though.'

'That's fine. You can stay up here and rest if you'd rather. You've been through enough today without having to listen to that noisy bunch.'

'Don't be silly. I love your family, you know I do.'

He rolls his eyes. 'So do I, but I wish they'd come one at a time rather than en masse. It wouldn't be a problem, but Uncle Jeff and Auntie Lynne were round at Mum's when I phoned, then they phoned my cousin Patrick, and he's working nearby. And I'd already phoned David, so ...'

'Is David coming too?' I move to get out of bed, wincing at how sore I am. I literally feel like I've been kicked up the bum by a horse.

'Yes, but later, when he's finished work. He said he'd bring Siobhan and the twins so that will be good for you,' he says to Daisy, tickling her tummy. She curls up, giggling, and accidentally spills her juice on his top.

'Sorry, Daddy.'

'Never mind, honey. It'll dry.' He gives it a rub then turns to go as there's a knock at the door. 'This'll be them now.'

'Okay, give me five minutes to get ready,' I say, standing up with a wince. 'Mum, you can take the baby downstairs if you like.'

'Oh no, you must introduce her to everyone,' Mum says, standing up to go out of the room. 'I'll wait outside on the landing until you're ready.'

Aiden's family is noisy and cheerful and so full of love and kindness that I can't even begin to express how grateful I am to be a part of it. They've welcomed me with open arms, and they're just as welcoming to my mum and sister too. As I go downstairs

332

with Poppy and my mum and enter the lounge, a big cheer goes up and I'm surrounded by congratulations and well wishes. Poppy hardly stirs as I pass her to Aiden's mum for a cuddle, and I'm immediately enveloped by hugs from Aiden's aunt and uncle and dad. Someone's told the elderly couple that live in the end house at the top of the lane, and they arrive too, clutching flowers and a card. I sit in the armchair, absorbing all the joy and smile across at Aiden. He's watching me with such an expression of love on his face that my heart swells. I'll never regret following him to Ireland. I belong here. I belong with him. The only thing I regret is letting him go that first time he left. He offered me the world but I was too scared to take it back then. I often wonder where we'd be if I'd have gone with him. I'm no longer convinced we'd have fallen out and I'd have run home. In fact, I'm pretty sure we'd have made it. I don't know if I wasted those five years of my life in some kind of limbo, or if it was important for my career. The only thing I know is that I'm so grateful we got a second chance to build a life together, because I can't imagine living my life any other way.

Acknowledgements

To my wonderful editor Charlotte Mursell, thank you for being such a pleasure to work with and for championing this story. Thanks also to the rest of the team at HQ Digital who worked so hard in the production of this book, and to my fellow authors who are always there with words of encouragement.

Big love to my family for their continued love and support, and to you, the reader, without whom all the hours spent writing would be pretty pointless.

I adore Orla and Aiden and think they might be my favourites of all my characters so far. The initial idea for this story was sparked by my interest in hobbit or cob houses, and an early draft had Orla going to interview a man building a cob house by a river. However, my love of animals and nature won, and Aiden became a wildlife photographer. Otters are such beautiful, fascinating creatures and it's so wonderful that, thanks to conservation efforts and cleaner waterways, they've made such a comeback in recent years and can now be found in every county in the UK. I gained inspiration from reading *The Otters' Tale* by Simon Cooper, which is a beautifully written account of the otters that live around his angling farm in the south of England. I also dipped into the *Halcyon River Diaries* by Philippa Forrester and

Charlie Hamilton James. This was also a lovely TV series, so if you ever get the chance to watch it, please do. I love a good wildlife documentary! The amazing footage captured never ceases to amaze me. There are some superb wildlife photographers out there, and their work is vital in educating us all and inspiring a passion for nature and conservation.

For further information about the conservation of otters in the UK, visit www.ukwildottertrust.org

Dear Reader,

We hope you enjoyed reading this book. If you did, we'd be so appreciative if you left a review. It really helps us and the author to bring more books like this to you.

Here at HQ Digital we are dedicated to publishing fiction that will keep you turning the pages into the early hours. Don't want to miss a thing? To find out more about our books, promotions, discover exclusive content and enter competitions you can keep in touch in the following ways:

JOIN OUR COMMUNITY:

Sign up to our new email newsletter: hyperurl.co/hqnewsletter

Read our new blog www.hqstories.co.uk

: https://twitter.com/HQDigitalUK

: www.facebook.com/HQStories

BUDDING WRITER?

We're also looking for authors to join the HQ Digital family! Please submit your manuscript to:

www.hqstories.co.uk/want-to-write-for-us/

Thanks for reading, from the HQ Digital team

If you loved *The Five-Year Plan*, make sure you've read more heartwarming romances from Carla Burgess

CARLA BURGESS

Marry Me Tomorrow

Twelve days. Two gold rings. One BIG secret.

Emily needs a husband … fast. It's just a few days until
Christmas and to finally put a stop to her nagging mother's
matchmaking plans, Emily has convinced her that
she's already married!

And when her excited mum announces that she's coming to
stay, Emily can think of only one man to play the part:
gorgeous ex-soldier, Sam. It's the best part of her day, handing
him a coffee every morning – but then, Emily never expected
to offer him her hand in marriage, too …

All that's left is for Sam to say 'I do' – it's the perfect plan! So
why then, do her 'pretend' feelings for Sam seem far too *real*?

One lift. Two strangers. Anything could happen …

Elena thought that today would be just like any other day …
until the supermarket lift jams and she realises she's *stuck*.

And not just stuck in the lift. Stuck with her childhood crush,
Daniel Moore, who unfortunately seems to be just
as *gorgeous* as she remembered …

One flit. Two strangers. Anything could happen...

It's beginning to look a lot like Christmas at the little flower shop …

Florist Rachel Jones might spend every day making beautiful bridal bouquets at her little flower shop, but her own love life is wilting as quickly as a bunch of dead roses.

Luckily, the arrival of handsome detective Anthony Bascombe, the new tenant upstairs is the *perfect* distraction! Although there's a catch, Anthony isn't looking for love – he's looking for her ex-fiancé, Patrick …

But as the snow begins to fall and her little shop fills with mistletoe ready for Christmas, will Rachel manage to melt Anthony's heart?

She thought she'd never see him again …

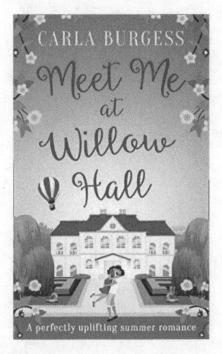

Rachel Jones' best friend's wedding is the perfect distraction from her own broken heart. That is, until the moment she squeezes into her bridesmaid dress and looks up to see the man who walked out of her life a year ago, Anthony Bascombe!

Still just as gorgeous as she remembers, it's clear Anthony's been keeping a secret from her and Rachel's determined to get to the bottom of it! The trouble is, the more time she spends around Anthony, the more she can't help falling for him …

But Anthony's already disappeared before, can Rachel trust that this time he's back for good?